TWISTED BLADE IN THE ARENA

T0161172

About the authors

Born in Switzerland, Oliver Frey a.k.a. Zack ended up in London and, after attending film school, plunged into gay art and publishing. Innumerable illustrations poured from his pen and brush for British magazines *HIM International*, *Vulcan*, *Teenage Dreams*, the *HIM Gay Library* series, and *Mister* magazine. For *HIM* he created the mold-breaking Rogue comic strip and later *The Street*, which was part of the inspiration behind cult TV series *Queer As Folk*. Some of his comic-strip work has been published recently by Bruno Gmünder: *Bike Boy, Hot For Boys – the Sexy Adventures of Rogue*, and *Bike Boy Rides Again*. Frey lives with life-long partner Roger Kean in a medieval town on the edge of Wales.

British-born author Roger Kean, who met Oliver at film school, has had careers as a movie cameraman, film editor, journalist, and magazine and book editor. As an author he has written books on historical subjects both factual and fictional, and gay fiction, including: *Felixitations*; *Thunderbolt– Torn Enemy of Rome*; *A Life Apart*; *Gregory's Story*; *Harry's Great Trek*; *What's A Boy Supposed to Do*.

Titles from Zack

Gil Graham & Mike Smith series
> *Boys of Vice City*
> *Boys of Disco City*
> *Boys of Two Cities*
> *Boys of the Fast Lane*
> *Boy of the West End*

Boys of Imperial Rome series
> *Deadly Circus of Desire*
> *The Satyr of Capri*
> *The Wrath of Seth*
> *Twisted Blade in the Arena*
> *Caradoc's Gold* (2017)

Other novels
> *Raw Recruits*
> *Desert Studs*
> *Blood and Lust*
> *The Warrior's Boy*
> *Mississippi Hustler* (as Rod Bellamy)
> *Mulholland Meat* (as Kip Nolan)

TWISTED BLADE IN THE ARENA

BRUNO GMÜNDER

Copyright © 2017 Bruno Gmünder GmbH
Kleiststraße 23-26, 10787 Berlin, Germany
Phone: +49 30 61 50 03-0
Fax: +49 30 61 50 03-20
info@brunogmuender.com

All text and artwork © 2017 Reckless Books-Zack/Oliver Frey & Roger Kean
www.zack-art.com

All rights reserved. No part of this book may be reproduced in any form or by any
means without the prior written consent of the Publisher.

All characters depicted are 18 years of age or older.

Printed in Germany
ISBN: 978-3-95985-281-4

More information about Bruno Gmünder books and authors:
www.brunogmuender.com

If you're still with us,
Les Armour,
this one's for you

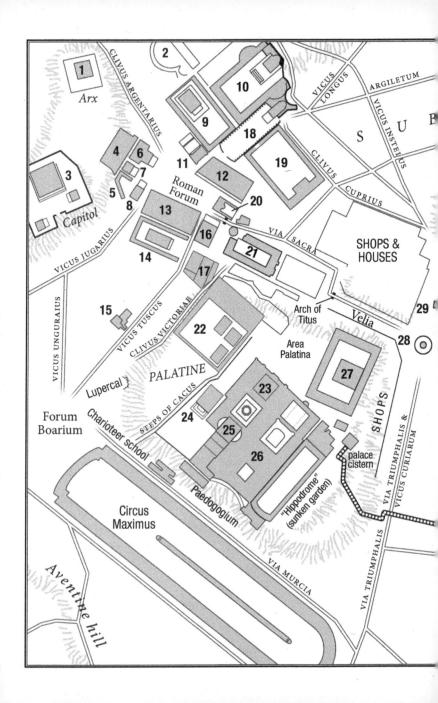

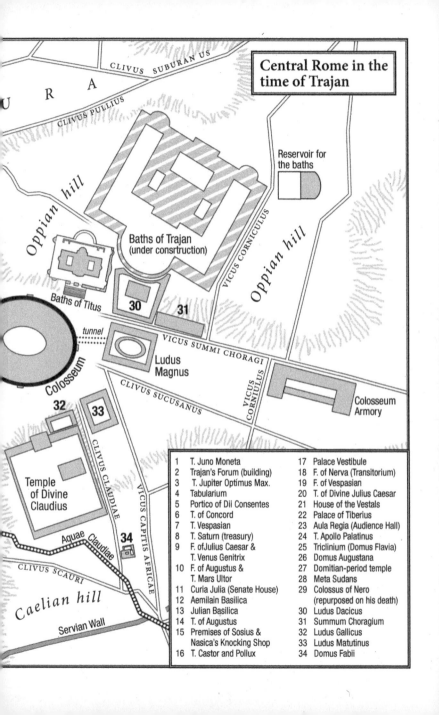

Central Rome in the time of Trajan

CLIVUS SUBURANUS

CLIVUS PULLIUS

Oppian hill

Baths of Trajan (under consrtruction)

Reservoir for the baths

VICUS CORNICULUS

Oppian hill

Baths of Titus

30   31

tunnel

VICUS SUMMI CHORAGI

Ludus Magnus

Colosseum

VICUS CORNICULUS

Colosseum Armory

CLIVUS SUCUSANUS

32   33

Temple of Divine Claudius

CLIVUS CLAUDIAE

VICUS CAPITIS AFRICAE

Aquae Claudiae

34

CLIVUS SCAURI

Caelian hill

Servian Wall

1 T. Juno Moneta	17 Palace Vestibule
2 Trajan's Forum (building)	18 F. of Nerva (Transitorium)
3 T. Jupiter Optimus Max.	19 F. of Vespasian
4 Tabularium	20 T. of Divine Julius Caesar
5 Portico of Dii Consentes	21 House of the Vestals
6 T. of Concord	22 Palace of Tiberius
7 T. Vespasian	23 Aula Regia (Audience Hall)
8 T. Saturn (treasury)	24 T. Apollo Palatinus
9 F. ofJulius Caesar &	25 Triclinium (Domus Flavia)
T. Venus Genitrix	26 Domus Augustana
10 F. of Augustus &	27 Domitian-period temple
T. Mars Ultor	28 Meta Sudans
11 Curia Julia (Senate House)	29 Colossus of Nero
12 Aemilain Basilica	(repurposed on his death)
13 Julian Basilica	30 Ludus Dacicus
14 T. of Augustus	31 Summum Choragium
15 Premises of Sosius &	32 Ludus Gallicus
Nasica's Knocking Shop	33 Ludus Matutinus
16 T. Castor and Pollux	34 Domus Fabii

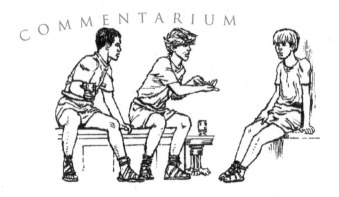

Quintus Caecilius Alba was telling his friend and lover, Junius Tullius Rufio, that he'd read about the old British saying: "the Law is an ass." Quintus explained to a deeply puzzled Rufio that those backward, barbarian Britons consider the Law to be a bit of a silly donkey. As the son of a senator, Quintus naturally disdains to handle real money, but to Rufio an *ass* (how it's pronounced) is a Roman coin—though more usually spelled *as* (plural *asses*). The Latin *aes rude*, meaning "rough bronze," was a form of currency way back in the mists of history, Quintus lectures. Rufio doesn't care much about this, as far as he's concerned the *as* is the basic coin of the Imperium, even though it's now cast in copper instead of bronze, with fractions such as the *semis* (½), *triens* (⅓), *quadrans* (¼), *uncia* (1/12) also a measure of weight (ounce). The *dupondis* has the value of 2 *asses*, the *sestertius* (2½ *asses*, plural *sesterces*), *quinarius* (5 *asses*), *denarius* (10 *asses*), and the *aureus* (250 *asses*— that's a lot of *as*).

Calculating costs is never a simple matter, but if it's any guide Junilla Tullia pays Eutychus somewhere between 600–800 *asses* a month for tutoring Rufio's young brother Cornelius Tullius Cato— that's when they can get the little brat up from his bed in the mornings; while Rufio and Quintus can enjoy a much longer lie-in during the winter for a strange reason.

Romans judge the passage of time by the use of hour-marked candles, an hourglass, or the infernal Greek inventions of the sundial and water clock, the latter called a *clepsydra*—"Although those slippery-sly Egyptians claim the water clock as their own invention," Quintus splutters indignantly. Meanwhile, Rufio has to explain to the cute German prince-hostage-slave Adalhard how Romans divide up the day into 24 *horae*, 12 hours of day and 12 hours of night, he tells him. "But our hours aren't fixed—your 'nine to five' in the office in Germania is like a stretchy band here in Rome. Since day begins with sunrise and night with sunset…"

Yes, yes, nods Adalhard, he's got that bit.

"And since the length of sunlight varies with the seasons, it follows that the length of the hour changes accordingly, *oder nicht*?"

Adalhard does follow this reasoning.

"A midsummer night is approximately a third of the whole day, a midwinter day only a third of the whole day, so at the winter solstice an hour is about 45 minutes, while at the summer solstice an hour is about 75 minutes. In general terms, the sixth hour of the day represents midday, the tenth hour—usually the hour at which guests start to arrive for formal dinners—is four o'clock in the afternoon."

It's clear to Adalhard that Rufio has gone and caught Quintus's hectoring-lecturing tone… *Zzzzzzz*

Adalhard's little nap might last for as little as a *secunda* (24 modern seconds) or perhaps as long as a *minuta* (24 modern minutes). When it comes to gladiatorial combat a *minuta* can be a lifetime of pain and a *secunda* the measure of a man's life in the arena. Hold on to that thought!

Finally—at Rufio's insistence—as a budding poet, Quintus would like to apologize in advance to any number of Roman rhymers, and also to point out that *gladiator* means "swordsman," from the short stabbing sword they use called a *gladius*, and that it's also vulgar for penis, in other words, "dick" or "cock"… and Flaccus feels like a boy.

Capua, 15th day of September, AD 108

Money changed hands along with a small phial. Britannicus saw nothing of the other's hooded features, a mere shade within the dark corridors of the amphitheater's underworks. Above their heads, through heavy masonry, came the muted roar of spectators hungry for blood. It sounded as if all of Capua was up there on the stone benches. The instructions Britannicus had received the day before assured the slave of the benefits of the phial's contents to his master: an additive that would infuse the gladiator with more stamina than his already prodigious levels and help ensure victory in the arena.

He went smartly past the cramped and noisy arming chamber where the lesser gladiators were crammed together. As their coarse banter faded, he reached the cubicles set aside for champions, more private spaces for the most celebrated fighters where they could prepare for combat in seclusion. Britannicus offered a cup of wine.

The traditional gesture touched his master. He sniffed appreciatively. "I don't know how you do it, but this is a fine Caecuban. Thank you, Britannicus." He quaffed the draught in one gulp. Britannicus took the cup from him and helped to fit and adjust his *manica*. The arm guard extended to the shoulder and left side of the gladiator's chest. Then he fitted the *galerus*, a metal shoulder shield to protect the neck and chin from an upswinging *gladius*. "Thank you. I will need it today, facing one of the *secutores*. Not, I hope, that huge Scythian bastard Bebryx. His reach is long." He smiled warmly at the Briton, at the way the boy's flaxen hair fell into oh-so grave eyes. They were well-matched opposites: the slave so white, the gladiator so black. "I shall be back for you before the sand is half-run through the glass." And with those words Capreolus swept out into the arena to the roar of the Capuan crowd.

Britannicus smiled to himself as the mob's noise settled into an expectant hush. He held the cup aloft, turned it upside down and let the remaining drops of dark wine fall to the stone floor. In the dust they looked like drops of blood. He scuffed them out. Beyond the walls, the clash of iron rang out.

Still smiling, he lowered his arms and took the cup to the basin to wash it out carefully. Capreolus was a tremendous fighter, always the victor, but a performance-boost couldn't hurt, and the man who had persuaded Britannicus of the potion's efficacy said that in offering it he was only protecting an investment. But Capreolus was too honest for his own good, in Britannicus's opinion, so he didn't want to risk his master finding anything suspicious in an unwashed cup, otherwise he'd go straight to the authorities and declare the fight unfair. And Britannicus certainly didn't want a nosy referee discovering that he had put something in the champion's wine to give him the promised advantage over his opponent.

For a moment it seemed the ground must cave in with the thumping and crashing as Capreolus, the black Nubian *retiarius*, leaped around Bebryx's helmeted head. Bebryx thrashed this way and that in an attempt to avoid lethal thrusts from the cruel trident. As a secutor he was thankful for the helmet with its face covering which protected him from the trident's prongs, but in rapid action its two eyeholes often made it hard to see where his opponent was. Due to his massive size he fought with an extra long gladius—almost the span of a cavalary sword—and one with unusually sharp edges for a thrusting weapon. He whirled, acquired target again, watched and waited for an opportunity to turn the tables on the black man. They clashed in a blur of flying limbs, half-deafened by the ringing of iron, and a fine haze of crimson droplets from nicks and open wounds.

As a giant beast baying for blood, the roars of the spectators rose to the heavens above Capua from Italy's second largest amphitheater. Bebryx flicked away sweat from his eyes with a vigorous shake of his head inside the confines of the helmet and readied himself for the next predictable move. He knew his adversary's style and fighting rhythm. And it came. Capreolus delivered three blows so rapid they would have slain a novice in the blink of an eye, but Bebryx was an adept and three-time champion adored by all of Capua.

Nevertheless, he only managed to avoid the last strike of the wicked tines by jinking violently sideways and throwing himself to the bloodied sand to roll over and over. All around the merciless gore-soaked theater of death his name sounded from a score thousand lips. For three years he had survived and prospered in a career that averaged ten months for even the most agile youngster. Yet it seemed Capreolus was learning new tricks in training from his *doctore* for in the next breathless moments the Nubian twice did the opposite of what Bebryx had expected and followed up ferociously on the advantage it gained him.

This last strike left Bebryx eating bloody grit on the floor of the arena again, desperately struggling to avoid the retiarius's trident or becoming entangled in his infernal fisherman's net. Looking up, he caught a glimpse of his adversary's balls and cock, tightly compressed like a black snake about to spring from the narrow confines of the inadequate pouch.

Capua was honored for its provincial celebration of the Ludi Romani festival by the presence of Consul Quintus Pompeius Falco to represent the absent Imperator Caesar Marcus Ulpius Nerva Traianus Augustus. Falco had decreed a primus exhibition—a bitter fight to the death. Bebryx had no intention of paying the ferryman yet—and one of them had to die—so it would be Capreolus the Nubian who would not be keeping his beautiful blond British boy warm tonight. The Nubian stabbed at him again, and again Bebryx dodged by rolling aside. On the fourth occasion, however, for just the blink of an eye, Capreolus lost balance. He seemed to falter and let his net trail as if he had lost the use of that arm. He recovered sufficiently to move his feet and ready another stabbing blow. Bebryx easily avoided the surprisingly clumsy maneuver. Capreolus staggered as he thrust a second time, but his aim went wide and he buried the points of his trident deep in the red-streaked sand.

Bebryx reached out, grasped a handful of gore, and in the flash of a lizard's tail hurled it into his opponent's face. The sand, made glutinous with spilled blood, clung and blinded. Shouting his rage, Capreolus lashed out about him. Bebryx rose easily to his feet as the crowd roared its approval. In his unseeing state, the Nubian stepped into the tangle of his own net. Faster than a striking snake Bebryx wrapped it around Capreolus's legs and pulled. The enraged fighter crashed to the arena floor in a welter of ebony limbs.

Adoring women in the crowd screamed and gasped their orgasmic excitement as Bebryx snatched up the trident and, reversing it, placed its razor-sharp tines at the throat of its owner. Capreolus cleared the sand from his eyes and glared up balefully at Bebryx.

"Kill!" roared the crowd as one. "Kill! Kill!"

Bebryx looked up at the imperial box, where the distant figure of the city's chief magistrate consulted Pompeius Falco.

"Kill! Kill! Kill! Kill!"

The consul stood up to gesture the deathblow. Bebryx leaned his full hefty weight on the end of the trident and felt it pierce tough black flesh. The razor-sharp points bored through skin, muscle, and bone as a fountain of blood blossomed from the major vessels torn apart by the thrust to end another life.

High in the amphitheater's stands money exchanged hands, a

thousand times more than Britannicus had received in the belief he was helping his lover and master to victory. Blood money for bets laid in the certainty of the winner, in the certainty of a planned-for loser. Fortuna was all very well in the arena, but she wasn't a guarantee—that required a human touch to ensure a happy outcome.

Blithely unaware that the fight had been a fraud, though puzzled at his opponent's uncharacteristic sudden clumsiness, Bebryx watched as three attendants dug their meat hooks deep in Capreolus's ruined neck and dragged the lifeless corpse away to the Porta Libitinensis—Libitina's gate, where the death goddess welcomed fallen gladiators through her one-way portal. Garlands and purses full of money landed about Bebryx's feet. Grateful gamblers usually threw in a portion of their winnings in tribute. As Bebryx finished saluting the imperial box and his adoring fans—all those salivating matrons—he considered with anticipation taking over Capreolus's lovely slave. Britannicus would make a fine gift to himself and otherwise the poor boy would be so lonely without his big Nubian to cuddle him in the increasingly chilly autumn nights.

O·N·E | I

Rome, 6th to 13th days of October AD 108

Damianus never showed much emotion, not that he didn't have feelings (apart from sheer terror that a clumsy slave would break an invaluable artefact and he'd get the blame) but he felt it a wise course to remain as expressionless as possible. So it was with great bemusement that Junilla Tullia found herself wrapped in her secretary's clutching arms. She had been away from the Tullius Emporium of Artistic Excellence before and never been greeted with such enthusiasm.

"How wonderful to have you back, domina!"

But then, she'd never been away for so long before or left her sister Velabria in charge either.

"Move it, Dammy," young Cato cried as he shoved past his mother and her bear-hugging amanuensis.

"Out the way, Dammy," said Rufio impatiently, following his little brother inside in front of a train of baggage-burdened slaves led by Zeno, Phocas, and Alexius. They all flowed, heads down like frantic market porters, around the immoveable island-nation of Aunty Velabria—all except the Tullii boys.

"There you are at last!" she boomed as she scooped both hapless youths into her iron embrace. "What time do you call this? It's the sixth day of October!" Her indignation flowed out as she released Cato and Rufio to flee toward the section of the sprawling domus housing the private apartments and sleeping chambers. "Damianus! Put my sister down instantly and behave like a rational human being… if that is even remotely possible. It's high time you got back, Junilla. I would never have agreed to mother your establishment along if I'd known you would be gadding about the provinces this long. My vineyards will be wrecks by the time I get back to Liguria."

"Don't exaggerate, Velabria dear. It's been less than five months and Egypt's a bit more than a mile down the Via Appia. Yes, Damianus, that's quite enough. There, there. Everything will be all right now. What have you done to him?" she aimed at her sister as Damianus slipped out toward the porch, a beatific expression plastered over his otherwise blank features. He was so wrapped in relief that he only narrowly avoided running into Flaccus Caepio.

"Done anything? *I* was the one doing everything. I don't know how you put up with him. And as for your slaves, well, you'd do better selling the lot, especially that waste of space Zeno. He doesn't know his place."

Aunty Velabria's voice reached the depths of the rambling Emporium domus, but mercifully at a dampened volume, though not quiet enough to prevent Rufio smiling at the thought of hunky Zeno no doubt running a mile from his temporary mistress's erotic advances. Aunty Velabria didn't take *No* for an answer, especially not a *ZeNo*, though the slave always had a beaming *Yes* for Rufio's occasional requirements. He smirked as she resumed her assault.

"Oh, and here comes the night watchman extraordinary," she snapped on seeing Flaccus standing just inside the entrance. "Why you took him along to Egypt, I'll never understand."

"Leave Flaccus alone," Junilla admonished. "He's been most valuable on a difficult and often very dangerous voyage. And he's no doubt tired, aren't you dear? So just drop all that stuff there and I'll get the Waste Of Space to deal with it. Now, off you go to your home, put your feet up and have a nice long rest."

Flaccus beamed at Junilla and divested himself of a forest of leather tubes containing scrolls of notes on all the antique statues, furniture, and other valuable objects still stored in Egypt awaiting the next sailing season. Their collection had been a primary reason for the Emperor and the Court's trip to the province. As Flaccus lowered the last case, Velabria started in on him again.

"Nice long rest! You, young man would be more gainfully employed in your cohort of the vigiles, putting out fires and arresting drunks than traipsing about the Imperium. And by Magna Mater's mammaries," Velabria shrieked. "Who is this... this *barbarian*?"

Junilla smiled to herself at her sister's ability to forget that only two generations separated them both from Gallic tribalism as she reached out a hand to pull close to her a young lad. His straight dark hair was oddly bleached to nearer a straw color at the front. His smoky eyes and cherubic cheeks contrasted oddly, though attractively, with his dusky skin. "This is Hephaestion—"

"A slave?"

Furrows crossed Junilla's normally smooth forehead. "Definitely not. Hephaestion is a... a long story for another time."

Another torrent of Aunty Velabria's invective reached into the depths of the Emporium domus. "Phew, that was a narrow escape," young Cato muttered. "Hopefully she'll be sent packing now we're back."

"Who's packing?"

The brothers stopped in surprise at the sight of a slender wisp of a boy standing in the corridor, revealed by the last of the slaves pattering off to distribute baggage in the various rooms.

"Felix," said Cato, a hint of well-met excitement in his tone.

Rufio gave the boy a sly wink. "Woof-Woof!"

The son of Clivius Ostiensus, headman of the powerful West Aventine Crossroads Club, gave both boys his familiar crooked grin. Rufio always found it hard to resist the feral look a broken incisor gave him—that and his tidy, helmet-like hair that in some lights lent him an uncanny resemblance to Quintus, a younger version of Rufio's noble friend... and lover.

Cato rushed up and exchanged a complex series of hand, arm, and finger clasps with Felix, the secret greeting of the Little Aventine Foxes. The loose confederation of gangs—when not properly engaged at a school—ran wild over the confusion of market gardens and unruly scrub land below the Aventine hill, hemmed in by the backs of the port warehouses and Mons Testaceus, the man-made hill of smashed earthenware containers past their best for transporting oil, wine, or grain. Rufio leaned casually against the wall, the sole of one boot lifted up to rest against it, content for the moment to be reminded of the sex he'd enjoyed with Woof-Woof (Felix's favorite position was doggy-style). "Here," Cato said, unstringing a charm from the silver chain around his neck that held his *bulla*. "You should have this back. It did bring me luck and kept me safe from… oh, too much to tell right now."

Felix took back the beautifully detailed winged phallus, the good-luck travel charm he'd given Cato when they set off for Egypt.

Rufio was mildly curious. "How did you know we were back, and how did you get past the dragon?"

"Oh Rufio, you can't expect to slip into Rome in company with imperial troops, pack animals, and the like," Felix said in between happy chuckles at the older boy's naivety. "The news was all over the Aventine before you left Ostia and I got here before you peeled away from the Emperor's train at the city gate. As for your dreadful Aunty Velabria, I came over the back wall." He shrugged narrow shoulders as if climbing from the roof of a Tiber Port warehouse fifty feet below the steep rocky hillside on which the Emporium was perched and then over the back wall of the property into the private garden courtyard was an everyday event.

"You will fall to your well-deserved death on the tiles below scaling that sheer wall." Rufio smothered a laugh and laid a proprietorial hand on the boy's shoulder.

"And who is this?" Felix swung around in Rufio's grip to stare at the dusky-skinned boy who had just appeared in the corridor behind them.

Cato huffed dismissively.

"That is Hephaestion,' Rufio said. 'And before you ask, he's a long story. Still, the best way to get acquainted is this way." And he swept

Hephaestion under one arm, Felix under the other, and headed for his bedchamber.

"Oh well, go ahead. Leave me to my own devices." Cato gave a theatrical sniff. "I can see you're gagging for it after such a long and tedious haul from Ostia."

Rufio threw his brother a casual middle finger over his shoulder as he guided Felix and Hephaestion into his bedroom, running fingers through thick, dark but sun-bleached hair—*so exotic on one hand*—and an equally generous, black crop—*on the other; so like Quintus...*

"Felix, meet Hephaestion..."

Rufio's hand cupped kneeling Woof-Woof's chin and gently urged him forward until the boy's lips met Hephaestion's bobbing hard-on as his other hand on the dusky new arrival's pert bottom pushed the two together.

"Say hello, Felix..."

Long pink tongue lapped up the smooth underside of the shaft pressed against his nose until eager upper lip slid over the proffered crown...

As was his habit, Rufio preferred action to words and had led the lads to his bed where he'd proceeded seductively to strip them, then got Felix into his favorite doggy position on all fours in front of a quickly rampant Hephaestion.

His teasing fingers deep in their tight asses got the boys going, pushing his spit-slick erection into Woof-Woof's yielding sphincter barely checked his enthusiastic enjoyment of the pretty newcomer's cock. Sounds of urgent sucking, fucking, and gasping filled the little room, and soon Rufio reached around Felix's slender waist to work him to spurting climax before pulling out and hauling Hephaestion away from the hungry mouth gorging on his erection and around behind doggy boy's gaping anus to take over shafting him. Rufio's own rampant meat invading his backside fueled the Graeco-Lybian-

Egyptian's pumping action and Felix collapsed in a gurgling heap as he was thoroughly had.

"Good to see you get to know each other so enthusiastically," rasped Rufio. *Yes! It's good to be back home—pity Quintus isn't here to join in.*

He ran a hand over his flat, hard belly under the loincloth that he'd untied and draped across his middle. It was fun to travel, but so much nicer to be home, to lie on a bed that wasn't rocking and rolling on the high seas. In a small niche cut into the thickness of the outer wall the sightless and slightly cross-eyed oriental eyes of Ramesses the Great stared serenely down at him, a reminder of the adorable Greek-Egyptian who had sold it to him, a reminder of the mindless sex they'd had in his shop. The name came back… Sekhemkhet-Adonis. His wandering hand found his idle cock.

Yes, good to be back. On the other hand, as a vigorous youth, Quintus Caecilius Alba resented being cooped up so much at home. Since his return from Egypt a week ago his father Lucius had insisted that Quintus should "not roam off like some lowly prole as you have been doing for most of this year." Which meant all he had to look forward to was sparring with other patrician adolescents—from horseback with long cavalry *spatha* swords and on foot with a *gladius*, the legionary's short stabbing sword—during his weekly weapons training at the *disciplina castra*.

His father's was an unworthy rebuke, and to refer to his recent voyage with Trajan as roaming like a prole was ridiculous. But it would be bad form to argue with the *pater familias*, even less so as the youngest of four brothers—his two older sisters Fabia the Younger and Julia, didn't count. The Nile tour had been a state affair, while Rufio and his mother Junilla made a collection of statuary to adorn Trajan's new civic projects in Rome. Quintus was taken along because as Rufio's lover Junilla considered him an honorary member of Familia Tullii and because Trajan wanted him along for... other reasons. Not that he was telling his father any of that, although his relationship with the most powerful man in the world was indirectly his father's fault in going along with Uncle Livy's shameful scheming. But Quintus didn't want to think about any of that.

"You must either take up the law or we must find you a legion that will have you in the capacity of junior tribune, my boy," his father insisted. "And before all that, I haven't forgotten that you are betrothed to Vipsania Metella. I may no longer need her extensive dowry, but additional wealth is never a hindrance." Quintus had fondly hoped that the subject would never again be raised; apparently a wish ignored. The words of his horrid brother Marcus over another tedious family dinner came back to him. "I'll bet your Vipsania will be as easily opened up and moist inside as this," he'd said before burying his mouth in the succulent pink heart of the fig he'd just opened. "I hear the Lady Vipsania is very beautiful,"

Quintus's Syrian body slave Ashur had said soon after. "How do you know?" Quintus demanded indignantly. Ashur shrugged. "All virgin girls of marriageable age are described as 'beautiful,' so I'm sure she must be." *Ashur, you were a great help.*

Marriage! By Juno's jiggling jugs he wasn't ready to settle down, wasn't sure he'd ever be ready. The thought of the virtually unknown Vipsania formed a leaden lump in his gut, as if he'd eaten a surfeit of lampreys and been unable to stick a feather down his throat in the *vomitorium*. Quintus didn't approve of the dietary antics that some of his father's senatorial cronies practiced at banquets, not that his father did either, to be fair. The Caecilii were an old-fashioned abstemious family in most matters other than the accrual of wealth. Except for Uncle Livy, of course, who exemplified gluttony, greed, and groping hands.

It didn't help his mood that he resented his lover Rufio's freedom to *roam* like a prole (*well, he is a pleb, after all*) whenever he pleased, though to be fair (he was trying to be principled, and failing rather) he knew that Rufio also had extensive responsibilities to his family's trade in antiquities and its party arranging business. He rolled onto his stomach and ground his hips against the bed, thinking of Rufio, missing him, and also of Ashur (sent out to get some sweet snacks). Actually, he resented most that Rufio was almost certainly having sex every day and night, either with Woof-Woof or Hephaestion. Probably with both at the same time, knowing Rufio. His mind slipped back to that apocalyptic day on the plateau above Memphis—not the battle that came after, the battle was the fateful bit, but the bit before that. Up the piebald pyramid of Snoferu. On top. With Rufio. And the lithe local guide-boy Hephaestion. Screwing him, fucking the boy's cock into Rufio's mouth. Skewering himself on Rufio at the same time. Nice times…

"Dominus? Were you talking to yourself?"

Ashur peered around the edge of the door with a plate of pastry delicacies in his hand and a hopeful expression on his face.

Quintus smiled lazily. "Daydreaming. Come on in. Put those on the side table and your ass down here next to me. Wait! Is that a honey cone I can see?"

'Yes, Quintus.' When they were alone Ashur was permitted to use his master's name, though he often took that liberty too far. "Would you like one?"

"Yes, but not for eating. Bring it over."

Ashur picked up the large pastry cone, its outer rim glistening with honey, and stood over Quintus, who slowly rolled over. In doing so the loincloth got left behind under his butt and his stiffening cock stuck up, swaying from side to side. Ashur grinned appreciatively.

"Up-end the cone over me... yes, like that. Ooh, it's cold!"

Ashur waggled the pastry case about until he'd quite coated his master's hard penis in honey and the runnels made it resemble a candle leaking molten wax down the shaft.

"Now warm me up."

Ashur lobbed the emptied cone back to its plate, dipped gracefully to his knees beside the bed, and dropped his mouth over the sticky cock. "Mmmm... tastes lovely and sweet, and... mmmm." Ashur burbled on happily as he licked Quintus's foreskin back and worked his prehensile tongue around the unsheathed crown, slurping up more honey where it ran down the thick, fleshy rod. Where the sweetness gathered richly in dark, short pubic hair Ashur lathed his tongue through it before licking down to the firm balls, and then back up the shaft to suck hard on the cock head.

When he sensed Quintus growing close to a climax, he glanced sideways and smiled slyly into his master's dark eyes. Without removing his lips from encircling the tip he said softly, "Will you fuck me, Quintus? Like you sometimes like to."

At the husky command, Ashur slipped off his tunic—as usual at home he wasn't wearing anything underneath—and eagerly climbed up beside Quintus. When Quintus didn't move, Ashur's grin grew broader. In a trice he was squatted up facing Quintus. He reached down to grip his master's cock and guide it, slippery with his own saliva and a faint coating of honey, into his hole. With a wiggle he positioned himself and then lowered his body. Quintus sighed with deep satisfaction as he felt Ashur's tight passage enfold his cock, the anus and internal muscles gripping and releasing in repeated rhythm.

Within moments they were both sighing like over-exercised horses, chariot racers fighting to the finish line in a lather of sweat. Quintus reached down to grasp Ashur's cock, bobbing in time with his frenzied up and down motion.

"Harder," Ashur moaned.

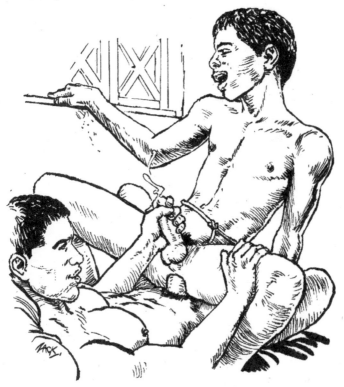

"Faster," Quintus groaned. And together they came, Quintus slamming his seed into Ashur, while the slave boy shot jets of thick cream at Quintus. The first splashed his shuddering abdomen, the second plastered his pectorals, the third slapped his chin and thick jizz ran down over his Adam's apple and into the hollow of his neck.

"I needed that," Quintus breathed as they eased apart.

"Me too." Ashur grinned. He bent down to lick Quintus clean of his own cum and then looked up sexily from under fluttering lashes. "Now would you actually like to *eat* one of the honey pastries I went to such trouble to fetch you?"

T·W·O | II

14th day of October AD 108

An eager crowd collected around the latest edition of the *Daily Gazette*. One of the publisher's copy slaves had just attached it to its usual position on a column in the outer arcade of the Aemilian Basilica. The items of most interest to those scrutinizing the details were the names of gladiators and charioteers recently added to the list of contests promised for the forthcoming Ludi Plebeii, the games dedicated to Jupiter Optimus Maximus and held between the 4th to 17th days of November. The Plebeian Games were also a subject of interest to four men gathered in a quiet corner of the basilica, though for a very different reason. The eldest peered closely at a small scroll as he talked to his colleagues.

"Tricostus did as he was bid at Nemausus. The fight ran for long enough to give good value, so the mob voted him mercy when he threw it. We cleared a cool quarter million sesterces on that one bout alone. The runner arrived at the eighth hour yesterday and confirmed the referee at Nemausus is happy to take more deals for Vestalia, and the games for Apollo, as well as the Victoriae Caesaris festival games next summer. I should get a list of participants well in time to make our dispositions and cost the… *remuneration*s."

"Our backs are covered? Publius Fabius Virius glared at the man they knew only as the Banker.

"Naturally. All our dealings in Gaul are handled through no less than three cutouts. Exactly as we do here in Italy."

"Gaul and Italy… it's all very well, but we need to expand into the wider market," Virius growled. "There are many venues in the Imperium."

The Banker only smirked in response, the thin-lipped smile of a Nile crocodile. "I have something to say about that, all in good time."

Senator Fabius Virius, the Banker, and two other men in togas, one a senatorial broad-striper like Virius the other an equestrian thin-striper, were gathered around a table in a quiet corner of the Aemilian Basilica. The four men called themselves the Summa, the top men of a shady organization usually abbreviated to the acronym S·A·D·A, which a very limited number of people outside the Summa knew stood for *Societas ad divitias augendas*, esentially a syndicate dedicated to the increase of its members' wealth… by any means. There were many similar institutions in the larger towns and cities, none entirely honest in their dealings, but few were as avaricious or vicious in the pursuit of riches as S·A·D·A—or as secretive. In the basilica the four were indistinguishable from the numerous legitimate moneylenders conducting business under the arcades, though there were many who said that *legitimate* and *moneylender* could never be synonymous.

Virius—he liked to think of himself as commandingly virile— had a short fuse at the best of times, but the way Cornelius Aemilius Papus, the other broad-striper, kept fiddling with his *latus clavus*, the thick purple stripe that marked them both out from other men as senators of Rome (or it would were Virius wearing his formal toga), was evidently a matter of overweening pride to Papus. From an ancient patrician family, Virius was of the top echelon of the Senate—a "conscript father," and he held *arrivistes* like Papus in low regard. The fop was new to the House. His adlection by Trajan came about in order to fill a vacancy, but also because the fiddly shit-face had plenty of "new" money, much more than the million sesterces held in property required to qualify as a senator. The signifying purple stripes of new men were always broader and brighter than tradition and good breeding required—presumably, Virius sniffed, to show off their improved social standing.

Virius found his mind wandering, something it was wont to do lately, and no wonder after what he'd been through recently. The year of the principal consuls Appius Annius Trebonius Gallus and Marcus Appius Bradua had been his *annus horribilis*. It had seen him reduced to associating with men such as Livius Caecilius Dio—like Virius, a senator and new member of s·a·d·a but not of the Summa. Livy was a loathsome toad and normally a rival to be shunned at all costs. Virius shuddered at the thought that the boorish idiot would almost certainly be lurking out in the Forum to accost him as to what information the Banker had presented. What Virius most wanted when the meeting was done was to fly straight back up the Caelian hill to Domus Fabii, to his adopted son Ambrosius, and fuck the boy stupid. Pliable Ambrosius had to stand in for Virius's wife Fabia, away in the south, no doubt spending what was left of the family purse. If he were honest, Ambrosius stood in for his wife even when the wretched woman was at home.

The Banker was speaking again and Virius dragged his attention back to the list of recent gladiatorial games and the yields from them. "These sums are just from Italian cities—not Gaul, Belgica, Germania, or Britannia," he added for emphasis. "They are for the summer months, followed by the accounted takings in sesterces from bets put on by placemen on the... *ahem*, arranged bouts. You can examine the detail later, but these are rounded figures in thousands: at Alba Fucens, a hundred and fifty; Altinum, two hundred; Capua over a four-day ludus, just short of a million; Egnatia, four hundred...

Virius agreed that he could inspect the detail at a later date and became lost in his thoughts again, bitter ruminations about the foundering of his fortunes through no fault of his own—and the reason he was now engaged in this tawdry business, clawing back wealth any way he could. Like any established patrician family since the mists of time Fabii wealth came from valuable agricultural estates, at least a half-score. They were dotted about the Italian peninsula and the northern ones included marble and stone quarries. With the advent of the imperial era ownership of quarries multiplied Fabii incomes. The Divine Augustus boasted he'd found Rome built of brick and left it clothed in marble, and since his reign emperor after emperor had glorified his name in high-quality stone.

For the past three generations Fabii riches increased many-fold through the supply of every conceivable kind of building material from north and south of the peninsula, although the value of business in Rome was worth ten times the rest of Italy put together. Now, with the spoils of Trajan's Dacian conquests filling the imperial treasury to overflowing, Caesar had embarked on the biggest civic regeneration of Rome since Augustus. Virius used his influence at every turn to ensure his bitter rivals in masonry, the Caecilii, were kept out of the best contracts.

That was when that piffling polliwog Livius Caecilius Dio screwed everything up. In theory, as pater familias, it was Livy's brother-in-law Lucius Caecilius Alba who controlled their business, but it was Livy who claimed to pull the levers. The slob came up with the notion of pandering Lucius's youngest son Quintus to Trajan—ever weak for a handsome and manly youngster—in return for a monopoly on imperial contracts. Virius conceded that the boy was a true-blooded beauty. He was never sure what he wanted more: kill Quintus or fuck his brains out—preferably both but the last first. But curses of Suadela! Trajan fell for Quintus, gave Livy what the slug had asked for and Fabii clients were cut out of all imperial contracts. There was at least a laugh in it. His own clever scheme burnt Livy because Trajan ensured—presumably at the insistence of his young amour—that brother-in-law Lucius and not Livy was named as principal in the deal. The son got it all for his father. Hah!

And when things couldn't possibly get worse there came the business with that lying bastard from the south, Kaeso Casca Malpensa. He promised the mint in return for Fabii senatorial influence—a not uncommon proposition. However Malpensa—unaware of Familia Fabii's fading power, something Virius was at pains to hide—had been as economical with the truth as Virius. It had to do with killing off the many Crossroads brotherhoods— effectively Rome's criminal underworld—so he could take over and freely sell drugs from the Orient, a market Malpensa claimed he'd cornered. Normally, Virius wouldn't have given the "barbarian" the time of day, but with his wealth draining away at an alarming rate Malpensa's promise of "untold riches" was too attractive to turn down. In a side plan of his own, Virius cajoled Livy to join forces with him because he needed a man inside Familia Caecilii to gain whatever Intelligence there was to be had regarding the imperial contracts in order to be ready to strike the instant of his financial restoration. It could have worked if it hadn't been for a most unfortunate coincidence involving a magnificent bronze statue of a satyr with a huge phallus he had purchased from the Tullius Emporium of Artistic Excellence. How was he to know it belonged to Malpensa and due to a clerical error on the Emporium's part it was supposed to be stored, not sold? Neither could he have known what the satyr contained in its hollow interior... †

Virius sighed inwardly. There was little to be gained in rehashing the subsequent humiliation and disaster, or the astonishing way in which Quintus Caecilius Alba and his red-headed catamite Rufio, son of the stupid bitch Junilla Tullia who sold him the thrice-damned statue in the first place—triumphed over adversity once again.

Virius desperately needed to restore his fortunes. His clients were deserting him (the most disloyal to those cock-sucking Caecilii) and what was he without a solid base of equestrian clients? Time-honored tradition forbade senators from engaging in trade but did not prevent them operating through the patronage of the equestrian class. In the political sphere a client canvassed the common citizens to vote for their patron in elections and if necessary bribed or threatened violence to ensure voters saw sense. In the commercial sphere Virius as patron used his senatorial influence to benefit his clients and supplied the funds for his Equestrian clients to handle the dirty day-to-day commerce according to their professional skills. They were well rewarded for their efforts, as much in social preferment and in legal protection when required as financially. Without clients Virius could not take advantage of his stone and marble quarries, and soon enough if his fortunes did not improve, he might have to sell off even those and more of his estates. It was unthinkable.

"…Paestum, a quarter million; Patavium, four hundred; and last but not least at Puteoli we netted just over a million." The Banker looked up from his scroll with a smile of bleak satisfaction. "Which means, my friends, there is more than sufficient in our purse for just about every bout in the Ludi Plebeii. Games in Rome always cost more in bribes and whatnot, but the yield is so much greater and we're comfortably able to cover the expense."

Flashing his *latus clavus*, Papus spoke in a reedy tone. He kept his eyes on the Banker, though his words were addressed to the equestrian narrow-striper seated at his side. "I do trust that you have your… helpers in readiness, Gaius Fabricius Luscinus?"

Virius knew Luscinus slightly. The young looking forty-year-old was known as the "hard man" of his patron Senator J— (who disdained the furtive business his client dealt with on his behalf but happily took his stipend from the profits and never objected to Luscinus manhandling his political opponents when the occasion arose). He evidently shared Virius's dislike of Papus although he smiled engagingly, but the sentiment never reached glacial eyes. Virius was only one of few who knew Luscinus relished a private cognomen: Panthera. The lion, tiger, leopard, and panther were members of the genus Panthera, predator of all animals, feline and deadly and a name to inspire fear in any who failed in their undertakings to Luscinus. So the thin-striper smiled tightly and flashed his *clavus angustus* at the snotty-nosed new senator, a man only two years his senior. His narrow purple stripe was considerably more faded than the one Papus stroked continuously between finger and thumb, impatiently waiting an answer, but then the Luscinus toga had probably seen a lot of laundering to remove bloodstains after much hard work. Papus had to be endured, however, because the snot had the wherewithal when it was urgently needed. S·A·D·A's many investors demanded instant access to profits, which put pressure on the cash flow and left insufficient liquidity for the many *pecuniae* to put in the pockets of referees, agents, lanistas, and sometimes gladiators. That is where men like Papus came in, with funds to ensure the desirable outcome of a fight… for a bigger cut of the eventual huge profits from the gambling of course.

"I am perfectly prepared, Cornelius," Luscinus said smoothly. "And Fabius Virius has also been most supportive." They exchanged polite nods while Papus frowned at the over-familiar use of his own praenomen. "I anticipate a problem-free operation at all the events, including across the river in Trans Tiberim."

"I presume by Trans Tiberim you mean the Naumachia, but hasn't there been a problem with the aqueduct supplying the basin?" Papus asked with the prim certitude of a nitpicker.

"When the Divine Augustus had the artificial lake dug out, his engineers failed to get the levels correct for the water supply, but Caesar Trajan has had the fault rectified recently. There will be no problem staging the naval battles."

"And the Ludus Magnus?" Papus wasn't giving up.

"That too is in hand, Cornelius. Mumius Bulbus, the lanista, is one of my clients, and Dannotalus Dolabella of the Ludus Gallicus owes me for many favors." Luscinus's smile was odd in that it made the corners of his lips turn down.

Papus's eyebrows shot up. It was not proper etiquette for one of the equestrian order to wave the fact of his having a clientele in the face of one in the senatorial order.

"Well, we have two weeks of the Plebeian Games coming up," the Banker said to relieve the tension between the two. He chewed his lips in a distinctly hungry manner. "An opportunity to replenish coffers. Luscinus, when can you get me a confirmed final list of prospective candidates in the various venues? I hate having to rely on the *Daily Gazette*. You know how they love to exaggerate and they're always confusing fact with fiction."

"Do we get a choice of bouts?" Virius wanted to know. "After all, this is home ground and many of us know the form of the most successful gladiators... and those who could do with a boost in their purses."

The Banker looked at Luscinus, who nodded. "As soon as I've pulled all the facts together, we can sit again and make dispositions. I will certainly heed any advice you would be gracious enough to offer, Fabius Virius."

Papus jerked his pointy chin up importantly. "I expect I shall have some wisdom to impart as well. For instance, will that big Nubian, what's his name? Capreolus, the *retiarius*, will he be performing? I had money on him at Interamna last March. A very promising fellow."

The Banker exchanged a quick look with Luscinus, who spoke up. "You didn't hear the outcome of the Capua games this month?"

Papus frowned. "No. What occurred?"

"His lanista wasn't willing to play harpustum," the Banker said quietly. "Or, rather, he was, but only for a huge *pecunium*. He argued he was owed the ridiculous increase for all the past favors he has done us. I would have advised approaching his opponent with a counter-offer, but Bebryx is rather proud of his integrity."

"I found a way around the problem," Luscinus added. "Sadly, for the Nubian, the bout was changed at the last moment into a fight to the death, so the trainer learned a sharper lesson than he might, and the upshot is that Capreolus is no longer with us. Sad really. I agree. He was looking good for the Plebeian Games."

Virius gave a low grunt of approval and nodded decisively as he stood. "It's a tough business. If that's all, I shall take my leave. You can fill me in on our expansion plans another day,' he said to the Banker. 'There is another pressing matter I need to attend.' *Like splaying Ambrosius out on my bed and seeking some urgent relief between his firm ass cheeks.*

"Would you not like to pause a moment, good senator?" the Banker murmured. "It was you, after all, who accused us of not making a move into more international waters."

With a faint sigh of well-bred impatience, Virius turned back to the table. "Well?"

The Banker sniffed in a self-satisfied way. "Thanks—in part—to Luscinus, most exciting news, I assure you."

And he started to inform them of some interesting developments.

Late autumn sun made the morning unexpectedly hot and stuffy but Livius Caecilius Dio was too eager to learn any outcome of the discussions from which, to his immense frustration, he was barred. Was he not supplying funding for this S·A·D·A the wretched Publius Fabius Virius had hauled him into? And why was he so incautious as to be so dragged after the last disaster the Fabian twat had embroiled him in? At least he'd escaped the Satyr of Capri fiasco with no more than bruised pride and the disappointment of not getting his hands on some of the "untold wealth" Malpensa had promised stupid Virius. Still, they were both out on their uppers. In his more honest moments, which he was pleased to say were infrequent, Livius admitted that he was in the same boat as his loathed colleague. Not quite as bad, though. At least his putrid brother-in-law Lucius Caecilius Alba had allowed him a hand in some minor aspects of their family businesses, and that earned the pittance he had offered to the potentially lucrative S·A·D·A operation … thanks to Virius's "good offices."

Just then he saw Virius materialize from the shade of the Aemilian Basilica's dark interior. A flash of amusement at the sight of the haughty senator forced to elbow his way through the cluster of commoners eagerly examining the latest edition of the *Daily Gazette* affixed to one of the columns almost eclipsed his excitement at getting hands on some new information. A little disheveled from the struggle, Virius spotted Livy and did nothing to hide a scowl of disapproval as he strode forward into the open.

"What is that rabble about?"

"They are anxious to see the latest names added to the games," Livy responded in a purposefully reasonable tone, the better to aggravate Virius. He knew he shouldn't do it because it might make the man even more close-mouthed, but Livy couldn't resist.

Virius glared, infuriated at being ambushed—as he'd predicted—by Caecilius Dio. "Why in Hades' name, *Livy*, don't they wait for the program notes on the day of the fights?" he snapped. He had a cloak draped over one arm, no doubt worn for the morning's chill breeze but now redundant in the unseasonal warmth. He draped it over his head with an upward glower at the bright sun.

"I thought we wanted them all worked up in advance over where to place their bets." The emphasis on the last word indicated Livy's eagerness to learn the outcome of whatever had passed between the Summa, even as he pushed aside his own irritation at Virius using his given name. Praenomina were for family and the most intimate of friends.

"That tightwad Banker never thinks of providing refreshment. I have a throat like the furred inside of a clogged drain." Virius pivoted his neck left and right in search of—

"Your two slaves are with my boy on the steps of Julius Caesar's temple. It's shady over there, *Publius*," Livy supplied the answer to the unspoken question, smirking at Fabius Virius's frown at the use of his praenomen. "Are you without your secretary Creon today?"

Livy's barely veiled amusement at his struggle through the mob of dirty commoners wthout his secretary to force a route through further irritated Virius. "I sent him on other more important business—"

"Are you going to give me some good news?" Livy asked, still smirking.

"—and my slaves are supposed to wait patiently for their master, ready to accompany him home," Virius grated out. "They are not yours to send off for a nice little shady rest period." Gimlet eyes pierced Livy. "I haven't the time now to impart much of our discussion…"

Indeed not, Livy thought wryly. *I bet you can't wait to fold that delicious Ambrosius of yours over a knee, prise apart what I'm sure must be delectable ass cheeks and get busy loosening the lad up for some hot afternoon diddly-do.* Oh yes, Livy knew all about the games Publius Fabius Virius liked to play with his adopted son when his formidable matron of a wife was off with the daughters spending whatever was left of his dwindled fortune on clothes and feasting down in the vacation resort of Baiae. He couldn't prevent a drip of sarcasm. "A crumb, maybe?"

Virius twitched his nose at the noisome smell that wafted past them from a nearby hot-sausage stall. "A crumb is all you deserve. Where's the stack of sesterces you promised me last week?"

"My dear brother Lucius doesn't see fit to pay me what he owes for my… labors." Livy spat out the word. "But I've been able to scrape together four score sesterces." Livy waved aside the objection before Virius could voice it. "I know it's not a fortune but every little helps. I should be able to hand over my share of the investment before the games start."

This hardly mollified Virius. He shook his head crossly, but decided to concede the point. "Very well. I can tell you that the admirable Gaius Fabricius Luscinus—"

"Our tame thin-striper?"

"Remember your place, Dio. He is not *your* thin-striper, and I'd advise not calling him tame to his face, if ever you meet. In any case Luscinus has managed to insert several of his… er, advisors, shall we say, into the M·G·M·F." At this Virius paused significantly, chin lifted, to peer down his long nose.

The importance of this little revelation wasn't lost on Livy. *Foedus gladiatorum orbis terrarum*—the World Gladiator Federation—the games' governing body. Rumors of international bout fixing were frequent and corruption was said to be endemic at the highest level. To Livy's knowledge, the Summa had previously failed to reach those who could really grease the wheels of fights arranged in such important arenas as those in Greece, Asia, Syria, Egypt, or Africa. Access to the top board of F·G·O·T could transform their fortunes dramatically. So many privately arranged games took place outside Italy, usually gifts of hopefuls in local elections to positions that would allow them to cream off the top of taxes. Under such circumstances, the provincial costs of arranging fighters and animals rarely topped fifty thousand sesterces, which meant the real quick turn-around-money came from gambling, and for those in the know gambling made the best returns from fixed bouts.

"Luscinus has sent an… an envoy, let's say, to our new province in the Orient where there is interest in advancing our possible fortunes."

"Arabia?" Livy looked dubious. "Is that really worth the effort?"

"Yes. And now I really must get on, but briefly, what news from within the scrolls of Familia Caecilii?"

Livy shrugged and patted his substantial belly and generally looked like one considering his options. He knew that Virius hated being reminded that he was reduced to consorting with one such as himself. For Livy's part, he much preferred the idiotic Virius in the role of rival, but the Fates had decided otherwise for the time being. He relented with a conspiratorial smile. "I do have some news on the Lucius front." He gave a quick glance to either side, which only had the effect of making them both look shifty.

Virius sighed. "Spill."

"Apollodorus of Damascus is commissioned to create a massive column for Trajan's new forum."

The sigh deepened. "I am also a senator, or has your mind turned to pulse porridge? We voted for the damned thing months ago in the probably vain hope that when he returned from Egypt Caesar would be pleased with us. I seem to remember you waving your hand in excited agreement when the extra cost for decorating the thing in reliefs celebrating his triumphs in the Dacian Wars was announced. Tell me something I don't know."

Livy drew himself up taller, which meant that his eyes came level with the thin mouth Virius pressed so tightly together that the blood fled his lips. "Ah, but the drums for the column were to be of granite—"

"I do recall."

"But what you can't know because only Lucius does—and now me—is that Apollodorus has since said that to carve the images he is designing in granite would be too difficult. So the specification has been changed to..." Livy paused for effect.

"Oh for Bona Dea's sake, what?"

"Carrara marble!" Livy pronounced with the satisfaction of a games editor aware that his spin on the next bout had his audience salivating in anticipation. He swayed back on his sandals. A smug expression pressed his eyes deeper into the rolls of his fat cheeks.

Virius lifted his chin and frowned. "*Your* family owns several quarries in Lungiana." His sour look said how much he wished he could wipe the self-satisfied expression off Livy's face. "But...? I sense a 'but' in that infantile grin."

Livy's smile vanished. "When I was rather more in control of our family matters I looked after the marble side of the business, so I can tell you that we don't have a quarry capable of producing what Apollodorus demands. The drums will be colossal, more than eleven feet across, and there will be twenty of them, plus the plinth. The Caecilii quarries can't produce such material. But you can. Your quarry near Colonnata has massive resources, I know."

Virius sniffed and contemplated. "Even so I doubt that Caesar will go back on undertakings given to the Caecilii."

"I'd say not, Virius, but you could sub-contract through Lucius, and if I pull the deal together it will put me back in with my brother-in-law and so in a much better position to further both our causes."

Virius gave a slow, thoughtful dip of his head in grudging acknowledgment. "All right. Do it. Grease the wheels of negotiation. I can be charming when I must. But bring me the money you pledged so I can add it in, which will give you some authority with the Summa. By the way, where did you come by it?"

The light wave of his hands said that Lucius was a man who knew a thing or two. "Oh that," he said airily, "I took a gamble on a bout at the last Capuan games and my chosen gladiator came up with the goods for me."

Virius narrowed his eyes. "Out of professional interest, who was that?"

"Giant Scythian, fellow called Bebryx."

When Virius stepped past the opened heavily ornamented door into the vestibule of his townhouse on the Caelian hill his thoughts were less on potential business prospects than on his adopted son Ambrosius's delicious ass, and what he'd do with it. Ignoring his hulking doorman, he called for his secretary. "Creon!" The man came scuttling obsequiously. "Be in my study in an hour, I need to dictate a letter to our man at Colonnata."

"Certainly, master—b-but I beg to inform that we've had a message from Baiae..." Creon stuttered to a halt.

"My wife, she's returning. When?"

Creon gulped, "Day after tomorrow, master."

"Right." Virius stomped on past his secretary, through the house and into the formal garden, shedding cloak and toga and dumping them into an approaching body slave's arms. *Curse the woman! Still, the vacation season is long over... she and the girls will be less of a drain on money here in Rome. Some hope...*

Woof!

There was Ambrosius, playing with his pet Molossus puppy.

There also stood the cursed Satyr of Capri. The once-toppled priapic bronze had been reinstalled on its pedestal, albeit slightly crookedly.

"Father!" The slender youngster rose and beamed at Virius, genuine pleasure in his delicate face.

"Ambrosius, just who I want to… see." *Fuck, of course…*

The statue's rampant monster cock never failed to inspire even though it now pointed down rather than straight out as it had done. "Come with me, boy."

He ruffled the hair at the nape of the slender neck and was rewarded with a knowing look and an elfin smile as the lad allowed Virius to nudge him toward the staircase to the upper floor. The enticing sway of the boy's bottom beneath his short tunic as they ascended fired Virius's lust. *I can't wait… must first take him quickly—a leisurely session can follow…*

Pursued by the excitable oversized puppy, he propelled his adoptive son up the steps and along the gallery into the conjugal bedroom, slammed the door shut just in time to keep the panting pet outside. *Now let's have you rough and hard, the way you like it!*

Virius swung Ambrosius around, back against the door, clamped hungry mouth over soft, parted lips, set his tongue to work. His rough hands slid under the tunic and kneaded the smooth ass cheeks, tore down the skimpy loincloth, freed the bobbing erection. To muffled gasps of surrender as he mauled the lad, he untied the knots at the shoulders that held up the open sided tunic, bared the heaving torso to the waist.

"Ah-h!" He abandoned the delicious, ravished mouth and chomped on vulnerable neck muscles, slurped over chest and nipples. While one hand groped and fondled between silky thighs, his other tugged the thin belt open, and soon the tunic dropped to join the loincloth around Ambrosius's ankles. *Delicate naked boy, hot for what I'm about to give you…*

He grasped the slim waist with both hands and heaved the

panting youth onto the large bed to lie splayed on his back. Not bothering to disrobe, Virius merely reached under his tunic to pull his engorged cock from silken underwear, then knelt between the boy's spread legs, ran fingers down inner thighs, savored the trembling flesh before hoisting them up and over, folding them to press the knees against heaving chest. This raised the naked bottom to an exposed, vulnerable position, its intimate center twitching enticingly. Virius plunged his mouth onto the inviting rosebud and munched and laved without restraint. *Sweet, spicy little thing... Open up, let me in! Oh...*

"U-uuh! Uh-hhr!" Ambrosius's pretty mouth gaped, his upper teeth bared in arousal.

Scratching on wood from outside. *Bark!* Woof! *Woof!* A frustrated puppy…

Can't wait—and you're ready for me—

Virius reared up, eased forward, guided his erection into position and, with his thumb, pushed his cock head down onto the boy's sopping sphincter. He grunted and plunged his thick, rippling meat in one fluid, squelching move deep inside. He didn't stop until his scrotum hit smooth ass cheeks. Ambrosius emitted a hiss and a grunt when the invader hit bottom.

Juicy, tight—!

Virius began to screw his adoptive son with vigor. Hands on his thighs for leverage as he pumped in and out, he pummeled the clutching channel, twisted and churned deep in a furious rhythm of fucking. The assault was fierce and came to a quick conclusion. To the lad's gurgled gasps and his own clenched-teeth grunts he lurched to desperate release, flooding the stuffed ass even as captive Ambrosius ejaculated to splatter cum over his own face. Breathless, Virius collapsed onto the boy, still feebly pumping inside him.

Just what I needed after this morning… and the boy loves it… Yes, your beautiful face is a picture of bliss… and your loving eyes plead for more… sweet Ambrosius.

Soon, Virius engaged the lad in a second, more leisurely but just as dominating dance of sex…

T·H·R·E·E | III

Rome, 5th to 9th days of November AD 108

For Quintus, the month since returning from Egypt had been divided between idleness, weapons training, and writing. Stylus to paper, he'd made edited copies for Trajan from his observations of the Nile voyage to Philae and back, and written some new poems, two of a decidedly erotic nature. Rufio had surprised Quintus half way up the Nile with his facility for producing imaginatively lewd drawings to illustrate the sexy poetry. "Ma knows this bookseller and publisher Sosius who does odd jobs on the side for senators with a taste in lurid literature," Rufio had claimed. "The biggest problem will be keeping up production when his army of copyists, bored stiff—literally—with Cicero, Virgil, and Horace, masturbate themselves silly instead of penning your words." Quintus was unsure as to how successful this venture might be, but it tickled his testicles to think of his poetry finding a wider market… albeit under a pen name of course.

There had been a private reading of his (more salubrious) poems before an audience of senators and magistrates held in the Curia of Pompey—fulfilment of the promise Trajan made on their final night at Elephantine in Upper Egypt. "We shall have a reading arranged on our return to Rome," he'd said.

Nerves almost undid Quintus as the day approached, and the presence of Rufio—the rascal's compulsory attendance was under strict imperial dictat—did nothing to calm him, nor did the presence of his bemused parents and—worse still—Vipsania Metella, whose hard-nosed family accompanied her. In addition to her mother and father, Vipsanius Numerius Metellus—no doubt present to examine the specimen who would soon take their daughter to the nuptial bedchamber—there were two brothers in their twenties: Cornelius and Drusus glared with expressions Quintus had last seen in the Forum Boarium on the faces of butchers about to castrate bulls. He had no idea whether the real Vipsania matched her portrait, the specially commissioned one he'd been shown when the topic of his marriage came up back in February, because a heavy veil under the hood of her palla concealed her face.

Still, the reading went well enough for Trajan to announce more such events. "I brought along a really sharp gladius," Rufio joked, "in case you felt the virtuous need to fall on its point."

Since the start of the Plebeian Games on the 4th day of November the Caecilii had broken their stay-at-home habit to attend many festivities. Quintus found it odd that such stuffy old-fashioned, not to say stuck-up, dyed-in-the-wool patrician parents put themselves out for a two-week festival of games and entertainment associated with the lower classes. On the other hand, mad Nero's fondness for the Ludi Plebeii decades ago had made the festival fashionable even among the upper classes.

Lucius Primus and Livius Secundus, his older army brothers, were on leave for the festival, but not Marcus. As the fourth son Marcus was really Quartus, but as Tertius had died in infancy Marcus was spared being known as a number and retained his namesake, a deceased paternal uncle. An optio aboard the flagship *Fortuna* for the voyage to Alexandria, Marcus had returned to the Misenum naval base after *Fortuna* brought the imperial party back to Italy. "Hey you poncing poetaster prick, be sure to keep your mouth stitched like you promised," he'd hissed at Quintus as they parted company at Ostia-Portus. It terrified him that his young brother might let slip by accident or on purpose how attractive a bed companion Trajan had found Marcus on the high seas.

"Such a fond farewell, dear brother," Quintus returned with a honeyed smile. "You're only pissed because you'll miss being poked by hard imperial dick-tat," he'd punned. He bounded jauntily to the jetty before Marcus could think of a suitable riposte. So it was a partly enlarged Caecilii family that attended races in the Circus Maximus on the second day of the festival. As was their custom, the five women sat separately from their menfolk: Mother Fabia, Fabia the Younger, Julia; and Maia and Aurelia, the wives of Primus and Secundus. From the reserved marble seats in the senatorial section Quintus looked back at the imperial box. His mind drifted to that fateful February day when his wicked Uncle Livy tried selling his nephew's charms to Trajan. *What a lot has happened in less than a year...the impression of a hawk's nose jutting up, a hand raised imperiously, the glitter of interest turned on me. I thought I would simply dissolve into a puddle at the Emperor's feet...*

And that day marked his second encounter with Rufio since the dreadful day at the Lupercalia (when—rampantly naked for the festival—the guttersnipe had dared lash him with the traditional bloodied goat thong normally intended for girls hoping to get pregnant). It was but a moment after meeting Caesar, when the clod coming up the steps from the imperial box ran headlong into him.

"Don't you ever look where you're going, or are you always too busy dashing about and striking out at people to see what's ahead of you?" The redheaded guttersnipe was unrepentant. "I'm in desperate need, so I'm off to the men's pisser. Do you want to join me? You look as though you're holding something in under duress." *I should have run him through with my spatha right there and then. Well...*

Scorpus, the sensational young charioteer from Rhodes, won the laurels in the biggest race of the day, an occurrence that had become as regular as the passage of the seasons. On the following days in the Colosseum ("I do wish you wouldn't use such plebeian slang, Quintus," his father complained. "Please call it by its proper name, Flavian Amphitheater") they watched full programs of wild animal hunts, dwarves bashing each other silly, condemned criminals tortured and executed, and proper gladiatorial combat. Quintus, who wasn't keen on the profligate shedding of blood for entertainment, irritated the Caecilii men by spending more time jotting things down on a wax tablet than in observing the carnage. But among the early novice fights of the fourth day's program he found a tyro simply labeled Regulus interesting. Fighting in the *murmillones* style with gladius, rectangular shield, helmet, arm and shin guards, Regulus showed promise. And Quintus couldn't help a natural attraction to those sharply edged, glistening muscles as they flexed and twisted. Regulus was young, strong, and *I wonder what he'd be like in bed…?*

He put away the unworthy thought, but idling there on the marble bench he felt a pleasant twitch in his loins as the after-image of Regulus metamorphosed into a cheery, loving picture of Rufio. The tingle of pleasure swelled in the anticipation of the night he'd spend in Rufio's bed when Trajan's thank you party at the Emporium was ended. *Tomorrow night!*

"Ma, he insisted there was to be no fuss, no bother, no flummery, and absolutely no courtly nonsense. Just a family get together over wine, food, and conversation. A relaxing opportunity to relive the best moments of our four-month trip to Egypt."

Words falling on deaf ears… well, not entirely. Junilla glared at her son. "Men! That's a typical attitude. You think because Trajan said 'informal' he meant he'll happily squat on dust-laden chairs in this higgledy-piggledy room of ours instead of reclining like a proper Roman to eat?"

"There's no dust anywhere. It's been polished out of existence."

In this Rufio was correct. Every household slave in the Tullius Emporium of Artistic Excellence had been scrubbing and polishing since the start of the Ludi Plebeii, and half the warehouse workmen had been hauling the everyday stuff out of the domus to replace it with fine furniture, antique statuary and decorative gewgaws awaiting sale. As the largest space in the house the *tablinum*—in reality a rambling family room of indeterminate shape—had to

47

do and now resembled a high-class *triclinium*, albeit with rather more couches and dining tables than virtuous Roman formality demanded. Quintus had pointed out as much when he dropped in that morning—before finding an excuse to dash off hurriedly in order to avoid being roped in to another round of polishing. "Laboring," he'd said stuffily, "is beneath a patrician senator's son." He made sure Rufio caught the smirk.

Junilla's glare brooked no dissent from hapless Rufio. "Go and make sure your bedroom is spotless."

"Trajan isn't going to see my bedroom, Ma."

The arched eyebrows spoke volumes of potential Celtic ire.

Rufio sniffed defensively. "Well, not tonight. He's used to beds the size of a legionary parade ground."

"Just go do it, and while you're at it check on Hephaestion's room, and then get that laggard brother of yours to tidy his as well."

Rufio departed, grumbling under his breath… Cato dusting? The boy was a whirlwind. He invented dust and grime. And Hephaestion? That had been a shock. The cocky little masturbator had weaseled his way into Junilla's affections after stowing away on *Cleopatra of the Nile* when they put in briefly at Memphis for supplies on the return journey. Over the days traveling the last stages to Alexandria, while staying out of Quintus and Rufio's sight, he persuaded her that Rufio had promised to look after him, to take him to Rome for a better life. Unlike Aunts Antonia and Velabria, their sister Junilla had a soft spot for waifs and strays and a tendency to collect them, in spite of being the tyrant she was with "feckless fools."

Rufio was horrified when he learned that the cute fuck from Snifferu's piebald pyramid was to be a part of the familia ("…he wants to learn the antiquities trade, pet…" *Yeah, probably to steal everything.* "He seems like a nice boy." *Yeah, in bed…*). His sex life was becoming too complicated, what with fending off the attentions of heart-sore Flaccus, coping with Woof-Woof Felix's need for a regular fucking, Quintus's slave Ashur (he and Quintus shared the boy sometimes) reminding him of that lubricious tryst on board *Cleopatra*, and now Hephaestion. Oh, and not of course to forget Quintus… beloved Quintus, who he hadn't seen enough of since getting back from Gyppo land.

They were eleven in all, a nicely compact, truly informal party reclining in no particular order, though Junilla insisted on Trajan taking the nearest thing to a place of honor. As the only woman present and hostess, she reclined next to Trajan, and on his other side there was Servilius Vata, the Praetorian Guard prefect on the tour of Egypt. The four large couches were arranged loosely around a large oval table of off-white-gray-green marble, which Damianus informed the party came from a haul brought in from Thessalonica and was handily waiting a buyer. To Trajan and Junilla's right Quintus, Rufio, and Hephaestion shared a couch (Hephaestion kept throwing Rufio sour looks every time he took the opportunity to touch Quintus, which he was doing rather too much to the Egyptian boy's thinking). Across the table were Cato, Eutychus—Cato's tutor while they were on the Egypt tour but kept on much to Cato's disgust—and the Emporium secretary Damianus, looking very fashionable in a light blue synthesis (but nervous in such exalted company). The fourth couch held only Flaccus because the other guest, Gnaeus Septimius Corbulo, was in the kitchens supervising the staff preparing the repast he'd promised Trajan that final night at the Source of the Nile, when the Emperor promised to pay for a feast in gratitude for everyone's efforts.

For this private occasion Trajan had discarded his twenty-four lictors, and the two Praetorian Guards Empress Pompeia Plotina had insisted accompany him were garbed in their lightweight togas over plain tunics and not military-issue uniform. They were also being looked after out in the kitchen area.

Cato nearly didn't make it to the party. In Egypt he had made friends with the Empress[†] and she was hosting an event of her own at the palace. "You must come, Cato," Plotina had insisted. "It is a party for disadvantaged children of Numidia, a cause close to my heart." Cato kicked up a stink on what he thought were reasonable grounds that he could go visit Plotina any other time, and he didn't give a dog's turd for disadvantaged Numidian brats. In the end Trajan intervened on his behalf to ensure his presence at the feast.

To emphasize the occasion's relaxed nature Trajan was dressed in a simple white army tunic, its only nod at his status being a thin purple strip at the hem and arms. Prefect Servilius Vata had chosen a fine pale blue tunic that rather matched Rufio's. Quintus looked resplendent in a severe white shoulder-buttoned tunic with a modest gold hem and wine-red cloak-style synthesis.

The atmosphere, abuzz with chat and the typical reminiscences of a shared journey into the unknown, may have been informal but the meal was not. Septimius may have been an army *frumentarius* in his earlier days—and in the capacity of securing food supplies, also a spy—but now he owned a *thermopolium*. The cookshop, though situated in a rough district of the Subura, nevertheless served some of the best food to be found in Rome—at least according to Rufio, who had first come across it when desperate for breakfast after a heavy-duty night of shagging two delicious Nubian lads at nearby Lucretia's Lupanar during the festival of Lupercalia.

Conversation died away in expectation as Septimius walked in, hands clasped. He sketched a bow in the direction of Trajan and Junilla, and cleared his throat.

"May I present my humble repast, which I could not have managed without the wonderful staff of the Tullius Emporium of Artistic Excellence—"

"Not to forget our other business: We Are Celebrations and Festivities!" Rufio shouted out.

"And *In Celebrationibus et Festivitates*—thank you. So, for *gustatio* we have jellyfish fresh from Antium this morning, steamed with bitter herbs and served with chopped hard-boiled quails' eggs;

a succulent sow's udder cooked in milk fragranced by an infusion of Cretan saffron; boiled honey mushrooms harvested from the trees around Tibur, glazed with garum made by the firm of Gracchus et filios of Lanuvium—they flavor their magnificent sauce with aromatic herbs, such as dill, coriander, fennel, celery, mint, and oregano; and finally we have a dish of sea urchins broiled with spices of the Orient, topped by an egg sauce of my own secret recipe."

A general smacking of lips and *hmmm*-ing went around the gathering.

"For *primae mensae* we have fallow Appenine deer from the forested hills of Etruria roasted with an onion sauce, Egyptian dates, raisins, honey, and a particularly delicious olive oil freshly pressed on the Ligurian coast at Imperia. Then there is a boiled ostrich with a sweet-spicy sauce; turtle doves clay-baked in their feathers; a brace of roasted parrots; dormice stuffed with pine kernels and finely minced wild hog from Samnium—one of your favorites, Caesar, I know; a good air-cured ham from Cremona boiled with figs, bay leaves, glazed with honey and then baked in a salted pastry crust; and last but not least, a beautiful flamingo which I have slow-simmered with dates in a rich Falernian."

More drawn-out *hmmmm*-ing and lip smacking.

"I felt that after such rich fare, the *secundae* should be fresh and modest, so we have a fricassee of roses in a flaky pastry; stoned dates—this time some really fat, juicy specimens from Jericho—stuffed with hazel nuts and pine kernels, fried in honey; and a popular dish we all remember served on *Cleopatra of the Nile*, my own take on hot African sweet-wine cakes drenched in a citrus-flavored honey."

"I say, Septimius, could you just run down the list again for me?" Flaccus beamed happily around the company.

Laughter for Flaccus and applause for Septimius drowned out the clatter of kitchen slaves (several borrowed from neighbors for the occasion) rushing in with dishes of the first course. Everyone set to with a will.

Trajan had saved up a number of surprises, which he produced like a stage conjurer once servants had removed the last vestiges of the feast and left intricately carved cases of ivory containing wooden toothpicks for each couch. First came the production of a set of eight beautiful silver goblets carried in by one of the guardsmen. "I wish to gift these eight wine cups to you, Junilla. They were presented to me before we departed Alexandria by the city's finest silversmith, the Greek artist Epigonus of Tralles."

Quintus and Rufio exchanged faintly disturbed looks and shuffled uneasily on their couch.

"Oh, Caesar, they are gorgeous." Junilla held one aloft to admire the intricate workmanship of entwined figures. "Just look what these two fine boys are up to… oh in two different positions as well, one scene on each side. So realistic, you can almost make out the facial features. Very erotic… and look here, there's a young boy peeking in, the naughty thing—"

"That's me," Cato exclaimed, grabbing one of the vessels. "He saw me and—*uggh*!"

Rufio's flung napkin cut Cato off abruptly. Rufio gave the company a sickly grin. "My poor little brother. The wine has gone to his head."

Quintus wanted the floor to swallow him, but with Cato effectively gagged the goblets passed around to generally admiring comment… until Flaccus got his hands on one. He stared at it, heavy brows drawn into a single straight line. He looked across at Quintus and Rufio. "Why, isn't that amazing?" He held the vessel out toward the two boys, squinting around its circumference. "The likeness! Why I would swear it could be you two depicted here. Surely that's Rufio on top in this one and… well I never."

Cato's snort matched his smirk, and he had to use Rufio's napkin to stifle a fit of giggles.

"That fucker Greek promised we wouldn't be recognizable," Rufio whispered in Quintus's ear.

"Looks like the bastard lied." Quintus sighed. "In our youthful folly we believed him and posed and now we'll never be allowed to live it down. Those goblets will go on forever—"

"Good fuck, though, wasn't it?" Rufio sniggered.

Quintus glanced up, his cheeks burning, and caught Trajan's benign smile and the hint of a wink. The Emperor waved his hand for quiet. If his gift to Junilla had floored her son and his lover, his next surprise was a real shocker. "For their fortitude and loyalty," he announced, "I grant to Junius Tullius Rufio and Quintus Caecilius Alba a stipend from the Imperial Treasury of one talent of gold each." Before either could express astonished gratitude, Trajan waved a hand and one of the guardsmen ushered in the slender form of a blond-haired boy wearing a gold slave collar and neat tunic. "One more gift to you, Rufio—and because he will be an extra hand to help your mother—I give you one of my personal slaves who will serve you faithfully."

Rufio wasn't sure where to put himself. If his sex life had become tangled, he had the feeling Trajan (probably laughing inwardly) had just made it even more complex. "Oh dominus! I am so happy to be yours," exclaimed the handsome German hostage-prince named Adalhard. He pushed in between Rufio and Quintus, all cocky smiles and fluttering eyelashes for them both. Hephaestion's huff of displeasure could be heard clearly. Adalhard's takes-one-to-know-one look wasn't intended to disarm.

"And finally," Trajan continued, "an extra treat for us all. After his amazing run of wins for the Greens in the Circus so far this Ludi Plebeii, may I present as an honored guest the most laureled victor of the track… Scorpus!"

Cheers, applause, greetings made the idol of a generation smile shyly as he emerged from where he'd been waiting in the Emporium's hallway a short while, ready to make his entrance. He glanced around and his pale gray eyes instantly lit on Rufio, recognized from the unanticipated blowjob he'd given when Rufio delivered Scorpus a phallic pendant of good fortune last February from Lady J—, one of the charioteer's innumerable female admirers. He found space beside Septimius and the company settled back to exchanging travel anecdotes and toasting the Rhodian idol of the Circus.

The occasional exchange of sly looks between the charioteer and Rufio hadn't escaped a sharp Alban eye. In a quiet aside Quintus asked, "Does the scorpion have a sting in his tail?"

Rufio dug a toe into the top of Quintus's thigh and winked. "Who knows? You might get lucky enough to find out... later."

It was done. Trajan was returned to the palace and the mantle of imperial responsibility and the other guests gone. Rufio and Quintus were cuddled up in Rufio's bed having somehow persuaded the complications in Rufio's sex life to get lost... all but one. For a short while Rufio fulfilled his veiled promise of earlier and introduced Quintus to the delights of jockey sex with a happily accommodating Scorpus.

The three had retreated to Rufio's bedchamber after he forcibly removed the rest of the ménage ("more of a menagerie," Quintus complained) with the unstated intention of extending the evening into something more physical. It was the people's champion who mentioned the idea of a *triga*. In the circus, races involving a *biga*, the chariot drawn by two horses, and the more popular *quadriga* of four horses, were the norm, "which make always a triga unsual," Scorpus said, mangling his Latin and waggling his pale brows suggestively. "Intimate more than the quadriga, fun much more than a biga."

"And how does it work?" asked an intrigued Quintus. Rufio just laughed softly.

From a pocket in his tunic Scorpus produced three toothpicks he'd taken from the triclinium and snapped two into different lengths. Then he arranged them in an even topped row between thumb and fingers. He gave Quintus and Rufio a sly grin. "In this race we run horses in line ahead instead of row… that would bore be. Longest wins and gets be middle stallion, next long gets at back, shortest goes in lead. Quintus, you choose, then Rufio of the Reds. I get what left."

Brows drawn, lips tightly pursed, Quintus plucked a toothpick.

"Ooh, Quintus get middle place!"

Rufio took his turn and pulled out what was clearly the medium length pick.

"You get back, so you screw Quintus who…" Scorpus held up the shortest fragment of toothpick, "fuck me!" He wiggled his butt like a puppy.

"So apart from the pleasure of having a length of patrician cock up your ass, what do you get out of it?" Rufio demanded with his best innocent expression.

"We are on our fours, like race horse, so Quintus reach-around, keep me happy, then when you two win your race…" Scorpus dipped into the pocket again and produced a dupondis, "you throw, see who must suck me over the finish line." And with that he pulled the tunic up over his head, tossed it aside, and bent forward on hands and knees, discarding loincloth in the process to reveal hard butt cheeks, cleft, and an asshole that might have been shaven, such hair as there was so pale. He spat copiously on his left palm and reached back to lubricate himself.

Rufio grinned at Quintus. "Come on, winner, get ready."

Quintus stripped and clambered up behind the charioteer, his cock already twitching to a nice hard-on. He followed the lead of Scorpus, letting a long bead of saliva drop to his cockhead as he felt Rufio grab his waist and ready himself behind in a similar way. Without further ceremony Rufio slipped his cock into Quintus, who felt it ream open his passage in a now familiar and welcome way. He gasped and let Rufio's momentum carry his own rampant erection deep into Scorpus. The charioteer echoed Quintus with a harsh exhalation and an indrawn whoop of pleasure. Quintus held

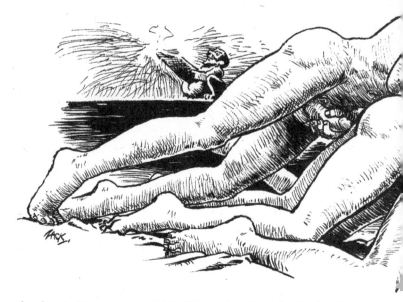

hard onto Scorpus around his slight waist, his right hand seeking the Rhodian's cock, finding it, shorter than mighty Rufio, but thick of girth, and incredibly hard, like the rod of iron running through a gladius hilt.

For several enjoyable minutes the three boys fucked in unison, Quintus keeping Scorpus "happy" as his own orgasm mounted through the thrust and friction of the chariot driver's gripping ass and the internal drubbing Rufio was giving him. Quintus came first. He dropped his head sideways onto the Rhodian's hard back and pumped jizz into him five, six, eight times, felt the explosion of his lover's cum in his own insides and the frantic banging of hips against his buttocks as Rufio emptied his balls with wheezing grunts of exquisite effort.

For a while silence reigned, broken only by quietly heaving lungs. Scorpus was first to break free. He scrabbled around still on his knees to face Quintus, who could see just how hard he was. His unusually pale gray eyes were alive with wicked humor and

he smirked as he showed the dupondis in his outstretched palm.
"Call it!" The coin flashed in low lamplight as it turned end over
end, reached the apex of its flight and fell back. Scorpus caught it,
covered it from sight.

"Venus!" Rufio called out.

In fact it was Pax seated, holding an olive branch upward in her
right hand, scepter in left, with a begging Dacian kneeling at her
feet, but it was the head of Trajan that lay revealed in Scorpus's
hand. "Rufio lose, Quintus win. Lucky Quintus take Scorpus cock
and fellate him."

Quintus shrugged, knelt forward gamely and, egged on by Rufio
stroking his back and ass, lowered his head to the ready cock every
maiden who frequented the circus dreamt of possessing and as
many men as women had. Quintus closed his eyes dreamily and
closed slicked lips around the smooth, bulbous helmet. The taste of
scorpion sexual heat filled his head…

That had been a half hour ago by the candle. Still aroused from the heady scent of charioteer, the aromas of victory, more relaxed lovemaking seemed imminent, but first they were discussing the proposition Scorpus had made—his "gift" to Rufio. "I have a tip, dead cert it is," he had begun. "There is brilliant young gladiator. I introduce you. You are expert at arena?"

"No," Rufio admitted.

Quintus nodded when Scorpus turned his sultry questioning look on him, hoping he wouldn't press for the kind of knowledgable detail Primus and Secundus would have no problem in answering. "Is he so promising?"

"Promise? He a Scorpus of the arena soon will be!"

The modesty was so becoming.

"For the festival, he at the Ludus Magnus has been these days."

Quintus found following the Rhodian's tortured Latin a chore and suspected it was a put on. No doubt his patrons found it exotic. His next words suggested the boy could read minds.

"He a decent patron lack, you know, to make sure best weapons he has, and clothes to look good in arena. The *ludi magister*... he care nothing stuff like that and all lanistas not bother such things either. Anyway, he start to compete at highest level and this new boy his sponsor absolute fortune will you make.' Scorpus stared wide-eyed with enthusiasm at Rufio. "So sponsor him, wrong you cannot go. Make fortune soon."

"What do you think?" Rufio said as soon as they were alone.

It be splendid, Scorpus had assured them. *This murmillo be your blade in the arena!*

"Madness. Lowlifes, gladiators they be, in need much of training expensive," Quintus spluttered in poor imitation of Scorpus. "Anyway, what do you know about gladiatorial combat?" he added, returning to his normal delivery.

"Not much. I like the races, the thrills and spills, but never had time for the fights, all that gratuitous slaughter. Not like you, I suppose?"

Quintus didn't feel like revealing his unpatrician indifference to commercial combat, but he pursed his lips and wouldn't look directly at Rufio. He shrugged. "I know my types."

Rufio brightened and grinned. "We're quick learners. Anyway, what can there be to it, being a sponsor? And thanks to Caesar's generosity, we now have the wherewithal."

A frown creased Quintus's brow. "Are you being serious? On the word of a… a—"

"Circus driver?"

"Low-born, boneheaded stable lad." He paused as Rufio patted his naked thigh with understanding plebeian condescension. "He never even mentioned the man's name, and—speaking of gladiators…" And because he seemed to be in a mood of mimickry, in a bad imitation of Rufio Quintus intoned, " 'The gods spare us! I tell you this, Quintus, after what we went through with Malpensa's fighting beauties in Rome, I swear by the colossal prick of Cernunnos I'll never have another thing to do with gladiators.' Do you remember saying that, that last night at Elephantine?"

A guileless expression fleeted across Rufio's face. "Did I? I'm sure I would have said 'cock,' not 'prick.' "

"You did, and what do you mean by: '*we* have the wherewithal'?"

"You'd go halves with me, wouldn't you? I'd need your common sense to keep me on the straight and narrow." Rufio fluttered his long, red-gold lashes and stroked the skin of Quintus's inner thigh just under his balls.

After a moment the frown melted away at the obvious flattery. And then Quintus smiled. "You! Straight and narrow? Now I've heard everything."

And with that, Quintus pressed Rufio back onto his pillow and laid lips on his with mean intent.

Rome & Nova Traiana Bostra, 11th day of November AD 108

Scorpus confused Quintus. It was all very well romping around with the charioteer on Rufio's bed, satiated after a gargantuan feast, but he still could not work out how to behave toward the Rhodian, who in spite of being Rome's current sporting hero, was nevertheless only a slave in effect… well, a recently freed one. Should a patrician and son of a senator consort in public with a lowborn *auriga*, literally a puller of a horse's bridle, a mere jockey-boy? Did having his cock stuck up Scorpion ass give the *quadriga* driver, eternal victor of the *ludi circenses*, a hold over him? It was all right for Rufio; he was a prole and the lower classes always got on, didn't they? But Scorpus seemed cockily sure of himself, which was probably Rufio's bad example. Quintus could still feel the bristly rub of the boy's buzz-cut against his inner thighs as Scorpus whorled his tongue in a delicious circling motion over his balls. But as though such intimacy meant he could consider himself an equal, the charioteer hadn't once addressed Quintus as dominus. He decided to find comfort in the fact that the young man's admirers—male or female—had to pay in expensive presents to have sex with the little godling, and there was something of a frisson in having had him and watched Rufio screw him after.

"For your thoughts a sestertius?" Scorpus grinned up at Quintus. "So serious your face, dominus."

Damn and copulation, the bastard does *read minds!*

'You'll need a golden aureus for the poetic reflections of Quintus Caecilius Alba," Rufio quipped.

Having walked down the valley between the Palatine and Caelian hills, they had reached the Colosseum and now skirted its great circumference in an easterly direction toward the Ludus Magnus. Beyond the bulk of the huge amphitheater a brume of grime and smoke hefted into the air from the building site of Trajan's new baths where they bit into the side of the adjacent Oppian hill. Quintus sniffed at the dust but hurriedly turned it into one of mild disdain as he attempted a haughty tone of voice. "I'm thinking if we're to meet this paragon of arena arts we should surely know his name. Hello, what's this?" he interrupted himself.

The crash of hobnailed boots on paving brought them to a sudden halt. A cohort the Praetorian Guard rounded the far corner of the Ludus Magnus and marched toward where they stood. "That's unusual," Quintus observed as the Praetorians cut across the plaza in a slow circle around the Colosseum. "Why are they wearing full military gear in the city?"

Rufio wrinkled his nose. "Some ceremonial event in the palace?"

"Hate them fuckers in toga or parade gear." Scorpus spat on the ground. "I forget name," he added. "Gaius."

"Huh?"

"Gladiator. Gaius… something."

"Well, *there's* something," Quintus muttered. "Gaius is *such* a rare name in Rome."

The sarcasm flew over the charioteer's straw-colored brush-head like a badly aimed spear. By contrast Rufio shook his unruly burnished locks at Scorpus. "Don't let any of those guardsmen see that *falx* you're not hiding very well." He nodded surreptitiously at the curved knife charioteers used to cut themselves free of the reins in the case of a crash in the Circus.

"They all know me," Scorpus said dismissively, but he put a hand to the hilt and shoved the knife back under the fold of his Green-faction cloak.

It wasn't cold enough for a cape, but Scorpus liked to show off his allegiance, Quintus thought. The Praetorians clumped past. *I bet every one of them knows every inch of you.* Off-duty guardsmen were said to enjoy fucking charioteers, even the freed ones. It wasn't a charitable thought but he was not convinced that there could be much return on any money invested in a gladiator, less still in a beginner, thank you Scorpus. "Come on." He waved a hand at the back of the cohort as wheeled left around the Meta Sudans and disappeared up the sloping Velia along the Via Sacra, obviously headed to the Forum and the Palace vestibule.

Scorpus led the way left around the western end of the Ludus Magnus, past its grand entrance used only when consuls or the Emperor paid a visit, into Vicus Summi Choragium. This short street took its name from the long, four-story pile of a building just beyond their destination in which the *choragia*—the machinery, scenery items, and props—used in the Colosseum were stored and administered by an army of slaves and imperial freedmen. The less imposing northern entrance to the ludus faced another training school, but its façade did little to shelter the street from the thick fog of dust pouring down the slopes of the Oppian hill. Through the ludus entryway, wide stairs led through the thickness of the building into the large central peristyle, which enclosed a raised, elliptical *cavea* of sufficient capacity for a select audience to watch training or warm-up bouts. Trajan sometimes held private showings for important senators and foreign guests, which was why he had spent a considerable sum in upgrading the seating and general facilities.

Before them, close to the portico columns, the marble-clad outer wall of the *cavea* rose the height of two men, only broken opposite the entry steps from where a few more steps led down to the sanded arena floor. The portal allowed stage props to be brought in, Quintus presumed, since it was wider than required to give gladiators access to the arena. Through the gap he could see the opposing side of the portico and counted fourteen travertine columns supporting the longer side of the upper floor and twelve on the shorter ends. Judging by the gaps between columns he judged the interior dimensions to be approximately 328 by 260 paces. At each corner between the arena's curve and the portico small fountains set in low triangular pools played soothing tunes. In the same area two sets of sixteen stone steps gave access to the highest tier of the *cavea*.

With the arena apparently deserted of combatants and no cries of spectators encouraging blows, it was quiet and the enclosure of the two-storied building cut off Rome's outside rush. And then the peace was shattered by voices raised in furious discussion, which almost drowned out the nearest fountain's tinkling song. Quintus furrowed his brow at the loud exchange arising between a gaunt giant of a figure clad head to foot in black leather and an extraordinarily hairy side of beef in a breechclout brandishing a wooden sword. The bellowing bull had one booted foot set back in the shallow triangular bowl of the fountain, the other planted firmly against one of the columns holding up the second floor.

Scorpus waved at the tall man whose leather cap drawn tight around his ears by fastenings under his chin lent him a frightening appearance. The two broke off whatever they were arguing about to stare at the newcomers. "Mumius Bulbus, chief lanista," Scorpus hissed. "Be nice. He make everything work around here."

"Who's the other?"

"Ursus. Bulbus's backstop."

Quintus cut off Rufio's snort of amusement, though judging by the vast bulge on show he couldn't help agreeing that what lay underneath must be a very effective stopper. But levity, he thought, was inadvisable as the two approached. Quintus wondered whether Ursus was the man's name or nickname, because his shaggy body certainly resembled that of a big brown bear.

"Are you here to cause mischief," Bulbus demanded in a disconcertingly croaky voice as he closed in. In spite of his grim expression and snarky smile, more of a grimace really, he seemed unthreatening.

Ursus lumbered up, dragging the point of his sword along the stone floor, then alarmingly waved it aloft, both arms spread wide,

63

and a moment later he engulfed the short figure of Scorpus, who disappeared as though a woolen rug had swallowed him whole. A grumbling roar emerged from the beast's throat as he shook the charioteer about before releasing him with a massive pat on the back that sent Scorpus sprawling into the arms of Quintus. "He's in love with me," Scorpus whispered.

"Wow…"

"Cock big like club of Heraclius."

"I'm sure you're right," Quintus managed faintly as he disentangled himself from Scorpus and—should Ursus take it into his head to greet him in similar style—found refuge behind Rufio. "Wipe that grin off your stupid Celtic face before we're devoured."

Rufio's smile broadened until the faint scattering of freckles on his cheeks stretched into thin lines. "I bet you when he's aroused he'd resemble the Satyr of Capri," he whispered from the corner of his quirking mouth.

"In what way?" Quintus was unable to quite hide his own grin. "The Satyr was handsome."

"Beauty is in the eye of the beholder, my pretty Alban."

"I do the poetry around here, and how many times do I have to say that my family has nothing to do with Alba Longa."

"Bulbus, I bring two *muneraria*, I tell you, to buy the *auctoratus*."

Rufio turned a surprised glance on Quintus. "The gladiator's a volunteer?"

Bulbus cracked a smile, a slight parting of almost invisible lips to reveal brown incisors. Quintus didn't like the way he kept stroking the handle of his coiled whip, or the lizard-like gaze that held a degree of contempt as he regarded them. "Just one fighter? I don't call anyone who sponsors just *one* gladiator a munerarius. That's for owners of a troupe of whoring fighters." He eyed Quintus and Rufio with a curled lip. "And two? Hah! They are but boys," he threw out at Scorpus. "Pretty boys the both, and not shaving yet, I'll warrant."

"With pretty money much, dominus."

Oh, he's quick to bow before the lanista, a man who consorts with the lowest of creatures, worse even than an actor, nothing more than a pimp of male flesh. Quintus kept a tightly polite face, hiding his nerves at being appraised for his "wealth." Bulbus looked like the kind of man to take advantage… no, rephrase that—as a lanista of course he'd seize any leverage whenever it was presented. Quintus drew himself up into a proper patrician stance and prepared to defend his and Rufio's qualities as muneraria, sponsors of a gladiator. Rufio beat him to it.

"Sir! You see before you two who are at Caesar's bosom, and valued courtiers. Men who by their own hand saved the Emperor and his family from the evil Acacus, uncovered the secrets of evil Malpensa and saved Rome from destruction, not to mention destroying the evil kingdom-to-be of Caesarion, self-proclaimed pharaoh of Egypt. I don't think a gladiator will pose much of a problem to such as we." He gave Quintus a hearty clap on the back that nearly projected him into the arms of Ursus.

Bulbus shrugged. I have more important matters to attend to than listen to the boastful drizzle of a child, his body language said.

A flurry of activity at the other end of the ludus drew Quintus's attention. He turned to see a file of gladiators crossing the walkway from rooms at the back and entering the arena wielding assorted, blunted practice weapons in hand. They were under the close supervision of four *doctores*, a grizzled quartet of hardened arena survivors and definitely not the kind he'd want to meet in a narrow alley on a dark night. They looked the kind of ruffians politicians hired to bully votes from commoners whenever elections were on the cards.

Bulbus grunted dismissively. "The lad's a *novicus*, but he acquitted himself well in the last Colosseum fight. You know the way," he said to Scorpus, and then added with a sour grin, "Don't let him chew up your two muneraria—he can be touchy." He turned and strode past them toward where the last of the troupe was disappearing between the rising sides of the stands, muttering as he went. "Whoreson spoiled brats, think they can work the arena and make a fortune and then…"

Quintus wasn't sure whether the lanista was referring to he and Rufio or the mysterious "certain bet" of Scorpus in whom they were supposed to invest some of the unexpected windfall from Trajan in order to make a "real" fortune.

Ursus scraped out a gruff rumbling that might have been a sentence and ambled off after the lanista with a parting grip on Scorpus's neck.

Quintus wasn't at all convinced of the easy money to be made from forking out cash on some asshole. "I mean, it's bad enough to be forced into arena slavery, but who in their right mind would do it for… for fun?" he muttered to Rufio, unwilling to say it out loud and risk insulting Scorpus and his "certain bet." And yet, the thought that he might just make a living outside the Familia Caecilii was a tickle in the soul that wouldn't go away. After all, owning a gladiator wasn't exactly like being in trade, was it?

"This is way," Scorpus commanded. And they followed him through an opening into a narrow hall beyond the portico that ran from the main entryway the remaining length of the building and gave access to a series of cells. Hinged bars that could be bolted in place offered little in the way of privacy for those they housed, but all stood open. The lax security surprised Quintus, considering the dangerous nature of gladiators, little better than mine slaves. Once again, Scorpus read his mind.

"Here, gladiators only short time, from schools in country, for big festival. Slave fighters indentured to Ludus Magnus all over other side. Much bigger guard."

"The visitors might still run off, though," Rufio objected.

Quintus shook his head. "They wouldn't get far. There are two barracks just over the street in front of that mess where the new baths are coming along. I know one houses the marines on detachment from Misenum because my brother Marcus had to spend a few months there—"

"Marines?" Rufio looked incredulous. "Long way from the sea."

"They're in charge of the *velum*."

Rufio looked blank.

"Oh, I keep forgetting. You're a landlubber. The awning that protects spectators in the Colosseum from the elements. Its sections are like sails... sailors?"

"You're a landsman as well," Rufio pointed out indignantly.

"Anyway, they and the militia in the second barracks would soon recapture any runaways."

Most of the cells passed were empty, their occupants out on the sand, but in the fifth a youthful, short-haired figure sat in the near-dark on his wooden bench-bed. He was hunched over his knees, fiddling with a short length of cord. At the scrape of footwear on the stone floor, he raised his head.

"Regulus!" Quintus breathed in surprised recognition. Maybe a return on the investment didn't matter after all...

* * *

As he stalked along the length of the Forum—trailing his secretary Creon and Sallustius, a household slave, in his wake—Fabius Virius was not in the best of moods. Whenever was he in these days of continued austerity? So Sallustius tugging at his secretary's arm occasioned a sharp clip about the slave's head. "What's the idiot want?" he demanded of Creon.

Rubbing his stinging ear ruefully, Sallustius pointed at the long portico of the Aemilian Basilica, the spaces between the columns as busy as usual. Amid the throng a waving hand caught his attention. The Banker.

"Remain here," he said to Creon. "On second thoughts, take Sallustius over to the market and purchase some fruit. Late pears. If they have any, some of those Persian pears." He didn't want Creon overhearing any private Summa business, but regretted his secretary's absence for it meant once again having to forge his own way through the grubby press of people. It didn't improve his mood. "What?"

The peremptory tone failed to discompose the Banker, whose mien retained its customary blankness. Virius admired the man as he might regard the appalling swiftness of a lion fastening on its victim but he hated the man's unreadable quality. "I have received some information," he said quietly. "I am unsure whether it is useful or not, or even relevant, but it might be something we can use to bring pressure to bear in certain quarters should the necessity arise."

Virius shifted weight from one foot to the other impatienty. "Yes?"

"It concerns your friend Caecilius Dio—"

"He is *not* my friend. I spit on the bloated toad. Unfortunately I need his dubious support for… other matters at the moment. What about him?"

"Are you aware of the novicus called Regulus?"

Virius stroked his smooth chin. "Yes, he's shown spirit and some skill in the arena, if I remember correctly. But what has he to do with—"

"As with many aspiring beginners, Regulus was housed in and attached to the Ludus Magnus for the duration of the games and, though as you correctly point out he shows promise, no out-of-town owner of fighters has picked up his option. It looked as though he might end up another practice butt at the Ludus Magnus for visiting champions, but now it seems he has sponsorship."

Virius blew out a huff of impatience.

"A little bird who labors in the ludus informed Luscinus that your friend Dio's nephew and some colleague were overheard taking a financial stake in Regulus."

"Caecilius Dio has several nephews," Virius snapped, eyes narrowed and brows drawn into a dark line.

"The youngest son of Lucius Caecilius Alba."

"Quintus!" A shudder ran through Virius. All that he'd lost due to that little cunny and his... *colleague*—strange word to describe a lowborn barbarian prole—came flooding back. And yet... "You think there might be some benefit, something to be gained?"

"The young are easily swayed. His uncle must have some influence he can bring to bear. I'm sure you can persuade him to convince his nephew to turn this association to our benefit. And winner or loser, it would be most useful to have his owners in our pocket."

Virius stared at the Banker, and then nodded briskly. The redheaded brattish offspring of Junilla Tullia would have to be sidelined somehow; far too streetwise, he would see through any plan the banker might have in mind to swell the coffers of S·A·D·A and try to scupper it if for no better reason than to thwart the Fabii. "I will have words with his Uncle Livius and see what can be arranged. I'm quite sure Quintus will do as he is bid. Meantime, I think I should speak with Regulus. Better me than Gaius Fabricius Luscinus, for he is more frightening than I. Are there the funds to grease his palm?"

For once the Banker looked mildly alarmed. "Is making a direct approach to the boy at this time wise?"

"Oh don't worry. I don't intend to try bribing him to throw a fight. When it comes to it surely Luscinus or one of his minions will be the logical choice for smoothing the way forward. No, I have something quite different in mind: an offer coming from Regulus I doubt Quintus Caecilius Alba will be able to refuse... seduction."

"I'm sure you know best," the Banker said to himself as he watched Virius stride away humming a popular pantomime tune that featured an over-sexed adolescent boy tupping a wooden puppet.

Almost two months before this meeting in Rome between Virius and the Banker, far away across the sea two men had confronted each other over a different and yet entirely connected matter, one that was to have a bearing on later events.

The Initiator glowered at the Intruder from under bushy eyebrows a mix of salt and pepper. Deep suspicion filled the dark orbits of his eyes, and perhaps a touch of fear that he was doing well to hold in. "Where did you get this? And what business is it of yours?"

The Intruder's disconcertingly bland expression never altered. "There's no point ripping it up. As you know, it's a copy lacking your seal, but I have the original... with your seal."

"Who are you?"

"I'm not important, Aurelius Aquila, but my principals are. Did you not receive instructions from Panthera last month?" The Intruder didn't wait for an answer to his rhetorical question. "Yet you proceeded with this contract."

At hearing the name, Aquila blenched, lending his swarthy skin a gray pallor. He shivered, but it wasn't the cold wind blowing from the desert across Nova Traiana Bostra. Aquila was descended from a mix of Greek, Nabataean, and some Roman ancestry, and so adopted a Roman name and Roman manners to fit with the new masters of his world. To those who didn't know him well he was one among the many Roman traders who had come to the capital of the former Kingdom of Nabataea. On the death of King Rabbel II

Soter two years previously, Trajan had ended the country's century of irregular vassalage, neutered Soter's son Prince Obodas politically, and annexed Nabataea. The new province, designated Arabia Petraea, came under the Emperor's direct control, not the Senate's, and enjoyed the protection of *legio* III Cyrenaica. As Nova Traiana Bostra sat atop a vital trading crossroads it had quickly benefited from imperial funds. Gaius Claudius Severus, the imperial governor, had wasted no time in beginning construction of a major new road— the Via Traiana Nova—to link Damascus to the north, through Bostra, to the Red Sea. Many new building projects indicated a swift increase in mercantile wealth, including the massive theater, nearing completion. This monument was on Aquila's mind.

He was a seller of cloth, a tailor, and naturally inclined to keep a low profile, but as one of the governor's unofficial procurators he was a member of a small elite that arranged and helped finance many social matters. These included chariot races and the games, a position that offered him many opportunities to line his own purse. Lacking a purpose-built amphitheater, the generous orchestra of the new theater was soon to stage Bostra's first commemorative games.

"Severus relies a great deal on me and as a part of his purview he represents the F·G·O·T here in Arabia," he told the Intruder.

A tiny puff of breath issued from between pursed lips. "Invoking the governor's name will not help, and don't waste your breath informing me that Nicantinous—your son, I believe—is the legionaries' favorite wrestler. The men of III Cyrenaica are like soldiers all over the Imperium and they will happily cheer whichever youth wins, and so will Claudius Severus. Against instruction you initiated a contract with that snake Sponsianus for his boy Demetrius to throw the fight, in return for… how much is it? For a pittance. Why, you couldn't even buy a flea-ridden donkey for this sum. But of course, that's the point. You intend to make the real money from selling the fix to your cronies. What are you asking? Twenty per cent of their winnings, thirty, more?"

Aquila was feeling his years and the Intruder's worrying calmness was making him grow weaker than he liked. He had a lot invested in Nicantinous, years of training since the boy was a toddler. It had cost. Someone had to pay. "Panthera's message told me to make agreement with Barbastia and his boy Apollonarius, but that cunning bastard has cheated me before—"

"So you thought you could deceive Panthera and deal instead with Sponsianus, as was suspected. You weren't perhaps to know that Sponsianus has crossed us before."

The expression might be bland, but the eyes were feral and Aquila wondered whether this wasn't Panthera himself he faced in his cloth cutting room.

"Because he is so far away in Rome, you thought." For a moment the thin lips almost sneered. "You can't elude him, panthers have eyes everywhere and my principals have hands in all places, even this wretched backwater. Still," he said in a lowered voice that failed to promise any respite, "you weren't to know that I had a berth on a military ship that brought me swiftly to Caesarea, or that my *issu* gave me access to the *cursus publicus*, a horse change at every stage from there to Tiberias and on to Bostra, where I discover Barbastia has no contract to fix anything. Sponsianus's name came up. Didn't take me long to track him down and mentioning s·a·d·a's interest in his deal with you had a beneficial effect. He was… happy, I think that's the right word, to hand over the document that proves your treachery."

Aquila sighed. He was a clothier, a tailor, not a fighter like his son of seventeen years. The celebratory games in honor of the Emperor had been widely advertised as the most propitious event in the new capital's short history… well, its Roman history. "What do you want of me?"

"Enter into the same agreement with Barbastia you were requested to make, but reword the detail so it is Nicantinous who takes the three falls and on the final smackdown he will yield the fight to

Apollonarius. Of course, you won't say a word about the change to anyone."

"But that will cost me—"

"Your son will receive the fee you stipulated with Sponsianus."

"That will break me, not to mention what others will say when their bets fail!"

"Should your son take it into his head to be a proper sportsman—I understand this Apollonarius isn't the brightest spark in Jupiter's armory of thunderbolts—the penalty will be ten times the fee value, to be delivered without delay or any of your inventive excuses… and I should add that S·A·D·A will feel the need to bring in more amenable procurators for future arrangements.

Aquila spluttered his frustration, and fear, but gamely tried one last thrust. "I will report this to the World Federation."

At last, that produced a full-scale sardonic smile. "Really, Aurelius Aquila? I don't think so. Do you imagine the *Foedus gladiatorum orbis terrarum* turning a blind eye to your previous match-fixing escapades? The humble itinerant tailor has a previous reputation, doesn't he? In Egypt, in Pannonia, in Galatia, even briefly in Rome itself… my goodness, all over the Imperium." The smile vanished as quickly as it had appeared. "Do as you're told. May I take back your acquiescence to Panthera?"

Aquila nodded. Nicantinous would never forgive him, losing a fight against that wet sop Apollonarius, a weakling who'd flee from a goose if it barked at him.

Rome, 11th and 12th days of November AD 108

Some fifteen hundred miles from Nova Traiana Bostra and three months ahead another contract was claiming the interest of young Ashur. While Quintus was off out with Rufio and that compact hunk of a charioteer Ashur was doing just what any good body slave would do for his master. He was spying on his young master's father.

Lucius and a porcine barrel of a man were ensconced in the *tablinum*. In between keeping a wary eye out for Pallas, Lucius Caecilius Alba's secretary—"my amanuensis," Lucius grandly called him as though he were some kind of Cicero and Pallas his Tiro— Ashur listened carefully to the rumbling voice of Vipsania's father. The two *patres familias* were haggling over the dowry, the one Lucius had told Quintus he no longer needed, but was damned if he'd forgo. The suggested sum sounded like a lot, but not enough in Ashur's humble opinion to reflect the wondrousness of his adored Quintus.

"Two hundred and fifty thousand sesterces?" Quintus exclaimed two hours later, on his return from the Ludus Magnus. "She's worth as much as that?"

"That's what the property portofolly added up to," Ashur said.

"Portfolio," Quintus corrected. In spite of his surprise his mind seemed to be on other matters.

"Yes. It was…" Ashur pursed his lips and gazed at the ceiling. "An insula block of apartments on a 'rather nice part of the Cispian hill,'" he said in a gravelly imitation of Metellus, "'a large farm outside Veii, and a smaller one with a village attached near Labicum.'" He dropped back to his own light tenor. "He told your father that those properties are worth two hundred thousand. And there's another fifty thousand in value for a large four-story insula in Ostia close by the junction of the Cardo Maximus and Decumanus—"

"So very central—"

"With a nice view of the forum one side and a row of taverns and eateries the other. He said the farms and apartments bring in a handsome income annually in addition."

"And they did the deal?"

Ashur nodded. "She really must be very beautiful for all that." Quintus shrugged irritably, clearly bored by the subject of his impending nuptials. Ashur sniffed dismissively. "The family is beneath you. The Caecilii are patrician and isn't he a mere equestrian?"

"What? Oh, I see. Vipsanius Numerius Metellus is pretty big, you know. He has the position of *praefectus annonae*. Being controller of the city's grain supply makes him one of Rome's most powerful men. And he's appointed by the Emperor, directly." A frown crossed Quintus's brow. "You were eavesdropping."

"I thought you'd like to know." Ashur cast his eyes to the floor in a show of fake contrition.

"So… did they discuss anything else?"

"I was pressed close to the wall outside the *tablinum*, though I had to keep an eye out in case Pallas turned up. For a while the subject of the dowry seemed of less interest to Metellus than boasting about some aqueduct he's building… I thought you said he dealt in grain. I heard him say, 'I shall have the Aqua Traiana delivered within the budget. Great Caesar has consented to consecrate it himself, and release its blessings in the forthcoming year. Think of it,' he said to your father, 'a grand waterway stretching twenty-four miles from…'" Ashur petered out, the details a bit hazy.

Quintus snorted disgust. "The man's an egotist, over fond of his *consummate* skills. He was talking about the new aqueduct that comes from Lake Sabatinus and he certainly isn't responsible for its twenty-four miles. Braggart!"

"I know," Ashur broke in excitedly. "Your pater, he told him. 'Thanks to the efficient supply of building materials for aqueduct and mills by my clients and our engineers,' he said." Ashur's brow furrowed. "What did he mean by 'mills'?"

"There's a series of water mills on the Janiculum hillside just before the aqueduct runs into its main cistern. They're for grinding flour more efficiently for the bakers. That's all Metellus is responsible for, the mills."

"That makes sense then. He said he would increase the supply of flour threefold, and your pa said, 'In which case, my dear Metellus, you should have no problem agreeing to the value of the dowry,' and after that I had to scarper for a bit until Pallas, who came up with a scroll, was safely tucked inside with them."

Quintus nodded. He chewed his lower lip. "Did they set a date for the engagement formalities?"

Ashur instinctively followed suit and bit his own lip.

Quintus grabbed him by the scruff of his tunic. "Well?"

"Not exactly, Quin— dominus."

"I'll fuck you stupid if you don't tell me."

"In that case, I'll keep my trap well and truly shut—ow! All right, all right. That Numerius Metellus, your father-in-law to be, is a man in a rush. He told your pa that the marriage has been delayed long enough already and could we dispense with the engagement formalities and can we just get on with it. The girl's pining for you something dreadful, he said."

"He didn't?"

Ashur nodded and gently unclasped the strangling hands from his neck. "He did, and then Pallas came out with what I assumed was the sealed marriage contract and I had to duck out of his way. But I'm sure I heard the date set for the wedding."

Quintus reeled back in horror. "Tell me at least in June. You know the month is propitious, what with being identified with Juno and that?"

Ashur shook his head.

Whatever had been dogging Quintus earlier fled and he suddenly look alarmed and wide awake to impending peril. "Sooner?"

Ashur nodded.

"You're really asking for that fuck, aren't you?"

"Please."

He groaned. "I suppose I'm the last to know."

"Just before you got back Maia and Aurelia hurried off with Fabia and Julia and the mistress on a buying spree, while Primus and Secundus were loading Festus down with togas to go to the fullers—"

"When?" Quintus screamed.

"The 14th day before the Kalends of January."

"By Pluto's purple prick, the 19th day of December—the third day of Saturnalia! That's barely a month away."

"Married in days of December's cheer / Love's star shines brighter from year to year." Ashur's singsong recital broke off abruptly as he ducked under the killing blow. "You will look so handsome in that new deep maroon synthesis and a lightweight toga of pure, virginal white," he added, half laughing.

A bit crushed by this news, Quintus slumped onto the edge of his bed. "I'm glad you find this all so amusing. There's another saying: A December bride will be fond of novelty, entertaining but extravagant. That's all I need, a woman seeking novelty in bed and spending a fortune."

"A Saturnalia wedding is lucky. Anyway, how did you find your young gladiator?" Ashur obviously thought a change of conversational direction might help. "You looked a bit preoccupied when you returned home."

Quintus stared at the opposite wall, eyes slightly glazed. "That Regulus is probably the handsomest man I ever met."

If the statement hurt Ashur's self-regard, he didn't show it. Even though Quintus allowed his Syrian body slave a lot of leeway he sensed levity would not be welcome. Nevertheless he couldn't resist pointing out that he thought Tullius Rufio was supposed to be his master's most handsome man.

For a moment, Quintus appeared flustered. "Of course, even though that low-born, proletarian, flamehead calls me a pompous—"

"Patrician prick," Ashur finished, helpfully.

Quintus glowered but made no move to respond or hit Ashur. He sighed instead. "He carries himself like a noble and those flashing eyes shout of an exciting danger."

"You've always called him a common pleb."

"Regulus, not Rufio!"

This was worrying, Ashur thought. Quintus hadn't sighed like that since he'd finally admitted to having fallen for Rufio, a social disaster he'd kept from his family apart from that cunny Marcus. Just as well Quintus had something equally terrible to hold over his older brother.

"Besides, Rufio's got Woof-Woof and Hephaestion and now Adalhard to keep him amused."

"Does he know you're lusting after this Regulus?"

Quintus growled. "Don't push your luck, Ashur, or I might have to remind you that you are a slave."

Oh dear. Quintus had fallen for the young gladiator but it sounded as if the cheap arena brawler hadn't responded favorably. Anger fended off Ashur's natural jealousy at the thought of Quintus lusting after another slave. Rufio was one thing (who serviced Ashur as well as Quintus on occasion), but how dare a low gladiator refuse to do his master's bidding? "You did agree to sponsor him?"

Dark eyes blinked in mild confusion. "Who?"

Ashur sighed as well, one more of frustration. "The gladiator, Reg-*u*-lus. Or is it an outright purchase?"

Quintus picked idly at a nail. "It turns out he's *auctoratus*. Get the file."

Ashur's brows disappeared under the bangs framing his forehead. "Are you serious? I thought he would be some street rat or a difficult slave sold to a ludus. Who in their right mind would volunteer for the arena?" Unthinkingly, Ashur handed Quintus the nail file and just as vacantly his master set about dealing with the problem. Neither seemed to have noticed that it was Ashur's job to handle the manicure.

"That's what I said." The rasp of file on nail filled the air. "It turns out that some men, even well-born equestrians, crave a bit of kinky excitement, and not everyone wants to sign up as a soldier for half their life. " He looked up suddenly. "Might even be like me, you know? The youngest son, a hundred brothers ahead of him, all the usual slots filled, so nothing for it but to take to a life on the sand."

"A short life. And you don't have a hundred brothers ahead of you," Ashur pointed out with annoying reasonableness.

"No. Three's enough. It'll be a stint in the army as a junior tribune for me and then if I'm *really* lucky several years practicing law in the courts." Quintus blew out a disgusted breath between pursed lips. He handed the nail file to Ashur.

"With a lovely wife to console you." The words and tone were half sad, half mean.

"Shit! Yes. Vipsania. I suppose having sex with a girl is similar to having it with another man…"

"Except you're supposed to be the dominant one." Ashur allowed a wicked glint of a smile to touch his eyes. "And you go one way and the other with Rufio, I know."

"You let that on to anyone and I'll sell you to a ludus with instructions for you to be thrown to the lions. Better still, I heard that the Colosseum *ludi magister* is expecting a score of Nile crocodiles soon. You know the way those critters smile when they're hungry."

Ashur shuddered and sat quickly beside Quintus. He ran fingers lightly up and down the tense back and pouted the way he knew his master couldn't resist. "You wouldn't, Quintus," he murmured, dragging the words out seductively. "You can use me to practice, you know… ready for Vipsania."

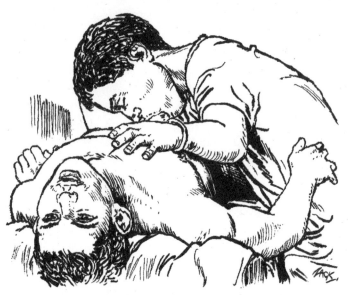

After a minute, Quintus bowed to the inevitable, let the tension flow out of his muscles, and flopped back on the bed, content to let Ashur slowly divest him of his clothes. Ashur stroked firm flesh, still sweat-damp from the long uphill walk from the Colosseum, until his right hand encountered the stiffening erection of his master's cock. He encircled it in a firm grip and rode his fist up and down, slowly leaning over Quintus's prone form until his lips kissed the noble crown, slipped down around the retreating foreskin, and Ashur began to suck.

"It matters not who I am, but who I represent," the elegantly dressed senator said. "And you have no need of knowing that either."

Regulus kept a polite silence after his first and redundant question, for he already knew the identity of his mysterious visitor, but he kept that knowledge from showing in his expression. Not a rich man seeking illicit sex with a young gladiator, though busy eyes betrayed a lustful interest from the otherwise calm demeanor. No, this was a noble after something more than sex. There was a bribe coming, but for what precisely? When the deal came, it wasn't what Regulus had anticipated.

"One of your new muneraria, the dark-haired one, is… shall we say, fit and handsome? It would not be too tough an assignment for you to… make him feel comfortable with you."

Regulus chewed the inside of his lip thoughtfully for a moment. "I'm not sure I understand, dominus."

A sharp hand reached out, struck like a snake, and grasped his chin painfully. It wouldn't have taken much to have the man on the floor crying for mercy, but Regulus knew better. He submitted physically while glaring resistance at the hard eyes staring into his.

"I will make it worth your while, boy. Starting today, some coins to better the fare you get, and more to follow. Let's be clear. You know exactly what I want. You are to seduce Quintus Caecilius Alba. I want him eating out of your hand, or your ass, or whatever suits, so long as you keep your other munerus as far away from him as possible."

"How do I do that?" Regulus twisted free of the grip.

"I'm confident your wiles will be sufficient." The cold stare was the fabrication of generations of aristocratic ancestors. It should have reduced the auctoratus to a quivering plebeian heap, but Regulus resisted… and then lowered his eyes. "And if your skills as a seducer prove less than adequate, well… there are other means to bring to bear. Here." The open palm held a glint of several denarii. "Let's not talk of other means. We have high ambitions for your successes in the arena. There will certainly be another who will come to see you at the appointed time and he will have a different proposal to make to your benefit. Meanwhile, do not think for the space of a single breath that you are not watched to ensure your compliance. Should you disappoint, the cessation of inducements will be the least painful consequence of your failure."

Shouted commands from outside echoed off the stone. Doctores ordering the men out to practice.

"I will leave you now. We understand each other?"

"Yes, dominus." Regulus shoved the coins under his thin mattress. He had a much better hiding place but did not wish the senator to see him use it. He knew too that Bulbus would be along soon to demand his cut. These people, he was learning, were all in it together, one way or another.

The hollow clash of weapons against shields echoed off the pillared portico of the Ludus Magnus, accompanied by volcanic gouts of blown breath and harsh inhalations. Steam from heaving lungs misted the chill air. The same cold burned up from the hard, stone seat into his butt, even through the woolen tunic Quintus had thought to put on, but the shiver that ran through him was occasioned by the sight he'd had of a hooded figure hurrying away from the ludus entrance as he arrived. He couldn't be certain but for a briefest of glimpses of the shaded face he thought he recognized his family's arch-enemy, Publius Fabius Virius. Surely not, though. What would the stuffed-toga senator be doing skulking about the Ludus Magnus?

He returned his attention to the action below his position on the arena *cavea*, eyes fixed on the agile murmillo weaving around and ducking under his sparring partner's clumsy strikes. Even to his untrained eye, having Regulus pitted against a *provocator* seemed unfair. With their legionary armor *provocatores* usually only fought each other. Protected by his *cardiophylax* breastplate and large legionary shield, the man had an unfair advantage over Regulus. Each wielded a gladius and when they clashed the wooden practice swords made a hollow clacking sound like the jousting of tortoises that rebounded from the mostly empty benches. Across the arena from Quintus disparate groups of gladiators, visiting competitors in the festival, waited their turns on the sand with their doctores.

He knew he should be at home on the Aventine preparing for tomorrow: Trajan's celebration feast held in the Domus Flaviana. Every year on the 13th day of November, tenth of the Games, Caesar invited the magistrates, senators, and their adult male offspring to attend a feast in honor of Jupiter. Since mad Nero instituted the event, it represented the upper classes' main involvement in the Plebeian Games. Technically a minor last year, Quintus had avoided what he considered to be an ordeal, but since February when he put on the *toga virilis* that proclaimed his adulthood his father now expected a perfect turnout of all his available sons... and no doubt awful Uncle Livy. And then there were the wretched horse brasses. Lucius had deputed Quintus with supervising the slaves charged with cleaning and polishing the ceremonial saddles and fittings for Primus and Secundus, military tribunes obligated to take part in the traditional cavalry parade on the day following the feast.

A wild cry of triumph brought Quintus back to the battle below. Astonishingly, Regulus had his opponent on the floor, gladius at his throat. A sharp crack made Quintus start. He glanced sideways in time to see Bulbus flicking the tip of his whip back. It signaled the end of the practice bout. Quintus slipped away down the steps, hoping to catch Regulus as he emerged from the arena. While waiting, his thoughts slipped back to what he should have been doing. It was all Rufio's fault, of course, that he was acting irresponsibly. Quintus's inherited patrician sense of duty had never been irksome before meeting Rufio. The layabout had no understanding of obligation— unless you counted his partial efforts at helping with his mother's businesses—but his rough and ready ways had rubbed off. A fresh wind of dissent blew through Quintus. *I'll check in on the stable slaves on the way back. It will be soon enough. And how long can it take for Ashur to wrap me in a toga ready for the damned feast?* His rebellious thoughts gave wing to what he'd already done... skive off his responsibilities—at least for a short while—in order to return to where the itch needed scratching: the Ludus Magnus.

"Ah... my master returns. One dominus, anyway. Where's the other? The wild redhead?"

Regulus tugged off his helmet with its fish crest and flicked his head to clear aside the forelock of black hair plastered to his forehead that was channeling sweat into his flashing eyes. The sight robbed Quintus of breath and voice. The provocator shoved his way past Regulus, evidently angered at losing to a youngster, and glowered at Quintus before disappearing into the gloom under the portico.

"Prick and slob."

Quintus hoped Regulus meant his recent adversary. He nodded brusquely and turned from the arena entrance to stride purposefully under the portico arcade. Quintus trailed after him, dodging guards and other gladiators going about their business, stifling a sense of inadequacy the gladiator aroused in his breast, suppressing the anger that followed. Weak sunlight flickering between the arcade columns, threw the bare torso in front of him into seductive relief; strong thighs and legs glistened with sweat. He hadn't felt like this before… but was that really the truth? Hadn't there been the same confusing sense of allure and revulsion with Rufio at first?

Wooden gladius, *manica* and *galerus* clattered onto the narrow bench that acted as seat and bed above a small wooden chest placed on the gritty floor. Regulus sat and glowered from under lowered brows at Quintus. For his part, standing in the doorway, Quintus found it hard to drag his eyes up from the protuberant lump pushing against the front of the young gladiator's scant, tight loincloth.

Regulus inclined his head slightly. An unspoken question.

In a tight voice, Quintus said, "I… I thought to check in on you. We never got around to discussing things."

"Such as?"

Quintus waved at the equipment. "Better stuff, you know, for the final days of games."

"Not much time left to do anything about that." One black eyebrow arched and a sly smile caught briefly at a corner of his full lips. "Less of course you have a tame armorer prepared to work through the night?"

Quintus admitted he didn't. "But I have some good quality military gear of my own. From the cadets. I mean, we're pretty much the same size."

Regulus wiped a hand across his brow, pushing that recalcitrant lock back again. "Cadets, hey?"

Quintus didn't fail to hear the faintly mocking tone and a worm of suspicion wriggled deep in his gut. For a lowbred novice in the arena, Regulus lacked deference. Indeed he radiated an assurance at odds with his status as a volunteer, bound to the arena by his own misfortune... whatever that was. And his manner of speech, abrupt, a little coarse, but Quintus suspected it wasn't really quite his own. But the sheer glory of the gladiator swept any faint misgivings aside. "I'm still too young to gain a position as a junior tribune." *Why am I defending my situation against this... my property?* "My colleague, Tullius Rufio, may be able to lay hands on some decent kit in time. If not," Quintus aimed for a nonchalant shrug, "we can certainly arrange matters for future games."

"Tell me about my other... dominus."

The switch took Quintus surprise. It was time to take control. He walked into the small cell and in the absence of anything else possible, sat on the bench beside Regulus. The animal sweat of exercise filled his nostrils with hot leather from the armor straps Regulus still wore. It wasn't quite the stance of power he'd wanted to aim for, but then, he hadn't really thought any of this through amid the confusion of his feelings for Rufio and the undeniable lure of sex emanating from the gladiator, heightened by the quiet amusement clear in his expression.

"Do I make you nervous, dominus?"

"No!" Quintus replied too sharply. "Why... why should you?"

Regulus got up, shucked off the leather harness and stood, legs spread slightly apart, facing Quintus. He reached out to a high shelf cut into the wall and Quintus saw there was a pitcher there beside a crude, pottery cup. "I'm afraid I can't offer you wine." He poured some water into the cup, raised it to his lips and sipped. Then held it out.

Quintus knew he was being tested, which was wrong. He was the boss here. Tentatively, he took the proffered cup and carefully sipped a tiny quantity of water. He handed back the cup. "Look here," he started, in the tone reserved for dealing with those beneath his station. "I came to finalize certain aspects of our relationship, which Tullius Rufio and I consider we left a little, how shall I put it—?"

"Hung out in the air to dry?"

"Yes. Vague perhaps. Like you, we are new to this business, but I assure you we're quick learners," he added, unconsciously echoing Rufio, and in haste to cut off the response he saw forming on the gladiator's lips. "Have no fear there. We're in this for the money, and nothing else." He left the lie floating, running out of words at increasing amusement Regulus seemed unable to conceal.

"Nothing else?" Dark eyes the color of burnt almonds regarded Quintus and the lowered lids seemed to beckon.

Some inclination of how Rufio would handle this situation came to Quintus, but Rufio's solution was beyond his usually modest character. Nevertheless... He stood and closed the gap between them, swallowed, spoke softly. "Yes. Something else. I—" *I'm attracted to you, fuckit...* "Gaius is your given name?"

Nostrils flared sensuously as a lion sensing its mate... or prey. Regulus tipped his finely sculpted head slightly to the side, as if seeing Quintus for the first time and reading the unspoken desire. "Yes, Gaius At— Gaius Regulus."

The hesitation struck an odd note, the suppression of a family name that a commoner would not likely possess, but the gladiator's all too real presence swamped any suspicion, even more so when he raised his sword arm and traced a line gently across the top of Quintus's brow. "So fine." The enigmatic pronouncement as much as the sensuous touch sent a hot flush cascading down through his body and straight to every filament of sense in his groin. Regulus allowed himself a tight smile of appreciation. "The other thugs I find myself incarcerated with in this place tell many stories of their lanistas, their domini, their muneraria, and the things they make them do." He turned away to hang the harness on an iron spike

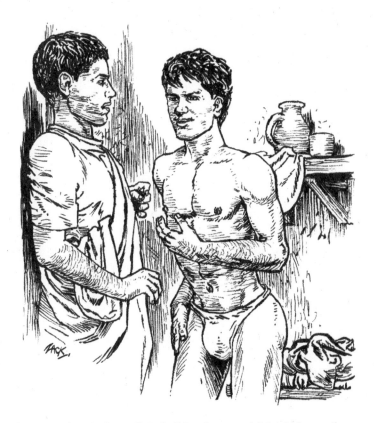

hammered into the wall. I shall be the envy of the ludus, to have such a well-set, good-looking and oh-so-young master to take care of me." He glanced over his shoulder. "Two, of course."

Quintus huffed and looked down at the stone floor, a streak of guilt merging with the heat radiating from his loins. "Oh, Tullius. Of course. But I expect he'll leave me to handle most… er, decisions regarding you, and such like."

"If I don't make you nervous, dominus, why do you stand so far off from me?" Mischief lit up eyes narrowed seductively. "It's quite usual for the munerarius to… sample the inner strength of his gladiator." Regulus cast those beckoning eyes down modestly.

"I confess I am attracted," Quintus finally admitted aloud, and gasped faintly when Regulus took him in his arms. Straining loincloth ground against tunic and toga, bunched at the front by Quintus's sudden physical reaction. But before he could follow through, Regulus released him and slipped past to lean down on the edge of his hard bench-bed. Quintus saw the heaving of his chest by the rapid rise and fall of his back. The voice came unevenly, muffled by what sounded like raw emotion.

"You cannot know the relief I feel, dominus, to have someone who has lust in their heart for me take over my care. To have a patron who has feelings for me, it… it is beyond hope. My life has been mean and hard, discarded by my family to fare for myself, leaving me with an evil choice between living off the streets or servitude to a ludus." He glanced over his muscled arm to ensure Quintus was listening. "Many there are who would say there is little to choose between those life options. But I saw greater honor in surviving the arena to one day win my *rudis*, my staff of freedom, and perhaps become a trainer, and so signed away my youth to the rigors of gladiatorial combat."

Quintus laid a hand on the quivering biceps. "You will have all you require of me… Gaius."

Regulus straightened, and reached for the water cup. He toasted Quintus and held it out. Quintus took it, making sure he drank from the same spot on the rim Regulus had used.

"I am humbled that our life-forces march so closely in step, dominus, that you understand deep in your heart how I must preserve my strength for the final hours of practice and the fights ahead of me in the days to come, but then, after…" The dark eyes flashed with promise. "Shall we find our hearts entwined in empyrean realms?"

It was in a somewhat unsatisfied state of mind that Quintus returned to his duties at Domus Alba, blessedly not missed by brothers or father. His balls ached with unslaked lust, confused as to whether Regulus felt any attraction for him, whether his coy looks indicated a genuine come-on or were the outward artifices of a slave obliged to pretend possible affection. Rufio never minded paying for sex when it suited him, but Quintus was not like that, he needed the physical to be a manifestation of genuine affection (he didn't equate buying a cheap alabaster head of Ramesses the Great from slinky Sekhemkhet-Adonis as a payment for the fun they'd enjoyed that afternoon in Memphis). At the same time he was trying to encompass the dark hints Regulus had thrown out about the unpleasant things that happened to young gladiators who didn't toe the line, though Regulus refused to elaborate what things and what kind of line needed to be toed. And there was that niggling doubt aroused by the gladiator's fluency—*empyrean realms?*—which slipped out at odd moments as if glimpsed through a narrow gap in a fence and that seemed out of kilter with his lowborn status.

Thoughts dark with unrequited lust and uncertainty, Quintus slipped quietly to his own chamber through the public rooms echoing with hidden industry. He hoped to find some time to pen a new poem for Rufio to illustrate, his muse fired by the illicit visit to the Ludus Magnus. If it went well, he'd send Ashur over to the Emporium to hand the stanzas to Rufio. Normally it would be the ideal excuse to see his friend, but... Rufio would probably be entangled with Hephaestion, or the blond German prince Adalhard, or maybe Felix, who seemed practically to live there these days. Who was he fooling? This was Rufio, so maybe all of them at once. Quintus steered clear of admitting that his meeting with Regulus might have something to do with avoiding Rufio right now.

S·I·X | VI

Rome, Ides & 14th day of November AD 108

Gaius Atilius Regulus upended the bucket over his head, shook thick, black curls of hair vigorously to send a cloudburst of droplets flying in all directions. He was still cursing his clumsiness at almost blurting out his family name in front of Caecilius Alba, a *gens* the uppercrust twit would surely recognize. Had he done enough to engage the patrician boy's lustful interest? He thought so, hoped so. It wasn't just the loss of future payments Fabius Virius had dangled— yes, he knew the man well enough by sight—that concerned him, it was the very real threat of promised violence for failure. But how to proceed without getting dragged into any unwanted acts of sexual congress. It was all very well tempting Quintus with flirtation, come-to-bed eyes, and withheld promise as he'd so far managed, but prick teasing could go only so far. Regulus was only too well aware that his status, barely better than that of a slave, meant he'd be the one expected to bend over and accept priapic Quintus up his asshole, or worse still (perhaps?) offer up his mouth. He ran hands over his chest and stomach to sweep away most of the water and shivered in the cold. But the demands had been specific, so there was no way of avoiding going through with… the sex.

"Hey, you runt! Mind where you spray your stinking piss."

Regulus glared from under his stitched-up brows at the hulking Scythian. Regulus was on the first of two "down days," no fights arranged, so he'd only been in the practice ring, whereas Bebryx was back from the Colosseum, bringing the gore stench of the arena with him in to the washing area. The older gladiator's British slave was sluicing his master down, so what did a few more drops of water matter? But Regulus stifled a retort. From the unfortunate example of others he'd learned it wasn't wise to rile Bebryx. When Ajax, a big, buff, and boastful Ionian, took exception at the Scythian and his "white worm of a slave" sitting down at the table Ajax called his own, it took less than a count of ten and the Ionian's beard had made its acquaintance with the refectory's sharp flagstones. That was at breakfast. Bebryx hadn't been in the best of moods. Rumors speculated that even though the secutor had wiped out his opponent in the afternoon bout in the Colosseum for some reason he took little satisfaction in it. Regulus overheard one sniggered whisper after Bebryx had left. "Perhaps the retiarius he faced, that little Egyptian shit Narmer, maybe he didn't put up much of a fight before he died."

More than the advantage of his overlong gladius, just maybe the match was fixed so the Scythian bastard would win, Regulus thought sourly. If so, it certainly wasn't the first and it wouldn't be the last.

Good temper was in short supply. There was a lot to be done in preparing for the Emperor's banquet later in the day and too many interruptions. Since her return from the Bay of Naples Fabia had been making demands on his body, rather more than Fabius Virius was prepared to allow, particularly since it made bedding Ambrosius all the more difficult. And now he had to face Livius Caecilius Dio invading his home like some cheap client waving his petition. "I'm counting on you keeping a close watch on the brat," Virius snapped.

The two senators stood beside a pillar in the atrium which offered an illusion of privacy from the desultory gathering of Fabian clients. "After all, and forgive my bluntness," Virius added without a hint of apology, "Quintus is not as naïve as you make out, he's pulled the woolen toga over your head a few times now."

Livy choked back a splutter of indignation at the exaggeration, a little mollified by the satisfaction of seeing just how thin on the ground were Virius's clients, so many abandoning his patronage after his recent string of misfortunes. "Leave Quintus to me. He only needs a guiding hand from one who knows the arena. As long as you've done your side of the business…?"

Virius nodded briskly. "It's not asking much. I'll give your nephew that, he's a very fuckable brat and Regulus is a good match. It didn't need much coin to persuade him to seduce his new munerarius." Virius injected sarcastic venom into the word. "But your task…" he prodded Livy's chest, "is to observe, to see that an affair develops, the better to keep your nephew's mind off that redheaded cockhound who trails after him like a mangy dog. You may think Quintus naïve, but his catamite friend is no fool. As a co-patron he would be just the one to sniff out anything not quite above board. It's best we keep them separated, at least long enough to suit our purposes, and what better than a fiery love affair between one of the owners and the gladiator?"

"Quintus doesn't take advice on matters of the heart from me—"

"Too chaste or too chased?" Virius barked a frog-like sound, a laugh at his own wit. Livy's black scowl reminded them that others were close enough to listen in. Virius lowered his voice again. "I was thinking more of cock than heart, but you're right. An intense involvement is what we need to see. I shall be watching this evening in the Domus Flaviana to make sure you are talking to your beloved nephew. Oh, and keep him as far away from Caesar as possible. We don't need imperial favor interfering again."

Like pitted olives squashed between bread rolls, Livy's eyes narrowed in their cushions of fat, but his sneer looked unconvincing. "Just make sure you have a firm hand on Regulus. Something about him doesn't quite ring true, but at the moment I can't put my finger on it."

"Young men who indenture themselves to a ludus aren't ten to the as, but neither are they so rare."

Livy shook his jowls. "I shall find out what's off about him."

"Stop being an old woman, Dio."

"Just remember that I warned you."

Chair after chair deposited the great and good of Rome in the Area Palatina, men of the senatorial and senior equestrian classes nodding politely to acquaintances, stiffly ignoring rivals or those of opposing factions. Praetorian Guards in full uniform acted as harassed valets, keeping the chains of litter slaves on the move, clearing the crowded space to make room for new arrivals. Quintus shivered in spite of the weight of his formal toga. Torches placed along the outer portico of Domus Tiberiana did little to dispel the gloom of the palace that old Tiberius barely ever inhabited, preferring his country estates and the island retreat of Capri, the very thought of which filled Quintus with shudders of horror†.

He followed close behind his father, proud of bearing in his thick-stripe toga, and his brothers Lucius Primus and Livius Secundus, resplendent in their military tribune uniforms under maroon-dyed cloaks (but without swords, of course). Unbelievably, he could wish that Marcus was at his side instead of being stuck down in Misenum, because he was the one brother who also hated Uncle Livy. Marcus had once suggested that Livy would love to get a hand up his young brother's tunic. "You can tell by the look in his eyes whenever he enters a room and sees you," he'd joked. Quintus had every reason to know just how true that remark was... still was. Were he present, Quintus would have kept Marcus between himself and Livy. But as the stream of dignitaries led by senior magistrates filed through the massive Aula Regia, and sandaled footfalls echoed around the marbled vastness of the three-story audience hall, Livy cut him off from the rest.

"A word, nephew."

Alarm fired Revulsion's arrow through Quintus. He saw that Livy wanted to maneuver him into one of the arched alcoves lining the side of the chamber—the last thing he wanted to happen. To avoid being diverted from the train of dignitaries exiting the hall ahead, Quintus slipped sideways around his uncle and stepped out into the great peristyle. Undeterred, Livy headed him off to the side of the central fountain and pool away from the path the noble multitude was taking. A parade of blazing torches suspened under the colonnades turned the fountain into a glittering cascade, flashing shards of crisp light that acted like a barrier from the others. In mild despair Quintus watched the rest of his family merge with the sea of senators as they were swallowed up through the double row of Corinthian columns into the huge triclinium of the Domus Flaviana. In moments the Caecilli would take up position, ready to greet the Emperor's appearance from the Domus Augustana.

"What do you want, Uncle?" Quintus kept peering around the corpulent figure at the last stragglers vanishing inside the triclinium.

"You know I am well-informed of many things, especially if it bears on our noble family, Nephew."

This wasn't news to Quintus. He didn't think Livy required a response, so he simply sighed.

"You have been seen at the Ludus Magnus, dear boy." Silence. "Don't give me that sullen look, Quintus. You know I have only your best interests at heart. Think of how I engineered your introduction to our dearly beloved Trajan Caesar."

Quintus almost choked on the bile that rose into his throat, which at least stifled the choking laugh that threatened to erupt at mention of this blatant chicanery. "You pimped me. And not for my benefit, *dearest* Uncle."

"Now, now, that's all in the past, but don't be so ungrateful. Look at what became of that introduction."

Nothing good for you, as it turned out! "What about the Ludus?"

"Ah, so you don't deny it. Good. I have friends everywhere, dear boy, and friends of friends who have an… an interest, shall we say? Yes, an interest in helping you make the most of your investment in this youngster called Regulus. I'm not particularly happy that he seems to have sprung into being fully formed like an Epicurean epigram from the mouth of Cicero, but there are colleagues who feel he may go far and—"

"What's this about? Really?"

Livy shook his jowls mirthfully. "Oh nothing, my boy. I would hate to think of you losing your investment, so I thought I'd offer a snippet of wisdom." He leaned in so close that Quintus was obliged to step back to avoid the blast of luncheon garlic. "Patronage is so much more than supplying better food than the awful fare the training schools feed their slave fighters, and more elegant armor and weapons. It requires a degree of physicality, my boy." The voice hardened. "Which I know you understand perfectly well. Make the gladiator your man, if you know what I mean. Reliant on you emotionally as well as financially. Dominate and press him to your will." Livy's eyes slid slyly down the length of Quintus to settle on his middle, safely tucked away beneath loincloth, tunic, and toga. Even so, Quintus felt his cock and balls shrink from the gaze.

"I— I don't understand."

"Oh yes you do. Seduce him. Make sure he's loyal and will do whatever is asked of him… as at some point it will be. And…" Livy straightened up and started to turn away, much to Quintus's relief. "And keep your… what shall I call him? Your partner, that saffron-top brat, keep him well away from Regulus. He's a dreadful influence. You know better than any what an unrestrained whorehound he is. You wouldn't want Regulus slipping from your domination. We wouldn't want that, as a family."

"Family?" Quintus was bewildered at the thought that anyone knew about his and Rufio's "investment" in the "certain bet" Scorpus had handed them on a plate and couldn't for the life of him imagine his father Lucius approving in the least. "You haven't said anything?"

Livy tapped the side of his fat nose. "It will be our secret, my dearest Quintus. As long as you behave in this matter as I advise. Understood?"

Quintus understood the barely veiled threat, but he did not comprehend what lay behind it.

95

Livy slipped in unremarked among the Caecilii waiting at respectful attention beside their appointed couches, but his father berated Quintus for his tardy appearance. "You're hardly ahead of the Emperor's appearance. You know that all young men making their first attendance at this feast must be presented to Caesar at the start of the banquet. I don't want our illustrious name mocked for your incompetent absence. You have already done more than enough to arouse Caesar's ire," Lucius grumbled sotto voce. He seemed to have a muddled perspective on the matters that had entangled his son in the Emperor's affairs, including a wilful forgetfulness as to his—admittedly unwitting—role in Uncle Livy's wicked plans that had gone so disastrously wrong for Livy and so splendidly well for Lucius.

"Yes, Father." He glanced between serried ranks of senators, motionless like so many beehive-shaped cones of salt in their strict formals, at the august surroundings. Columns of marble in alternating Numidian yellow and Phrygian purple supported a ceiling of richly painted panels set between ribs of cedar wood adorned in lapis lazuli. Since the Nile journey, he was able to recognize Egyptian granite sparkling with myriad glints of feldspar, quartz, and mica, while the exquisitely patterned floor was an expanse of marble in pink, blushing red, and sea-green malachite. Warmth radiated from the underfloor heating system. Somewhere in the depths of the palace underworks slaves toiled to keep the *hypocaust* furnaces burning to heat the air forced through tubes below the marble and up through the walls. Slaves, however, were not foremost on Quintus's mind, for at that moment a herald announced Caesar. The head of House Ulpius swept grandly into the great dining room in company with Hadrian and several men of the inner court.

Immediately, more heralds summoned the handful of youths newly admitted to the ranks of manhood to line up and pass before their Emperor. Quintus was fourth in the row to bend his knee in a formal bow and cite the short oath of allegiance as a member of the patriciate. Into his lowered view came a long-fingered hand. The signet finger bore the great ring of state. He felt Trajan's hand fall lightly on his shoulder and the squeeze that followed. He didn't, however, think any of his fellows received the added whispered words in the familiar, pleasant baritone brushed with its tinge of Iberian provincial accent: "I shall soon send for you and Rufio. It's been too long since our last soirée…"

* * *

Rufio's tuneless whistling would never put the birds to shame crowding the plane trees lining Vicus Portae Naeviae as he climbed the slight incline to the plateau of Aventine Minor. Behind him, the arcade of the Marcian Aqueduct sliced off the rest of the city from view. Patting the cap end of a leather tube tucked under his arm created a drum rhythm to the tune in his head. He was eager to show off the latest illustrations he'd just finished in a fever of inspiration at reading the couple of short poems Quintus had sent with Ashur two days before. The body slave's excuse for him making the wordy delivery in place of his master barely registered. Moments

after being ushered into Rufio's presence, Ashur was flat on his back, Graeco-Egypto-Libyan cock rammed down his throat and Rufio's big, hard dick up his ass as the fucker muttered something about Quintus not minding sharing him.

At the fizzling memory the whistling reached a new pitch. The new drawings had gone quickly, but he hadn't thought to bother Quintus yesterday, knowing that the poor sap would be all tits-over-ass with preparations for and attending Trajan's big bash to mark something weird the nobs always got up to in their stiff formals on the Ides of November. He'd muttered something about a cavalry parade for today, but that he wasn't involved in all that ancient nonsense when men proved they were leaders of men of the Equestrian Order by showing off their mounts; just as well, Rufio thought: he wasn't fond of horses. But the tone of the two poems had aroused his curiosity. *Something's got his groin all a-twitch, some of the damn sexiest things he's ever penned... and so romantic as well!* He hoped his friend wasn't suffering a hangover after honoring whatever the palace shindig was all about... yes, Jupiter, of course, with no doubt endless libations of wine.

He broke off to grin cheekily at a rough but cute boy swaggering down the slope toward the Vicus Porta Raudusculana, the main thoroughfare that cut through the Aventine hill on its way to join the road to Ostia. The boy's dress indicated a lowly status, but its scantiness on this unexpectedly warm November day lent him a seductive appearance. Rufio's wink wasn't missed either. He paused in his stride to give Rufio the eye.

"Whatcha got in there, then?" Freckled face, fair hair like badly cut corn stalks, and a suddenly wicked grin.

Mmm, very forward. Rufio matched the expression with a gaze that said he was mentally undressing the young man. *It worked a treat with Quintus, and look how he hated me on sight.* "A scroll."

"Oh there's a surprise." The lad sighed theatrically. "I meant what's you got on the scroll?"

Rufio twisted his face in regret. "Oh I' sorry. I— I can't show you... not here... in public."

Interest glimmered in widened eyes. "I seen you before, all that red hair. I know! In The Two Balling Fighters, that tavern over t'other side of Aventine. Go on, tell me. If you won't let me see what's on it, tell me about it."

Rufio squinched his lips together to show he was reluctant but considering the request while unselfconsciously rearranging his cock and balls under the hem of his tunic. "It's an erotic poem written by a friend," he said finally, with a becoming blush.

The boy's interest faded a bit. "Poetry..." a hint of dismissal.

"With appropriate drawings by me," Rufio added proudly.

The eyes lit up again. "Go *on*, let's see."

"I told you. Not here, but..." he leaned in close so that his lips almost brushed the boy's ear, "...if you want to drop by the Emporium of Artistic Excellence, maybe then. You can't miss it, at the end of the Street of the Cork Sellers, off Vicus Platanonis."

A wave of straw-colored hair fell across twinkling brown eyes at the nod of recognition. "Not far from The Two Balling Fighters."

As Rufio continued on his way he wondered why he had done that. Didn't he have enough domestic strife as it was without adding another sexy flibbertigibbet to the mix? Truth to tell, he was happy to be out of the house for a while, away from the clinging charms of Hephaestion and the less than enjoyable friction between that curly-haired mini-monster and Felix. Poor Woof-Woof hadn't taken the Egyptian-Libyan-semi-Greek's insertion into the Tullius family and Rufio's bed very well. And as for the handsome German hostage prince, the palace slave given him by Trajan, Felix didn't take to Adalhard at all.

"I don't mind Quintus," he'd complained, "because he's nice to me and cares, but the half-breed and the barbarian, well…" There were no words. Felix pouted and accepted a quick doggy-fuck by way of compensation while Hephaestion was out doing chores for Junilla and Adalhard was demonstrating to Damianus his suitability as a secretary's amanuensis. Yes, it was good to be away from the angst for a bit, going to visit Quintus to show him the results of his artistic renderings. That's when it clicked. *Our visit and arrangement with Regulus obviously excited his muse no end! Oh Quintus, you dirty dog, you've fallen for a bit of rough-brawler trade. Must've been that session with Scorpus got those delicious patrician balls itching.*

And there was another matter he needed to raise. A real hangover, this time from the Egyptian trip… one for Quintus. He picked up the tune from the point that the attractive youth going the other way had so rudely interrupted and started tootling again. He could tease Quintus that he would soon have his hands full with the boy who walked like an Egyptian and gulled Quintus into buying some cheap tourist tat, that shitty alabaster bust of Ramesses the Great, apparently… though it might have been any Egyptian pharaoh so poor was the carving. The alabaster seller Sekhemkhet-Adonis ("Call me Sek") had done some of his own worming just like Hephaestion at that short (but obviously not brief enough) halt the cruise-boat *Cleopatra of the Nile* made at Memphis. He'd smarmed Junilla that she could make a fortune selling finely carved honey-colored Egyptian alabaster to the Roman rich, and for that she would need an expert on hand in Rome, *etc, etc, blah, blah*. A letter announcing his arrival as soon as the new sailing season opened was delivered only the day before. The postscript added that he hoped to renew his acquaintance with "the delectable Quintus" and eagerly anticipated future intimate delights.

"He's coming to Rome?" Quintus looked gratifyingly anxious on hearing the news.

"Not for a bit. Ships won't be sailing now until spring. And that's when I get busy helping Ma with all that statuary and stuff Trajan collected. You could wrap the entire Roman Forum in the manifest. Anyway, it's all right. I shan't mind you having him left, right, and center—"

"But I don't want…" Quintus spluttered helplessly.

"No, of course not," Rufio soothed. Quintus's bared, quivering arm deserved a gentle rub. "Not at least while you have the hots for that gladiator."

"Don't *you* start as well."

Rufio paused in his response, mouth half open. "As well?"

A frown darkened Quintus's brow. He raised both shoulders defensively. "At the feast. Uncle Livy was goading me on about Regulus—"

"How did he know?"

"He just does know, and he was hinting heavily that it would be in my interests if I formed a… well, a strong relationship with our investment, but I think he really meant *his* interests."

It was Rufio's turn to frown. "What interests? What could your wicked Uncle Livy want with a gladiator… apart from the obvious?"

"Good question." Quintus gave a proper shrug of irritation. "He's up to no good again, but I don't know why." He fixed Rufio with a glare. "Anyway, there's him egging me on to get into a gladiator's loincloth and now you're saying I'm hot on Regulus."

Rufio decided to forget the machinations of Livius Caecilius Dio. "You do too. It's in every word you wrote. Look." He unrolled the short length of scroll, weighted down the ends, and watched Quintus struggle to forget the Egyptian alabaster seller's threatened appearance. They were standing over a long marble table set against a wall at the back of the atrium. The place was so quiet it felt as though they had the house to themselves. With Lucius Caecilius Alba's morning client session long over, the brothers out on their own business or pleasure, and the women of the household all demurely ensconced in their own apartments, weaving or doing something virtuously useful, Rufio hoped, the slaves—including it seemed Ashur—had made themselves scarce. Just as well; his rare visits to Domus Alba always made him feel nervous, too many people flitting this way and that, dusting, polishing, admonishing.

Quintus cast eyes over the artwork adorning his neat script.

Rufio waited with expectant impatience. He had endured the usual reluctance of Tredegus, the doorman and only other apparent human in residence, to admit him. On the few occasions Rufio had presented himself at the Domus Alba threshold it was a game they played: he brashly announcing himself, Tredegus always failing to recognize him. Slaves in patrician households breathed in the airs and graces of their masters, thought themselves better than mere plebeians, though the door slave had not yet been rude enough to call Rufio a prole or compare him to an actor, an *infame*, the lowest of the low. And to be fair Tredegus did have some reason to be obstructive to the lout who had drunkenly bloodied his nose before lamming into Quintus barely a year ago.†

"Well?"

Quintus looked up a touch of awe in his eyes. "Did anyone ever tell you that you have a very dirty imagination?"

Rufio tilted his head. "Which means?"

"It scintillates."

"Is that a long word for it's fucking amazing?"

"With everything so far and this new scroll, have we got enough now to show this tame bookseller of yours?"

"Ma's tame scribbler pimp, and I'm not sure he's all that easy a screw. Publishers are a bunch of conniving thieves, you know."

"Have we?"

"Enough to make him cream his loincloth? I'll bet. Let's take the stuff to show him tomorrow." For a moment Rufio almost looked vulnerable. "*Do* you like them, really?"

The smile belied the uncaring shrug. Quintus turned back to the manuscript and pointed to one of the colored drawings. "Have you actually tried out that position with… er, one or two of your menagerie? I mean it looks fascinating but rather exhausting and maybe, just maybe impossible?"

Rufio smirked and waggled a flaming eyebrow. "I thought I'd wait until we were alone and give it a go. What do you say?"

For an answer, Quintus freed the scroll and popped it back in its tube, and then with a smoldering come-to-bed glance over his shoulders, strode off toward his bedchamber.

"Do you think it's treason to have seen…" Cato lowered his voice to a low murmur so that Felix had to lean close to hear him above the grumble and grind of the Roman streets. "To have seen the Emperor having sex?" he whispered, drawing out the last word's sibilants.

Felix straightened up with a start. "Must be!" Shock turned to prurient curiosity. "Are you saying you have?"

Cato's dark brown bird's nest of hair rustled as he nodded with a matter-of-fact toss of the head. "On the voyage to Egypt."

Felix licked his lips and then tongued the gap between his incisors made when a bigger gang member of the Aventine Foxes punched him out and cracked one of them. "Was it with the Empress?"

Cato grinned manically and shook his head in a vigorous denial.

"No! The brother of Quintus, Marcus. The one who's in the marines."

"By the hairy balls of Bacchus! Really? What were they doing?" Felix's aroused interest seemed to have overcome his nervousness at discussing a potentially treasonous subject.

The two lads were returning from a joint lesson in rhetoric held at a private school. Junilla wanted her youngest to get a decent education, "not like your wastrel brother," she'd told him with an amiable smile. He wasn't convinced being landed with the continued attentions of Eutychus were worth the effort, and was glad they managed to lose the tutor way down the hill when he paused to buy a honey pastry at a cookshop. Felix was similarly dubious as to the lessons' value. As headman of the West Aventine Crossroads Club, Clivius wanted his son to become an advocate and make a name for himself in the law courts. Felix suspected this had more to do with having a lawyer in the family who wouldn't charge the usual ruinous fees for getting Clivius off any future unpleasantness that might arise from running the rackets than any regard for his son's future—Felix Clivius Ostienus, Àdvocatus!

The Vulpeculae, the Little Foxes of the Aventine who ran wild in the scrubby wasteland lying between the the Aventine hill's southwestern slopes, Mons Testaceus, the river wharves, and the tombs lining Via Ostiensis, knew Felix by several other names: sometimes Diastemi or Gap Tooth because of his broken incisor which gave him the feral look that really interested some men; more often Felix Vulpus, the lucky fox—for when it came to sex the younger boys thought he was—but he'd always particularly liked Rufio calling him Woof-Woof, testimony to his love of being taken doggy style. Now, he glanced around furtively, but no one was near enough to overhear their conversation in spite of the crowded Vicus Armilustri. Still, Cato kept to a conspiratorial whisper.

"What were they doing? They were pretty firmly stuck together."

Felix licked his lips. "Did one of them have his cock in the other's asshole? And who was on top?"

"Oh the Emperor was mounted on top. Marcus was getting rammed pretty hard. There was much puffing and groaning, but I heard one of the sailors come clumping up from the rowing decks so I had to scarper and unfortunately missed the ending."

They walked in silence for a while, each lost in thoughts of what Cato had witnessed.

"What's it like?"

A raised eyebrow. "What's *what* like?" Felix asked.

"Fucking. Doing it."

The eyebrow dropped and sort of scrunched together with its companion. A sniff accompanied Felix's high moral tone. "You're too young to be talking about stuff like that."

"I'm getting my *toga virilis* in the New Year." Cato's voice wobbled with indignation, part treble still, part swooping down to an untried bass register.

"You're still in the Little Foxes."

"So were you, when you started hanging around the Two Balling Fighters and places like that, and I know what for as well."

Felix shrugged. "I didn't get much pocket money off my father."

"Look here, I not only saw Trajan knocking off Marcus, I've seen Quintus and my brother screwing like bunny rabbits in front of some Greek artist in Alexandria. Seen it but not done it. So. What's it like?"

The twitch of Felix's nose showed he would give in. A smile tucked into the corners of his lips. "It feels wonderful. When he slips his hard cock right inside you and starts to move in and out, or when you wrap your lips around an aroused legionary helmet."

"You've never done it with a woman?"

Felix shrugged again. "Never been interested. Besides, I like to take it and last I heard women aren't much good for giving you that, not like your br— like Rufio." Felix took on a dreamy expression for a brief moment. "Oh, it feels weird talking to you about having sex with your brother."

Cato took his turn to shrug a nonchalant shoulder. "S'all right with me." He widened his eyes as they circumnavigated a vegetable stall taking up too much of the narrow sidewalk. "Do you get your thing nicely gripped, like when I do it with my hand?"

"Yes, but better, lovely and warm and slippery, and Rufio always hits a spot deep inside that sends sparks like signal flares off in my head, just before he makes me come, and I feel him shooting into me… Oh sorry. Is this too much?"

"No, no! So how many times have you been fucked and by how many different men?"

Felix hummed and hahed for a moment, totting up sums on his fingers. "I've taken it up the ass… maybe ten, fifteen times, by… hmm, four different payers."

"Rufio pays you?" The idea seemed to shock Cato.

"No. I let him do me for free because I… well, he's just so adorable."

Cato's snort of laughter was typically that of a younger brother for his older sibling.

"It's true. Ask Quintus. He's a noble and he adores Rufio too."

"I know." Cato grinned to himself. "I used to work Quintus up by sitting on his lap and fiddling with him, you know, just shuffling around to get him lustful. Never worked, though. He was so embarrassed." Cato burst out into a full-throated chuckle at the memory. "Almost as bad as Flaccus." He recovered and then asked, "But you've fucked someone?"

"A couple of times. One of my pick-ups at the tavern asked for it that way and there was one of the Foxes who wanted to try it, so I obliged. He was a bit of a cunny really but he wriggled nicely. It was all right."

Vicus Armilustri bent to the left and became Vicus Platanonis. Some fifty paces beyond that point the Street of the Cork Sellers ran off to the right. The boys paused at the junction. Felix was aimed across the top of the Aventine toward the Crossroads Club and

Lares' shrine run by his father, Cato to the Emporium at the end of the street, which was little more than a curving alleyway.

"What's it like, getting shagged in the mouth?"

"Where'd you hear words like that?" Felix scratched behind his ear, nodded with sudden insight. "Rufio, I suppose. Hmm, I love oral sex. For me, if I'm getting it, it's the best way to come." He leaned in close. "It makes you feel just... *eeuurrgh!*" The shiver was eloquent enough without further elaboration. "And if I'm sucking, I love the vibration as the man starts to ejaculate—"

"But the taste...?" Cato screwed up his face.

"Never eaten your own?"

"Well... once."

"And?"

Another shrug. "It was all right, but someone else's stuff...?"

"Everyone tastes a bit different. Depends what they've eaten or drunk. A good quality wine works well, but dirty cheap *posca* turns it sour. Anyway, best for me is shooting when I'm getting screwed hard. You wouldn't know it to look at his oh-so-innocent patrician face, but Quintus fucks like a onager firing a shot."

Cato's eyes widened to saucers of avid interest at the image of the dread artillery weapon that when fired had the kick of the wild ass after which it was named. "Really? He did you too. When?"

"You know when there was all that trouble with the gladiators from down south, nearly knocked off all the Crossroads Club bosses? It was a day the three of us were lying about in your *tablinum*, nothing better to do, and well… it just started. I sucked Quintus while Rufio fucked me and when he'd done his bit, Quintus plugged me." Felix sighed in a long exhalation. "That was some afternoon, that was."

"Where was I?"

"Um… I think you were still being held by those mercenary gladiator bastards."

Cato gave Felix a scandalized glare. "The three of you were happily screwing your brains out like bunnies high on Cyrenian silphium while I was chained up in a cellar, threatened with rape and death!"

All Felix could do was shake his head and spread his hands in a helpless gesture of apology. "There wasn't really anything we could do right then. We didn't know where they were holding you. Well, we did, I know, but not precisely in which bit of wherever it was. Anyway, it was me really found out where you were and helped free you."

Cato humphed. "I'd better head home or Ma will have me ground up like a terrine."

Felix's hand detained Cato. "You never said."

"What?"

"When you get around to it, whether it'll be with a woman or a man."

"Haha… as long as I get it, I won't much care!"

And with that parting shot, Cato darted off down the alley, waving over his shoulder. Felix raised a hand in response at the disappearing back, stroked down the erection bunching the front of his tunic, and then continued on his way along Vicus Platanonis.

S·E·V·E·N | VII

15th day of November AD 108

"I've always wondered," Rufio began, "why this is called the Forum of Nerva when he didn't build it; according to Ma he didn't anyway."

Quintus wrinkled his nose and shook his head in weary sorrow. "As a Roman you are supposed to know your history."

"When it's convenient, you're always quick to remind me that on Ma's side I'm descended from barbarian Celts. And don't sigh in that long-suffering sigh way."

Quintus breathed out nasally. "Before Domitian Caesar started to fill in the narrow gap between his father Vespasian's Forum of Peace…" with his right hand he indicated the towering wall where an opening led into the garden forum… "and the older Forum of Divine Augustus on our left…" pointing at the great connecting arch… "Via Argiletum was a street of cobblers and booksellers. After Domitian's death it was his successor Nerva who dedicated the new *Forum Transitorium*, so called because it still connects the Subura in the north to the Roman Forum. But everyone just calls it Nerva's Forum."

Lecture concluded, Rufio looked both ways along the long, narrow space lined by tall, fluted, statue-topped columns. Crowds packed the thoroughfare as usual. Looking over his shoulder, he could just make out the backs of the Aemilian Basilica and Senate House, which butted onto Divine Julius Caesar's forum; ahead, the temple of Minerva dominated the Suburan end. "So what happened to the Argiletum?"

"You're standing on it. Domitian covered over this stretch of it." Quintus could see Rufio was still confused about the forum's name. He must have passed through this way to the Subura numerous times, but probably never gave it much of a thought… of course. "Look, Domitian was a cruel tyrant and when his wife and chamberlain bumped him off the Senate damned his name. Then the senators asked elderly Nerva to take the purple."

"So Nerva was a good egg?"

"Exactly! Don't you remember him?" Quintus glanced sideways in exasperation.

"I was only seven when he popped it."

"So was I! But I damn well remember when it happened."

"Because you're a patrician pri—. You mentioned booksellers."

"Since you managed to forget to ask your Ma where this snake Sosius has his place of business, I assumed it would be somewhere along here. I suppose you've never noticed, but the forum—and the Argiletum beyond—still houses shoemakers and booksellers." He searched the length of the forum. Unlike the other imperial forums there were no arcades to shelter under and along both sides a ramshackle collection of stalls made a visual clutter at odds with the austere elegance of their monumental surroundings.

Quintus strode up to a rickety table covered in tattered scrolls and addressed the man bent over behind it. "I say my good fellow, tell me does Sosius have a selling spot here?" The wizened creature, garbed in a shapeless robe of indeterminate brown, partly straightened up, coughed, and ejected a stream of phlegm that matched the color of his tatty garment. Quintus stepped smartly out of its trajectory into Rufio who steadied him. The greasy discharge splatted down on the paving stones just where Quintus had been standing. When the man shook his head it set the straggly, oiled ringlets of hair hiding his ears to whipping about comically.

"Since Titus sacked Jerusalem the Jews don't seem fond of Romans," Rufio said quietly.

"Thank you for sharing that wisdom," Quintus snapped. He straightened his cloak, tunic, and dignity. "Funny how sometimes you do remember some history."

The scroll seller cleared his throat again with the force of the cloaca maxima releasing a clot of effluent into the Tiber. "Yonder," he spat out. The second spurt of sputum joined its fellow in an expanding puddle. He flapped a hand in Rufio's face and Quintus interpreted the gesture as a pointer across the forum.

"Sosius. Oh gracious no," said the young man manning the stall the expectorating Jew had indicated. He had to shout to be heard above the crowd's roar, buying, selling, or just plain walking to and fro in the echoing space. "You can find him at the copy workshop on Vicus Tuscus. It's halfway down on the right. You can't miss it."

"You can't miss it," Quintus mimicked savagely.

"We've walked up and down this fucking hill twice," Rufio complained as they started again from the top.

To reach Vicus Tuscus the two hopeful authors of quality pornography had tramped back across the Roman Forum, through the gap between the temple of Castor and Pollux on the left and the Julian Basilica on the right, past the grating set under the steps of the basilica from which the stench of human waste rose up in an almost visible miasma from the Cloaca Maxima. From there Vicus Tuscus climbed the Velabrum's steep slope before plunging downhill to the Circus Maximus and Forum Boarium.

They might have kept this up for half the day, for when they were up they were up and when they were down they were down, and when they were only halfway up, they were neither up nor down— which is where they ran into a man struggling to keep together a jumble of scrolls and leather tubes. He staggered precipitously under his burden from a narrow doorway set deep between a tavern and…

"Nasica's Knocking Shop," Rufio said in joyous recognition as he dodged the scroll carrier and gave the large erect phallus cut in stone at the doorway's side a fond rub for good luck.

"Is this Sosius's place?" Quintus asked the human donkey somewhat more practically. "I think that was a yes," he added as the fellow lumbered off up the slope toward the Forum. "Will you stop stroking that thing. People will think you're needy."

Rufio gave Quintus his best shit-eating grin. "Have you ever known me not? Mind, I only tried Nasica's once on a recommendation from my asshole friend Octavian, and what would he know? He only goes with strumpets. Nasica's boys aren't very hot. Too many drawn from the dregs of the Paedagogium if you ask me."

"I'm not asking, and *that* isn't the entryway we're interested in." Quintus threatened violence with the scroll case. "Or has a chunk of erectile stone made you forget what we're about?"

With a last squeeze of the unhooded limestone cock's tip, Rufio sidled into the bookseller's domain, followed closely by Quintus, suddenly nervous of the reaction their work might receive. At the end of the narrow passageway a tatty drape covered an opening. Sensing that his friend's mind was more on what might be happening in the bordello next door than on their business, Quintus pushed past and peered around the curtain into a large windowless room. His first thought was that the place was on fire due to the thick smoky curds coiling and writhing under the ceiling. When his stinging eyes cleared a bit he made out row after row of heads bowed over tables like a classroom of schoolboys at their lessons. Only these were men of all ages, from thickly haired youths to venerable graybeards, some balding, others like polished bullets under oil lamps suspended overhead from chains stretched from one side to the other, as many as there were rows of copy desks.

The cheap lamps were the source of so much acrid smoke. Not that it seemed to bother the educated slaves. Quintus counted twenty copyists. Their pens skittering across papyrus rolls made a sound like an army of cockroaches on the march. Glancing to his left he took in a wall of shelves stacked with scrolls and leather buckets holding yet more loose scrolls. In front, seated in a large cane-weave armchair on a raised platform, a heavily bearded Greek was dictating an author's manuscript to the scribes.

Rufio pushed through beside Quintus, blinking furiously at the thick atmosphere, and at this second irruption the Greek stopped his sonorous reading. Instantly, silence fell on the room. Twenty pens ceased scratching. The corps of cockroaches halted. Oil lamps hissed. Forty curious eyes flicked up.

"Um… sorry. We're looking for Sosius?"

This unaccustomed quiet civility from Rufio struck Quintus dumb.

The reciter peered at them sternly from under bushy brows drawn together in a frown. "Our production is on a deadline and not to be interrupted." His voice came as a deep bass grumble compared to the lighter tenor of his dictation.

"Sosius. Please?" Rufio even fluttered his long cinnamon lashes. A trick that never failed to amuse Quintus since Rufio was too tomcat to ever succeed as a coquette.

With a long-suffering sigh that would have done Quintus justice, the Greek raised an arm and pointed across the shrouded room to another curtain, this one in rather better condition than the one they had just pushed aside. Rufio nodded a polite thank you and slipped across in front of the dais toward the farther door, nodding apologetically at the rows of unblinking eyes following his passage.

Quintus went hot on his heels, dipping his head at the phalanx of scribes, their scrutiny having followed Rufio as far as they could, whipped heads back to follow his way across the room like spectators at a harpustum game. As he slipped through the door covering, the army of locusts resumed marching and the sonorous voice of the reader followed him. "Let us get back to Acheloüs wrestling with Herculius: *'With difficulty I thrust my arms, pouring with sweat from the great effort it took, under him, and, with difficulty, freed his firm hold on my body. He pressed me hard, as I gasped for breath, prevented me from gathering my strength, and gripped my neck…'*"

Sosius was not at all what Quintus expected. Since he'd first heard the name in Egypt he imagined a roly-poly, greasy, fat bastard overdressed in a fake toga with a fake hairdo, fingers swollen with a clutter of ostentatious rings, a touch of rouge applied to the cheeks above several chins—instead, as he got to his feet behind his work table Sosius was revealed to be tall and thinner than the rake the guardian of the Lupercal Cave used to sweep leaves from its opening. He reminded Quintus of an aging racehorse, with a long, pinched equine face, an impression helped by the lank forelock that fell like a mane at an angle over his brow from an otherwise military short-cropped hairstyle.

"How may I help you, young gentlemen?"

The voice only added to the horsey impression, a high-pitched neigh and a strange rhythm to the words, as if broken up by the pace of the gallop. Normally the voluble one, Rufio was suddenly tongue-tied. He glanced nervously at Quintus, who realized he was expected to act the confident patrician. "You know my friend's mother, I think. The Lady Junilla Tullia. We have some work to show you."

Sosius lifted a long bony hand and pressed the first two fingertips thoughtfully to his lips. He stared at Rufio. "I see the resemblance."

Quintus uncapped the leather tube, drew out the scroll they had worked on, and held the ends down with a couple of scroll weights carved in the likenesses of Apollo as god of knowledge and wisdom. The publisher's eyes widened. Rufio's drawings drew his attention and Quintus was forced to point to the poem they were illustrating.

"Hmm…" Sosius bent over to peer more closely. "The Tree," he read the title aloud. He scanned a few lines. "Mmm-hmm…

" 'I thought his long slim legs and thighs
I with my tendrils did surprise;
His belly, buttocks, and his waist
By my soft nervelets were embraced.
About his head with writhing tongue
Rich clusters of kisses I behung
So that my Calvus seemed to me
Young Bacchus ravished by his tree.'

"Well, it has something, I should say," he muttered darkly before continuing to read aloud.

"'My curls about his neck did crawl,
And arms and hands they did enthrall,
So that he could not freely stir
I had him trapped, my prisoner.
I dreamed this throbbing part of mine
Was changed to a creeping vine,
Which crawling across my beloved Calvus

Made way to enter his dainty anus.
But when I crept with eager lips to hide
My tongue in those parts he kept unespied,
Such fleeting pleasures there I took
That with the fancy I awoke;
And found (ah me!) this flesh of mine
More as a wooden stock than like a vine.'"

Sosius stood straight and eyed them both. "You have a way with words… which one?"

Quintus indicated himself modestly.

"And these… these, well… I have never seen illuminations quite so, er… direct, shall we say?" He gave a stern look. "I'm very strong on fact-checking. I assume all these positions have been tried and tested?" At the embarrassed mutual nod, he asked, "Is this all you have, my boys?" His veiled eyes tried to hide an interest.

"We can provide as much as you will take, Sosius," said the suddenly vocal Rufio in a quiet businesslike tone.

"How much would you pay to publish?" Quintus asked with a touch of eagerness.

Rufio stepped in front of him, standing painfully on his toe, determined to take over the commercial side of things. But Quintus's enthusiasm had played into the publisher's hand. Sosius recovered his gloomy mien and neighed dismissively.

"Ah-hah well, as you must understand, it's one thing to copy words on a production line such as I have, but reproducing many detailed illustrations is a very time-consuming and an extremely costly task." He returned to the other side of his table, scratching his pointy chin as if considering the fate of the Imperium. We could look, perhaps, at going as high as, hmmm, five asses for each sold copy, accumulated and paid twice annually—"

A sharp snap interrupted Sosius in mid-flow. Rufio had freed the two Apollos from their weighty task and the released ends of the sample scroll rebounded on each other. Snatching the scroll tube from Quintus, he replaced the pornographic masterpiece, slapped the cap down firmly, and turned for the door. A bewildered Quintus looked at his friend and then at Sosius.

"We'll see what Crassus of Sicily has to offer," Rufio threw over his shoulder with a flourish of flame-hued hair.

"That saw-toothed shark!" Sosius's whinnying shriek of outrage was perfectly theatrical. "He will rob you boys blind, if masturbation doesn't take your sight first."

Rufio turned, half through the curtains. "As you are trying to do."

Quintus thought his head would fall off if he kept swinging from Rufio to Sosius and back again as they glared at each other.

Eventually, Rufio broke the silence. "The finished book will be thirty feet long, so great value for money. We'll want ten denarii and not a quadrans less, paid for all copies sold at the end of each month. And we're not paying for unsold copies or returns."

The publisher's thin mouth dropped open, revealing a bank of gray millstones. He spread his arms in a gesture of helplessness. "I can't pay for returns."

"They'll have cum stains on them." Rufio grinned, all teeth and lips, with a wink for Quintus.

"Two denarii, that's my last offer, and far too generous."

"Five denarii and one quinarius. Take it, or leave it to Crassus of—"

"Done! When can you deliver the first scroll for copying?"

Rufio looked across at Quintus, who coughed. "Er, I've got a few things I have to get through first, but… how about six months?"

"Three!" Rufio and Sosius were as one voice.

"Five. Can't do it any faster."

"Four!"

"All right, four then."

"Try it the other way around," Rufio ordered Hephaestion. He was seated at a small tripod table in his bedchamber, sketching lightly on a scroll stretched across it, the ends curled up on the floor on either side. Care was needed to weave the illustrations into the spaces between stanzas of Quintus's latest poem and around the edges. "Felix, you have to look as if you're rearing up to give some head to a person out of shot."

"It's not easy to pretend when there isn't one there." He gave Rufio a pout, his dark hair grown out at the front so it fell fetchingly across his burnt-umber brows.

"I can't do both things. Just imagine I'm standing in front of you. No, better still, Adalhard, make yourself useful. Wave your dick in front of Felix... yes, like that, but step sideways because you're not in this scene yet."

"Yes, and hold still," Hephaestion complained to Felix. "How'm I supposed to get it in with you wriggling like a ferret on heat."

The Graeco-Egypto-Libyan boy had discovered a liking for fucking and was more than happy to practice on Woof-Woof, but he and Felix were having trouble modeling for Rufio.

"My back just doesn't bend like that," Felix moaned.

"Hades' hand-job! Epigonus of Tralles didn't have this trouble with Quintus and me when we posed for his blasted cups. That's why I said try it the other way around." Exasperation burst from Rufio's lips. "Right! Hold it like that. Adalhard, stand back a bit more and get your cock out the way or I can't see Felix's *ecstatic* face. Mouth wide, Hephaestion, you're about to fill his tummy full of love... and jizz."

He and Quintus had quickly recognized that their joint method of working meant making the book up of several short sections, which could then be joined, as many longer books were, into a single scroll—and the copy slaves and whichever artists Sosius employed to faithfully reproduce Rufio's originals would have to do the same. As the boys bent their bodies into impossible positions an unfamiliar sensation troubled his usually light-hearted, sunny nature. The source of his unease lay with Quintus. They had certainly enjoyed a stormy start to their friendship, and then over the months and the scrapes they'd been in together an affection that went way beyond acquaintanceship had sprung up. But in the past couple of days he had seemed preoccupied and Rufio didn't think it was his impending nuptials—though Jupiter and Minerva alone knew it must dominate his thoughts, poor fucker (it exercised Rufio as to how they'd get on after). No, he feared his lover was falling for that admittedly totally screwable gladiator boy. He wanted to be wrong for he thought Regulus would be an emotional disaster for Quintus. And there was the wretch Livius Caecilius Dio sticking his limp prick in where it wasn't wanted. What was that all about?

He glanced up from ruminating to find his models had lost it. Hephaestion had Felix pinned face down beneath his slight weight and his ass, a slightly paler tan than the rest of his lithe body, was humping up and down at a furious pace.

Rufio sighed resignedly and waited for the boys to finish their business before he could continue working.

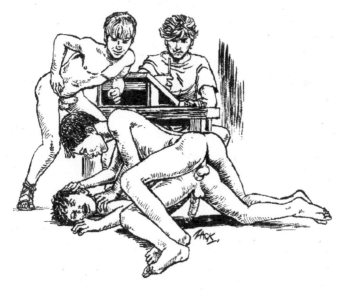

E·I·G·H·T | VIII

16th day of November AD 108

The day's editor, one of the two plebeian aediles, could have drawn him to confront a *Thraex*, a discipline Regulus had practiced against more than any other, but no, not the editor but the Fates decided on a *hoplomachus*—not so different from the Thracian style, though with a less head-enclosing helmet. The Greek "armed fighter" evidently fancied himself as one of those *decus puellarum, suspirium puellarum*, judging by the showily discordant colors of his quilted leg wrappings and bright yellow of his loincloth designed to draw attention to his evident manhood. Well he might be a "sight of joy to sighing girls" and make them lust for his embrace, but he was going to die, at least technically, if Regulus had anything to do with it.

As usual with the novicus class, this was yet another exhibition match: minor wounding permitted with blunted swords, but no fatalities. Nevertheless, He needed this "kill." He needed to be worthy of his new muneraria—well Quintus at least. Otherwise what was the point of his being here, putting himself in harm's way? Truth to tell, Regulus enjoyed the skill, cut, and thrust of well-matched fights, but he dismissed much of what the mob called "games" as pure butchery. Only that morning had he not watched convicted criminals thrown to lions and bears followed by more of the dispossessed matched only with knives? And to what point? The men, wretched *ordinarii* with no training, condemned to die in the arena, wore no body protection so their flesh was open to a thrust, and every blow told. But always among the bunch there was one bolder, more vicious, more desperate and no sooner did he kill, than the mob shouted for him to kill another, or to be killed.

Like his brethren of the arena, Regulus understood that the common people preferred this bloody murder to matches on level terms. "Of course they do," Bebryx had spat out to some tyro who'd questioned the spectators' irrationality as the big Scythian was breaking his fast. "These are scum who have never spoken our *sacramentum*, our sacred vow to ensure to be burned, to be bound, to be beaten, and to be killed by the sword. They like that no helmet or shield blocks a blade, and what use is skill or defense to the idle watcher? All these merely postpone the grisly deaths jaded palates desire for entertainment. 'Kill him,' they shout, 'beat him, burn him. Why is he too timid to fight? Why is he so frightened to kill? Why so reluctant to die?' They disgust me and dishonor our brotherhood, and lay low brave fighters of the *familia gladiatoria*."

Bebryx, Regulus thought, was nothing if not a pontificating prig when it came to "honor in the arena." Regulus saw precious little of that; the Scythian was naive or blind or both. He shook the thought away as he stood beside his opponent and saluted the editor and whichever member of Caesar's family occupied the imperial box. He suspected they would all be more preoccupied by whatever delicacies the slaves were offering than an exhibition match... even if the weapons were not blunted or, worse still, wooden practice swords.

The hoplomachus in his leggings, long shin-guards, and manica on his sword arm shook his gladius at the packed cavea and brandished his small, round shield, not much more than the span of two hands. His helmet, with its traditional plume of bright feathers on top and a single feather on each side of its wide brim, made him look jaunty. Regulus had to keep dancing to put off his adversary's aim, for the hoplomachus also carried a spear, which he would cast before closing for hand-to-hand combat.

They circled three times, each seeking an opening, and then the hoplomachus lowered his throwing arm, tensed and hurled the spear. Its leaf-shaped blade grew in size as it flew at Regulus. But he was prepared and even before the missile covered a quarter of its flight he leaped forward, fell to one knee and rolled under its potentially lethal trajectory, which brought him to his feet again right under his still unbalanced opponent. The spear that in the hands of an experienced gladiator could end a fight before it had really started was also a serious disadvantage to a novicus, and the hoplomachus was, if anything, more of a beginner than Regulus. He had no time to switch gladius from left hand to sword arm after the throw before Regulus swept a wide arc around his legs, thus avoiding the protective greaves to cut into the man's unguarded calf.

The hoplomachus staggered back, uttering a sharp cry barely heard above the baying of the crowd, *tuba*, *lituus*, and thundering water organ. In an instant Regulus sprang up from his crouch at the same time bringing his sword back to deliver a frontal thrust. His opponent blocked with his shield, but its small size only managed to deflect the gladius point from a serious blow to a painful slice across the ribs. He fell back again, but brought his gladius up savagely, in turn hoping to catch Regulus off balance. The blade scoured a line across the murmillio's tall legionary's shield and failed to find a better target. In turn, Regulus shoved hard with the shield, lifting it violently so that its upper rim lashed into the hoplomachus's unprotected chin. His shocked cry turned to a gurgle as he slumped to the sand.

Regulus stepped forward, stood over the fallen gladiator, sword point pressed to his opponent's throat just under the gashed jaw. Regardless of the rules, that this was an exhibition match between tyros, and ignoring the fact of blunted weapons, those in the massed stands who weren't more engaged in eating their lunch shouted for the killing blow, but the editor would never ignore an imperial edict. After a swift consultation with his imperial guest—Hadrian, Regulus thought—he stood, held his right arm, hand splayed, stiffly against his chest and then swept it widely to the right to signify the conclusion. Two arena medics ran out onto the sand to help the hoplomachus, but he stubbornly pushed them aside as he got to his feet—it was more his wounded pride that pained him than the cuts about the back of his legs. Regulus acknowledged the cries of praise and headed briskly for the gladiators' portal.

"You'll need more than luck, baby-buck, if you ever face me on the sand," Bebryx growled as they passed each other.

"And may Fortuna smile upon your gracious head too," Regulus muttered as the dark swallowed him up.

"You were magnificent!"

Regulus managed a smile for Quintus, who was still waving in his hand the libellus that, as a patron, gave him access to the Colosseum's cavernous underworks. He allowed the good-looking youth—out of breath from his dash from the stands above—to embrace him. He acknowledged his patron's lean body, hard with pride and something more urgent lower down. *Keep him on heat so the more controllable he will be.* That lizardly patrician's voice rattled around in Regulus's head. *Just don't give in all the way. Youths like Quintus lose interest all too quickly once the conquest has been made.* Regulus thought the senator was talking more about his own attitude than that of Quintus Caecilius Alba, but he had every good reason to both accept the man's inducement and the command that went with it.

"Are you happy I managed to commandeer an arming cell to yourself?"

Regulus was indeed happy about that; less so perhaps about the real reason Quintus wanted him split off from any of the others who had to share the temporary day-quarters in the Colosseum before returning along the gloomy cryptoporticus that linked the arena with the Ludus Magnus. But he permitted the hug and light kiss on his sweaty neck. It felt weird to have a patrician boy act like his personal slave, *but when the Ferryman rows…*

Gracchus of Capua was a surly bastard at the best of times. He treated his gladiators worse than shit, but as far as Bebryx was concerned there was one good side to the lanista: he was always so overawed by the fact of being in Rome, summoned at Caesar's express command, that his insecurity found outward expression by showing off. His swagger doubled, trebled, anything to make up for the fact that cretins like Bulbus cowed him inside.

And so Bebryx, as outstanding champion of Ludus Gracchus, benefited from an excess of his lanista's bluster. The prick had demanded one of the few suites on the airier upper floor of the Ludus Magnus maintained for the cream of gladiators. Bulbus was not a man to accede to polite requests so the resulting shouting match resembled the opening maneuvers of a real gladiatorial fight until Bulbus relented… in return for a percentage of Gracchus's audited winnings. In addition to being a natural bastard, he was a creative accountant, so Bulbus never received a fraction of what he thought he was entitled to, and absurdly Gracchus could bask in his champion's further elevation.

But Bebryx didn't feel he had really earned the right. Sure, he'd just wiped out that tough bitch-bastard Thraxus, a *retiarius* with six championships to his name this past year in prime games up and down the peninsula. But therein lay the problem. Thraxus was the third in a line of champions starting with that big black fucker Capreolus in Capua who caved in at the crucial moment. It was as if the will to fight had abruptly fled. It left the Scythian with an empty feeling in his stomach and a grave suspicion that he was missing something.

He would have to be mind-dead not to know that in gladiators' grimy habitations rumors of match fixing were rife, but no one had ever approached him with anything under the table. And were his recent victories the result underhandedness or just an extraordinary run of good fortune? Bebryx beseeched Fortuna for her grace, but he didn't believe in relying on her showering him with so much luck, and three such easy wins were too many to be coincidence.

Yes, it began with Capreolus—Bebryx wondered whether the Nubian's slave boy knew anything. Bebryx had received Britannicus as a prize from Gracchus, briefly grateful for a big win from betting on his victory over Capreolus. That hadn't been an easy relationship. Britannicus loved Capreolus like a puppy adores its master and hated Bebryx as his former master's murderer. The boy's attitude verged on the rude then, and was hardly much better now. Their first meeting had also been in much finer surroundings than a gladiator normally aspired to, another gift from the lanista. Britannicus was the envy of many a sex-starved gladiator at Capua, a Briton with an unpronounceable native name of the Trinovantes but the face and body of an angel, glowing pink-white, finely limbed with the bearing of a prince—which he might well be—and a bottom as delectable as two Persian peaches.

Bebryx had awaited his arrival with growing anticipation... but a dark scowl deformed the boy's expression. The moment he pushed through the curtained entrance to the inner chamber his glance took in the splendid furnishings with a fixed sneer on his delectable face. "Sit down," Bebryx commanded.

The boy did not move. "You called and I came, but I'm here because I have been ordered to. I know what you expect, to gloat in your victory. Well, you may relive it in my body, but the killer of my lover shall never possess my heart... or my respect."

Bebryx liked the boy's spirit but still stepped across and hit him with an open hand hard across the cheek. "You will do as you are told."

The boy picked himself up from the tiles with a crooked smile. "It is easy to slap boys around, gladiator. Is that the limit of your prowess?"

Bebryx held himself in check at the boy's calculated insolence. "I shan't listen to your childish taunts," he said eventually. "Undress."

"You don't want to force me surely? I can tell. You desire me."

Bebryx stared at the slave expressionlessly.

"You want me to love you as I loved Capreolus."

And damn the gorgeous vision's hard heart, it had been true then, and it still was now as once again, in an eerie repeat of that September day back in Capua, Britannicus came through the curtain covering. Bebryx's hefty cock twitched the front of his tunic.

In spite of the weeks Britannicus had served Bebryx he had yet to spear that beauteous ass. Something had held him back from taking the Briton. But not tonight. Tonight sodomy was on his mind.

The boy's usually blank expression eased slightly to be replaced with a jeering smile that grew as he saw an involuntary movement beneath his master's loincloth. "I fetch you food and drink, I test it to ensure none has the intention of poisoning you, I wash your clothes, I clean and polish your leathers and brass fittings, I warm the latrine seat for you, but I see you still demand pleasure—"

Patience ran out. "I have questions to put to you, boy, but they can wait." Bebryx reached out and grabbed Britannicus and pulled the tunic from him to admire the firmly muscled body with its pale Celtic skin gleaming like pearl in the lamplight. Desire washed over him. He crushed the boy to him, feeling the resisting, unresponsive body against his own, the limp cock pressed to his thigh, its shape clear in his mind. "I have your measure, boy. Admit it, you desire to be taken forcibly, to be laid out and dominated, to yield to my strength… Admit it!"

As he spoke that blank expression softened. Bebryx felt the pressure on his thigh increase as the boy's cock betrayed him. Bebryx led him to the great bed and they fell back on the downy mattress in a tangle of limbs, side by side. Britannicus slipped the tunic off Bebryx and ran fingers lightly over the hard, chiseled angles of oiled muscles. He followed the crisscross paths of numerous scars running across the cicatrice map of Roman violence that was the Scythian gladiator's body. With one hand he reached down and worked a hand under the loincloth, gradually pulling it loose and then free. He ran fingertips through the tight fur from which sprang the firm balls and the rigid tree-trunk cock. With his other hand he played over erect, inflamed nipples.

In a surprising reversal of the dominance he had so recently expounded, Bebryx lay back, supinely enjoying the sensation. He watched with delight as the boy's pink tongue flickered out between moist lips to probe the cone of a nipple and follow the line of an old sword wound. The boy's hands now actively worked on his cock, sweeping up roughly over his contracted balls to press down on his shaft and force the rampant meat into the hard band of stomach muscle. Britannicus continued this rhythm until finally his questing tongue tip ran up lightly over the thick purple business end. Bebryx sighed deeply as he felt the boy's cool mouth take all of him in, the enclosure of lips moving up and down his cock, breath burbling wetly over pulsing veins.

After a moment of this pleasure Bebryx sat up and pulled Britannicus off him.

"You'll take me to my climax if you keep that up, and I'm not ready yet,"

He grasped the slim waist and rolled the boy over. Britannicus looked up apprehensively. "We… we've never…"

"Your Nubian must have done that to you, surely? No, well never mind. I will be gentle with you."

Britannicus lay on his stomach as Bebryx knelt above him. He put his hands around the boy's waist and pulled the hard flat cheeks up toward him and then reached to the small tripod table beside the bed where he'd had the forethought to place a phial of olive oil scented with rosemary and cinnamon. A generous helping filled his palm and he coated his cock with one hand while transferring more of the unguent to that delicious crack. His dextrous ministrations produced a quiet groan from Britannicus, who humped his ass up off the bed against the pressure. Then for a few moments Bebryx allowed the angelic Briton to feel the smooth bifurcated head of his cock sliding sensuously up and down, playing at the entrance. He held back the moment of penetration until natural moisture mixed with the oil and eased the movement as his shaft slid home. Bebryx sensed the boy's wincing subside as he got deeper and deeper into him. Inch by inch Britannicus took all of his length, melting around him as the fucking increased. At

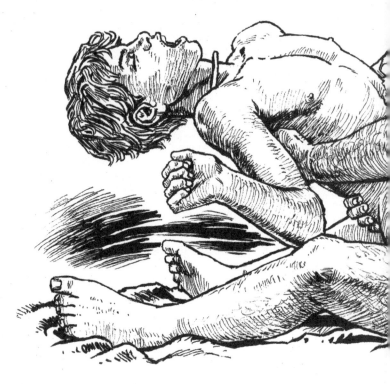

one moment Bebryx withdrew his cock almost completely before thrusting back up to the hilt.

Unintelligible barbarian invocations emerged muffled from where Britannicus's face was pushed deep into a cushion, moans of growing animal delight. But then Bebryx did withdraw. The boy looked around in surprise as Bebryx sat beside him on the bed. He pushed his back up against a bolster to support himself, and then indicated that Britannicus should sit on his lap facing him. The boy grinned when he understood. Britannicus placed his legs either side of Bebryx's waist. In this astraddle position the big Scythian eased his enormous prick back into the boy, who breathed out loudly as if the pressure pistoning up into his asshole was driving the air from

his slight body as he sat impaled on the gladiator. In this position, Bebryx—with all the flexibility and agility of an arena fighter—stretched his head down to take the boy in his mouth as he urged Britannicus to move up and down on him at the same time as the boy eagerly thrust his cock up into Bebryx's gaping mouth.

In this excitingly enervating position the interlocked thrust and counter-thrust increased as their mutual pleasure mounted inexorably. The boy's moans filled the room, his hands grasped at strained muscles slippery with sweat. They rocked, swayed, pushed until with exquisite agony they exploded, shooting their seed each into the other.

* * *

A brazier standing in a corner of the chamber radiated heat against November's sudden chill and made Bebryx feel pleasantly drowsy where he lay after the sexual workout, the light weight of Britannicus stretched out beside him. For once Britannicus hadn't held back. He barely heard the murmured words. "What?"

"You said you had questions," Britannicus repeated with more force.

Bebryx rolled over and sat halfway up, propped on one elbow. He regarded his slave from under lowered lids. Britannicus reclined in a loose-limbed way, relaxed now from his exertions. He turned lazy blue eyes on the gladiator.

"Yes. It was about Capreolus."

"Why would you want to talk about him? He's crossed the Styx to oblivion as you Romans think of the afterlife, and you put him there."

"Roman? I'm no more a Roman than you," Bebryx said, ignoring the jibe. "I want to know why he died." Fleetingly, Britannicus stiffened is posture and the reaction didn't escape Bebryx.

"You... you killed him—"

"But I shouldn't have, not so easily at least. Were you the last to be with him before he entered the arena?"

Britannicus sat up as well and turned to Bebryx with a defiant expression on his face. "Why are you asking?"

"Were you?"

The Briton cast his eyes down at the rumpled bed covering. "I suppose, apart from the arena guards and the men manning the doors and the—"

"They couldn't have given him anything."

Britannicus's pale skin became bloodless. "Given?"

In a blur, a meaty hand clamped down on Britannicus just below his Adam's apple and bore the slave back to the bed. Bebryx loomed over the boy. "What did you give him? Answer me!"

A rasping gurgle broke from the constricted throat. "You—you're hurting me." His eyes were wide with sudden terror.

"What?"

"I didn't! Master—*cough*…

"Capreolus faltered and grew weak. Gladiators don't take to the sand if they are ill, unless they have a death wish or they've been condemned to die. Someone gave him something that stole the strength from his body, and that someone had to be you." Bebryx slid his encircling fist higher up the boy's throat, pinning him firmly to the bed with the other hand. Britannicus wriggled and writhed, but to no avail. His face turned to a livid shade.

"No—please master—I didn't mean…"

Bebryx started back, easing the pressure on Britannicus's throat. "Mean what?" he asked with dangerous calm.

"Let me up, please!"

Suddenly freed, Britannicus skittered sideways on the bed, holding his sore throat, but no further than the sudden vise-like clamp on his ankle allowed. The ghost of a smile flitted across the Scythian gladiator's otherwise grim countenance. "What was it you *didn't mean*? Tell me, or I will exercise my right to end your miserable life."

"He told me it would enhance Capreolus, make him invincible in the ring."

"What?" Bebryx thundered.

"The— the potion." Tears started from the boy's eyes and for once Bebryx thought they might even be genuine. "It was supposed to ensure he was so strong you… you could not prevail, master." His voice trailed off miserably, eyes flicking everywhere but never to rest on Bebryx.

"Who gave you this, this potion?"

Britannicus shook his head.

The hand clamped around his throat again. Bebryx shook him violently.

"I— I didn't know him. Hooded. Please…?"

Bebryx relented and freed Britannicus again, frustrated. "How much were you paid for this treachery?"

A furious shaking of the head. "No, no money! He said it would make my mast— Capreolus a winner. Why would I need paying to make that happen?" He stopped abruptly in realization that whatever he said could not possibly put him in good standing with the man his actions were supposed to have helped Capreolus slaughter, there on the bloody arena floor of Capua. "I tell the truth. He stopped me the day before the fight and said he and his principals had money riding on my mast— Capreolus winning and he didn't like to leave matters to Fortuna, that if I administered the contents of a small phial he would bring the next day Capreolus would certainly gain a victory…" Britannicus shook his head, wetting Bebryx with his tears. "I would *never* have done anything to hurt him. Please, you must believe me. *Never!*"

"You took no care for *my* fate." In spite of the harsh words, the anger seemed to have abated. "This mysterious man tricked you."

The Briton's head slumped forward. He nodded miserably.

"And you have lived with your betrayal ever since."

More nods.

"For in the end, it was a betrayal." Bebryx sighed heavily. "Even if you did not know of it until it was too late." He slid his feet to the floor and sat on the edge of the bed, his bowed back to Britannicus. "You thought you were helping him to win and instead you helped slaughter him. For some consortium's financial gain. The bout was fixed." Bebryx stood abruptly, renewed fury in his posture and expression. "The fight was fixed and I, Bebryx of Scythia, I was made the fool. I was duped."

"It wasn't my fault," Britannicus said in a small, trembling voice.

Bebryx rounded on him. "Well in fact it *was* your fault. You were prepared to cheat." And then his anger deflated. "But you were being loyal to the one who you loved. You were duped, as was I. As I have been again, twice more. I know it!" He began to pace the room. "And what if someone again offers you a potion?"

Britannicus flung himself from the bed to the cold floor and fell at the

gladiator's feet. "Never again, master, I swear it!" He clung to Bebryx's ankles, sobbing until shudders ran up and down his bent spine.

Bebryx was lost in thought, but reached down to drag Britannicus up. "On your feet. Look at me." He waited until teary eyes gazed back. "If I have even the slightest whiff of suspicion that you might betray me, I will make sure you die in great pain, very slowly."

"I won't, ever." Britannicus nodded vigorously. "May Ankou take my dying breath should I ever—"

"Who the fuck's Ankou?"

"God of Death of my people, Bebryx."

"Well… that sounds … sufficient. Now we have business afoot. No one makes a fool of Bebryx of Scythia. I will have my vengeance and all who have a filthy hand in this wretched match fixing will die."

* * *

"Athenos informs me that Ceasar is asking what progress has been made on his gift," Pancratius, secretary to Chamberlain Athenos, spoke these words coolly to Epiphanes, secretary to the *rationibus* of the imperial *fiscus*.

The freedman so addressed returned the frosty glare with an equally chilly stare and a haughty sniff. "I passed the matter of Caesar's gift to the office of the *praetores aerarii*. In my opinion this is not a matter for the Emperor's fiscal purse. Obviously, great Caesar intended the gift to be paid to..." he shuffled a stack of scrolls about importantly, finding the right one with a smile of quiet satisfaction. "To Junius Tullius Rufio and Quintus Caecilius Alba from the *Aerarium populi Romani*—it's clearly a matter for the public treasury. Check progress of the paperwork with Philo, secretary to the chief praetor there."

"When was it that you passed on the papers?"

"Three market days ago? Maybe four? I'm too busy to recall every item."

"Very well," Pancratius sighed. "I will chase Philo... whenever I get a moment to do so."

N.I.N.E | IX

16th & 17th days of November AD 108

"Dominus," Zeno began haltingly, a hint of wonder in his eyes, "that is surely not possible." The workshop slave flexed his bulky arm muscles and then twisted his torso painfully, half-giggling with effort as he tried to imitate the position of a character in the illustration he was studying with avid curiosity.

He knew he shouldn't do it, but Rufio was unable to resist the temptation of teasing the big handsome lunk. He was taking advantage of the store manager's absence. Piso was off slave-driving Zeno's fellow laborers Phokas and Alexius in the unloading of freshly arrived antiques: some valuable pieces from Epirus that came across the Adriatic to the southern port of Brundisium and from there the cases were driven up to Rome. Piso was anxious to inspect for any damage after Damianus had passed on Junilla's explicit instructions on how to convert into a terrine the detached testicles of any Emporium worker who broke something. If there were any damage, he wanted it blamed on *Logisticae Tabellarius*, one of the commercial haulers they regularly used.

Just as Zeno's contortions reached an impasse with gravity, mouth opened in a wide *O* as if swallowing a carrot whole, there came a loud scratching at the doorpost. A short, slight figure stood silhouetted in the opening. In his surprise, Zeno folded gracelessly to the floor, leaving Rufio doubled up with laughter while doing his best not to damage the portion of scroll depicting the activities of Hephaestion, Felix, and Adalhard from the last modeling session. Master and slave turned to face the unexpected visitor.

Fair hair and a wicked, toothy smile greeted Rufio as he suppressed his laughter at Zeno's antics. "You did say to pop in," came the not-quite-familiar voice with its common sounding accent. "And you'd show me what was on that scroll. Remember?" A flop of straw-colored hair fell into amused brown eyes as the flibbertigibbet lad encountered on Vicus Portae Naeviae nodded at Zeno. "What's he doing? Is it a beating?" Excitement showed in a cheerful grin and freckles dancing on his cheeks. He pushed off the doorpost and walked across the warehouse toward them. "Don't let me stop you. I love to see a good beating."

Rufio returned the grin with a smirk. "Oh it was a punishment all right. Zeno down there… oh, get up! He was trying out this…" He turned the visible part of the scroll so the young visitor could see in the light pouring in from the yard behind him and waited with sly anticipation. The boy leaned forward, eyes suddenly popping from between pale, widely spread lashes.

"Hey… that's… intricate."

Not a word Rufio would have thought in the boy's vocabulary, but definitely not inaccurate.

The boy stepped back, shaking his head, laughing at Rufio, laughing at Zeno. "You drew this?"

"I told you. I illuminate my friend's poems."

A shake of the head. "Ugh, not poetry, please, boring stuff, but *that*, that's poetry in motion!"

Rufio sniffed, looked the intruder up and down and then smirked at Zeno. "It really needs four to make *this* one work, but…" he shuffled the scroll along a foot or so and showed Zeno another picture. The Emporium slave smiled even more broadly than Rufio, his eyes eating up the vision of youthful confusion.

"Why you look at me both, like that? What?" The boy glanced at the drawing, understanding dawning. "Oh no, I'm not like that."

But Zeno had him in a tight grip before the lad knew what had happened. "Everyone's *like* that. Curious. What's your name?" Rufio wanted to know.

136

"C-C-Celer…"

"Hah! Well you weren't quick enough, were you?" Zeno chortled at his own wit. The boy was pressed to his knees and squirmed in the grip, but it looked more a token than a serious rejection of what was obviously going to happen.

"See this?" Rufio thrust the drawing in Celer's face. He nodded, looked up fearfully. Rufio's experience in such matters made him certain the expression was faked. "And this next?"

"Yes…"

"Hold him steady, Zeno." With slow deliberation, Rufio raised the hem of his tunic and loosened the belt holding up his loincloth, which was already unable to contain the aroused rod of flesh rising up.

"Brazen balls of Bacchus, it's a big one! I'll never manage to fit that—*mmummph!*"

"Ooh, yes, nice and tight. I think, Celer the Unquick, you have done this before. Mmmm, yes. Lick the tip and around the seam, yesss…"

"Does it feel good, dominus?" Zeno asked eagerly.

Celer gagged momentarily, regained breath, and advanced down Rufio's length as far as he could manage until his extended mouth splayed out wetly like an eager lamprey sucking on its prey. Swollen lips reached the root of swollen cock and Celer rotated his head to provide even more sensation, proving Rufio's presumption of his experience in the delivery of fellatio. "Mmmm…" he answered Zeno. "Lovely tight, velvety mouth." Rufio placed both hands on the back of Celer's flaxen head and began to thrust in and out of the boy's mouth. "Oh yes, Zeno, very good and so unexpected. I'm sure he'll give you a go after, but now… part two. Turn him around."

Rufio pulled his engorged cock from Celer's mouth with a satisfying plop and as Zeno tugged him to his feet and swiveled him to about-face, Rufio pulled the tatty, mid-length tunic up and over Celer's bent back to reveal he wore nothing underneath. In the light from the doorway the boy's ass cheeks glowed like two colliding moons.

On Rufio's command, Zeno whipped his own rigid shaft out and slapped it against Celer's face. The boy gaped. Rufio knew what his thoughts must be: how in Hades' name will I ever fit that bull-cock in my mouth? But with a hollow *pfflupp*, Zeno plugged him at the same time Rufio rammed his saliva-lubricated cock up into Celer's back passage. A muffled squeak emanated from between spread lips around Zeno's girth, and in a trice master and slave had the boy mounted at both ends like a suckling piglet on the roasting spit.

All the pretence of fright at the thought of sex Celer showed earlier had dissolved as the three moved in harmonious motion. In between suffering indrawn breaths Rufio ground out, "Drawing's… all very… well, but doing… it is… so much… more satisfying."

"And fulfilling, dominu*sss*… and… and I am about to fill this boy with a… massive load… of cum. Oh…"

Celer spluttered, gagged, swallowed, groaned and moaned and

swallowed as Rufio slapped his reddened ass cheeks, then reached both arms around his waist to grip the boy's long, slender and very hard drooling dick. Celer responded with ever-louder explosions of pleasure and suddenly packed Rufio's hands out with thick creamy cum at the instant his fucker detonated deep inside him.

"Well that was pleasantly exhausting," Rufio said after they had somewhat recovered.

"I suppose that's what I get for accepting an invitation to look at a strange man's etchings," Celer said in a mock-regretful tone.

Rufio nodded pleasantly, acknowledging the fun they had all had, but at the same time a wash of melancholy splashed his soul and he didn't have to search far for the cause: Quintus. Gods, he was missing the poncy patrician prick. Here they were, working together like never before on these stupid poems and drawings and somehow never so far apart. Rufio determined to march across the Aventine and confront his… his lover.

The unmistakeable aroma of damp rug wafted along the darkened lower corridor of the Ludus Magnus, not a part of the large complex much seen by Trajan's guests come for the thrills of intimate fights to the death he liked to put on for visiting provincial senators. Bebryx pressed himself close into a corner where a rough-hewn support column met the basement wall. A greater flare of light than the few sconces down here parsimonious Bulbus permitted announced the proximity of someone carrying a sputtering torch.

"Aaagghh!" Ursus grunted in momentary alarm on sighting Bebryx. Then he growled angrily. "Wha ya hiding fer?"

"Waiting for you, as it happens, Ursus my friend."

A huge furry hand thrust a hank of hair back up over the broad forehead. Black, piggy eyes glowered from bloodshot whites. "Friend? Huh, since when?" Ursus, about as wide as he was tall, pressed in close enough that hot spits from the flaming brand burned Bebryx's cheek and competed with a gust of sour onions.

"Gargh, it's hard enough understanding you at a distance." Bebryx danced sideways into the freer air of the passageway. "I wanted to thank you for keeping that Catalaunian asshole Flatucias away from my table. It restored my appetite not to have his stench assailing my nostrils when I'm trying to eat the crap we're given here."

"Huh?

"Rome! Capital of the world. I've had better fare at Capua, even at Aternum, and trust me, that's a place the gods forsook when they divided land from sea."

"Hah…?"

"I've a reward in mind for you."

"Present?" Ursus panted.

Britannicus had almost vomited when Bebryx told him what he might have to do. "Rumors of the size of what he hides between his legs are greatly exaggerated."

"How do you know?"

"That Samnite fighter told me. You know he's a pig."

"And hairy as one of those bears they bait in the arena."

"I meant the Samnite, not Ursus. Under all that shag he has a sweet nature."

Britannicus stared at his master in mute horror.

"Oh for Saturn's sacred shit, Ursus doesn't know how to use it. All you'll have to do is stroke his pelt and whisper nice things in his ear—"

"If I can find one."

"I need you to be nice to him. Just the once. Anyone would think I was ordering you to your death."

"Present?" Ursus repeated eagerly.

At the mention of Britannicus, the big fellow beamed and hopped a little jig.

"Just one ring of the hour-candle," Bebryx warned. "And no rough stuff."

Ursus nodded his shaggy head and then went still. He cast a

suspicious look in the gladiator's direction. "Wha you going to want more, hey?"

"More? Oh, nothing much. But I bet you know just about everything that goes on here. Like which senators or equestrians or magistrates have favorites and who they are." Bebryx risked leaning in a little closer. "Britannicus has always said how much you excite him. I bet you do well out of backhanders." Bebryx winked conspiratorially.

"Oh haha, yes. Britannicus?"

"Maybe a half hour extra… if you can tell me who I should speak to, you know? To find out how I can make more money. Which fighters are…" he rubbed thumb and forefinger together in the universal gesture for being on the make.

"Two hours?" Ursus wheedled.

Bebryx smiled. "So, give me names."

"Britannicus first?"

A sigh of irritation escaped the gladiator's lips, but Bebryx knew better than to either rile Ursus or try to outbid him. He nodded.

* * *

"Ashur, be a good lad, and fuck off," Rufio said, but kindly. "I need time alone with Quintus."

"Well someone needs to sort him out. It's that cursed gladiator's got to him."

Rufio patted the slave's ass paternally. "Just make sure Tredegus doesn't go announcing my presence to everyone." It was the doorman's job to notify his master of any visitor, whomsoever they were calling to see, and the last thing Rufio needed was Lucius Caecilius Alba crashing in on his youngest son. Being in Domus Alba always made him feel edgy, now he had even better reason for nervousness. He tried to stop slapping his thigh with the leather scroll case he'd brought along as an excuse for the visit and made his way toward where he knew Quintus was supposed to be consulting his erotic muse. Quintus had his back to the door when Rufio silently pushed it fully open. The poet heard nothing, leant over his worktable, apparently absorbed in reading whatever he'd written.

Rufio closed the door softly and rushed Quintus before he could fully turn around, tossing the scroll tube on the adjacent bed. "Good. Got you to myself." He furrowed his brow sexily as Quintus tried to twist in the firm grip about his waist. Rufio clasped hands over the hard stomach and nestled his crotch against the hard butt, wiggling suggestively through his clothes and those of Quintus.

"Whoa, there! Hold your horses," Quintus remonstrated hoarsely. "You want Pallas or one of my sisters rushing in?"

"They won't. I told Ashur to keep everyone at bay. You've been avoiding me, sending Ashur with stuff instead of coming yourself."

"*Stuff*? Stuff, is it?"

"And aren't you supposed to be the sensible one—"

"Nice to know how highly you think of my work."

"—stopping me being the *stupidus* with gladiator decisions?"

He released Quintus, who decided it was time to take back some control. "I've been busy. It was you and that Sosius set me up with an impossible deadline." Making out like he'd spent all his time writing rather than pining for Regulus. For an answer, Rufio flung himself down on the rucked bed, buried his head in the pillow and sniffed deeply.

"Mmm, smells of you."

"Thanks, I think…" Quintus relented and sat beside Rufio's lasciviously sprawled body and stroked his raised hip.

Rufio sighed and began fiddling with the clasp of Quintus's belt. "You've been a bit distant lately." His voice rose at the end as if asking a question.

"Huh, you've been busy too, no doubt bedding one, two, three, all of your menagerie."

Rufio ignored the accusation. "I'd far rather spend time with you." He pulled the belt loose and, after hesitating a moment as if he were going to reject the invitation, Quintus rolled over to make it easier for Rufio to hike his tunic up and loosen the folds of loincloth. "I think I'm going to eat your ass first," Rufio murmured, relishing the expanse of muscled stomach and taut thighs as the unwinding of the linen revealed more. Quintus pushed up and grappled back. For minutes they rolled and tumbled around the bed, wrestling each other for supremacy, giggling like schoolboys, laughing with the freshness of months ago, for a while all other problems forgotten.

Quintus had the edge in military cadet strength, but he was content to lose eventually and let Rufio pin him on his back and straddle his chest. The freckled cheeks glowed with sexual excitement. Quintus's hands were trapped, but he wriggled one free and grabbed Rufio's cock through his loincloth where it angled upward, enticingly covered. "Cheat!" Rufio sniggered and started tugging Quintus's tunic up over his head, trapping him in its folds. Quintus's muffled voice complained. "Now you're not being fair. Get off me and off the bed."

Rufio did as he was ordered as Quintus struggled free of his tunic and glared in mock anger at his still-clothed attacker. For his part, Rufio swayed his hips sideways in a frankly provocative pose.

Quintus rolled over to the edge of his bed, reached out to slide hands under the hem of Rufio's pale blue tunic, followed by his head. He ran his tongue over the lightly tanned skin of the abdominal V, finally letting it rest on the waistband of the saffron-colored breeches, flicking to and fro. Then he moved down and tongued the hard shape of the Rufio's big cock, wetting the fabric. Rufio reciprocated by swaying his torso against the pressure of Quintus's questing mouth. After a minute of this delight, Quintus unclasped the restraining belt buckle, flipped the loincloth down and let Rufio's oh-so-familiar cock bob up into his waiting mouth. "Mmmm," was all he said, kissing and lipping the pink rose of Rufio's foreskin and the pointed plum-shaped head hiding inside the sheath.

He lay back and let Rufio shed the rest of his clothes, loving the way his eight, gently inward curving inches jutted so stiffly upright and so hard that the partly sheathed cock head tucked up against his flat belly. Time to take control again, a touch of Woof-Woofery... "Kneel up on the bed doggy style," Quintus commanded, husky of voice, and then softly: "Instead of you doing it, I'm going to tongue fuck you."

This change of scenario found no complaint from Rufio who clambered back on the bed eagerly and stuck his rounded butt into the air. Quintus began by licking all around the firm rounds of Rufio's cute ass cheeks and the top of his muscled thighs. With deliberate slowness, he swirled his tongue around, nearer and nearer as Rufio wriggled appreciatively, giving encouraging little whimpers. And then Quintus hit the sweet spot, inhaling Rufio's sexy musk as he flicked the tip of his tongue around the flaring sphincter ring. Rufio flexed his whole body, inviting Quintus to ever more exertion, and gave vent to a long hissing breath as the busy tongue finally penetrated. Quintus rotated his head violently to drive his tongue as deep as it could go and treated himself and Rufio to sheer bliss for more time than it would take to cross the Forum on a law day.

And then they began a slow dance into ever more intimate entanglements.

Next day people thronged Rome's major thoroughfares in their thousands. The 17th day of November marked the final celebrations of the Ludi Plebeii with races, theatrical mimes, music, and gladiatorial games; so much on offer it made a tough choice as to what to see. The Summa's inner cadre was scattered about between the Circus Maximus and the Colosseum, determined to make the most of this last day of easy money. Luscinus had assured his colleagues at an early morning gathering in the Aemilian Basilica that everything was in place for a profitable conclusion.

"What of this young Regulus?" the Banker wanted to know.

Virius jumped in. "The first moves have been instigated and the seedling watered. Growth should be forthcoming rapidly, in time for whatever aedile or local magistrate decides to hold games. We need his… muneraria—if you can call a spoiled adolescent brat and his catamite 'owners'—to attach him to a suitable lanista as soon as possible after his last appearance today." He left the others to interpret the underlying meaning of the word *suitable*. "There isn't a lot of leverage with a novicus when it comes to gamblers' interest in bouts so the quicker we move him to a professional standing the better. I shall ensure Livius Caecilius Dio brings pressure to bear on his nephew to this end."

"Thank you, Virius Fabius." The Banker nodded, but then added, "I was more interested in the boy's provenance. We know so little. He seems to have sprung fully formed at the start of the Ludi Plebeii." He turned his pale gaze on Luscinus.

"I have a rat inside the Ludus Magnus, fellow Senators…" a tight nod of reluctant recognition at Cornelius Aemilius Papus, "…and I've yet to hear a hint of intelligence as to his background, other than what he claims: born of a legionary discharged under suspicious circumstances (unstated) who turned brick-layer and a Vicus Patricius whore. They lived somewhere beyond the Praetorian Camp, off Via Nomentana. The father was killed in a building accident working on a tomb for one of the Claudian family and so threw his only son on the mercy of his own wits. Mother vanished long before."

"And what of his strength?" Papus added sourly. "Are you sure he had no military training? He fights with a competence I would have thought beyond a tyro of his young years."

"I have my eye on the boy, Senator. At this moment in time, he is of less concern than several other factors, including developments in some far-flung provinces."

"Very well," the Banker murmured, "perhaps you would be so good as to bring us up to date on…"

Virius allowed the voices of his fellow conspirators to fade away, as he turned his thoughts to the day ahead. He dispelled an unwelcome vision of fat Fabia pressing her less than charming bosom against his face and replaced the image with the upturned, waiting ass cheeks of Ambrosius.

Unlike the Summa's wide choice of venues, there was only one option for Rufio and Quintus. The final fights in the Colosseum were scheduled for the morning so that the maximum number of spectators would be free in the later hours to attend the torchlit Circus Maximus for the last races. The boys fought their way through the crowds shuffling through the Arch of Titus and then down the Via Sacra through the Velia toward the massive amphitheater.

"I told you we should have come along the other way, east of the Palatine down the Vicus Curiarium and Via Triumphalis," Quintus grumbled as he sighted the tip of the Meta Sudans above the heads of those in front.

"You came to mine, as we agreed, and through the Velabrum and Forum's quicker… well, usually," Rufio admitted grudgingly. He continued in his unspoken concern for his friend. After yesterday's pleasant sojourn in Domus Alba amid sweaty bed coverings, Quintus appeared to have reverted to this unusual moodiness shot through with sudden and out-of-character bursts of agitation. Brittle smiles, as if a puppet master were working his cheek muscles in an uneven rhythm, accompanied these brief flashes of animation.

"Here." Quintus handed Rufio his libellus, the small token marking them out as owners of gladiators. "We can use the fifth *vomitorium* and—" He paused at Rufio's gasp.

"But Quintus, this gives us access to the *podium*!"

"Are you feeling under-dressed?" Quintus grinned meanly as he elbowed past a matron and three children fighting over a pastry.

"But I'll be sitting with senators."

"The pinnacle of Roman society."

147

"And rubbing shoulders with the Emperor—"

"Well face it, you've rubbed more than Caesar's shoulder, Rufio."

"—and Vestal Virgins." For once, Rufio looked quite discomposed. He fiddled with the folds of his best tunic. "I'll feel quite weird and uncomfortable surrounded by thick-stripers, on better seats than all those thin-striper equestrians seated behind us in the *maenianum primum* looking down their long noses in haughty disdain at me."

Not much interested in the bloody sport, on the few occasions he'd attended games, Rufio and his whoring friends Crispin and Octavian fought for a spot in the sixteen rows of the *maenianum secundum* along with the rest of the great unwashed, foreign visitors, and witless slow-eyed out-of-town stumblies. Still, they had a better view there than the women (excepting the Vestals and womenfolk of the court) had, stuck way up behind the Corinthian colonnade in the *meanianum summum in ligneis*—literally: up top on bleachers of wood.

"Tweaking haughty equestrian noses never seemed to bother you before. Anyway, it's only a half-day," Quintus soothed. "You see. Many senators will be less formally dressed than normal, even if Trajan does attend."

And in keeping with the shortened schedule, the wild beast hunts and comic relief of the last handful of unarmored convicts slaughtering each other were kept to a merciful minimum. Amid the arean floor staff with their hooked poles for dragging away the bodies roved two men dressed like Dis Pater, dread god of the dead, and Charon, Ferryman of the Underworld, with their massive hammers to inflict fatal blows to the heads of the fallen who still showed any signs of life. When the last criminal corpse slid through Porta Libitinensis—the Gate of Death—more slaves rushed out with baskets of sand and rakes to cover and smooth over the gore.

When the six *novicii* ran out into the arena for the three advertised exhibition matches light snacks and early luncheons appeared on napkined laps all around the vast cavea. Rufio expressed annoyance, but Quintus—the man of great experience—simply shrugged it off. "It's always the same. I suppose you can't blame them. The mob want blood and spilled guts, not skill in weapons handling."

"Yes, but the fucking senators are all nibbling away as well," Rufio grumbled, keeping his voice low to avoid causing any offense. He also noticed that his hitherto glum-jumpy friend was now glowing, perched on the edge of his senatorial cushion (they only had hard, splintery wood to sit on up in the *maenianum secundum*), eyes glued to every step, parry, and thrust their man was making, his expression rapt.

Yes, Ashur's right. My boy has it something bad. And there was me hoping it was just a bit of understandable lust…

Regulus and his opponent were well matched and the ringing sound of clashing blades rose above the chattering, lunching crowd.

"What happens if he gets hurt?" Rufio looked concerned. "I mean all that money we're supposed to make."

"It's not likely… well, maybe a minor cut. The blades are blunt. It's only an exhibition bout for beginners. Oh, good blow! Did you see that? The crosswise counter-slice and riposte parry with double longitudinal twist!"

Rufio sighed. Boys and their swords. At last Regulus had his man down on the sand making the traditional signals for mercy.

"Come on, quick!" Quintus was up and pushing along the block of seats. Fortunately, the harassed *locarius* who showed them their places had made them sit close to the nearest exit stairway. As he went, Quintus threw out short apologies to the three men in the way whose snacking he was interrupting. And then Rufio was running up the steps behind him to the curved passage that separated the podium from the equestrians' seating tiers above the head-high wall that ran all the way around the cavea. Moments later they were plunged into the deep gloom of the lower passageways, down more, narrower brick steps to the arming levels, Quintus clearing the way through armed guards with his waved libellus.

A flaring sconce lit the faces wreathed in sweat of murmillo, Thraex, scutarius, retiarius, and hoplomachus, excited or downcast as fitted the outcome of their bouts. Rufio watched Quintus grasp Regulus by the arm and all but embrace the gladiator—which would have been uncomfortable because of his armor—and help remove his helm. He nodded to himself, stepped between two of the young intervening gladiators to reach Quintus. "Ahem… I'll leave you to give Regulus notes. Other matters to attend to, you know? Will I see you at the Circus? No…?"

He might as well have been speaking to the wall for all the effect his words had. Switching from nod to shake of the head, Rufio left Quintus and Regulus and set off back along the passage, completely lost in the underworks maze.

17th & 18th days of November AD 108

"Watch where you're going. Who the fuck are you?" The voice came as an ear-splitting warble, distorted by enclosing metal, that echoed off the grim brickwork. Suspicion flowered like a sudden burst of flame in eyes made all the more terrible for glaring through two small holes in a fright of a faceplate.

Instinctively, Rufio took a step back from the terrifying apparition towering over him with an aggressive outward lean, but his natural assertiveness refused to let him cower before the... *Secutor. I think. They're the ones with big legionary shields... I think.* "Who are *you*?"

The figure made a sudden move, but before Rufio could flinch, he grounded the curved, oblong shield with a grating noise on the stone floor and whipped the unfastened helmet from his shaggy head. He shook his hair out and glared indignantly, the impudent question having evidently astonished him. "I? I am Bebryx the Scythian. It is I, as the secutor set above all others, who terrorizes any who dare face me. Bebryx before whom all shake in their sweat-pooled boots and pray for a swift, merciful death. Here, take this." He held out the large helm, but it was not an order aimed at Rufio. An ethereally beautiful adolescent boy stepped out from behind the gladiator and obediently did as he was bid.

Rufio goggled at the slender figure, pale as fine Carian marble. He was torn between wanting to ravish the fair-haired vision and falling on his back, waving his legs in the air to entice the brutish fighter to drop on him and thrust his fleshy gladius straight up his ass. "Bebryx," he said faintly, "I see."

"Everyone knows me... everyone who is anyone, that is." The

suspicion returned with a vengeance. "But I don't know you, or what you are here for. You are not one of the arena staff, nor of the Ludus Magnus."

Struggling for a sensible answer, Rufio suddenly came to his senses and remembered that he did have a right to be there. "I… I am here to meet with the auctoratus Regulus. You see he is—"

"That little piss-pot! What would you have with him? His virginity, perhaps. Haha, He hasn't enough between his legs to excite a Thracian worm… but wait!" The expression of ridicule metamorphosed instantly to one of suspicion again. "You are one of *them*."

"I'm not sure what you mean."

"Yes," came the drawn out growl of understanding. "Those who whisper treachery in willing ears, who deal in special potions."

"No, really, I am his munerarius, well one of—"

"Pah! I have no time for this. I have a cringing fisherman shivering for me on the sands of glory, waiting for me to fillet his worthless sack of flesh. But I warn you," pointing a blunt finger at Rufio, "I will be back and wanting more answers from you. Note his features, Britannicus. And don't think you can hide from Bebryx. I have your scent and I will make sure you will never again bribe any fighter, not even a shit-faced cunny like Regulus."

Mouth agape, Rufio stepped smartly aside as Bebryx swept up his massive shield and clomped down the passageway, his gorgeous slave Britannicus trotting at his heels, weighed down by the bowl-shaped helmet. The explicit threat didn't overly concern Rufio. He didn't know much about gladiators, but if they were anything like charioteers their boasts were all hot air and bluster. What niggled was the implicit suggestion that he was down there on some errand of ill intent. *Bribes? Incentives for what?* "I think I know who might be able to help me understand," he muttered aloud at the grimy bricks that ran with the excrudescence of violent death, but they didn't hold the answer.

The spaces of the Ludus Magnus rang with the sounds of men leaving, returning, the creak of leather and clatter of discarded arms under the barked commands of doctores and hired guards, the shuffle of booted feet and slapping of arms in the sudden chill after the heat of combat. Oaths muffled and shouted accompanied taunts and gruff laughter. The cell looked uninviting, but Quintus didn't care. He followed Regulus through the opening, thankful that the pelt-covered bed sat alongside the longer wall where, tucked into the corner, it was more or less out of sight of any passing along the passage outside. Regulus threw down his murmillo's fish-crested helmet on the end of the bed.

They had exchanged little in the way of words on the gloomy journey through the cryptoporticus from the Colosseum, but hot from his victory the young gladiator radiated some of that warmth over Quintus. By small gestures, light touches, slow-eyed looks, Regulus conveyed a willingness that sent bolts of Jupiter's lightning sparking through Quintus. Now, reaching a modicum of privacy, his juices were running wild and he felt uninhibited in a way alien to his usual sensibility—other than in Rufio's presence... a pang of regret? But the all-too-solid presence of this handsome, rugged champion of the ring overwhelmed his customary rectitude.

Regulus turned and grinned as Quintus threw aside his cloak and pulled the tunic over his head. He stood naked but for the slight loincloth which at the front betrayed his arousal. After a pause, Regulus closed in and embraced him.

"Whoa! Your metalware's freezing cold."

"Why don't you take it off, then?" Regulus teased. He stood still, arms at his sides, daring Quintus to undress him.

There really wasn't much to do: Quintus tackled the manica first. Buckles loosed, belts slipped from loops, curved shin-guards clattered to the ground, lone gaiter followed. He tore away the fighter's protective loincloth, ridiculously eager to finally set eyes on what lay hidden beneath. He loosed his own which fell to the floor in a tangle with that of Regulus. And they were naked, skin-to-skin, thickening cocks pressed between them.

"Boots?"

Quintus gave a dimpled smile. He bent down and in a frenzy tugged at the offending footwear. Regulus hopped about laughing, and fell back onto the narrow bed, narrowly missing his discarded helmet. With his boots flung casually aside, Regulus pulled Quintus down beside him and rather more gently removed his sandals. And then to Quintus's surprise he leaned right over, lifted Quintus's right foot and placed his mouth over the big toe.

"Whoo, that's…" Quintus fell back full length on the bed, while leaving the right leg bent up so as not to interrupt the sucking. The helmet made a dull clang as it hit the ground and rolled away.

The contrast could not have been starker: compact limbs and lithe torso of marbled whiteness enrobed by the great ball of dark, shaggy hair; muffled whimpers attempting tenderness against guttural

animal grunts. The saving grace, were there such a condition in this hirsute hell, was that Bebryx had spoken the truth… after a fashion. Ursus seemed content to run his horny hands all over Britannicus (they were as hard as horn as well as hot to trot) but not to expect much in return. True, there was a tree trunk of hardness somewhere down there—however, this really was a case of being unable to see the wood for the trees, or bushes more aptly in this case—but the great bear had made no attempt to insert it anywhere. Britannicus prayed that would continue to be the case and that his sacrifice would be worth the price he was paying for Bebryx to extract whatever information he hoped to gather from Under Lanista Ursus.

But a child's stone's throw from where Britannicus yielded to hairy fondles, Regulus' drew in a sharp breath that found its echo in a jerk from Quintus, his cock pressed hard against the unyielding bed's surface. He squirmed forward, his entire body alive with lust and felt his foreskin drag back against the pleasurably prickly animal pelt—a bearskin, he thought. He made enough headway to get to work on Regulus's balls and the shaft of the gladiator's ready cock. It mattered not that Regulus seemed to prefer lying back and letting Quintus get on with whatever he wanted to do without responding much above the occasional wiggle of his torso or the shake of a leg. Quintus wanted only to concentrate and make Regulus feel loved, wanted, and subsumed in the sensation of sexual abandon. Through the medium of mouth, tongue, fingers, and bodily contact he desired to hurl himself into the loss of self the act of love could induce and in so doing make Regulus his own.

He threw Regulus's right leg up and over his own body, stretching Regulus's buttocks apart so he could reach with his tongue into that most private part which no less than Caesar himself had introduced him to. So delighted was he with the growing body reactions he forgot that Trajan and Rufio were the only ones to be so treated. If there was betrayal in this, Quintus was too besotted to feel it.

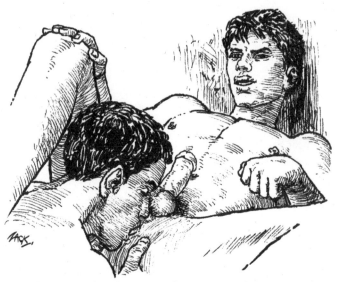

Regulus moaned with increased urgency so that Quintus knew his tongue had to go there, his lips must lap at the gateway, and they did. He forced Regulus's other leg up and worked up into the crack of the fully exposed ass, probed, flicked, forced until his tongue tip reached the winking muscular ring. Regulus responded by wiggling his legs in an uncontrolled way, which delighted Quintus and the thrill ran right down to his aching balls.

"Quit the complaining. Did he actually do anything to you? I don't see you walking like a cavalryman just off his horse after a week's hard riding or swaying like a sailor freshly arrived on shore."

"He pawed me. All over." Britannicus pouted as he kept patting arms, legs, and rubbing his neat belly, as if ascertaining that all the bits were present and correct. "Did you get what you wanted, master?" he said sourly.

Somewhat absently, Bebryx pulled his slave close and placed an arm about his slight shoulders. "We are set to join the ludus of Dolabella."

"Is that in Capua?"

"No, here, in Rome. He runs the Ludus Gallicus. My victories give me the power of choice and I chose Dolabella to pay that croaking frog Gracchus to transfer my contract. I need to be in Rome to make best use of what your playtime with Ursus will grant me."

Will... Britannicus hoped that didn't mean more Ursus groping. He shrugged under the—admittedly comforting—weight of Bebryx's arm and wondered petulantly how his master would feel wrapped up in those great big hairy limbs. For his part Bebryx was going over again the information he'd screwed out of Gracchus when the lanista made the mistake of coming up to that magnificent suite on the top floor of the Ludus Magnus without a single guard for his protection. It was a complacency Bebryx took immediate advantage of. He pinned the lanista to a couch at the point of his very sharp eating knife and demanded of him what he knew about the way Capreolus lost focus and so died at his hand. In terror of his life, Gracchus spilled the lentils and the outcome was the more important aspect of why the Capuan lanista had been willing to enter into a transfer agreement with Dolabella. Bebryx got a promotion to a prestigious Roman ludus and in return promised never to reveal his former master's secret.

Things had gone badly for him, Gracchus said, when during a drunken tavern brawl he'd been tricked into shouting some unwise comments about the Emperor's manhood. It so happened that an equestrian magistrate visiting from Rome was conveniently present to hear the treasonous obscenities. Gracchus described this man as "frightening, prowling like a caged beast waiting to pounce and shred my flesh before I would be thrown to the lions in my own arena." There was a get-out-of jail-free clause, of course. The penance had been to pay a minion to persuade Britannicus to unwittingly poison Capreolus. The only name this specter went by was Panthera, Gracchus told Bebryx.

* * *

Quintus returned his attention to the ridged, veined weapon, now oozing like a nymphaeum. Quintus's tongue slipped around the cock head like a schoolboy tasting a chunk of honeycomb. Regulus groaned from deep inside, a rising rumble so low it could have been the first portent of an earthquake. Quintus firmed his hands around Regulus's hot balls and squeezed as he dropped his lips down the throbbing shaft, the taste of his urge-juice strong and heady. Up and down quickly with the lips, clever flicks of his tongue over the fount.

Regulus yielded his pent-up breath in a guttural grunt and loosed his seed in a gush that flooded Quintus's mouth and throat, a hot reward for his loving efforts. He gulped and sucked it down, every jerk as it came spurting out. As the flow slowed, Quintus continued

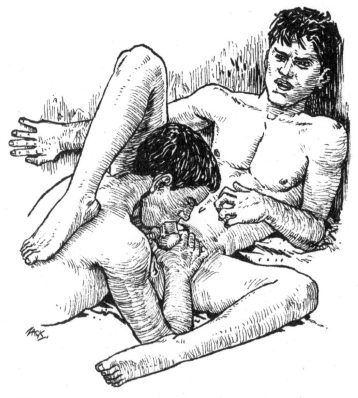

to roll his lips around Regulus's cock head to coax from it the last after shots of pleasure, lost in his own happiness at having made his lover feel so good. He would do anything for this hard-limbed fighting machine.

"Ask for anything," he breathed, still relishing the cummy taste of of his first Regulus orgasm.

Dark eyes regarded Quintus evenly. He tucked in a corner of his mouth, a considering smile. "I'll think on that," he said quietly.

* * *

Given the naturally vibrant color of his hair, turning up at the Greens' headquarters on the following day was a rash thing for Rufio to do, but he was keen to talk to Scorpus. He felt that the charioteer might be able to throw some light on the suspicions aroused by Bebryx's obscure comments. The young champion of the *ludi circenses* had topped off the final day of races in the Circus Maximus with a close-run but predictable victory. It was one which a po-faced Quintus endured with evident impatience, eager to be off again to "supervise the arrangements for our Regulus now the games are over," but an imperial dictat had pinned him to a seat in the lesser ranges of the imperial box. As a supporter of the Reds (obviously), Rufio kept his exhortations to a minimum—at least until the race started and the roar of a quarter-million voices took flight—for both Hadrian and Trajan were well known to support the Green faction.

It was late afternoon when the final twelve *quadrigae* lined up in the starting gates. Already in the darkest corners of the giant stadium could be seen lit braziers. Under the arches of the starting-pens glowed the faction colors, three teams of each, blue and white, red and green, alternating in position as decided by the toss of coins. Drivers and staff advertised their teams in dress and headware and badges of appropriate color. A swarm of grooms to each chariot held fast to mouths and reins, all the while inciting the steeds, stimulating them with encouraging pats and, while holding them back, whispering words into pricked ears to instil a rapturous frenzy.

"Look how they chafe at the barrier," Rufio exclaimed, pointing unnecessarily at the barrier lowered across the front of the gates. He nudged Quintus in the ribs, trying to ignore what instinct told him was the truth—he was sure he could smell the scent of sex on Quintus. "See how the vapor steams through the wooden bars. I was down at the rear of the gates once, looking for Scorpus as it happens, and the space is filled with the horses' panting breath. They push and bustle, they drag back as if in fear and then strain forward again as if in a rage, and rear against the traces... and Caesar's dropped the napkin! They're away!"

At the blare of the herald's trumpet, the barrier sprang up and the impatient teams launched into the field. At a mad sprint they furrowed into the narrow space between the nearest *meta* turning point and the outer wall, fighting for the best initial position close to the spina. Finally, Quintus showed a faint glimmer of enthusiasm. The races had never caught his interest they way they did Rufio. "They lack novelty and variety," he told his friend in an idle moment. This had surprised Rufio since it was Quintus who boasted of his horsemanship, where Rufio hated "nags" as a means of transport and was little more than a hindrance in the saddle. "I mean if you've seen one race, there's nothing left for you to see. And all those grown men—like my father and stupid brothers—thousands upon thousands of them, screaming and waving at running horses with men laying over the pole between them. If it were the drivers' skill or that of their steeds that attracted them I could see some point, but it's just the colors. That's what they back. All praise to Neptune that I am no slave to this so-called sport—"

"Neptune? I thought he looked after the sea?"

"And horses, you ignorant Celt... *Neptunus Equester*? Anyway, while my brothers waste their leisure as well as their earnings, I'm at my happiest occupying my time with a pen."

"And being very stuffy with it," Rufio had retorted; though lately he couldn't really accuse Quintus of that crime, not after all the

Gaius-on-Gaius raunchy lines that had poured from his pen. And occupying his time with Regulus as well, he thought.

The ground gave way under the thunder of wheels and the dust that swirled in their tracks smirched the air. The charioteers wielded the reins and plied the lash, stretched forward over the chariots so low that they struck the horses' withers. In such a prone position it was impossible to decide whether they were more supported by the pole or by the wheels. From the imperial box the "ships of the circus" flew out of sight as they traversed the open part on the other side of the central spina, then becoming hemmed in at the end. At the first turning post one of the Reds spurred ahead of a Blue and White team, leaving Scorpus forced into fourth place on the outer track, with his fellow Greens and the other six chariots following in his dust.

"Not doing so well, is he?" said Quintus with perverse satisfaction.

"Nonsense. You know nothing. Stick to arena combat. He's keeping a tight rein on his team. That's consummate skill, that is, keeping ahead of the pack, tucked in just behind the front runners, wisely reserving the strength of his steeds for the final lap."

"Hmm…"

The hoarse roar from applauding partisans stirred Rufio's heart, and the contestants, both horses and men, were warmed by the race. From the heights of the spina, to which the racers clung as close as possible for the best advantage, *sparsores*—young boys hired as "sprinklers" by the four factions—threw down water from jugs onto the horses' noses to help the beasts with their strained breathing in the rising dust. Once round, all fighting for position, then a second time, followed by the third lap and the fourth without serious incident. By then the mob was praying for the thrill of a "shipwreck," as the Circus crowd called an accident, and the collective prayer was answered. Out in the lead, the Red driver had unwisely allowed the outside pair of his team to pull too wide of the approaching meta. Close in his dust, the first Blue charioteer attempted to overtake by accelerating through the gap. Blues supporters all stood as if their energy and wildness of shouting could speed him through. But he left it a breath too late. Red went into the turn, cutting across the Blue driver's path. Rufio yelled his encouragement for the timely rally as the Blue driver lost control of his inner pair of horses, terrified at the sudden proximity of the high spina wall flying right past their eyes. While they made it around the tight turn, the chariot behind them did not.

The frail craft dashed against the stonework. Wood dissolved into smithereens. Tethered to his flying team by the traces tied around his waist, the driver smashed into the spina wall just at the turning point. The hapless man bounced brokenly off and was thrown forward at full pelt to the sand. The bang must have stunned him, for he was clearly unable to use his falx to sever the reins and so his four horses dragged his twisting, torqueing body at a furious pace behind. Around the meta they went and in a trice the inner wheel of the Red chariot passed right over his bloodied form. A great groan of despair from the Blues' supporters arose from all around the mighty stadium, while the Reds gave vent to ecstatic screams of delight.

A small army of slaves rushed out from the outer wall and began to drag away the wreck and the lifeless charioteer. They worked at a frenzied pace, well aware that if they were not clear by the time the racers returned around on the next lap many of them would become part of another shipwreck, probably at the cost of their dispensable lives. As to the driverless team of four, they ran on, now clearing more to the outer track.

On went the race, through the fifth lap and into the sixth—Red, White, and Scorpus in third position, all vying for first place. Now the return half of the sixth course was completed and the crowd was already clamoring for the award of the prizes. Rufio was torn between favoring his Reds—their man Endymion of Ephesus (sex god on legs to Rufio) still hanging onto his lead—and backing the sexy Green, for who he also felt a great admiration. "See how he dupes the others by holding back," Rufio lectured Quintus. It was true. Scorpus's adversaries, with no fear of any effort from him, were scouring the track in front with never a care, when suddenly Scorpus pulled hard on the curbs all together, tautened his chest, planted his feet firmly in front, and chafed the mouths of his swift steeds as he used his whip to encourage, never to lash. At this sudden threat, the driver of the White team, clinging to the shortest route round the turning-post, was hustled by Scorpus coming up close on the outside. The White team, unnerved by the unexpected maneuver, lost their harmony. As Scorpus saw him pass before him in disorder, he got ahead of his rival by remaining where he was, cunningly reining up. The White driver, exulting in the public plaudits and believing he had fought off Scorpus, ran closer to the spectators. He realized his error a heartbeat too late, and having gone awry he was forced to turn sharply aslant to make the turn. It cost him several heartbeats and, cutting neatly inside, Scorpus sped straight past his swerving rival, hard behind the leading Red chariot.

They hurtled around the meta into the final straight, neck and neck. No longer needing the inside track for advantage, Scorpus bent to his team and urged them to give everything left, which proved to be a crucial ounce more than Endymion's too-early overrun Red team could manage.

As Scorpus drew level, Endymion in reckless desperation shamelessly made for his bitter rival's wheel with a sidelong dash. It was his undoing. The sudden over-steer tangled his horses and they were brought down. A multitude of intruding legs entered the wheels, and the twelve spokes were crowded. Amid shouts of glee and horror, the revolving rim shattered the entangled feet, snapped bones with audible cracks and shrieks of equine terror. Endymion was flung from his chariot, which fell on top of him so that he was unable to fling himself from the path of the following White team. The charioteer was unable to avoid riding straight over the top of the race's second victim. Hooves hammered the bent figure and wheels jounced Endymion's body and jerked him about as a lion in the arena tosses its victim before devouring the corpse.

Rufio was sad at the disaster. "Risk of the game," Quintus said unfeelingly. That tragedy had been the day before...

"Sixty thousand sesterces for the first prize... that's a lot of things you can do," Rufio said admiringly when he finally caught up with Scorpus. About his waist the charioteer still wore the purple silken victor's ribbons presented to him by the Emperor. Their ends flapped in the breeze, a bright contrast to the brilliant green apparel that made him look like an exotic plant. They stood in a spot of relative calm amid the clamor of the city stables. A large stud farm some few miles up the Via Flaminia housed many more horses, but in the city the Green Faction's headquarters was a large, two-story rectangle surrounding an inner court off the Via Recta on the Campus Martius, under the shadow of the Capitol.

"Hah! You say lot. You no idea, Rufio my Red friend (sorry for Endymion). You know how many in this place have fingers in my prize moneys? You think I keep all what I win? I do not. There is the buyers, there is the trainers, the doctors, horse-doctors, harness-men, clerks, older grooms, club-servants who does entertainments for visiting bigwigs, oh and don't forget the chariot-makers—"

"Why do they deserve anything? These things are nothing but flimsy baskets on wheels!"

"True, but great skill is basket weaving. And there are two domini, our bossmen do the business on top. Yes, even they greedy bastards, Apollo bless their hearts, take something." He gave a cheeky grin and leaned in close. "That is why I must have other earning." He grasped Rufio's arm and jerked him out of the way of a groom walking a skittish stallion up and down in an effort to calm the horrible thing. Rufio gave the animal plenty of room. It had a big snarling lips revealing overlarge, square teeth that looked if they clamped on his juicy arm would never let go.

The interruption seemed to jog the charioteer's memory and he beamed. "Your certain bet, that Regulus, I hear he won everything! Yes? Just like I said. Now you start to make money proper."

"What did you mean, 'other earning'?"

Scorpus gave a careless shrug as one man of the world to another. "Like I say, you make proper money," this accompanied by a waggle of an upturned palm behind his back. "That way I always win."

Rufio snorted disagreement. "I've seen you lose a few races."

"Ah, but that the point, my friend." Scorpus repeated the waggle, going further by adding a sly wink. "Even when I lose it means I win. Like you and Quintus soon do with Regulus. You see?"

Rufio had an uncomfortable feeling he did see but Scorpus misunderstood his silence as bafflement.

"Look, don't fret; you don't approach them, they come to you soon enough. Anyway, that no real problem, not like this bad magic." He held out a small, misshapen tablet. To Rufio's eye it looked like a fragment of animal bone, perhaps a small bit of pelvis. Rufio took it gingerly and peered at the tiny letters inscribed on it in a scratchy hand. He gasped as its import registered. He started to read the words out, but Scorpus shushed him urgently. "Not to speak aloud!"

I beseech, demon, whoever you are, and I demand of you this day that you torture and kill the horses of the Greens, and that you cause collisions and kill the drivers, Scorpus, Felix, Primulus and Clarus.

Rufio looked up, the blood drained from his face. "That's awful. But what…?" he spread arms wide in a helpless gesture. "When did you get this?"

"Oh, yesterday at first light," Scorpus replied airily. "A groom, he finds it is nailed on the gatepost."

"Magic is punishable by crucifixion, but what did you do?"

Scorpus examined a hangnail, nibbled at the cuticle and spat out the offending bit. "The main horse-doctor, he is our weird man, you know, a follower of the Jewish magician they call Christos? He take the curse," he said, grabbing it back from Rufio, "and speak the counter-magic spell of Holy Spirit over it and *poof*! All gone. As you see," indicating his very alive person. "Now it's one more for the collection."

"This happens often?" Rufio looked appalled.

Another eloquently unconcerned shrug. "Now and then. Always the horse-doctor he make the magic go away. Easy to see why so many now follow the Jewish magician, special as he bring people back to life after they dead. Maybe Endymion a follower?"

Wisely, Rufio decided to avoid any further investigation of this disturbing aspect to sporting life. But as he waved a farewell, he decided he needed more expert advice on making "proper money."

Philo, as his name implied, thought himself a great lover, and his position as *rationalis* to the public treasury gave him many opportunities to put erotic theory into lubricious practice (everyone needed funding, after all). Pancratius loathed him. "Oh, that strange gift to a couple of…" he riffled through some papyrus sheets of neatly written notes. "Nonentities? No, clearly it is not a matter for the public purse," Philo sibilated through barely moving lips.

Pancratius spluttered. "But it is Caesar's gift!"

"Absolutely, dear, dear Pan, which is why I forwarded the papers to Themistocles, you know? Chief assayer of *congiaria et donativa*. It's his department that issues money gifts to the public."

"Olympus and Hades! They take forever to deliberate over the addition of a single denarius. What will I tell Athenos?"

"I would suggest you pop over to the old Tiberian palace and make life unpleasant for Themistocles. But you know what he's like, thinks he's above the law."

"When did you send the papers?"

"Oh…three market days ago? I'm too busy to recall every item."

"Very well," Pancratius sighed. "I will chase Themistocles… whenever I get a moment to do so."

E·L·E·V·E·N | XI

Rome & Cappadocia, 19th day of November AD 108

"*Pedicabere, fur, semel; sed idem si deprensus eris bis, irrumabo. Quod si tertia furta molieris, ut poenam patiare et hanc et illam, pedicaberis irrumaberisque,*" Cato read out. He looked up at his brother. "Which thief are you thinking of 'swiving' and then 'irrumating'? And is swiving a poetic word for sodomy?"

"Give me that, you pricklet." Rufio snatched from Cato's hands the latest piece of scroll dropped off, he presumed, by Ashur. "You're not supposed to be reading any of that."

"Then I suggest you don't leave it lying around where *thieving* hands may find it, my priapic pet," Junilla said. She had just emerged from her private cubbyhole at the other end of the rambling tablinum-cum-atrium-cum-dining room. "Is that something Quintus wrote? Where's he been lately? Haven't seen hide or hair. And why are you in such a snarky mood these past couple of days? Have you two had a fight? You should be supportive, you wretched Celt. Poor Quintus, facing marriage to a girl he's never seen beyond a probably flattering portrait."

"He's spending all his spare time with our 'investment,' that cunning Regulus fellow."

"Speaking of spending, how much have you so far?"

Rufio frowned. "What?"

"Spent?"

"Nothing yet. Last I heard, Quintus was seeking advice on which banker we should approach to take out a short-term loan against the promise of Trajan's grant. It's taking ages to come through."

"Wouldn't it be more appropriate to have a thief thrown to the beasts in the arena?" Cato demanded. "Or maybe your Regulus could chop him to pieces." He thrust an imaginary sword into an invisible gut.

"What are you driveling on about?"

"Now don't take out your bad mood on your brother, Rufio, and don't go showing him any more of that smutty poetry. Save it up for Sosius and his lascivious customers. And you, my little sage-flavored sausage," she said to Cato, "be off to your afternoon lessons. Eutychus is outside waiting."

As he swung down Vicus Armilustri in the latter part of the seventh hour according to the sundial set in front of the Temple of Liber, shortly after this exchange, Rufio considered the lines Quintus had written that had so excited Cato's prurient interest. He wondered how best to illuminate a poem about a young thief's suitable punishment. The hero of the piece, if he caught the lad, would bugger him for a first theft, and if again arrested he would make the boy suck him off. But if the boy returned to plunder a third time the villain would suffer both penalties: pedicate and irrumate, though Quintus hadn't specified in which order the ass fuck and the face fuck should happen or if a slave should be present to hold the boy down for his punishments. He was still pondering this matter when he emerged from Nerva's Forum and plunged into the steeply rising labyrinthine streets of the Subura.

"I can offer you fare simple or extravagant, depending on your appetite, taste, and of course your pocket," Septimius was informing a corpulent equestrian seated at the counter of his thermpolium halfway up Clivus Suburanus. "How about lunching on slices of grilled plump kid, fresh in yesterday from the bucolic hillsides of Frusino. The great orator Cicero spent summers at his villa there in the Campania Romana, no doubt feasting on this delicacy. This kid is the tenderest of the flock, with more milk in him than blood. To complement the delicate flavor may I suggest some wild asparagus topped with lightly coddled hen's eggs, which I assure you were laid barely a turn of the hourglass ago. Perhaps a dish of grapes, pears and apples to end with?"

Septimius nodded a greeting over the would-be diner's shoulder. Rufio acknowledged it and hovered impatiently.

The customer, evidently something of a typical glutton, sniffed dismissively. "A fellow from my guild, the Collegium Bisellariorum," he said grandly, "praised your Dish Minerva. I'll have some of that."

Rufio had to wonder what it was the guildsmen of Makers of Chairs for the Gods actually did and why they needed a trade guild to protect their interests. Surely the gods extended their grateful arms protectively over the furniture carpenters in return for all those comfy chairs? When Septimius explained that the Minerva terrine was made from pike liver, pheasant brains, peacock brains, flamingo tongues, and lamprey roe, ingredients that came from every corner of the Imperium and that, desolated as he was, he could not serve it up without at least three months' notice, sometimes even more, the disgruntled customer pushed off, grumbling that cookshops were going to the dogs.

"I'll serve him up dog feces marinated in vintage cats' piss next time I see him," Septimius said with a grim smile. "And what are you after? And don't bluster me with being a newly inducted member of the Collegium Armarorium now you own half a gladiator."

"That's what I wanted to talk to you about." Rufio kept his gaze down on the counter where his fingers tapped on the marble in a mood of unusual diffidence.

"How about a small trout seared on the hot plate. Nice and simple and line-caught well above the Bridge of Agrippa."

Rufio was well aware of Septimius's disapproval of fish caught *intra duos pontes*, the stretch of river between the two bridges just above the Tiber island and below the Cloaca Maxima. Gourmands claimed the outpouring of effluent from the great sewer gave fish that dined on so much human shit an irresistible flavor. Septimius claimed it made those unwary enough to eat the flesh sick.

"I'm really not hungry."

Septimius slapped down a small bowl of porridge and one of his Everyday Basic sausages. "Pork and bread meal fragranced by the slightest trace of sage. Now, tell me what's got you so despondent. You haven't caught the clap off one of Lucretia's lupanaria-boys have you?" He waved a hand in the general direction of the infamous brothel run by a dear old friend of Rufio's mother (not that the connection gave him any concessions when it came to the cost of entry). "Ah, at last, a faint grin... almost a smile?"

Rufio shook his head. He scooped up some porridge with the end of his sausage and chewed thoughtfully for a moment. He swallowed. "I know it's very unRoman of me, but I've never bothered with gladiatorial fights, but something Scorpus said got me to thinking. There's a lot of money rides on the outcome of races for gamblers, so I suppose it does in the arena?"

"Of course." Septimius took up a cloth and started wiping down the counter surface. "Millions and milllions of sesterces change hands during the year at official games all over the Imperium."

Rufio chewed a bit more before speaking slowly around sausage. "So it would make sense to some unscrupulous people to know the outcome of a fight or a race in advance. Bet heavily against a fighter you *know* is going to lose. Even better if he's a champion."

"Bout fixing." Septimius threw the cloth down into a metal bowl filled with water. He glanced up sideloing at Rufio hunched against the counter. "Are you surprised?"

"I suppose not."

"After all, the antiquities trade isn't exactly free of guile, is it? And I imagine in your mother's other business, arranging festivities and parties, there is unequal competition."

A nod acknowledged the truth of this observation.

"When we were in Alexandria, while you and Quintus were traipsing around the sights and mooning over Alexander's tomb—"

"Mooning's a bit strong."

"—I was busy making inquiries of former *frumentiarii* cronies of mine, for the benefit of Caesar's security of course, but those old army spies know a thing or two about the fight scene wherever they end up. Like who's up and coming or on their last legs; who's willing to sell out and throw a fight; or the lanistas who for a cut will arrange a fight. I know it's illegal to gamble outside of officially sanctioned fesstivals, but they had some solid tips on who was throwing fights and I made a killing while we were there. A right bundle it was."

At this confession Rufio looked up sharply. "Did you? I didn't know that." He tried to keep the scandalized tone out of his words, but Septimius wasn't fooled.

"Now there's me surprised, and me thinking you a man of the world, young Tullius. Gambling and sharp practice go on all the while. If you'd told me your mate Quintus was disapproving, I'd have understood. Patricians are good at twisting the system to suit their own ends while keeping their noses clean and well above the stench of everyday commerce… like securing the outcome of a fight to line their pockets while tush-tushing any who might get caught."

"Quintus isn't like that." A sudden rush to his friend's defense. "It's just that Scorpus said because Regulus has been victorious in all his exhibition matches it means that now we'll be able to start making *real* money. I admit that when he said Regulus would be a certain bet to return us a fortune on the investment of being his patrons, I thought he meant from prize money—"

"And from good bets you make. *Cert-ain* bets…" Septimius said, drawing out the two syllables.

Rufio polished off the sausage and porridge and ran a sticky hand through his curly red locks. "So this fixing, it goes on a lot?"

"All the time— I'll be right with you," Septimius called out to a new arrival, hungry for a late luncheon. He leaned across the counter to bring his head close to Rufio's. "Look, there's many a man makes a tidy bit on the side from fixed matches because there are cartels all over the place who let their people know what's what, but be careful—the men who make the real big money, the ones who run the game, they are not nice people to cross."

"You know who they are?" Rufio asked, wonderingly.

Septimius straightened up. "That's not a part of my world now, Rufio. Just be cautious. Don't make waves. But also, don't trust anyone, especially not the F·G·O·T—they maybe the governing body, but the collegium is rotten through with seceretive cartels using it as a screen for their criminal activities. I must go… no, keep your coins. Instead, just tell me in advance when Regulus is going to beat the shit out of his first real opponent." And with a sly tap of his nose, Septimius crossed over to take his new customer's order.

Rufio started off down the hill toward the imperial forums going over what he'd just heard. Surely Septimius was exaggerating the dangers, acting like an old woman suddenly. Not like him at all. He took a deep breath and filled his chest. He decided not to pass on what Septimius had told him to Quintus, who would just scoff at such fears. Time to check in with the wayward boy to see if he'd got any further with advice on a bridging loan to tide them over.

Rufio's blithe assumption might have taken a bad knocking if he had been capable of seeing across the intervening 1,400 miles to the northern shore of Rome's province of Cappadocia.

Easterly winds blowing across the Pontus Euxinus might be drenching the port city's streets in chilly rain, but here inside councilor Metellus Scivus's town house it was warm and cozy. Trapezus might be a prosperous bustling trading place, exporter of ironware, wine, and honey from its mountainous hinterland, and a Roman naval base; it might have civilized basics such as an aqueduct, baths, temples, and a modest but popular arena—but in the eyes of the Enforcer it was a piddling provincial dump on the furthermost eastern reaches of the Imperium and nothing like Rome. Perhaps its only redeeming curiosity was that it lay on the trading route that snaked east beyond the known world to lands populated by monsters and people of strange appearance whence exotic goods arrived to be sold to wealthy sophisticates… *And here I am cuddling two delightful newly arrived imports with almond eyes, even as I attend business for* S·A·D·A.

The golden lamp light, the brazier-fueled warmth and comfortable furnishings softened the rough rock walls of Scivus's ample basement storage room, lined on two sides with amphoras of local wine. Rather rotund, Metellus Scivus sat behind a bulky desk, back to the wall, nervously gripping a goblet of his wine. The Enforcer deemed the vintage acceptable. He was comfortably nestled in ample soft cushions, a pretty boy lounging either side of him. Conciliatory gifts from Metellus, they were beauties the likes of which he'd never set eyes on before. It was their faces: exquisitely delicate with dainty yet firm mouths, widely spaced little nostrils, gentle high cheekbones—and the most exotic eyes, pools of liquid black, inscrutably alien, within strangely slanted, seemingly foldless lids of translucent ivory colored skin beneath elegantly arched brows. All this and cascades of jet-black lustrous hair. The faces alone had taken his breath away, now lounging between them, the warmth of their slim bodies through semi-transparent silk promised delights to come…

They'll fetch me a fortune back in Rome!

The elephant in the room spoiling his mood was the young brute, wrists chained behind his lower back, torn tunic around his ankles, wearing nothing but a loincloth, firmly in the grip of two strongmen.

"Well, Xanthos, what am I to do with you? You've caused your master Scivus and myself a good deal of trouble—"

"All I did was fight! Gave it my all—"

"—and won. Which was not the plan."

The young thug's face beneath unkempt curly hair contorted with belligerence, anger, frustration.

"I-I couldn't! The shame—I just couldn't *lose!*" His muscles bunched and strained against his captors. "Sorry! I have my-my pride! I—"

Was that a hint of fear? Vulnerability made the lad quite appealing for lovers of rough trade, supposed the Enforcer, his fingers touching smooth thighs pressed against him.

"Expensive pride. Which we will destroy."

A slight nod, and his henchmen went into oft-practiced action. They tore the loincloth from their victim's waist and, holding him firmly by his arms, roughly caressed his face in mock adoration. He flinched at the touch, eyes darting from one to the other. He emitted an involuntary hiss when they ran their hands down his front and back with forceful strokes to finally grope his cock and balls, kneading, twisting, jerking. Then, suddenly, their hands pulled back, bunched, and landed a twin-fisted blow to his midriff that doubled him over with a strangled cry.

The Enforcer's exotic boys clutched him in fright and even Scivus, who must have expected violence, recoiled in shock.

"My men will teach you true shame... and they love their job."

One of them yanked the chain that bound the boy's wrists to jerk his arms up his back and held him bent over. His mate kicked the prisoner's legs apart and pulled his clenched ass cheeks wide open with a grunt of anticipation. While he fingered the exposed sphincter, he deftly removed his leather belt and quickly had it coiled in his fist.

The whipping began, steady, methodical, forceful; the target the upturned buttocks...

Scivus gulped wine in convulsive swallows, rapt eyes on the naked, twitching body. The Enforcer languorously busied himself with his pretty gifts, distracting them from the sordid spectacle, the slapping, the whimpers... his seductive fingers caressing and exploring, gently arousing...

With shivering pleasure, the Enforcer had just attained smooth naked boy flesh within their loose silken clothes and had both of the exotic boys lolling supine in the embrace of the pillows when the slapping stopped. Only the pained whimpers remained. He looked up at the clinking of chains when the two tormentors hauled Xanthos upright between them.

The next part of the young gladiator's humiliation loomed.

His trembling body glistened with sweat now, and angry weals adorned his lower back, buttocks, and upper thighs. His handsome face was a tear-streaked picture of clenched-teeth suffering. The men holding him upright leaned close, their lewd smirking turning them from tormentors to seducers.

Their fingers began a cruel dance of arousal on the youth's shuddering body. They took their time… gentle swirls, feather-light caresses soothed his pain-wracked skin… from chest to flanks to belly to thighs… from raw buttocks to spine to shoulder blades. The Enforcer admired their skill as he saw the lad's face slowly register confused awareness…

"Nice boy. Learned your lesson, haven't yer…" one torturer's coarse voice gurgled obscenely.

Agile fingers increased the intensity of their seductive roaming over the sweaty flesh… teased, rubbed, pinched the youth's nipples to erection, fingernails raked down his midriff, worried at his bellybutton, then ran up his inner thighs… and there it was: the first unmistakable twitch of his prick. Settling back, eyes on the unfolding corruption, the Enforcer's fingers resumed their appreciative exploration of his submissive boys' naked softness.

"Yer likes this, don'tcha?"

His men kneaded their victim's lower belly, fingers in his thick pubic bush. Another twitch of the swelling cock… then they were lightly stroking the underside of his exposed head and shaft… rewarded by a jerky stiffening, which they soon plied to a full erection. The youth's nostrils flared and his lips parted with a whimper. Grinning, the men now started masturbating him and playing with his balls, while not neglecting to torment his swollen nipples. The boy's head lolled back as he sagged against them, and they continued their erotic assault. His whimpers turned to groans and gasps as his erection was coaxed and bullied, his balls squeezed and pulled. Fingers wormed between his tormented buttocks to ply his slippery asshole, and his body jerked in their grip and moans became yelps then gurgles of defeat as he was invaded.

"Right little slut, ain'cha, love your asshole poked, bitch…"

The Enforcer gazed in fascination even as his own fingers were arousing delicate nipples, fluttering bellies, and his mysterious catches were undulating in pleasurable abandon.

He saw that one of the strongmen had pulled his engorged phallus from under his tunic and now stepped behind the youth. In one smooth move he prised the sweaty ass open and pushed his shaft in and up to the hilt. The boy's eyes snapped open in shock and outrage, and a gurgled gasp escaped his gaping mouth. His legs squirmed as he spasmed to accommodate the intruder, even as it began to pump

in a steady fucking motion. The man had his hips in a firm grip and his mate never let up tormenting the lad's erection as he was shafted.

While Scivus goggled in queasy shock at what was being done to his gladiator, to the sounds of slapping flesh and rhythmic gasping of the rutting the Enforcer returned his full attention to enjoying his playthings. His busy fingers had coaxed the boys' pricks to bobbing erections and he now probed the intimate delights hidden beneath the plump balls, delicately teasing the little rosebuds within the warm embrace of firm cheeks…

Delicious pleasure to be had tonight in private. For now, let me see… taste… your exotic juices. He began to fondle the vulnerable erections with real intent.

Xanthos had by now been transformed from thug to helpless youth in the throes of sexual abandon, spluttering at every ruthless thrust deep inside him. "Want some more, eh, boy…?" The man snarled and winked at his companion, who abandoned their victim's drooling cock and stooped to snake his strong hands under the boy's knees. With deceptive ease he lifted the legs up and folded them against his chest and over his shoulders.

"Try two of us up your boy cunny!" Rough hands cupped the lad's stuffed ass in position as the second erection was pressed and forced into his stretched sphincter. Xanthos's mouth gaped wide open in mute agony. Bit by bit the cocks adjusted, and the newcomer abruptly slid in to the hilt. A keening whine came from the boy sandwiched between the men, and the fucking resumed… "Nice—tight—juicy hole—you got, boy bitch!"

As the gladiator was ravished and Scivus hid behind his goblet, the Enforcer leant forward and slid his mouth over the first enticing prick… suckled it, fingers fondling delicate balls… his other hand kept the second boy aroused… while his hungry mouth rapidly caused an eruption of hot, delicious seed and writhing limbs, little gasps of orgasm from the first beauty. *Exquisite…!*

A quick glance to savor the obscene sight of Xanthos's ass bumping on twinned shafts of meat… then he dipped his head to feast on the second boy's straining cock. His forceful tongue and lips… expert fingers between opened thighs… a twitch of smooth belly… and he was milking his plaything dry… *a mere foretaste of what I've planned for you both later!*

Cries, whimpers, squelching sounds drew his attention back to where the young gladiator who had thwarted his organization's business plan in this godforsaken port at the shit end of the Imperium was being punished, taught a lesson. The furious fuck (if two cocks crammed into one asshole could be vigorous) was coming to a climax. His men grunted, their buttocks clenched, and cum oozed from where their shafts disappeared inside Xanthos. His sweaty, folded up body, shuddered, jerked, and a plaintive groan escaped his slack mouth as he succumbed and splattered his chest in his own orgasm, his trapped erection bucking, rubbing against his taut stomach. The Enforcer saw tears welling from the defeated youth's scrunched up eyes. The men pulled out of him and let him crumple to his knees on the stone floor, a miserable, shamed, sobbing wreck.

"Where's your pride now, Xanthos? You're no better than a catamite, slut boy who likes it rough."

The Enforcer stood in front of him as the youth was hauled to his feet... stepped up close and grabbed his sweaty scrotum, tugged it... produced a wicked looking blade, brought it up for him to see.

"N-no—*no!* Please, *please!* Not—" Xanthos goggled in horror, as a rough hand pulled his slithery cock clear of the target. "You forfeited any right to your balls when you disobeyed clear orders from your master—"

"It was a m-m-mistake. P-please... *Mercy!*" There was no escape, the wretched boy was trapped. "I'll d-do anything. I beg you, dominus. *Dominus!*"

Scivus looked on in alarm, ashen-faced.

"*Not that!* Give me a-another chance..." He choked on his words when the knife dropped to caress the stretched skin linking his captive member to his trapped scrotum. "No— I'll follow all orders—always, always. Just please... *spare me!*" The Enforcer gave another tug—then released the sweaty balls, and took a step back.

"Very well, young man. You're reprieved... for now. Fall short one more time and I will personally relieve you of much more than your pride and joy." He fixed nervous Scivus with a flinty look.

"As a sign of goodwill and to encourage you in your rehabilitation, Scivus has agreed to reward you with a handsome sum."

Scivus blanched at this unexpected news and manfully choked back a startled respponse.

"Accept it and do well for us, Xanthos. You won't regret it. I shall follow your progress with great interest..." The Enforcer turned toward his pretty gifts from the Orient. "Scivus, my man—show me and my young friends to my quarters. I will be dining in private tonight."

* * *

"What do you mean, the *aerarium militare*!" Pancratius yelled at an unmoved Themistocles. "What's Caesar's bequest to do with the military exchequer?"

"There is no requirement to shout." A burst of sunlight shafted through a high window and bounced off Themistocles' shiny bald pate, almost blinding Pancratius. "I noted one beneficiary has the status and age to be a junior military tribune," Themistocles said. "We at *congiaria et donativa* handle public finance gifts not military hand-outs. I suggest you contact Theron Cunctator at *militare*, get him to fork out the money."

"When did you send Theron *the Delayer* the paperwork?"

"Oh, several market days ago, I think." Themistocles' long nose twitched imperiously at the sound of grinding teeth echoing off the gloomy walls as Pancratius stomped away.

T·W·E·L·V·E | XII

23rd to 25th days of November AD 108

Once again secreted behind a column at a corner of the impluvium in the Domus Fabii's atrium, Livius Caecilius Dio had just suggested the lanista of the Ludus Gallicus as the best person to oversee the advancement of Regulus… and to exercise real control over the boy.

Virius sniffed noisily, a mannerism inseperable from his dismissive attitude to any opinion other than his own. "He runs a tight school, I suppose, and he's firmly in the hands of our prowling Panther, even more so than that irrumating cloaca Bulbus."

Keeping an uncharacteristically tight rein on the irritation which always burned in his throat at Virius's *I am the only fount of common knowledge* tone, Livy said, "It *is* why I mentioned Dannotalus Dolabella. I shall have words with my nephew accordingly."

"He's listening to you now, is he?"

Livy ignored the sarcasm. "The stupid prick knows next to nothing about gladiators or their training, or anything. In fact I swear nothing at all unless it's iambic, anapaestic, dactylic, or trochaic, or perhaps guttersnipe plebs with hair the color of a common hennaed prostitute. I shall ensure he does what works for us, immediately after I take my leave. Indeed, I must to my dear brother-in-law to press again your suit for delivering marble for the Column. He is warming to the idea," Livy lied.

The capital-C could only mean Trajan's monument to celebrate his victories over the Dacian tribes, planned by Apollodorus of Damascus to soar to the heavens from between the libraries—one Latin, one Greek—sited at the northwestern end of his gargantuan complex of forum, temple, and shopping arcades.

"See that you do succeed, Dio, or I promise that you will deeply regret the failure. Now I must attend to the *rest* of my clients."

Livy would have visibly bridled at the snide implication he was a client of Virius if he weren't too fat for such a physical expression. Instead he contented himself at counting only five men pressing Virius with requests and receiving instructions… hardly what he'd call an impressive clientele. There was a time when scores of eager equestrians and freedmen would have crammed into this atrium and it was satisfying to see Virius so bereft of status. But for the moment their fortunes seemed inextricably linked and when it came down to the line, Livy couldn't work out who he hated the more: his brother-in-law Lucius Caecilius Alba or Publius Fabius Virius.

"But Lucius my dear, dearest brother, our Lungiana quarries—"

"*My* quarries, Livius," Quintus heard his father interrupt sharply. "And don't 'brother' me." The days when Livy cowed his father had been swept away after Caesar decided to give everything to the Alban Caecilli, cutting out Livy as well as the Fabii and all other potential rivals for the lucrative business of supplying stone and building materials for the massive imperial infrastructure program.

The brothers-in-law had never gotten along, but it was always Livy who ruled the roost until his devious scheme to do Lucius down and line his own purse by pimping Quintus to Trajan as an inducement to secure the monopoly went badly awry. *Did my uncle ever really think Trajan was so easily swayed, or fooled by such a transparent scheme? I thank Fortuna that Caesar liked me enough not to have me executed on the spot for being Livy's unwilling tool.*

"*Your* quarries," Livy persisted, "don't have sufficiently large deposits of pure, white Carrara that Apollodorus insists on having. You know that. The veins may be very refined but are too narrow. The quarry at Colonnata in the possession of Publius Fabius Virius can produce what's required, so why not sub-contract his people?"

"What's in it for you?" Quintus whispered harshly.

Ashur shushed him. They were eavesdropping, pressed close to the wall nearest the tablinum, having happened accidentally on the discussion. Quintus had suppressed his disdain at "sneaking around like a slave" and followed Ashur's sneaky lead. It was clear that his father wasn't at all keen on dealing with the Caecilii's arch-rival.

"Must I remind you," Lucius went on, "that Fabius Virius has ever been out to do damage to this family?"

"At least have Pallas speak to Creon, our people and his," Livy wheedled. "Surely it's better to cut Virius in and take a percentage— and keep the whip hand—than end up with nothing at all and have the contract go to the Fabii anyway?"

"What's the greasy cunny up to now?" Quintus wondered softly. He discovered nothing more, for at that moment there was a final heated exchange and footsteps approached the partly shut door. There was just enough time to step back far enough to emerge from the shadows striding forward, innocent of expression, as if he and Ashur were simply crossing the atrium on business of their own. Livy looked startled to see them there, but recovered swiftly. His several chins competed in a complex dance as his face creased into a beaming smile of welcome. Quintus felt a stone drop into his bowel and it churned. A smile like that was not a good sign.

"Ah, my dearest boy and my most favorite nephew. Well met. I was contemplating seeking you out—"

"For what?" Quintus glared back, unwilling to relax under Livy's uncomfortably affable demeanor. It was an expression unfamiliar to his uncle and kept hovering uncertainly between amiability and something murkier—a cocktail of lust, greed, and maybe dyspepsia— an unpleasantly shimmering chimera.

Livy bore down on Quintus and a quailing Ashur like a ship under full sail in the vast envelope of an expensive looking synthesis. Before he could prevent it his uncle's embrace engulfed Quintus in a silky squall. "Get lost," Livy snapped at Ashur over his shoulder. "I have important matters to impart to to my nephew."

In the first hour of the day the sun had barely risen, not that any would know if it did from the cloud haze covering the city. That was when Zeno came to summon Rufio. The slave found him in the largest of the Emporium's several storehouses—the one the Satyr of Capri briefly inhabited before its erroneous sale to Fabius Virius. Every time he looked at the vacant spot where the huge, rampant bronze had stood it reminded Rufio of Ambrosius, the delectably seductive adopted son of Virius. Not only had Rufio—utterly beguiled by those limpid sex-smoked eyes—enjoyed a sweaty, squinchy, sucky-fucky hour with the lithe youth, he and Quintus had later taken the lad to triplicate delight as well.

"It's master Quintus, dominus," Zeno said, breaking into Rufio's erotic interlude.

"Really?" *Sudela's seductive socks, but he's early!* A flush of excitement ran up and down his spine. Hoping that early meant eager, he thanked Zeno and set off across the already busy yard, dodging statues on wheeled carts, a massively ugly candelabrum clutched fearfully to a worker's chest, a pyramid of tripod tables wobbling between two dusty joinery slaves. Even though they were supposed to be partners in the patronage of Regulus, the waves of coolness Quintus had given off in recent days on the few occasions they had come face to face made him wary of sparking off a confrontation. It was the fault of Regulus, of course, but Rufio was sure the infatuation would blow itself out and until it did he'd thought it better to leave Quintus alone. Yes, better to keep his head down and get on illustrating the poems Ashur delivered. That at least they still had in common. Nevertheless, as he took the three steps up into the porch in a single leap he could not suppress the hope of finding himself restored to Quintus's affections again.

As he burst into the tablinum he saw at once that he might be disappointed. Quintus paced the uneven floor in impatient steps. At the intrusion he stopped and regarded his partner with the stern patrician gaze Rufio hadn't seen directed in his direction in many months, unless Quintus had been teasing him. "I had a lecture yesterday afternnon from Uncle Livy," he opened in a flat tone. Rufio crossed the room in a few strides and made to hug Quintus, who accepted the embrace but quickly pulled away in a businesslike manner. "You know we need to enrol Regulus somewhere he can begin serious training for real fights—"

"And dear Uncle Livy's told you of the right school?" Rufio said, automatically stepping back. No one knew better how much Quintus distrusted the man, so his curt nod in acknowledgment of the attempt at flippancy came as a surprise.

"Yes, the Ludus Gallicus."

Rufio shrugged. He didn't know of it. "Sounds more like a place they train Gauls." He grinned and tapped his chest. "Like me, a descendant of that noble race—"

"You really don't know anything—"

"I know the price of antiques from Delos to Delphi," Rufio snapped, stung at the tone of the response. This wasn't his Quintus, affectionate, ironic Quintus, gentle with his taunting. "I know the worth of statuary from Londinium to Leptis Magna, from Colonia Agrippinensis to Ceasarea, Tonbriga to—"

"I've no doubt the Divine Julius Caesar would have happily dragged a few of your forebears in there," Quintus fired back in a raised voice. "He it was who first displayed your Gaulish ancestors in the arena." He quieted, face flushed, and took on a familiar lecturing tone. "You see the Gauls he fought and conquered were more heavily armed than any foes Rome had faced to that point, so the Ludus Gallicus was named after them as a school for any heavily armed gladiator—like Regulus, a murmillo, and Samnites and hoplomachi—"

"My, my, but aren't we the expert all of a sudden."

Quintus colored even more, spots of hot anger on his cheeks. "One of us has to take an interest. It was your idea in the first place."

"Oh, fuck off, Quintus! I try and you keep freezing me out."

"I do not!"

A scrape at the door stopped worse words being uttered. The entryway darkened. Flaccus stuck his head around the corner and glanced in warily. "Not fighting are you?" His grin indicated that he couldn't believe they would ever be out of sorts with each other. "I need to get something agreed with your lady-mother, Rufio. Before I have to report in for duty on the Viminal."

"Flaccus Caepio, come in." For once Rufio was happy to see the vigilis and waved him forward, relieved at the interruption. *By Fortuna, a timely arrival of the lecherous nightwatchman!* "Take the weight off your overburdened caligae. She went off with Dammy, but said not for long. Anyway," he said to Quintus, "where is this Ludus Gallopus and how much will it cost us?"

Quintus made a visible attempt to calm his breathing. "It's one of the four main schools surrounding the Colosseum, tucked under the Temple of Divine Claudius, next to the Ludus Matutinus, which is next—"

"To the Ludus Magnus. I know that, at least. I didn't know the building on the Velia side was a ludus. It looks too small. You said one of four, what's the fourth?"

"The Ludus Dacicus, for Thracian-style fighters. It's the other side of the Colosseum, next to the Baths of Titus, just below where Trajan's new baths are coming along."

"And you learned all this from Uncle Livy?" Rufio asked with overdone wonder.

Flaccus gently chided him. "It's fairly common knowledge, Rufio,"

Not to me, and I guarantee Quintus knew no more either, at least not until yesterday. Rufio sighed and kept the thought to himself. "So how does it work?" he asked Quintus.

"Livy has what he calls 'a connection' with the lanista so he can get us a good deal. He says that big Scythian brute, the one who slaughtered his way through all the Plebeian Games, has persuaded his ludus in Capua to transfer him to the place, so it must be worthwhile for Regulus."

"Huh, a good connection for Uncle Livy, no doubt. Which big brute?"

"Bebryx."

Rufio started at the name. The stench of the gloomy underworks assailed him again. *Those who whisper treachery in willing ears, who deal in special potions.* It would be sensible to mention his misgivings about the whole business of being gladiator owners, but he didn't think Quintus was in the mood to hear vague rumors. He went and perched on the edge of a table where he could keep both the others in view and tried to rekindle some good humor in Quintus. "Does he have any good connections to a nice banker who will give us a bridging loan at a favorable rate? I tried Ma's friendly moneybags but he turns out to be more grasping than Lucretia, and by the pudendum of Venus, that's saying something."

"Gods," Flaccus blurted out in agreement, "that woman's purse is tighter than Juno Moneta's minge. No one can be that mean—oh…" His face went scarlet. "I mean Lucretia, not, not…"

A strangulated scoff broke from Rufio and he stopped swinging his leg to double over. "I know you'd never compare my mother to Juno Moneta's…" he spluttered when he was able, at poor Flaccus. "Well he is." Rufio grinned. "I don't know how she gets good rates of interest out of him." Even Quintus permitted himself a smile to tickle the corners of his mouth. Rufio recovered his composure. "Actually, I suppose I don't want to know how Ma wheedles a decent rate of interest from him."

"Lanistas aren't exactly noted for being kindly souls either," Quintus said. "And I don't suppose my uncle's claim of a connection means the lanista being nice and friendly. Mind you, after Bulbus…?"

"Gallicus, huh?" Flaccus broke in as he settled his big frame on a stool. "That's Dannotalus Dolabella that is, the lanista there.

187

You want to watch him. He's like 'em all, of course, but worse, an *infame*—a cur, lower than a butcher or a pimp, and a despicable price gouger. Leastways, that's what we hear in the barracks." He looked at both boys in turn, daring either to contradict him. "But Libo, my mate on the Watch, says he runs a tight school, he does."

"Bound to be a criminal then if your lot in the vigiles know anything about him." Rufio loved to needle Flaccus because he could, playing on the man's eternal crush on him.

"That's as may be, Rufio. He's a freedman, got his manumission from that Servius Cornelius Dolabella Petronianus, who as a consul gave his name to the year† along with Domitian who-we-don't-talk-about-any-more. I was just nine then, remember it well. Domitian we-don't-talk-about-any-more started the Capitoline Games that year and I got taken to see the fun. Back then they came from all over the Imperium, the contestants did. Poets—like Quintus here—speakers in the Greek style, historians, you name it they were there, not like now."

"Sounds like a bundle of fun," Rufio said dismissively. "I prefer a bit of racing."

"Complete bastards, though."

"Huh? Who? The contestants or the Dolabellas?" Rufio wanted to know.

"Not the *Dolabellas*," Quintus broke in, having evidently made sense of Flaccus's non sequitur. The Patriciate was a subject Quintus definitely did know about. "The *Gens Cornelia*," he insisted, "were—are—a pretty bad bunch. Loads of consuls in their past, but some of them were a byword for turncoats, forever switching sides in the civil wars to their own benefit."

"Not like the Caecilii?" Rufio gave a cheeky grin.

"Definitely not."

It amused him how much Quintus was permitted to run his own family down, calling them stuffy old stick-in-the-mud conservatives, but if anyone else cast aspersions in their direction

† The year was AD 86

up went his back and his upper lip pursed stiffer than a boy-whore's dick at the prospect of money.

"Anyway, I meant Dannotalus Dolabella, or not so much him as his people," said Flaccus. "The Mandubii tribe, they're called. Bunch of hopped up, no-good—"

Even in his black mood Quintus snorted with repressed laughter. "Careful, Flaccus. The Mandubii are a tribe of the Gallic nation. For all we know, the ginger-haired monster squatting on the table over there might even have been one once."

Another wash of embarrassment spread across Flaccus's face, and he stuttered an apology. "I think I meant that particular bastard is a poor specimen of his obviously very fine Gallic tribe. I meant no offense," he said.

The transformation Quintus had made from sternness to… well, a little bit lighter, made Rufio happy, but the matter of finances still loomed. He sighed. "None taken, Flaccus my fiery fire-fighter, but all these fine compliments to my ancestry aren't going to find us a bridging loan, and I don't fancy getting into debt with a hopped up, no-good Mandubian lanista. What can be taking the Palatine stylus-pushers so long, do you think? I mean it would be rude to go and ask Trajan to hurry them up, wouldn't it?"

"I wouldn't dare to do that," Flaccus spoke up, alarmed at the idea. "He might think you're questioning his generosity, or something. Anyway, bureaucrats are the same wherever, always passing bits of paperwork from in-tray to out-tray and on to some other bastard functionary's in-tray. You should hear Centurion Varro go on about the delay in his pension coming through—"

"But we need ready coin from someplace. Quintus?"

"I can't get advice from my father. He still doesn't know anything about Regulus, and Uncle Livy swore not to tell him—"

"You can take that to the bank."

"But I *could* ask him. After all, he did run the Caecilii clientele up until we, well… you know, the thing with Trajan."

"Isn't that rather like asking Locusta to cook you up a tasty dish of mushrooms?"

"I'm shocked you know the name of the infamous poisoner of the Emperor Claudius!" Quintus arched an eyebrow.

"I *am* acquainted with *some* history, you know. Anyway, my point is valid, sort of."

Quintus nodded. "Yes, but Livy clearly has a vested interest, even if I can't work out what it is… yet."

I think I can, Rufio thought, *but I can't see where all the pieces fit in… yet.*

"If we're agreed, Rufio, I shall now to the Ludus Magnus and see to the transition of Regulus to the tender care of this Dannotalus Dolabella. Then we will see how extensively Uncle Livy's writ runs. I'll send word if there's anything needs your stamp on it."

Warning growls, shuddering roars, squeals of terror or fury mingled into a single baying of strange, exotic beasts filled the air along with the fetid smell of animals kept in close confinement. The noise and stink from the Ludus Matutinus increased as Rufio descended the narrow lane that ran alongside the temple of Divine Claudius, done in by mushrooms. As the road dipped lower, so the great platform supporting the vast temple gardens seemed to rise up until it almost blotted out a dull sky. The lane opened between the two training schools—Matutinus on the right and Gallicus on the left—onto the wide expanse of pavement encircling the Colosseum.

He had gone on this roundabout route from the Aventine on purpose. It took him up steep Clivus Scaurus to the summit of the exlcusive Caelian hill and so past the Domus Fabiii. However, his hope of bumping into Ambrosius proved to be vain. He was sure he heard a dog barking, surely the deep canine voice of Lossy? He even considered hammering on the grand front door, but thought better of it. Quintus expected a prompt report: "Everything you have ordered us to do will be done!" Rufio declaimed in a stern military tone. He raised his right arm and slapped his upper chest firmly in salute, grinning at passersby. A surly Quintus had sent him to check on Regulus after his transfer from the Ludus Magnus, now emptied of gladiators from all over Italy whose owners had been handsomely paid for their attendance at the Ludi Plebeii. There was the matter of adding the stamp of his signet ring to the agreement between them and the school, "and make sure Dolabella has housed him properly, like we agreed," Quintus had commanded. "I don't trust that man any farther than Cato could throw a stone."

"Don't put him to the test," Rufio retorted with a snort. "With his sling Cato can hurl a stone a very long way."

Harsh shouts of men rose above the dark coughs of large cats, screeches, bellows, snorts, and trumpeting of strange creatures—training sessions were well under way in Ludus Matutinus. "Why's it called Morning School?" he'd asked Quintus and received another lecture from newly acquired knowledge that the training school took its name from the word *morning*.

"Because that is the time of day when the *venatores*—the wild beast hunts—are scheduled in the arena." These, Quintus went on to say, often followed *bestiarii* events when prisoners condemned to death were sent into the arena armed with little more than blunted spears to face wild animals like African lions, packs of feral dogs, or half-starved bears. Rufio couldn't think of a nastier way to die than to be a ravenous lion's breakfast. So it was with some relief he passed through the outer entrance and into the restive calm of Ludus Gallicus.

Relative calm. He found the dull thudding of wooden weapons a trifle more comforting. It was more human than the alien sounds of wild animals. A short, narrow cobblestone passage ended at firmly closed and barred double doors, and the sounds of combat—slapping feet, human grunts of exertion, and the hard blows of practice swords and harsh obscenities of the doctore—came from the other side. There seemed nowhere else to go. As he puzzled about what to do, the sudden clatter of drawn bolts drew his eyes sharply to his right, where in the gloom under the barrel vault a small door appeared in the wall as if by magic. Drawn to the muted sounds of combat, he hadn't noticed it. He took two paces and reached out for the large ring set in the wood when it was suddenly flung back. Rufio's heart raced at the shock. It was all he could do to stifle the shriek of disgust which sprang up his throat as he recoiled from the horrible sight that greeted him.

"Who are you?" At the intrusion Theron did not even bother to look up from the tablet on which he was scratching out a solo game of *terni lapilli* as if it were a document of great import.

"Z-Zosimus, dominus," the young man stammered.

"Ah yes, The Survivor." Theron glanced up with a strained smile at his own pun on the clerk's name. "I'm told you are a clever snake when it comes to burying inconvenient fiscal matters under a forest of consolidated trust funds?" Zosimus gulped so his prominent Adam's apple bounced up and down in a manner Theron took as an affirmative. "Good. Take this…" he held out a well-worn scroll with several signatures scrawled on its margins. "It details some *gratiae principis* Caesar has made to some… some people of no apparent consequence. Obviously an oversight brought about by the eternal burdensome weight of government. Make it go away, bury it in some multi-layered escrow or a non-transferable financial instrument."

Zosimus took the scroll as if it were a poisonous serpent. "Dom-dominus… what should I do if any should come seeking its whereabouts?"

Theron flapped his hands as if it were no concern of his. "No one will, but should it occur, send them to see Callias at the *aerarium sanctum*. He can never remember anything he's received and can never find anything when he has."

T·H·I·R·T·E·E·N | XIII

25th day of November AD 108

In the open doorway stood an apparition which Rufio's horrified mind told him was the Terror of the Grotto come back from its watery grave under Capri. A weak light flowing around the grotesque figure revealed a different kind of monster. He started back and peered at a face that resembled a squashed turnip. Either side of a buckled bump in the middle were two dark holes staring back, not quite level as if a heavy hand had twisted the head out of alignment.

Rufio's first impression that he and the misshapen creature were of the same height was dispelled the instant the thing stepped down onto the cobbles. What Rufio first took for wiry vegetable roots stuck to the top of his crown turned out to be hair. When a slight breeze coming from the plaza caused the clumps to wave it only added to the creepiness. Gimlet eyes glared up. "Yes?"

Rufio swallowed down his fright and regained his breath. "I am an owner." He drew himself up to his full height, which made him one and a half heads taller than the ugly little leguminous fellow barring his way. "Um… I am Junius Tullius Rufio, Munerarius."

Turniphead rocked from side to side in an aggressive manner.

Remembering how Quintus did it, he spoke more firmly. "I'm here to see the gladiator, my good man. Gaius Regulus. He was transferred yesterday from over the road."

"You has to speak wiv the boss. The lanista," Turniphead added in case Rufio didn't understand, which would have been entirely possible given the creature's strangulated vowels. His voice sounded similar to the noise Rufio imagined cattle made stomping around in a greasy bog.

"Then… be so good as to show me the way to where I may speak to Dannotalus Dolabella."

"Got appointment?"

"No, I haven't, no need. My business partner, Caecilius Alba—" *always best to flatten 'em with a nobby patrician name,* "—will have informed your dominus to expect me."

"No appointment, no way in." More rocking.

It was a lawcourt day so Rufio decided to restrain his annoyance. A market day, oh that would have been different and this wretch stretched out on the cobbles, blood and brains leaking… "And from whom would I obtain this appointment?"

A nod of the disjointed head back at the gaping doorway. "Secerterry. In there."

Rufio reined in a desire to squash the rude fellow's face ever further. "But you said I can't go in there without an appointment, and if I have to go in there to get an appointment but I can't go in there without an appointment, how in the name of Neptune's niggardly numbnuts do I get one?"

"Conundrum, innit? Mebbe you should write?"

"Con-*un*-drum! Out of my way you half-witted cur, son of bi—"

"Are you Tullius?"

Rufio lowered his arm and glowered above the tufty, buckled and still rocking head at the powerful man who had appeared in the doorway just in time to prevent murder.

"Let the man pass, Rapa."

Rapa by name, *rapa* by appearance; Rufio walked around the turnip and the man above stepped back inside to allow him entry.

"I take it you are not the *secerterry*?"

A mirthless smile, more a thinning of the lips, greeted this sally. "Greetings, Tullius Rufio. I am Dolabella. It's just as well I heard what was going on."

"It certainly is. I was about to brain the dolt."

Dolabella continued as if he hadn't heard the threat. "Otherwise Rapa would have turned you into a bloody lump of ground beef. He has a temper on him."

Rufio just stared blankly at the man for a moment as the humor of the situation caught up with his disbelief. His face broke into a smile. "That paltry poltroon?"

"I assure you, Tullius, Rapa can convert a man three times his size into minced dogmeat in the space of a few breaths, as he has done on numerous occasions. In his time he was the most feared man in the arena. Don't let size—or ugliness—deceive you." He sighed. "Unfortunately he has this notion that he is the ludus doorman. Come."

Rufio stepped around Rapa, who turned on the spot so he could continue to glare threateningly, burbles of menace issuing from his twisted lips. Dolabella led the way through the dimly lit outer lobby to an arcade spanning one side of a training area that measured not a great deal more than the palaestra at the Baths of Nero. "You see we are limited for space, but it forces the gladiators into close proximity, a boon when it comes to a melee rather than one-on-one bouts. Your man Regulus is in the last-but-one cell on this wing." Dolabella pointed along the arcade at the far corner. "There are stairs at the end there down to the accommodation level."

"Have you put him though his paces yet?"

The humorless smile returned. "Regulus has done a hundred

push-ups and run rings, as we call it here… a hundred laps around the perimeter."

"That doesn't sound like much…?"

"When you're wearing the equivalent weight of four legionary kits on your shoulders, it's quite a lot. Weapons work will commence this afternoon. I know you are eager to be able to match him against some real opposition to begin making financial gains." He spread his arms in a helpless gesture. "After all, the cost of keeping your own gladiator at a ludus in Rome is not cheap. I have my own investment costs to cover after that thieving crow Gracchus of Capua overpriced his champion Bebryx on the transfer list."

Rufio changed the subject. He didn't fancy running into Bebryx. "My colleague Caecilius Alba said there was some paperwork to complete?"

Dolabella led the way to a narrow stairway set between ranges of storerooms. It came out onto a wide balcony overlooking the exercise yard. Seats scattered about for muneraria and their guests so that they might observe practice bouts were covered against the possibility of rain. To the other side more rooms ran along three sides of the yard, the fourth side closed off by the rising side of the base to the temple of Divine Claudius. Opposite the stairs to the left was the long armory behind its thick bars; to the other a long narrow room was evidently the lanista's place of work. Three small windows in the outer wall let in wintry light and gave a view of the towering Colosseum.

Dolabella weighted down a scroll and pointed at the base. "The wording is standard between the ludus…that's me in effect…and you as the muneraria, the top six paragraphs; all of us with the auctoratus, the last three. I am unclear as to his precise status. Volunteers are one of four types: social outcasts, men dispossessed by the state, bankrupts, or men on the run. Are you clear which?"

Rufio wasn't, but he avoided showing his lack of knowledge. "It doesn't matter. Regulus was recommended to us by no less than Scorpus of Rhodes."

Dolabella raised an eyebrow and seemed to accept this as a satisfactory answer. He waved a hand at the scroll. "His clauses are the usual: the minumum and maximum number of fights in any month, the quality and frequency of food, his style of fighting, murmillo I think, his level of burial club contributions and the tax levied on those, plus your indemnity in the case of his death in a contest at the express order of the Emperor. Oh and the penalties for his breaking the contract: burning, shackling, whipping with rods, killing with steel, the usual."

"What's this?" Rufio pointed to a third wax seal beside that of Quintus and Dolabella.

"As I understand you lack the funds, he is standing in as your guarantor for payments to the ludus." He scrutinized Rufio through narrowed eyes. "You knew of this?"

"Of course." *What the fuck is* Uncle *Livy doing in on this?*

After appending his own seal to the contract, Rufio was still pondering on that and why Quintus had not told him while descending two flights to the lowest level where the cells were like a honeycomb under the palaestra and upper floors of the ludus.

He found Regulus slumped back on a rush bed, forearm covering his eyes. At the sound of Rufio's footfall, he lowered the arm enough to squint over it at the unbarred doorway. Meager daylight entered the cell down a cunningly placed chute that must somehow pierce through the ceilings and floors above to add to the flickering torches on the hallway outside.

"Ah, dominus Rufio." He sat up easily. "The accommodation is not as luxurious as the Ludus Magnus."

"What do you know about Bebryx?"

The question took Regulus aback. He leaned against the wall, almost insolently.

"He's a hairy-assed barbarian with a short temper, pretty much like nearly everyone in this place. Why? What else is it you would like to know?"

"Is he… a trouble-maker?"

Regulus shrugged.

"I ran into him, literally, in the cryptoporticus one of the last days of the Plebeian Games and mentioned your name to explain my presence."

"Why should a slave question you?"

Rufio wondered at the tone and delivery of this telling little question—not surprise at a slave's effrontery but anger; surely the reaction of one used to seeing himself in a much higher station of society? It raised the question of which section of Rome's social strata Regulus really came from. Dolabella's words came back: social outcast, dispossessed, bankrupt, or on the run? He put it aside for the moment. "He mistook me for someone else, and my motives for being there. It doesn't matter. I can report to my colleague that you are here and… well, as comfortable as it's ever likely to be."

Regulus regarded Rufio with a level gaze as he spoke. "Colleague? Forgive me dominus, but I thought I detected something more… intimate? Between you."

"What's that to you?" Rufio snapped, instantly regretting giving away more with the retort than he would have liked.

Regulus dropped his eyes. "Apologies, dominus Rufio. It's just that in a world of such strife it is enjoyable to encounter consistency of fellowship. It gives one a sense of comfort."

Rufio stared at his property, trying to fathom what it was Regulus was after. Slumped he might be, but cowed he was not as was evident from his calling him *Dominus Rufio* in so familiar manner instead of simply *dominus*—like it was a taunt. And in his very pitiable repose there was an underlying coyness that amounted to flirting. It didn't normally trouble Rufio that he often saw what aroused Quintus, or vice versa. They had become used to sharing sexual escapades, and by the penetrating prick of Priapus he would as happily fuck with the handsome Regulus as any he could recall, relish making all those hard-edged muscles, magnificent in their grimy oiliness, melt before the rage of his sexual heat… and yet in this case he found it disturbing.

"Comfort!" He made the word as razor sharp as the gladiator's flexing sinews, no longer relaxed on the straw paliasse. "We don't need you to be comfortable, Regulus. We need action and victory. And you don't fool me with fluttering lashes. I know you are working some magic on Quintus. Be sure it is not evil. Speaking of which, has anyone approached you with… blandishments, promises of assured future victory? Anything along the lines Bebryx seems to think commonplace within the profession?"

The eyes came back up in a flash. For a heartbeat the look was guarded, as if he'd caught Regulus out in a lie, and then the expression softened into an innocent smile. "I don't know to what you refer, dominus. No person has made any approach to me about a thing, except…" he shrugged, "…weapons practice after our meager lunch. And, speaking of which, the other day you mentioned some better armor for me to appear in."

There was a touch of steel in the reminder.

"That's for Quintus to arrange." As he turned to leave, Rufio added, "I told the lanista to give you freedom on those days when most gladiators gather at the Velia end of the Colosseum to flirt with all those sighing maidens flocking to the Meta Sudans."

Rugulus rocked up to his knees in a suitably deferential position, but there was nothing ingratiating in his attitude. "I am deeply gratified, dominus, though I assure you, I have no need of a marble cone suggestively sweating water to arouse me to my duty."

As Rufio departed, his last impression was of dark eyes looking up from below lowered lashes and ferociously hooked brows offset by the faintest hint of a smile on full lips.

Another pair of eyes followed Rufio's progress along the arcade to the exit. Bebryx recalled the shock of red hair as it alternately glowed and dimmed in the passage behind the peristyle columns.

He was too busy engaged in fending blows from two hoplomachi to go after the scheming bastard who did the dirty work of the fixers, but if he had appeared here now, surely he would again. And then he would answer to Bebryx the Scythian...

The artisan who long ago painted the crude figure of a soldier in arms had tried bravely for what was once the popular impression of an ancient Etruscan warrior. Hard to make out now because the Rex Etruscorum's sign faded years ago to a gray wash some considered tasteful and others plain worn out. It swung above the door that opened onto the small three-sided space where Vicus Platononis crossed two other streets. This was the heart of Aventine Major, the center of Rome's 13th Region. Against the bar's street wall facing the triangular square a deep niche housed the shrine to the local Lares, the divine spirits and protectors of the neighborhood community.

King of Etruria was headquarters to the West Aventine Crossroads Club, guardians of the shrine and the district, and home to its patron, the redoubtable Clivius Ostiensis. Many in authority regarded him as little more than a gangster, controlling the protection racket into which every local business paid. While everyone from senators to slaves was welcome to pay their respects to the Lares, few were allowed within the precincts of the bar without invitation or a good business offer to Clivius or to make payments to his accountant Decimus. But after the business with Malpensa† Clivius had granted Rufio and Quintus honorary membership and the bar made a useful neutral meeting ground without the baggage of parental interference. It was also home to Felix, for Clivius was Woof-Woof's dad.

Crossroads brethren—a lot of them legionary veterans and in reality enforcers—crowded the bar along with those granted the right of a drink after paying up their monthly dues. Clivius Ostiensus sat in a corner near the back with Decimus while Rufio—just back up the hill from his visit to the Ludus Gallicus—and Quintus were in a huddle with Felix on stools nearer the front of the bar.

"Your wicked uncle's acting as guarantor." Rufio was aggrieved. "Why didn't I know and anyway, isn't the niggardly nugget of numbscullery broke?"

"Skullduggery."

"What?"

"It's what you meant," Quintus replied patiently. "I've no idea what numbscullery is and besides, alliteration doesn't become you."

"Your poetry must have rubbed off on me."

Quintus huffed. "I don't do alliteration."

"You uncle?" Refio returned to the point.

"He ambushed me outside the house the other day—after I'd left you at the Emporium—when I was on my way to see Regulus moved. He went out of his way to harangue me on the need for ready sums to pay Dolabella for housing at the Ludus Gallicus. I didn't need his lecture—"

"Pot and kettle have any meaning?"

"Stuff it. Anyway, he'd discovered the source of our finance and—"

"How?"

"Something about having been to school with Athenos, Trajan's chamberlain, old school *bulla* and all that."

"It leaked."

Felix placed a hand on Rufio's arm. "It would have come out eventually, surely? After all, there were a lot of us present at the Emporium when Caesar made the grant to you both."

Rufio sniffed in irritation. "Suppose so. At least it's good to hear it wasn't any of our lot leaked it. Not that it was a real secret, just that when you hit big winnings like that you don't need every Titus, Decimus and Herennius begging on your arm."

Felix hastily removed his hand.

"I didn't mean you. You know you're almost part of the family." He glanced back at Quintus. "Pity we didn't know just how slowly the wheels of bureaucracy work on the Palatine."

"That was Livy's real point, that we might still be waiting an age.

Says he knows how these things up there. So it seemed like a good moment to ask him about a loan to tide us over. You're right, of course, he hasn't two asses to scrape together these days, but he said he could easily persuade someone to help out for a modest interest rate of ten percentum per annum."

"Outrageous!" Rufio glared at both his friends.

"In the meantime, he said, he would act as guarantor until he was able to arrange a deal with this person. He said Dolabella would accept it because he and Livy have done business before and because anyway it would only be for a few market days."

"So who is this generous patron of us newly rich but unable to lay their hands on our assets?"

Quintus paused, chewing his lower lip. When he looked up at Rufio it was in expectation of an explosion. "Publius Fabius Virius."

Rufio fell back against Felix, doubled up, choking with laughter. "Oh Quintus," he started, trying to recover his breath, "you really missed your true vocation as a comedian."

"He was serious," Quintus said in a stiff voice. He straightened his posture into an oratorical pose.

"Well *we* can't be, hoo…" Rufio wiped tears from his eyes. "The man is worse than a blood-sucking swamp-rat. Besides, didn't he end up out of pocket like Livius when your uncle's plan for you to fuck Trajan went wrong?"

"Don't be coarse. I don't know what his situation was or is. Obviously since the Caecilli and the Fabii are serious rivals I can't like him but I can take his money—"

"At ten percentum?" Felix broke in. "What happens if the treasury officials take too long in activating Caesar's bequest? You'll be ruined before your Regulus even makes his first kill and earns you anything on prize money or successful bets. What about my father?"

"What?" Quintus and Rufio exclaimed at the same time.

Felix waved a hand behind him at where the wiry accountant, hunched over his books, was in deep conversation with his boss.

"I'm sure he won't charge that huge rate of interest. After all, he owes you both a lot."

"Maybe, but I can't imagine after that business with Malpensa and his army of gladiators trying to take over the Crossroads Clubs' business affairs he would have a hard-on for anyone investing in a… gladiator." Rufio opened his arms to emphasize the hoplesness of such a request.

"You're wrong there. He and Bestia and Copertius, you know, heads of the Quirinal and Velabrum brethren, have been in talks about getting into the games business, but the *Munus gladiatorum mundi foederatio* won't even deign to answer their application."

"I'm not surprised," Rufio interjected. "That bunch is run by stuck-up magistartes, senators, and former consuls. They wouldn't let a gang of crim— er, businessmen like your dad and his mates become muneraria. Lanistas maybe, but not respected troupe owners."

"But Quintus is a senator's son and a patrician of ancient lineage," Felix pointed out. You would be an ideal front, Quintus."

"Front!" said a clearly affronted Quintus. "I thought we were going into this on our own. I'm beginning to regret ever listening to that idiot jockey boy Scorpus."

"Didn't mind fucking him, though." Rufio sniggered at Quintus's sudden discomposure. "Have you had Regulus yet?"

"Mind your own business."

"So that means you have, and if you don't mind, it actually is my own business. Oh, lighten up you Caecilian cock-hound. I don't mind what you two get up to," Rufio added in a voice that suggested he did. "We'll still be our own bosses."

"And call the shots," Felix said enthusiastically.

"You ask him, though." Rufio glanced uneasily over his shoulder at Clivius who was in the process of pinning a man to the tabletop by his throat. "He can be a bit scary."

"Leave it to me. After all, one day I am going to act for him in the courts as his lawyer and it's a diplomat's skill that wins cases."

He smiled bravely. A slight figure about to take up arms. With a brief wave, he set off to weave a route between rowdy racketeers toward where Clivius was letting the chastened debtor to his feet. He gave the man an encouraging pat on the cheek. Quintus had to sway back on his stool out of the man's path as he fled past their table, the expression plastered on his face of a convict given unexpected remission from his sins escaping the lions' jaws.

F·O·U·R·T·E·E·N | XIV

Kalends (1st) and 2nd days of December AD 108

All three seemed unusually subdued. Trajan regarded the handsome boys through eyes narrowed with puzzlement. So different to each other and yet in their unique ways normally so close… certainly they were among the most delectable of his stable of regular sex partners. It was always a delight to loosen up the stiff patrician attitudes of Quintus while reining in the unbridled lustiness of Rufio and bringing them both to a mutual and tumultuous climax. Usually. This afternoon he noted an edginess to their conversation and the tension between the friends had cast a pall over proceedings. Yes, he had ridden them in turn as his "chariot steeds" after a languorous warm-up of entangled limbs, taut in their youth, eager to please, and yet somehow a bit quiet, particularly Rufio.

Trajan leapt to his feet and strode across the wide expanse of rug-covered marble floor with a lithe athleticism that belied his fifty-five years. He stood beside a glass window and looked down three floors into the deep-set peristyle garden at the center of the Domus Augustana. At repose he actually resembled the statue that had been sent recently to every quarter of the Imperium, except that showed him garbed as Imperator, resplendent in a triumphing general's ceremonial armor, while now he was splendidly naked. "I find it easy to relax with you two rascals. There are few with who I can be off guard, with who I may discuss subjects an ocean away from politics."

Rufio rolled onto his stomach and arched his back in a feline manner so his firm ass humped up off the bed cheekily. "We aim to please, Caesar."

"What would please you to discuss, Caesar?" Quintus asked with a faint smile—really his first of the day.

"You can start by telling me what ails my Firehound and my Mars." He enjoyed the flinch Quintus failed to repress at the reference to his role as the God of War in a pageant created to please Prince Obodas of Nabataea that Trajan had forced him into. To an adolescent patrician—a prickly species at the best of times—acting was for the lowest of low-lifes—*infames*, but Quintus had acquitted himself well despite driving the choreographer Sponsus Terpsichorus to professional suicide.

"He's getting married." Rufio's voice carried in a flat tone. He raised and lowered a leg like a signals officer semaphoring a different message.

Trajan swept up a light tunic from a couch on the way back to the bed. He sat between Rufio and Quintus, who was perched uneasily on the edge of the huge bed. "Congratulations! Do I know the lady?"

"Vipsania, daughter of, Numerius Metellus," said Rufio.

"Ah, my *praefectus annonae*. A good match."

"Yes, Caesar," Quintus admitted without much enthusiasm.

"And this is what is eating the two of you?"

The sighs came at the same time.

"No."

"Yes."

"No, Rufio?" Trajan reached out and fetched the nearest ass cheek a good slap, leaving behind a red handprint.

"Ow! Well…" He turned over and sat up. "Of course I'd prefer it if Quintus wasn't marrying—"

"Cramp your style?" Trajan grinned meanly and turned to Quintus. "And what does the prospective bridegroom have to say?"

Quintus shrugged. "I don't have a choice. She came to that reading at the Curia of Pompey, but I couldn't see anything under that veil, so I still have no idea what she looks like. May resemble the back end of a plaustrum for all I know."

"It won't matter. Marriage is sacred. You'll make it work. So that's the reason for the long faces, is it?"

Quintus nodded and after a moment so did Rufio, but he shuffled uncomfortably. Trajan sensed there was more to it, at least as far as Rufio was concerned, something neither was saying. When they were dismissed and made to leave after dressing Trajan signaled Rufio to remain. "I want you to take Lady Junilla a message."

He watched Quintus pass through the tall double doors held open by the two Batavians who had been on bodyguard duty outside, and wondered what the Emperor wanted of his mother.

When they were alone Trajan pressed him. "There's no message, I just wanted a moment alone with you. I understand that marriage signals a change in life—Divine Augustus made it patrician and equestrian duty to produce many offspring—but many are married and still follow where their natural instincts lead. There's more to the tension I sense between you and Quintus than an impending wedding. I'll have the truth now."

And Rufio poured out his heart. He told Trajan about Regulus and that—to his utter consternation, given his usually carefree attitude to life and sex—he couldn't help being jealous of the gladiator or fearful that Quintus was being led astray. He talked for a long while, so much so that it came home just how much Quintus had come to be a part of his life, his very being. He even admitted that his growing suspicion that Regulus was not what he claimed to be might be a reflection of his jealousy.

When the words dried up, Trajan stroked his chin thoughtfully, the other hand resting lightly on Rufio's shoulder. "What lies between you and Quintus must stay with you. Even if I had a magic solution, it would be unwise to intervene, and let's face it, a Caesar may order his senators and knights to engage in marital relations for the procreation of the Imperium, but even an emperor cannot tell a man where to express his emotional love. However, if your fears for the wellbeing of Quintus are well founded there is a way for this young man to prove himself worthy or to show that he harbors an alternative motive for being a gladiator. Surely his real intentions will be revealed when he finally faces an opponent in the arena with sharpened blades. You may be aware that Sanatruces, the King of Osrhoene and Armenia is a guest in the palace and I have promised him some entertainment in a few days. It will be a small gathering at the Ludus Magnus to watch some fights. We shall command your Gaius Regulus to show his colors and fight. From what you tell me of his progress and build Thraxus should be a good match."

Gods alive! Quintus will be horrified! Is Regulus ready for a real battle?

Rufio did not voice his alarm, though unworthily, considering what he'd just heard, he wondered whether now was a good time to bring up those talents of gold and when might they be likely to lay hands on it all. And then the warning Flaccus had uttered gave him cause to swallow the query. The funds would come in their own good time, meanwhile they would have to bite tongues and bow before vile Virius… unless Felix and his father came through.

He bowed to take his leave, thanking Trajan for his kindness.

"Did I say those fights will be to the death? No half measures. That should rattle any snakes from the rushes. Athenos will make arrangements. Farewell Rufio, until next time."

Hiding in plain sight wasn't a tactic Ursus understood but he had received a message on the kalends from Bebryx suggesting they should accidentally bump into each other on the following day amid the crowds gathered around the Meta Sudans. Parading muscled thighs, arms, bulging ceremonial loincloths and little else, gladiators on day-release from all four schools mingled with gaily chattering young women, all employing their own tactics to lose their chaperones or push aside the older matrons hoping for a wicked liaison with a handsome hunk of swordsman. In a complex interchange of coyness and lewdness the erotic dance swirled around the circular pool, inspired by the massive conical phallus of the Sweating Fountain. Its marbled form oozed water from small orifices up and down its length that glistened in the wintry sunlight like male pre-cum cascading down its slick sides.

Stripped of revealing armor, few could spot an individual gladiator's fighting style and it was beside the point anyway when what was on everyone's mind was to get laid before the day's end. Young warriors from every corner of the Imperium relaxed in multicultural nonchalance against the fountain's low parapet or practiced crouches, squats, push-ups, hip flexors, leg presses, and other assorted exercises to show off their assets… and asses.

Amid this scrimmage of lust and laughter, Bebryx was just another gladiator, albeit one many women present were willing to swoon over. They kept their distance however when the dark presence of Ursus swaggered through the crowd.

"I know I said we should bump into each other but there's no need to collide with me, you great oaf."

"Luff you too," Ursus growled.

"Don't make it obvious you're talking to me," Bebryx hissed from the side of his mouth. He guided the Ludus Magnus under-lanista over to the rim of the basin and casually perched there. "What have you got for me?"

Ursus grunted.

"I didn't get that."

"You said not to be obvious."

"Nor obscure, damn your hairy hide."

"The man you seek is even now in the Ludus Gallicus. Not the one approached the auctoratus Regulus before in the Magnus, another who speaks now with Dolabella."

"With a pile of red hair?"

Ursus pushed some of his own haystack from his eyes and blinked in confusion. "Red? No. Very dark and short. Important man. Deals with Bulbus from time to time and Dolabella I know, maybe many others. Only man I ever know makes Bulbus nervous."

Bebryx whistled softly between his teeth and wondered what kind of man could make Bulbus quake. "Who is he?" He was annoyed it wasn't the copper-topped prick he'd run into before the last Colosseum fight, the one he'd seen sneaking away from the Ludus Gallicus, no doubt after offering Regulus bribes or some such. That cocky fucker needed taking down a peg or two, pretending he hadn't had a clue as to who Bebryx was. His time would come soon and it wouldn't be a pleasant end for a petty criminal who brought the noble profession into disrepute.

"This one's bad," Ursus grunted from the corner of lips concealed behind a ratty mustache that resembled two spurs of a hairy waterfall. "Not the usual piss-ant fixer with a hand-out for the lanista and a prostitute bribe for the owner."

"Who?" Bebryx snapped, forgetting his own insistence on not attracting attention.

"Ever heard of Panthera?"

He stiffened at the name.

Bebryx and Ursus were too involved in not being seen to be talking to each other that they never noticed two others trying hard to blend in with the swirling sex circus around them. Closer observation would have revealed Regulus making pretty eyes at a modestly dressed maiden who played the coquette rather well. Even closer and an eavesdropper might have made out that their exchanged sweet-nothings were exactly that: nothing. Nothing at least to do with amorous intentions… and was there a family resemblance?

It seemed that finally the young gladiator overstepped the virginal girl's boundaries. She delivered to his cheek a resounding slap and flounced off in a high dudgeon. Had Bebryx wandered around the circumference of the Meta Sudans at the right moment, he might have seen a suppressed smile suffuse the reddened cheek of the tyro. But Bebryx was headed off across the plaza toward the Ludus Gallicus with the stride of a man on a mission, so he never saw Regulus turn and come across from the other side of the Sweaty Turning Point to follow in his footsteps, neither of them knowing the other had concluded a secret rendezvous.

Bebryx was first to be checked in through the part-opened double doors to the ludus training yard. The two heavily armed security guards were surly by profession as Salutis Procuratio, the security firm Dolabella preferred to employ, boasted. Bebryx ignored their muttered taunts and lewd smiles, suggestions that he hadn't returned with a whore for fun, and walked purposefully down the long arcade to the stairway leading to the upper levels. At the top another two guards barred his way, suddenly drawn swords crossed.

"Back down, Bebryx," the taller of the two snarled. "You know you're not permitted up here without the dominus sending for you."

"He has a visitor I need to speak with." It was a try and Bebryx knew it wouldn't wash. He attempted to peer between the guards at the long office, hoping to catch sight, however brief a glimpse, of the face or profile of the man Panthera. Nothing.

"Down the steps!"

He nodded, and turned to descend the narrow stairway. He had taken but a step when the rectangle of light at the bottom darkened momentarily as someone walking along the arcade passed by the stairs. Bebryx slipped quietly down and peered around the corner of the wall at the bottom in time to see the youth reach the lower stairs to the cells. It was the tyro Regulus. But instead of going on down, the boy started back as if someone out of Bebryx's sight had confronted him at the top of the steps. The big Scythian could move silently as a cat when he needed. He slipped outside the boy's line of vision behind the line of arcade columns and pulled up behind the last between him and where Regulus stood at the top of the steps down to the subterranean level, still in a pose of wariness. Bebryx caught the exchange of words.

"Who are you?"

"Hush, boy. I am the Other."

Regulus stepped back a pace from whoever was confronting him, which drew the man out just enough for Bebryx to see him.

"I— I was told to expect you," he heard Regulus say in a hushed voice.

"Were you." It wasn't a question. The stranger was certain of his standing.

"There was a man told me—"

"I know. Take me to your cell."

"Dolabella doesn't allow strangers."

"Hah! Don't concern yourself about about Dolabella. I just informed him of my intention to speak with you, boy."

Bebryx's eyes widened. He had been ensconced with Dolabella, just as Ursus claimed. So this was the man who made even Mumius Bulbus nervous. Panthera—obviously not his real name—looked to be in his late thirties, no spring chicken, but he exuded a feline grace that promised a stygian cavern of horrors for any who fell foul of his wishes. Nothing a trained gladiator should fear, but

Bebryx knew that not every battle was won by virtue of physical prowess. The brethren of the arena fought for the honor of it, the time-wreathed battle of like souls; then there were those who killed without compunction, without warning, for no better reason than the sheer enjoyment of ending another's life. This Panthera exuded a quietly commanding air, the brooding sense of the coiled torsion spring of a ballista; he smiled, but his eyes were cold bullets of pain.

Regulus followed the man down, the voices faded. Bebryx stepped back under the peristyle arcade and quietly followed. He had every right to be abroad in the lower hallways so his presence, should he be discovered, would not arouse suspicion. A moment's stealth brought him close enough to catch the conversation from the cell.

"That's very generous of you, dominus," Regulus was saying, "but I cannot… my honor?"

By his tone, Bebryx imagined Regulus with his head stretched forward and tilted up earnestly. His interlocutor was not having any of it.

"Honor?" Panthera made it sound like a dirty word. Bebryx bridled. "You are an *infame*, a nothing, a boy from the gutter with, I grant you, guts and skill, but if you ever wish to progress, to earn your way back to freedom you woul do well to heed my words… and take the offer. Do well at the start and then you must throw the fight."

"Which fight? No one said anything about a fight yet."

Was that eagerness or fear in the boy's voice? Bebryx could not tell; in his experience both emotions often sounded the same.

"The Ides of January. Octavius Vindex craves the rank of praetor for Ostia next year and is prepared to show how well he can put on games should he persuade the common mass to vote for him. Dolabella has the time to get you prepared to put up a convincing match."

There was a long pause, and then the boy's voice came low, uncertain. "How will I know that I will not be…"

"Killed? Your opponent will be chosen as one less skilled and sure to lose. One thing is certain, however. Refuse to cooperate and you will meet a sticky end. Do as I bid and great wealth will one day be yours. We look after our own. Well? Your answer."

Bebryx was bursting to break up this corrupt meeting. He even wanted to throw his arm of protection around the novicus, so angry was he at what was being proposed: carefully leak the chosen opponent's poorer form and let his lack of appeal persuade many spectators to stake everything on Regulus winning. But in the arranged outcome only the selected stake-takers in the know would benefit, as well as those bankers whose minions handled many thousands of sesterces in bets—and all bankers were cheats. It took all his willpower to refrain from shoving his way in and beating the shit to a pulp… that and an underlying fear he hated admitting to. A gladiator attacking a citizen was a capital offense, and this Panthera oozed a confidence born of wealth, priviledge, and something far more sinister—a power based on having control over life and death.

He consoled himself with the realization that no good would come of his intervention, not if the lanista was in on the business as well. He would have to bide his time. Perhaps he could inspire a second Spartacan revolt?

"It's all very well, dominus," Regulus was saying, "but what of my patrons?"

"Say nothing. It is better for all that neither side of the equation speaks of these matters."

"You mean they are in your sway?"

Regulus sounded as disappointed as Bebryx felt exonerated. His suspicion of that redheaded sneak was proved correct.

"As I say, it's not your concern. They are taken care of. Do we have a deal? You really have no choice, Gaius Regulus."

Regulus dropped his voice in reply, but Bebryx caught the tone of aquiescence.

Pancratius wrung his hands in frustration and worry. "What in the name of Juno Moneta is the request doing here at the *aerarium sanctium*?" he shouted at old man seated behind a mound of scrolls. Callias was so ancient he could tell those conned into listening to him every detail of working for Pallas, the financial secretary to the Emperor Claudius, while instantly forgetting the reason why the eager-to-escape unfortunate had come to see him.

"Oh dear... I'm sure I've seen this, but... Let me look into it for you."

"I have Athenos on my back. Caesar has been chasing up progress. If I don't sort this out, we'll all be for the silver mines in some blasted place like... like Sarmizegethusa."

Callias glanced up in rheumy-eyed horror. "Where in Hades is that? I can't even pronounce it."

"How much silver do you expect us to put up, hey?" Bestia asked in an aggressive tone. The bossman of the Quirinal Crossroads jerked his head at Copertius of the Velabrum brotherhood, looking for support. "We'd need a silver mine of our own to match what those fuckwit, upper-class tits spend on winning. I passed the notion by my main patron, Agrippa Menenius Lanatus, and he just looked at me like I had taken leave of my senses."

"It's a good idea, though," Copertius said

Testa who ran the Crossroads Club on the Viminal nodded his head in agreement. "S'not like it's all that much up front, Bestia. And we've all had ideas on breaking into the games."

"Look at them," Rufio said under cover of his hand so Bestia's deaf sidekick couldn't read his lips. "Jealous as green-eyed maidens fighting over a spare cock when it comes to protecting their territorial rackets."

"Which way's it going?" Quintus wondered aloud.

"My father's pressing hard, and the Aventine's promised more silver for the kitty than any of the others," Felix threw in. "It'll be all right and you will be able to stick a finger up to your uncle."

"Ugh!" Quintus screwed up his face in disgust. Rufio almost burst out laughing at the expression that disfigured his friend's handsome face. "I wouldn't even want to despoil my spatha sticking that up his ass, thank you Felix!"

The three boys fell silent, watching the men at the table in the corner always reserved for Clivius. Low growly mutterings erupted now and then mounting occasionally to throaty outbursts. It was like watching dogs unsure whether they should have agreed to share a juicy bone. In spite of the time of year, thanks to the crowd of lieutenants and soldiers attending their Crossroads Club bosses, the King of Etruria's backroom was hot and humid.

The hour-candle Quintus was observing had burned through two rings before Clivius approached through the haze of alcohol and lamp smoke to say: "It's yours, lads: a bridging loan at two percentum per annum. Money up front in your hands tonight. Can't say fairer than that, and in return you sign your gladiator lad to our consortium in a private agreement so you still appear on the register as his muneraria. After that... well, I doubt there'll be much trouble recruiting a stable of lanistas and fighters. There are so many unhappy at the way the F·G·O·T lords it over everyone."

"Won't there be trouble with the fixer rings?" Rufio asked.

"Hah! Sure to be. They have their thugs, I'll be bound, but not as many as us lot can gather together. I bet you haven't forgotten the punishment we handed out to that Malpensa asshole, after all, you was right in the thick of it. Oh, and there's another condition. When he's done his studies, you hire Felix as your advocatus for the games' side of things. Problem with that?"

"None," said Rufio happily.

Felix grinned back so much his broken incisor gleamed.

"I can't wait to tell dear Uncle Livy," Quintus said with a laugh, one of the first he'd given for some time.

"And we can both go to the Ludus Gallicus," Rufio crowed, "and tell Dolabella to redraw the contract to get Livy's seal off the document as guarantor. Hahaha!"

3rd to 6th days of December AD 108

Blades rang in the close confines of the ludus exercise yard and echoed from the rock wall forming the base of Divine Claudius's temple. The sound of combat reached easily to the upper floor of the ludus where Quintus and Rufio were closeted with Dannotalus Dolabella. If the lanista was surprised at the alteration the muneraria wanted to the contract he showed no expression of it. If anything, he appeared happy to remove the seal of Livius Caecilius Dio when Quintus presented him with a leather bag bulging with coins, each one a gold aureus. They, however, were surprised at what he told them when Quintus remarked on the unusual fact of Regulus sparring with real weapons rather than blunted or wooden swords. At least they both looked shocked, but inwardly Rufio felt pretty bad.

"My apologies." Dolabella sketched a contrite bow, more a slight dip of his chin. "You were both so eager to make contractual changes, it quite slipped my mind to let you know of the greatest possible honor. A big surprise, but word was brought before dawn this morning that Caesar has commanded the presence of your Regulus to confront Thraxus."

"What!" Quintus almost staggered as he took in the words. "But… but he's barely begun serious training. He's still a novicus. When?"

"On the 5th day—"

"Of this month? That's in two days!" He turned to Rufio with a helpless expression.

After a quick swallow, Rufio tried an appeal to patrician duty. "It *is* a great honor, Quintus, to be asked to celebrate the visit of King Sanatruces of Oshroene and Armenia—"

"How do you know that?" Quintus snapped out. His narrowed eyes registered a sudden suspicion. "I haven't heard anything about a state visit."

"As I understand, it is a private, informal visit," said Dolabella.

"I suppose," Quintus conceded. "The Parthians are rumored to have spies everywhere and with trouble brewing in Mesopotamia again…" he trailed off.

"It is the first visit of an Armenian king since his predecessor Tiridates came to Rome to salute Nero," Dolabella stated flatly, as if it might mollify Quintus.

It failed to do that, as Rufio could have told Dolabella. Quintus preferred to deliver historical homilies, not to be in receipt of them. He turned on Rufio. "If there was no fanfare how did you know?"

Rufio cast his eyes down and shuffled uncomfortably. "Trajan told me," he whispered for Quintus's ears alone.

"When we were there… after I left you?"

"Yes. Sorry. Should have said something, but…"

Quintus glared angrily for a moment and then straightend his shoulders, swinging round to Dolabella. "Well, I suppose a private exhibition match before foreign royalty and at the Emperor's command would be a good experience for Regulus."

"It would be rude, not to say possibly treasonous, to refuse." Dolabella smiled wolfishly. "And that's why I had them out with real weapons the moment the imperial page from the office of Athenos departed." The lanista gazed at Quintus with the fascination of one imparting sensational news and eager to see the reaction it caused. "It will be *sine missione*."

"What's that mean?" Rufio asked anxiously on catching Quintus's bleak expression of shock.

"To the death." Quintus scowled sourly at Dolabella. Tipping his head at Rufio, he added, "He doesn't know the ins and outs of the noble game." Quintus did not sound as if he thought there were anything noble about what was in store for Regulus.

"When did you hear about this?" The Banker's normally expressionless face almost gave away his inner anger. It fascinated Virius to see the gnomic man disconcerted. He quickly recovered his composure and nodded to Luscinus. "Continue."

"I came immediately here from Ludus Gallicus the moment Dolabella informed me of the imperial command bout. I knew of no planned games, or indeed of the somewhat secretive arrival of this Oshroenian client-king."

"Is it coincidence that Regulus has been selected, and what can you tell us about… Thraxus is it?"

"They are both tyros, well matched I'd say. As for coincidence, I find people who believe in them often die because of them."

"I agree. We must protect our investment in Regulus," the Banker said with finality.

It was the turn of Luscinus to look uneasy. "I counsel against interfering with a fight decreed by imperial fiat, my friends." He looked around at the Banker, at Virius and Papus.

The last two nodded faint agreement. "Far too risky," Papus said. "It would smack of treason."

"And this comes on top of what Fabius Virius has just informed me before you came in," the Banker continued. "The nephew of his friend Caecilius Dio—"

"I insist, Banker, Livius is no friend of mine. A barely tolerated associate at best, and unfortunately an incompetent to boot."

"Very well!" the Banker snapped. He failed to repress another slight slip of his perennial mask of assumed indifference. "It appears that our efforts through Dio to ensnare his nephew Caecilius Alba and his associate Tullius Rufio by placing them in our debt has run into an unexpected hitch."

"And the relevance of these 'interfering' young men?" Papus said in a cool voice.

"They have become joint patrons to Regulus."

"I didn't know about this." Papus gave his Summa colleagues an affronted look. "Why would they take on the onerous role of muneraria without adequate funds? I presume that to be the case since you mention 'ensnaring' them."

Virius waved the blade of his right hand edgeways as if dismissing the matter. "Dio, as the patrician boy's uncle—the other isn't even of equestrian rank—uncovered an interesting nugget. Apparently, for services rendered to Caesar—don't ask—he had awarded each boy a substantial award in gold and for some reason known only to the unformed, puerile mind, they decided to invest it in a gladiator... Regulus."

"But as we all know," the Banker broke in, "the wheels of Palatine bureaucracy grind exceeding slow, so those two have fallen into arrears for many costs including ludus housing, food, weapons training, you name it. In addition, as an auctoratus Regulus is entitled to payment from his owners. I'm not sure these callow youths knew that."

"Regulus is a promising talent who may be used in the future both as a winner and as a loser when required," Luscinus added. "But I have yet to hear as to what the 'hitch' might be."

Ignoring Luscinus, Papus gave the Banker an understanding nod. "Do you have people inside the fiscal departments who can be persuaded to slow payment even further?"

The Banker allowed himself a rare phlegmy laugh, though the merriment never reached his bloodless lips or his eyes. "Is the Emperor a Roman? Don't worry. Those stylus scratchers will bury it. It's natural for exchequer freedmen to hang onto every coin they can. The gift will be dropped into a clerical hole and forgotten. That is not the hitch of which I spoke." His piercing gaze roved from Luscinus to settle enquiringly on Virius.

"Thanks to funds supplied by our friend," Virius indicated the Banker, "I provided the wherewithal for Dio to offer his credentials to Dolabella as guarantor to the boys, the first hook into their future loyalty to our cause." He spoke past Papus to address Luscinus directly. "I learned earlier from the lanista that Quintus and Rufio overturned that by providing all the coin required to house Regulus at the Ludus Gallicus for the foreseeable future—capital they did not possess the day before. And that's the hitch."

"And from where did these mysterious funds materialize?"

"I made haste to confront Livius, but the idiot had no clue other than to confirm that Caesar's gift has yet to be given."

"I've had my ear to the floor and made a few delicate inquiries," the Banker said. "Mutterings in the dawn light fluttering around the basilica at the start of business suggest new assets are being pressed to float on the market. As Fabricius Luscinus has made us aware in the recent past, several Crossroads Clubs have wanted to 'invest' in the games. For 'invest' read 'muscle in on' the business side of all the Imperium's *ludi*. To this point the *Foedus gladiatorum orbis terrarium* has rejected any official application. Sensibly, the governing body considers that those people are nothing more than common criminals, though rarely with a common cause…"

"But something's occurred to bring about a change?" Luscinus said with a suddenly enlightened tone and expression, one which quickly hardened to anger. "You suspect one or more clubs have ganged up and are using the patrician Caecilius Alba as a respectable front? Yes, that makes sense, backing him and his pleb friend. If true, this is disturbing news."

"You have the means to confirm the suspicion?"

Luscinus pondered the question a moment. "Yes," he replied, drawing out the word. "Yes, I should be able to discover what's going on. And if what you suspect is proven, it won't be good news for some young patrons who fancy themselves as muneraria."

As he was returned to the very cell in the Ludus Magnus he had so recently vacated, Regulus was surprised to get a friendly—almost affectionate—pat on the back of the head from Ursus. "Hurr, back again so soon. You be good little victor now. Got coin on you, hurrr."

221

Every muscle, every sinew, every cartilage ached from two days' intensive practice sessions under Dolabella's taskmaster doctore. Everything Regulus thought he knew about fighting a Thraex had been turned upside down, inside out, and put together again in a new way. The doctore grunted that he might just survive to fight another day if he could remember at least half what he'd just been shown. Dolabella too had managed some encouragement: "Fight well and be victor, boy. A lot of people have invested in your future, so you'd better not get returned here in a sack."

Regulus wsn't sure he wanted to concentrate on victory to be nothing more than a pawn in the money making games of others, but he felt a modicum of loyalty to Quintus, and maybe the redheaded big head too, even though they were in the pay of the game fixers, as Panthera had indicated. "Not that I'm in any position to cast moral stones," he grunted. More unnerving than the lanista's idea of reassurance was the caution he received in a low growl from the Scythian bastard as Regulus passed the bars of his cell. "By imperial command, boy, so no guarantees for your victory, no fat bastards fiddling the outcome of this fight."

"What are you saying, Scythian?"

"You know, you snail. Still, I'd worry less about your opponent than those you choose to keep company with. Trust no one," Bebryx hissed. "And I mean… no *one*," he added darkly. There might have been more in the same strain but Salutis Procuratio's security guards shoved Regulus on past to the stairwell.

Not even the extensive powers of the combined Cossroads Clubs could prevent Regulus meeting Thraxus in the private enclave of the Ludus Magnus. Quintus burned that Rufio had known about the bout but kept it to himself, even worse that the fight was *sine missione*. What use was a dead Regulus to them? What was he thinking? He could not bear the thought of Regulus getting killed. But there was to be no tame exhibition match for the bloodthirsty barbarian from the wilds of Mesopotamia. Client-king of Osrhoene and Armenia he might be, but Sanatruces was descended from the Persian Arsacid dynasty, Quintus knew. Proud men who had battled Rome for generations, warlords not to be trusted, men who craved the blood of others as babies craved the milk of their wet nurses.

How could Regulus—should it come to that—expect mercy from one fabled to have survived as a child when he was taken by Avde, sister of King Agbar of Edessa (himself a confessed convert to the atheist sect of Christians), from there to Armenia through the Kordvats Mountains, where the party was caught in a blizzard. They battled the snow storm for three days and three bitter nights and Sanatruces survived thanks to some strange white-coated animal that kept the child warm. None could say what nature of creature it was but perhaps the clue was in his name. In the barbarian tongue Sanatruk meant "Dog's Gift."

This was the man who would happily have Regulus slit from stomach to sternum at the wave of his no doubt heavily beringed hand. There were times when Quintus wished he knew less about history and was less the scholar when it came to strange people and their customs. "I can't go," he told Rufio firmly.

"You can't *not* go," Rufio remonstrated. "Trajan has commanded it. We're the patrons of Regulus, his owners. We have to be present. Besides," he took Quintus by the arm, "there's nothing to worry about. Regulus will make mincemeat of this Thraxus. Trust me."

"I won't be able to look."

"You'll look very silly hiding behind a cushion. You're a true-blood Roman. Wear your toga with pride at your gladiator's certain achievement, and put your sticky old patrician *virtus* on display.

"I wasn't aware you had an invitation from the Palatine," Mummius Bulbus said to the thin striper he knew as Panthera but also as Gaius Fabricius Luscinus, strongarm man for Senator J—, and not a person to be crossed. Bulbus would not normally confront Luscinus but it was a different matter when the Emperor and no doubt many guests were due any moment, all cocooned by Trajan's Batavian bodyguards and a cohort of Praetorians.

"I have no wish to sit with the imperial party, Bulbus. Just find me a warm spot on the upper level where I might observe the fights without being seen."

"Which bout are you most interested in, or is it all?"

Luscinus stared hard at the lanista. "All of them, but let's say the third may pique my interest most. Always useful to see youngsters coming through."

Bulbus shook his head and the unfastened thongs of his leather skull cap rattled against his pointy chin. "I don't know what it is about that Regulus that's getting so many people itching in their underwear."

That gave Luscinus pause for thought. He leaned in close, eyes narrowed to spear-blade slits. "Who has been expressing interest, Bulbus? You know you are supposed to inform me of anything, anything at all that might be useful to know."

"It was one of the Viminal goons. The training schools don't pay any monthly dues because those low-lifes don't like mucking it with trained fighters, so bit of a surprise. Turns out he was fishing for information and... willing to pay for it. Now there's a turn-up for the books! Seems like they were kept out of something cooking elsewhere among rival Crossroads Clubs."

"I see." Luscinus stepped back out of the lanista's face. "Just make sure I'm informed promptly next time. *Prompt*, as in 'immediately'?"

"All right, I know, but this goon only showed his face... well, not an hour ago. How'm I supposed to get news to you that fast, huh?"

"Try Mercury; they're a better courier service."

Heat from braziers placed at intervals on lower levels of the cavea wafted upward, although the day was unusually warm. A low sun flooded the Ludus Magnus so that one end of the oval arena dazzled

224

while the other was in shadow. Cosseted on piles of embroidered cushions, the invited guests were a sea of multi-colored apparel with more formal white scattered about. By leaning forward from his position at the edge of the gathering, Quintus could see around the curvature of the marble benches the rugged profile of Hadrian seated on the other side of King Sanatruces and Trajan. With primped hair in the Greek fashion the self-styled "prince" had happily accepted the joint roles of editor and referee. No hope of mercy there. He loved a fitting end for a defeated fighter. Beyond Hadrian and his waving editor's rod were the two late-year consuls, Gaius Julius Bassus and Gnaeus Afranius Dexter.

On the higher rows behind Trajan and the king clustered the many courtiers, hangers-on, discreetly attired Praetorians, several aediles, praetors, and the prefects of the Urban Cohorts and the Vigiles… pointedly not acknowledging each other. He strained his neck back to see if his soon-to-be father-in-law was present, but it seemed this particular show was not of interest to the *praefectus annonae*: "Probably busy counting sheaves of wheat," Rufio quipped at the mention of his absence.

Quintus was in no mood for humor. The opening bouts were messy. In the first, two provocators hacked at each other with their swords, hammering blows off shields, clumsy *cardiophylax* breastplates, and helmets. Blood soon flowed from cuts to unprotected flesh, but the weight of armor quickly tired both combatants. To cries of spectator anticipation, the taller of the two bore his opponent to one knee and rained down blows until the other raised a finger to signal his surrender. Hadrian's decision was a foregone conclusion. Quintus shut his eyes as the victor pushed his gladius to the hilt into the soft spot between his victim's neck and shoulder. He yanked it free with a flourish and a fountain of jugular blood.

The second and more athletic bout was between a secutor and retiarius, but ended as bloodily when the net fighter trapped his opponent in his web, pulled the legs from under him, and buried his trident's cruel tines in the exposed neck: another for the welcoming arms of Libitina.

The attendants had barely dragged away the secutor's corpse and tidied the gore-covered sand before Thraxus and Regulus appeared. Rufio nudged Quintus in some excitement. "We're on," he said quite unneccesarily. Bile rose and threatened to choke Quintus. "You have to look. Trajan has his eye on us."

As his professional name suggested, Thraxus was attired in the Thracian manner, a Thraex armed with a *parmula*, the small circular shield of his style, and a very short curved sword, the Thracian *sica*, which was similar to the falx Scorpus carried to cut himself loose of the chariot traces in the event of a "shipwreck." In skilled hands the sica's honed blade could cause awful damage to an opponent's unarmored back. He wore armored greaves to protect his shins, a padded manica on shoulder and sword arm, a wide protective groin belt above a wine-red loincloth, and legionary caligae on his feet. Thraxus wore the same broad rimmed helmet enclosing the entire head as a hoplomachus, distinguished by the representation of a griffin on the front of the crest that proclaimed him a companion of the avenging goddess Nemesis.

Though there was so much noise arising from the small crowd of dignitaries he need not have bothered, Rufio whispered, "He looks sumptuous, almost eatable." He did not mean Thraxus.

Quintus glimpsed through sheltering fingers and had to agree. Regulus was indeed magnificent. As he stepped from the shade into sunlight, his oiled muscles gleamed like polished bronze in contrast to the cold-blue-hued steel of the naked gladius held in easy grip at his side.

"Are you pleased that I found those silver decorations in our warehouse for his *balteus*?"

Quintus nodded, his throat too congested to make a comment. The leather belt, glittering with borrowed insignia, secured a bulging loincloth dyed a striking yellow. Several leather thongs looped around from just under the armpit to above his wrist reinforced the thickly padded manica that protected his sword arm. Thick padding under bright leather wrapped around the lower legs would allow him to kick out at his opponent; otherwise the murmillo fought barefooted. In his other hand he held by its top rim a large rectangular *scutum*, the legionary shield with its curved surface marked with steel lightning blazes against a saffron-colored leather covering. And hooked from the thumb by its chin traces, the murmillo's large, ornate bronze helmet with its jutting rim to protect the chin, enclosing visor, and broad brim was topped by a horsehair crest.

"Look how his eyes flash with exuberance."

Quintus saw it differently. He thought it was an expression of fear. *Perhaps I'm projecting my own anxiety*. He consoled himself with that notion as the two young men stood side by side, legs planted, shoulders back, looking up at Trajan. Hadrian gave the sign, the gladiators parted and donned their helmets, swiftly securing them, and before Quintus could take another breath the fight was begun.

They circled warily, each taking the other's measure, balanced easily on bent legs. Above them most spectators started to exchange wagers on the outcome. Quintus saw Trajan in smiling debate with Sanatruces on one hand and Hadrian on the other. He had a horrible feeling Trajan was one of the *parmularii*—supporters of gladiators who used the small round shield—and so would not be rooting for Regulus.

In spite of wanting to cover his eyes from the sight, Quintus was riveted as Thraxus made the first attacking move, sidling in with the intention of taking Regulus in his blind spot and slashing at his vulnerable back with the deadly *sica*. At the last possible moment, Regulus spun around to lash out with his shield. Its sharp rim swept aside his opponent's parmula and left a nasty gash on the shield arm.

For the next half of a *minuta*, the two exchanged blade thrusts, with neither seeming to gain an advantage. Nevertheless the skill on display was evidently thrilling the select audience for cheers of encouragement rose from the cavea interwoven with shouts of alarm as Thraxus or Regulus landed a telling blow. They churned the sand into a plowed field in which Regulus with his bare feet had the advantage of better grip. It began to tell as they both tired, that he could make sharper turns and quicker recoveries. His double-brimmed helmet made a formidable weapon on its own and he used it to deliver several head butts with the sharpened edges that left Thraxus bleeding from nasty welts across back and bared chest.

Quintus felt his hastily eaten lunch rise up into his gorge when on one turn, Regulus tripped and fell back to the sand. He brought the scutum up to cover his torso as Thraxus leaped on him, his sica flashing in the lowering sunlight. Regulus rolled left, rolled right, pulled his legs up in a trice as Thraxus aimed his blade down. But then Regulus uncoiled and lashed out with his right leg in a classic murmillo sidekick. The heavy padding caught Thraxus under his helmeted chin, jerking his head back savagely. In a sudden moment of silence, everyone heard his pained grunt.

Regulus rolled again, over the barrel curve of his shield, and back to his feet. It was a lightning move that brought his gladius point up as he dove for Thraxus. The Thraex fought to recover from the unexpected kick but he was too late to bring his parmula up to deflect the thrust and the blade sliced deeply across his bared shoulder. As one, the spectators drew a collective breath before starting to yell.

Regulus! Regulus! Regulus!

He heard the acclamation as if down a long tunnel and peered through the moist visor grill in a daze to see the damage his gladius had wrought to his opponent. Blood flooded the sand at his feet. It pooled around the wrecked neck and shoulder. Thraxus's shattered collarbone poked up through torn flesh, a shocking white between welling rivers of carmine.

He was not sure he could go through with what must now follow. He heard Dolabella's voice hollowly repeating, "In a fight to the death there is no other way but to make a clean kill of the vanquished. You are not to let the Ludus Gallicus down by acting like a cowardly little child."

Regulus! Regulus! Kill! Kill!

For what seemed like an eternity but was really no more than a secunda, Regulus stared down into the pained gaze. Thraxus—a young man much as himself, a man he never really knew and now never would. Now he felt the full force of horror that his accursed mission had brought him.

Kill! Kill!

Thraxus squirmed at his feet and then looked up beseechingly. Regulus put the tip of his blade to the gap between the third and fourth rib as his doctore had taught, paused a breath, and then leaned down with all his strength. The edges of the gladius made a sickening hissing sound as they parted skin and muscle until the point pierced deep, sundering the heart of Thraxus, ending his life.

Rufio watched in some concern as Quintus gradually pulled himself together. He barely acknowledged Rufio's well intended I told you not to worry and said in a lame voice, "We must go to him. You know, to offer congratulations."

"No, you go. I can see him another day, when we discuss with Dolabella what happens next. After Saturnalia there will be more munera for him to attend, private and public, and we should organize with Dolabella." Rufio knew he was wittering on to fill space. He wanted to go home to the Emporium with Quintus, but knew it was a forlorn hope, so better Quintus went to Regulus on his own and they could… well, do whatever they wanted to do. No doubt the gladiator would be as randy as stallion set among a field of in-season mares after such a victory. He patted Quintus on the back. "Go. Give my compliments to our boy." And then he turned and made his way down from the cavea and out onto the street before anyone could sweep him up into an after-fight party.

* * *

When Quintus reached the cell at the back of the ludus peristyle, heart hammering with a sudden rush of desire, he was startled to see four Praetorian Guards leading Regulus away. "What's this?" he exclaimed.

"Aside, please," snapped the uncommonly polite centurion.

Regulus glanced back between two of his military escort. "I– I've been summoned—"

It's the baths for you, before you get to the Domus Augustana," the centurion said as they and Regulus disappeared up the steps to the street. Quintus stared after them. His balls ached with need, and irritation made his head bang inside like a hollow drum. "Damn Trajan," he spat out. "Damn his imperial prick. Well…" His spirit deflated. He kicked the wall. "And I thought he was one of the parmularii and wouldn't touch a murmillo with a galley sweep. You don't know it," he addressed the travertine facing, "but I don't have much time left for satisfying myself the way I want. Shit! My life is due to formally end in…" he counted mutely, "…fourteen days from now."

Hooded eyes observed from the shadows as the guardsmen escorted Regulus away and a saddened young man wearing a toga watched his departure. The young gladiator was now a known quality—he had taken the Summa's coin and there was no way back from that other than via the Porta Libitinensis, but it was soon time to introduce Quintus Caecilius Alba to the *Societas ad divitias augendas* and show him the error of his ways in approaching any Crossroads Club. He smiled grimly at the boy as his pent-up frustration exploded with a kick at the wall. The impotent fool.

S·I·X·T·E·E·N | XVI

6th to 18th days of December AD 108

Trajan's desire for a taste of victorious gladiator was to Ashur's benefit. When he finally dragged his lust-filled body home, Quintus was in desperate need of comfort. As Regulus discovered the joys of the world's most powerful man plowing his captive furrow, Ashur licked and sucked his way up and down his master's fevered flesh. After many secunda of this torment Quintus forced him onto his back, head lolling over the end of the bed, while he knelt on the floor and fucked Ashur's face as hard as he could. Ashur loved it. Quintus came twice in quick succession, his mind a whirl of confusion: visions of Rufio, of Regulus, of Trajan screwing his and Rufio's gladiator, all mingled and swirled about his head.

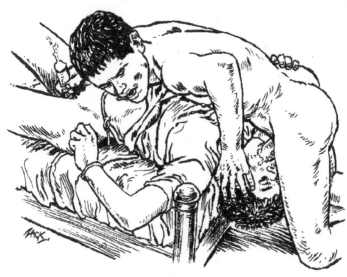

The following days passed in a blur: meetings with Clivius and his collaborators; sessions with Dolabella; confrontations with his uncle and a particularly unnerving conversation with a smoothtalking equestrian Livy introduced as Fabricius Luscinus, who was under the misapprehension that he, Luscinus, had a stake in Regulus.

As the Day of Impending Doom (as Quintus had come to call the wedding) grew closer, life became more complicated. Sosius was forever sending messengers demanding progress on the erotic scroll while Rufio pushed for new poems. His family was in a fever of prenuptial arrangements from the men to the women (although mercifully no one seemed the least bit interested in his contributing to their flurry). And there never seemed to be any time to actually have a quiet moment with a post-Emperor-impaled Regulus.

Rufio buried himself in work for his mother at the Emporium to keep his mind off those matters that would preoccupy his normally cheery thoughts otherwise: Regulus and his suspicions of corruption in the arena; concern as to what that meant for him and Quintus; the Regulus-Quintus love-lust affair; Quintus getting wed very soon and what on earth that would mean.

On the 16th day of December he joined Quintus at the Ludus Gallicus when Dolabella finally informed them that a certain Octavius Vindex had requested Regulus as a contestant on the Ides of January. The lanista required their consent. "Vindex has to put on a good show—the praetorship of Ostia with the new port coming along is an lucrative magistracy. The games will be a bribe to the plebs so they vote for him in the forthcoming elections. He saw Regulus in those games the Emperor put on for the Armenian king. Unless the crowd wills it otherwise, there will be no sine missione fights, but there will be good prize money for the owners of victorious gladiators… maybe more to be made on the side?"

Quintus had no idea what that meant and Rufio said nothing.

Dolabella grimaced. "I know you lads have found a new fountain of money from somewhere and it's not my business where you laid hands on it, but Caecilius Dio is anxious that you may be putting your heads into a lions' den and—"

"But it is *my* business."

Quintus gave a faint gasp of recognition. "Fabricius Luscinus! Uncle Livy brought you to Domus Alba."

"Can't have been good," Rufio muttered.

The man who now came forward from a corner of the long office where he had been hidden looked menacing—lean and hungry Rufio thought, but he did not quail before the glare. "What makes it any of your affair… whoever you are?" Rufio planted his hands on his hips aggressively and frowned. "I've seen you somewhere before as well, but I can't think where, or when."

"Ah, you are the pleb partner, I presume," Luscinus said with a sneer. "I've heard about you."

"Nothing good, I hope." Rufio shook his head and made his coppery locks fly as he grinned rudely at the man. Then the expression snapped off. "What do you want, coming out of a dark corner like a cat ambushing a mouse?"

"I'd advise politeness, Tullius," Dolabella warned and stepped forward is if about to intervene between them. "In our business, Fabricius Luscinus is known as—"

"Panthera. Yes, like a cat, known for my cunning, my stealth, my speed in attack, and for my ruthlessness." A Nile crocodile's grin was more humorous than the one the interloper gave Rufio. "My principals don't take kindly to interference from outsiders. You two are out of your depth and you are cutting across well-laid plans."

"Plans for what?" Quintus took a step to stand alongside Rufio.

"For your boy. Gaius Regulus. When we see talent in a beginner—and one who has sold his life to the arena as well—we take a great interest. There's no harm in your acting as muneraria, if that's your game, but only on our terms and by—"

233

"Who exactly *are* your principals?" Rufio interrupted, glancing suspiciously at Dolabella.

"That really isn't your business. As I was saying, you are welcome to act for Regulus, but on our terms... and that does not include taking money from unapproved sources, as it seems you have done. Were you not content with Caecilius Dio acting for you?"

"He's always in with Fabius Virius," Quintus pointed out.

"He's a snake. Actually they're both serpents," Rufio confirmed.

Luscinus-Panthera ignored the outburst. "The money's come from a consortium of Crossroads Clubs, hasn't it?"

In the silence the sounds of combat rose up from the yard.

"Tell me how many and which affiliations? The clubs aren't noted for their cooperation." He waited with pronounced patience. "So... no comment? Very well, for now you may go about your business. I shall consult with my principals, but know this: Regulus is already ours, and if you wish to continue your happy existence..." he smiled at Quintus, "yours on the *cursus honorum*, I suppose; yours..." he threw a derisive glance at at Rufio, "as a cleaner of public latrines or something similar—"

Dolabella caught Rufio's arm and held him in a powerful grip to prevent his reaching Luscinus.

"Hah! With a temper like that you should take instruction from the man holding you back, boy. I'm sure that flaming red hair would be popular in the arena. As I was saying: you will do well to drop your current bankers like hot brands and come see me. I can be very understanding for a first transgression. The Vindex munera in Ostia is arranged?"

Dolabella's curt nod acknowledged that it was.

"Good. Then we have nothing further to discuss until the New Year. Oh but… you two, you will be watched. Every move, and I'd advise warning your *former* bankers not to mess with s·a·d·a— we run the games in Rome and throughout the Imperium. The Crossroads Club patrons might think themselves big bad wolves, but we are everywhere, so very much bigger, so very much nastier."

Dolabella let Rufio loose once Panthera had left. He was spitting angry, unwilling to calm down when the lanista advised him to cool down. "Where does he think he gets off? And if that Fabius Virius is anything to do with it, I'll– I'll…"

"Do nothing. Take my advice, both of you. Sit back, let us get Regulus to top form, do as Panthera says, and come under his protection. It will be to your great advantage, and if it means anything to you hotheads, I don't know of any involved in the games who don't cooperate with him and the shadowy organization he represents. Its big money, and the few who have proved difficult haven't lasted long."

Their footwear echoed clatteringly off the walls of the narrow stairwell down to the exercise yard. Rufio was still so incensed he never saw the heavy form loom up over him until it was too late. The huge hand that clapped under his chin bore him up against the arcade's back wall, "What—! *Oww*—" and his head connected painfully with it.

"I saw him come down the steps! You were up there with that Panthera, plotting, I knew it!" Bebryx hissed "And I heard him and your boy talking days ago, conspiring. He said then that you are in his pay."

In the deep shade under the arcade the struggle was all but invisible to the gladiators training only paces away in the yard. Rufio wriggled furiously, but Bebryx had the height, weight, and strength. "What nonsense… are you… talking about?"

"Hey! Let him go!" Quintus yelled as he jumped down the last three steps. He raised an arm and swung furiously at the gladiator's midriff, delivering a powerful kidney chop. It barely registered. Bebryx easily swept him aside with his free hand and as the would-be rescuer sprawled on the ground he returned to shaking Rufio like a rag doll.

"Confess, you cur, tell me what Panthera is up to."

Quintus regained his feet and spoke up. "That man is nothing to do with us."

Bebryx continued to shake Rufio.

"He… oh fuck off and let me go! I've nothing to do with… Let–let me down, you great oaf, and I'll tell you."

At that moment two security guards strolled around the corner. Bebryx growled and relaxed his hold. The men had not seen the altercation but still approached cautiously, hands hovering above their sword hilts. One leered at Rufio. "Don't let him jump your bones, sonny, they get damned horny after being cooped up for the day. Har, har…"

Bebryx glowered at their backs as they vanished around the far end of the arcade. "Useless granny fuckers. Ten of them wouldn't stand up to me if I had a weapon in my hands." He seemed to have run out of fighting steam as if his anger had followed the guards.

"Look," Rufio began, his voice croaky as he rubbed his sore throat, "Regulus is our man, and that's all there is to it."

"You're in bed with that corrupt bastard."

"No!" both boys said at once. "In fact," Quintus went on, "we're on your side… that is if you're an honest man."

Bebryx gave a loud snort. "Honest? You jeer at my honor? Me, Bebryx the Scythian—"

"Oh here we go again," Rufio sighed. "Bebryx, ask Dolabella, he'll tell you we have nothing to do with this Panthera character, and we want nothing to do with him either."

"I don't suppose Dolabella will want to say anything," Quintus pointed out. "After all, his word's hardly to be trusted."

Rufio considered the logic of that for a moment. "Then you'll have to take our word for it, as honorable muneraria."

"Never known an honorable owner," Bebryx grumbled, but he seemed to have accepted their word, for the time being anyway.

"*That's* where I know him from," Rufio suddenly exclaimed. "I saw him with Senator J— when he visited the Emporium ages ago. What did you mean about Panthera conspiring with Regulus?"

"They are all in it, conspiring to make money from bent fights. Good men sacrificed for greed. Ask him. Ask your runt."

Rufio exchanged looks with Quintus, who dipped his head. "I don't believe it. Regulus is clean, I'm convinced, but if it will put your mind at rest I will go and question him."

"We should both go—"

Quintus cut him off. "I'd rather speak with him alone."

Rufio scowled, but he didn't want an argument in front of Bebryx. When Quintus left he turned to Bebryx. "If you're right and Regulus is willing to cheat I'll find out." *At least, if Quintus will let me. He's just not acting like himself…and I'm getting pretty pissed about it.*

Bebryx clapped him on the shoulder. "Hmm, maybe I misjudged. Seems we may be on the same side after all."

"Dominus," Regulus said, rising to his feet from where he had been executing rapid push-ups.

Quintus regarded him uneasily. "We have just spoken with a man called Luscinus, or Panthera, if you prefer."

Regulus adjusted the bulge in the front of his loincloth, all he was wearing. In spite of the damp chill of the cells, perspiration gilded his muscles which the floor exercise was intended to ease after the exertions of a recent training session. The movement appeared to be unconscious but Quintus did not miss it.

"Do you know who Panthera is?"

Regulus pursed his lips and scrunched his eyes in concentration, shook his head slightly. "I don't think I've heard the name."

"Well he appears to know you. He said, 'Regulus is already ours.' What could he mean by that?"

A picture of bewildered innocence greeted the question. "I have no idea, dominus."

Quintus frowned and stared down at the floor, pushed some of the rushes left and the right with his boot. *Uncle Livy's handiwork is evident all over this, ever since he wheedled the information about Regulus out of me.* He made up his mind. "He was just trying to disconcert us, and he succeeded. I'm convinced it all comes down to my wretched uncle's meddling."

"Your uncle, dominus?"

"Apologies, thinking out loud. Clearly you know nothing of such matters." He would have liked to linger but not with Rufio waiting upstairs. "It's not long now to your first proper fight. I'll be back as soon as I can to see to any needs." *After the Day of Doom, that is…*

"My day is empty when I don't see you," Regulus intoned softly.

Apollo's cock, but Regulus really got him going. Quintus paused a moment at the bottom of the stairs. He was still visibly aroused when at the top an agitated Rufio confronted him.

"Did he admit to anything?"

Quintus bridled. "Why would he when there's nothing to confess."

Rufio flushed at the sight of Quintus's hard-on tenting his tunic and he suddenly snapped. "What's wrong with you? You're so under his spell you can't any longer see what's real. Well I'm finished with it, and you. You sort everything out, you fucking loser!"

"Ma, where is everybody?" Cato looked up from the tablet on which he was writing out Latin declensions. He dropped the stylus with a clatter. Eutychus was a veritable tyrant when it came Latin literature, "and without grammar you are a nothing," the martinet argued—"*bellum, bellum, bellum, belli, bello, bello*… it's war!"

Across the table, Junilla was busy recording the last few days' income and outgoings. She didn't trust the company accounts to anyone. The professionals were as crooked as the bankers when it came to bookkeeping. "What day is it, pet?"

"The 18th day of December, Ma. You know that."

"*Mmm-hmm*, that's why there's no one around," she pointed out what should be obvious. "Or at least, no one of interest." She sighed softly, eyes turned to the ceiling. "It *is* the wedding of Quintus tomorrow, as you well know, you wicked truant."

Cato sighed in turn. "Don't remind me."

They were alone in the deserted Emporium. The last kitchen slave had been dismissed and gone to her alcove, and Rufio was off out. His ménage was off out with him. "I'd rather he was here with us tonight," Junilla continued aloud her inward thoughts. "I don't really know why he wants to celebrate his dearest friend's last day of freedom."

"Any excuse for a piss up."

"That's enough rude language from you, my pet. I worry over how it will affect Rufio," she mused. "We know very little about the woman Quintus is marrying. She may be the sort to sit with her spinning wheel and loom, quiet and virtuous, as demure as a temple mouse, or she might be a harridan, the kind of wife who never lets her husband out of the house on his own."

"Does that mean we won't see Quintus again?" Cato sniffed, wiped the back of a hand over his nose, examined the result, and then rubbed it on his tunic. He picked up his stylus and recommenced declining nouns in the wax—*filius, fili, filium, filii, filio*…

"I hope it won't be so bad as that." Junilla gave a short laugh to convince herself that everything would be all right. "But Quintus is a member of our family." She chuckled again. "Do you remember how stiff he was when Rufio first introduced hin to us?"

Cato glanced up, a cheery grin on his face. "Oh he was always stiff, Ma."

"I didn't mean that," she scolded. "I feel concern for him, but I've been more worried about Rufio. Those two have been off with each other lately and I'm sure it's the wedding. It's come between them."

"I'll bet they've done that often enough." Cato neatly ducked as the thrown apple core sailed over his tousled head. He gave a throaty chuckle but then turned serious. "I think they had a big argument. Over that gladiator. Never mind, I'll look after him," he soothed, though he did not say whether he meant Quintus or his brother.

Junilla pursed the corner of her mouth in faux disapproval of her youngest before returning to her books, a worry frown marking her broad brow as she tossed her head to flick aside a ringlet of auburn hair from her eyes. "*Tch-tch...* Dammy, what have you done here? He's put an item into the receivables that ought properly be in the chargeables." She scratched at the scroll. Her mind wasn't really on correcting her secretary's error. "I just hope Rufio is acting sensibly tonight."

* * *

Rufio pulled out of the writhing Nubian's squishy ass and toppled sideways onto jumbled pillows, his hand still firmly gripping the lad's jerking, sticky erection. He was utterly drunk. His head spun in sluggish revolutions, his surroundings were a moaning, gasping blur of bodies amid eddies of smoky lamplight, pulsing to a languid rhythm of syrupy music.

It had all seemed a good idea at the time—*well, in truth, it was never an* idea, *just a stupid reaction...* Drink a lot, fuck till you drop, lots of mates together. Pretend the row with Quintus never happened, pretend he isn't marrying some snobbish girl. *As if!*

Hiring the private function room at Lucretia's Lupanar had been quick. Mother's great friend. Special rates, *not*. Whore boys, dancers, musicians, drinks and snacks all easily organized. Friends, well, the likes of Felix, Hephaestion, Adalhard, Zeno, not-so-quick flibbertigibbet Celer and even hopelessly lusting Flaccus rounded up, and there you go: an orgy ready to sizzle! Pity he hadn't been

able to snaffle adorable Ambrosius, too... And the result? A mere piddling distraction from the tooth-aching truth. His ideal friend, his lover, lost to him... *Quintus really is getting married tomorrow.*

Rufio dimly recalled the jollities getting off to a quick start. The cute dancers, so lascivious on stage in their hardly existent costumes, seemed barely to have started their moves to the musicians' erotic tunes before being hauled off the little stage and all but devoured by the lusty party. Wine was guzzled, and the prettiest servers pounced on to be sampled.

Gods! He had drunk and fornicated with desperate abandon... screwed cheeky Celer, mouth-fucked Adalhard, was spitted by stolid Zeno... fleeting images of a slinky Syrian skewered both ends, mouth stuffed full of cock, what he assumed was Felix with two pricks up him, glistening Nubian beauties upended and ravished by Flaccus and, he thought, Hephaestion who had someone's face firmly clamped into his pert ass slurping away... All sorts of sensations whirled through him... the fractured memories of nibbling on taut flesh and nipples, invading helpless mouths, opening his thighs to penetration, swallowing cum, torturing slick balls... of abandoning himself to desperate lust. *Did I allow big, gentle Flaccus to finally have me? Where am I...?*

Rufio felt fingers worming their way into his aching ass—and his stomach heaved. Vomit surged and spewed from his slack lips, and his face fell into the acid puddle... *Quintus, Quintus! Why, why... you fucking aristocratic cunny! You... you...*

S·E·V·E·N·T·E·E·N | XVII

19th day of December AD 108

Having dispensed with the engagement ceremony—his father was obviously as eager as Numerius Metellus to get the business over and done with—Quintus had at least been spared the engagement ceremonies, the exchange of bride and groom gifts, and the kiss that traditionally sealed the formal arrangement. It also meant he still hadn't had a really good look at his "beautiful" bride to be, and since tradition also demanded she wear a veil throughout the wedding, the first time he would be able to see for himself the accuracy (or not) of that small portrait would be in the bridal bedchamber. He shuddered at the thought. She was bound to be a shrewish bitch; it was simply his luck.

Ashur was fussing over arranging the lightweight toga's folds over his master's broad shoulders and only half paying attention to the continuous grumbling. "There, I told you you'd look magnificent in white over the maroon synthesis. And those slippers…"

"They pinch." Quintus peered glumly down his nose at his bright-red leather footwear from Cypripedium Gucchius in the Saepta.

"You'll wear them in on the way over to Domus Numerii and your blushing bride, so expectant of—"

"Shut up. There's nothing worse than marriage, you Syrian idiot—"

"I know you're upset. But wedding-day nerves are to be—"

"The only reason for marriage is the absurd patrician necessity to produce children, otherwise no sane man would ever get married," Quintus spluttered. "You know what they say? A rich wife will be a tyrant and a poor one will spend all your money."

Ashur brushed hands over the toga folds in a proprietary manner. "Oh, it's not that bad. You haven't actually got any money yet."

"The only men who marry are those who can't avoid it—like me—or men burdened with the responsibility of continuing the family line—which Primus, Secundus, and Marcus can do—"

"So long as Marcus keeps his butt away from the Emper—"

"Or those who decide to found one, which isn't me, thank you. And don't speak treason."

"No, Quintus." Ashur stood back. "My, you look absolutely ravishing. Why not marry me?"

"Don't be absurd. You're a slave."

"Free me then."

"I'm more likely to murder you first. Anyway, Father hasn't formally made you over to me yet." He sighed with heartfelt distress. "So, shall we get on with it then? Bring on the *nuptiae*."

The public and religious rituals of Saturnalia were over and the 19th to 23rd days of December were given over to family matters and revelry. Familia Caecilii made a gay spectacle as they strolled in chattering procession down the slopes of the Aventine and up the eastern end of the Caelian to the sprawling Domus Numerii, accompanied by two pipe players. The trees were still weeping a few remaining leaves, which suited Quintus's desultory mood perfectly. As if herding him to prevent escape, his father and brothers formed a cordon wrapped around and a step behind behind his lead. The women followed. Maia and Aurelia, the wives of Lucius Primus and Livius Secundus, gossiped happily with their mother-in-law, Fabia the Elder, while her two daughters, Fabia the Younger and Julia, trailed closely behind in close discussion of their own nuptials due any day. Both girls had been betrothed when they were twelve and ten respectively.

"I bet you can't wait to get your leg over," Marcus said in that insufferably smug tone he used in addressing his young brother.

I bet you can't wait to get your ass in line for another poking by Trajan, Quintus said to his inner ear, but thought better of voicing it aloud. He wished the Misenum base commander had refused Marcus leave to attend the ceremony.

"I hope she knows the mare's position," Primus brayed coarsely, which turned into a snort at Maia's giggle.

Marcus amplified it in a giggling chortle that verged on a snort. "Now I ask you, how would a virgin have that kind of knowledge?"

"As long as she gives you a good roll in the bridal bed, Junior, that's all that matters," Secundus threw in with his own chuckle.

"Now, boys, leave Quintus alone," Lucius admonished his eldest sons, but couldn't help adding his own sestertius' worth. "I will expect to see a good stain of consummation on the bridal sheet before we sit down to breakfast tomorrow, Quintus."

With a suffused blush, Quintus shut his ears to the rest of the lewd imprecations and wished the whole day... and night... over.

A beaming janitor flung wide the doors of Domus Numerii and beckoned everyone in with a low, expansive sweep of his propitious right arm. Quintus treated the man to a sour grimace. In the atrium were gathered Vipsanius Numerius Metellus, his gaunt wife Vipsania the Elder, his sons Cornelius and Drusus—still regarding Quintus with glowering suspicion—as well as their wives, Quintus presumed, children, numerous aunts, uncles, cousins, and hangers-on hoping to gorge their stomachs on the free food. The volume of comingled voices in the enclosed area was deafening. He watched with barely hidden dismay as Vipsania the Elder gathered his mother into a loose embrace. Both mothers produced tear cups to capture for posterity the obligatory maternal gush of happiness at gain and sadness at the loss of their offspring.

The rest of the afternoon became a fog: Vipsania the Younger emerging to a blare of nose flutes (couldn't the Numerii have hired more tuneful musicians?), a weird vision in her straight-sided, hemless *tunica recta*, belted with a Knot of Hercules so elaborate Quintus had no idea how he'd untie when it came to the time; the almost indecently jolly *pronuba*, a matron who had only married once, accompanying Vipsania throughout the ceremony; the bright glare of Vipsania's traditional saffron-dyed wedding veil—quite impenetrable—and boots of matching color; standing beneath an arrangement of wheat sheaves symbolizing his new father-in-law's control of Rome's corn dole, muttering vows as ten witnesses observed the *patres familiae* signing the final contract; the crowded dining room, the chaos of food and wine and noise and far too much bonhomie and pats of his shoulder; the ritual exchange of kisses through Vipsania's veil, which might as well have been a curtain.

The cold air did a little to sober up Quintus as he staggered home through streets lit by torches held aloft by his rudely chanting brothers. He had to get back in time to receive the even noisier following procession consisting of the rest of his family, his bride and her attendants, her family, and the guests.

"You got the torch ready, Quintus?" Primus yelled as soon as the four men piled into the Domus Alba. The household staff scattered in all directions to their prepared stations ready to welcome the carousing wedding party. "Where's the 'joyous boy'? You did remember to send a 'joyous boy' to fetch some 'pure water', didn't you?"

Head awhirl, even though he'd tried hard not to imbibe too much of the watered wine, Quintus went in frantic search of Cato, the only Tullius allowed anywhere near his connubial day, and about the most joyous boy he'd been able to think of.

"Keep your hair on." Cato sprang out from behind a pillar, looking anything but joyous, waving a silver pitcher. A small gush of water topped the lip and splashed onto the tiles.

Quintus sniffed suspiciously. "Where'd you get it?"

"That fountain in the small square where Vicus Platononis crosses Tanners' Parade—"

"Night Soil Street," Quintus cried in horror. "It's supposed to be pure!"

Cato held the pitcher defensively in front of his chest. "No one pissed in it while I was looking."

"Torch, Quintus! They're coming."

Primus and Secundus grabbed Quintus by the arm and started

dragging him toward the entry hallway as Marcus thrust an unlit torch in his free hand. Cato kept close, muttering that the water was pure enough for any bride and that she wouldn't really drink it anyway, after all who in Hades' name ever drank water?

Quintus was aware of Ashur, face gleaming with happiness, dashing tears from his khol-blackened eyes, placing a small brazier near to hand. And then Quintus was firmly planted in the open doorway, Primus to one side, Secundus to the other, Marcus at his back to block the escape route. Out on the street, torches flared, musicians wailed, and the obscenely happy pronuba presented her charge. In the flickering light Vipsania resembled one of those chilled cream deserts with a melting saffron-colored topping the insanely rich had made for them using ice transported from the Alps. She extended an uncertain arm to offer Quintus the ritual torch lit from her family's hearth where on the evening before she would have sacrificed her childhood toys to the family Lares.

Primus jabbed Quintus in the ribs and prompted from the corner of his mouth, "*Aquae et ignis communicatio.*"

Quintus reacted with a start. He reached out, took the torch from Vipsania, and immediately handed it to Secundus. Then he lowered his own torch into the brazier at Ashur's side. It flared into life and he offered it to Vipsania. She took it wordlessly. He stuck his hand out, groping blindly behind him, suddenly grateful at Cato's thrusting the pitcher handle into his palm. He held it out. Vipsania accepted the pure water and, to Quintus's terror, raised it to her veiled face. He stifled a sigh of relief when she made a sipping gesture; no water passed her hidden lips, pure or more than decidedly otherwise. A rumble of approval escaped the gathering. The pronuba joyously echoed Primus. "*Aquae et ignis communicatio*, the gift of water and fire by which we live is shared!"

Quintus fell back as two of her relatives swept his bride up in their arms—it would have been an especially bad omen for her to trip on her first entry—and carried her chastely across the Domus Alba threshold to lower her before Quintus. And so Vipsania Metella was welcomed into her new home (temporary, since Quintus hoped against hope to find sapce and to set up home in one of his dowry properties). Quintus stared at the blank saffron curtain, lurid in the torchlight, and wondered what Vipsania was thinking behind it, freed now from her father's discipline to her husband's control. Two steps back, Dryantilla—the bride's pesonal maid—glared at Quintus as if warning him to lay no hand on her mistress.

The jab in the back came from Secundus. Quintus opened his eyes wider and stepped forward to take her hand in his own as he waited for the final invocation of this torturous process.

The saffron veil dipped slightly, and then Vipsania spoke in a surprisingly clear, crisp voice. "*Ubi tu Gaius, ego Gaia.*"

Quintus almost reeled at the traditional words. *Wherever you are, I'll be there. Oh gods above and haunting lemurs below, I hope not. What will Rufio think…?*

Quite how he and Vipsania ended up in his bedchamber, the space he'd shared for years with Ashur since childhood, and more recently with Rufio, he never knew. Amid much cheering, jeering, and salacious encouragement, the married couple were ushered from the atrium, through the halls, and finally shut in.

Alone at last.

Alone with his wife.

Despite what Quintus might have thought, the Joyous Boy was not the only Tullius in the vicinity on this connubial day. December's early dusk concealed the form of Rufio, wrapped in his darkest cloak, lying atop the crumbling remains of the Servian Wall, which marked the boundary of the Domus Alba gardens. The previous day's (night's?) orgy had left his rear end sore and his throat raw from wine and…other fluids. Outwardly, he shivered uncontrollably from the cold while Vulcan and a whole army of blacksmiths hammered out suits of armor in his overheated head. It throbbed

more than he could remember. He was determined to make his misery perfect on this perfectly miserable day. In some magical way he had believed something would occur, some barrier be raised, the hand of a benign god would intervene and leave Quintus single… and his to claim as his own. *Except there's damned Regulus hovering in the picture. Gods! Why did I lose my temper with Quintus so badly?* But the gods didn't fucking care, obviously. There had been no divine intervention, no miracle had occurred and the wedding had.

From his eyrie, Rufio could peer down through sore eyes into and along the arcaded passage that led to Quintus's bedroom where they had made love. Due to angle and distance, it was an imperfect view and so it was a brief glimpse he had of Quintus and the veiled woman his friend (*lover no longer?*) had married being pushed by eager family hands ceremoniously into the Chamber of Consummation. Most guests then returned to the atrium. Among the few who remained Rufio recognized Marcus and supposed others included the older brothers he had never met.

A part of him wanted to be able to pierce the walls to see what was going on; the other half shuddered to think of his Quintus having to go through with what was now inevitable. There were many occasions when as a child he and his mates Octavian and Crispin climbed walls, hid among tiles, perched precariously where they shouldn't be, spying, snooping, and with suppressed giggles typically acting as wild urchins. Perched on the wall it felt a bit like that, but if his old friends had actually been up there with him on this night, he would have had to avert his head lest they see the rivers of tears streaming down his cheeks. Junius Tullis Rufio crying. It beggared belief.

Sadly, he scrambled down from the wall to land in the grass at its foot and slipped away, lonely into the night.

Now that the reality of inevitability was upon him, it was not the face of Regulus Quintus sought for comfort but that of Rufio. *Struck by a wild, whipping redhead with… yes, with wicked cornflower-blue eyes. Big cock, though, and cocky with it… Ah, Rufio. Ah, Regulus…*

The actual consummation of the marriage was supposed to take place immediately in the bedroom, in the dark. Quintus had wished for darkness, but now he was relieved that Ashur had left a small night candle burning. Being alone in the dark with a strange woman would have been just too terrible. On the other hand, in the dim glow she would be bound to see how unmanly his manly equipment was; he couldn't recall a time before that it had been so limp—he'd been a walking erection since his ninth birthday.

Vipsania remained motionless with her back to the closed door, apparently ignoring the continued raucous sounds of lusty partying from the other side. He closed the distance, hand shaking, and raised the horrid saffron veil. In a short space of time, Quintus had faced down a crazed assassin, defeated a ghoul intent on stealing the essence of his youth, escaped the clutches of Neptune on a storm-tossed sea, fought a nest of gladiators intent on wiping him out, and struggled free of entombment in a pharaoh's mortuary temple, but none of these compared to the sheer terror that shook him to the core as he lifted that shroud from his wife's face.

Dark blue eyes, wide open, appraising, under black brush strokes of eyebrows glared back.

Full, artificially reddened lips pursed in a straight line suggestive of a combative personality.

Quintus completed the action of throwing the veil back over her shoulders. He knew the routine. Next came the ritual of that wretched knot of Hercules, a tangle that only the bride's mother could put together and only the husband—

"Don't think of touching me!" Her voice was surprisingly deep and sent a thrill of... what? Excitement? Fear?... through his body. He pulled the hand back sharply before she could slap him away. "I know what it means, the knot. The symbol that you are belted and bound to me, and which you must untie as you take me into your bed with the intention of ravishing my virginity."

She glanced around him at the truckle where he had tumbled with Ashur and with Rufio. It suddenly seemed ridiculously small for the purpose of connubial conjugation. To his alarm she took a pace forward and jabbed him on the breastbone. "Don't think I know nothing about you, Quintus Caecilius Alba. Your courageous reputation, dear husband, may precede you, but there are those of us who know you prefer to reserve your real heroics for your own kind."

The lump in Quintus's stomach lurched painfully. He felt frozen to the floor, but took a sticky step in retreat. "What?"

"When I first saw a portrait of your face and shoulders, I made a point of sneaking off one day to catch a proper look."

"How...?"

"And seeing as I'd be forced into some sort of match soon enough I decided it might as well be to someone easy on the eyes. Better still, one who had already found his Gaia..." a tiny smile eased her severe mouth, "or is he Gaius and you Gaia?"

"This... this is intolerable. Vipsania! You are mine to command—"

"Oh come off it, Quintus. Let's cut the crap and get a few matters straightened out between us. Our fathers may have made a contract, but it doesn't mean we need to abide by the spirit, as long as we appear to obey the word." She flung the veil aside. "Gods, but I hate that thing." She shook her head vigorously to loosen the ties and pins so that her lustrous dark locks flowed in a cascade to her shoulders. "That redhead…Tullius Rufio…don't deny it. You may never have set eyes on me, Quintus, I took care that you shouldn't when you were out, but I've seen you two together. I've seen the way you look at each other." She made cow-eyes in imitation.

Quintus fell back on his bed, mind churning, not least because she couldn't know how he'd let Regulus come between them until Rufio finally lost his temper over it. "So, what are you saying?"

Vipsania shook her head impatiently. "Isn't it obvious? You like Gaius on Gaius and I… I like Gaia on Gaia. Oh for Juno's sake! It's why I didn't kick up a fuss when dear pater got all enamored of a marriage into the Caecilii. Gods! It could have been that awful brother of yours, the unmarried one—"

"Marcus?"

"That's him. Ogling me all afternoon. I could feel his hands undressing me, his tongue licking my secret places, and—"

"Oh hang on." He felt nauseous at the thought.

"But you. Quintus. The one who would understand, who wouldn't care. Indeed, the one who wouldn't paw me, force me on my back and enter me forcibly…" A faint look of alarm crossed her features. "You wouldn't, would you?"

Quintus shook his head, which did nothing to settle the confused fluttering inside it.

"Good! So, you see, don't you? This is an ideal marriage for us. I can happily hold my parties with Gaia this and Gaia that while you go off screwing whichever Gaius you choose."

Gaius, why does it have to be Gaius…? He thrust an image of the gladiator from his mind. "And Ashur assured me you would be as innocent as the Alpine snow," Quintus said faintly. He also recognized that the portrait had failed to do her features justice. Vipsania fell on the pretty side of handsome, for a woman. However, Quintus decided to keep any compliments to himself for the time being.

"Who's Ashur, apart from a man with poor judgment?"

"My body slave."

"Who shares your bed."

It was a statement and Quintus could only shrug. "Well—"

"Naturally. Anyway, your Ashur is correct, as far as any Gaiuses go." She came and sat beside him. "It will be fine, my dear, dear, new husband. I'm sure we can keep up a fine front for everyone else."

This is a turn-up for the scrolls. What will Rufio say? But for the first time in several doom-laden days, Quintus saw a faint chink of light in his future. And then it blinked out again. "But my father is expecting to see a bloodied connubial sheet before much longer. I mean, are you…?"

She shook her head. "Gods no, lost that a couple of years ago in a rather delicious tangle with… well, you don't want to hear about all that. Can't you do that noble, heroic thing and nick yourself with a knife?"

"I suppose. No one would know, would they?"

"Course not. Our fathers will be out there all smiles outwardly, cursing all manner of horrors to visit upon the other should you fail to come up to expectations… or me for that matter. So let's show them the conclusive evidence of our consummation, And they'll all be *cooing* and *ahhing* tomorrow morning when they see me appear wearing my matron's costume, announcing I'm ready to become a mother, as I make an offering to your family's Lares and Penates— where is your larder, by the way?"

"It's on the other side of my father's office and— Wait! 'Ready to become a mother'? How are we ever going to get around not having children?"

Vipsania sprang to her feet in a pirouette, laughed lightly, a silvery sound from amid her more husky tones. "Oh there will be several months, maybe even a year or two before we need concern ourselves about that. Surely we can buy a baby somewhere? One that matches our appearances. Doesn't your family own a holiday home somewhere, or a farm, or some place we could disappear to for a couple of months after I've started stuffing a pillow under my tunic and palla? Then we return with a baby in tow, and a wet nurse, thank you, and a nanny to take care of the thing."

Quintus just stared at her.

"Don't look at me like that." She sighed. "It'll be just the same as adoption. Everyone does it. We'll see the boy is well brought up, wants for nothing, etcetera."

"Well, you seem to have thought of everything."

She smiled and sat back next to him, their thighs pressed together, mates having a chat. "I try. Come to that, can your Ashur keep his mouth shut? My Dryantilla is steadfast like the nymph of the oak for whom she's named and she exemplifies the word 'trustworthy,' but I don't know of any other slave I'd entrust with our secret and he's bound to find out. I'd hate to have to arrange a fatal accident—"

"That won't be necessary," Quintus interjected hastily. "Ashur's very loyal to me… and Rufio." For the first time since the door had been shut on them, Quintus cracked a grin. "Besides, I'd threaten him that I would withold his sex privileges and he'd never get another fucking if he ever thought of betraying my trust."

The silvery laugh rang out again, louder this time, causing a faint stir of interest from beyond the bedchamber door. Vipsania crossed to the tall dresser where rested a flagon of wine and two small goblets. She filled them, handed one to Quintus and raised her cup. "To our happy marriage, Quintus. Now, let's sound like we're making the beast with two backs."

Stifling the giggles that threatened at every moment, the two threw themselves in to a frenzy of convincing sound effects, accompanied by taking turns to thump the bed noisily. "Think you're doing it with that buff redhead of yours and coming to a splendidly vocal climax," Vipsania whispered.

"How do you know all this kind of thing?" Quintus hissed back between loud moans.

Vipsania raised her eyes to the ceiling in mock despair. "I told you I'm no virgin, you silly ass… Oh! Oh! My dearest… OH!"

Quintus joined in, shouting ecstatically into a bolster so that the half-muffled cries of sexual release sounded more convincing.

"Now, bloody the sheet for the sake of Bona Dea." With which Vipsania threw herself back on the bed in a languished, happily ravished pose amid tangled coverings while Quintus winced at the cut he made on his palm with the point of his eating knife. He smeared blood on the removed lower sheet and, winding a loincloth modestly about his waist, part-opened the door and waved the evidence to a massed cry of joy from the other side.

"Now perhaps they will leave us alone," she said firmly as he closed off the celebrating relatives, and then added as Quintus made to sit back on his bed, "You can't expect me to sleep on the floor…"

"Can't we just share, not touching, I mean for one night?"

The firm shake of Vipsania's head dispelled any thought of a comfortable sleep. "I shall have to demand a larger room so we can have a proper marriage bed, wide enough for us to each have our space. It's time father pushed Lucius Primus out, get him his own place. He has three rooms to himself and Maia, all larger than this, and they're hardly ever in Rome." He went to the dresser and pulled out some more bedding. "I suppose we'd better do some more heavy breathing, grunting and groaning, don't you?"

* * *

Marcus nudged Livius Secundus. "Hear that? Well away at it for a second time, they are."

"Oh to be young again, to be newly wed, dipping the wick for the first time."

Marcus stiffened in surprise and turned to look at his older brother. "First time? Are you saying you'd never done it before you married Aurelia?"

"What? No! Of course not. I can tell you that Aurelia had nothing to complain of, brother." Secundus harrumphed indignantly.

"I'm sure my bride won't either. We sailors have plenty of fun in port." Marcus swallowed thickly, his asshole tingling in memory of the reaming he'd received from Caesar… several times.

"Bacchus bare his buttocks, but they really are humping away. I never thought Quintus had it in him. I suppose we'd better leave the happy couple to it."

The brothers crept away, last of the party to take to their own beds. They never saw Ashur creep from the shadows minutes later and settle down, back to the marriage chamber door. Ear to the timbers, he could hear the snores coming from the other side, one higher-toned set from the bed over by the window, the other, deeper, right up against the door against which he leant.

He smiled a smugly satisfied smile.

E·I·G·H·T·E·E·N | XVIII

2nd to 4th days of January AD 109

The carnival atmosphere of Saturnalia brought the year to a raucous conclusion. Even stuffy Domus Alba echoed to merriment on the traditional "upside-down" day when masters became servants and waited on their slaves at meals.

And suddenly it was January in the year of the consuls Aulus Cornelius Palma Frontonianus and Publius Calvisius Tullus Ruso. Over the holiday period Quintus avoided the Emporium, justifying the absence from Rufio by telling himself he needed to help his new wife acclimatize to the Caecilii. The couple endured the bawdy breakfast following their night of frantic consummation, the blood-smeared sheet was duly admired, libations offered to the household Lares and the Penates, the spirits of the pantry, and numerous toasts were raised to the newlyweds. Come the evenings Quintus and Vipsania were happy to retire to his bedroom where they repeated the sound effects of married bliss before settling: her on his bed, he on hurriedly assembled blankets and a fleece covering.

"We really must get a place of our own," Vipsania had said on the first day of the year. They were closeted in a corner of the atrium, away from any family. "Perhaps we could move to the farm outside Veii that's a part of my dowry."

Quintus looked dubious.

"I'm joking. I'm a city girl. I think of the country as a short summer retreat when Rome gets too hot and smelly."

"What about the block of apartments that came with the dowry, on the Cispian hill? Does it boast a name?"

"Sunrise Cloisters," Vipsania answered after a moment's thought.

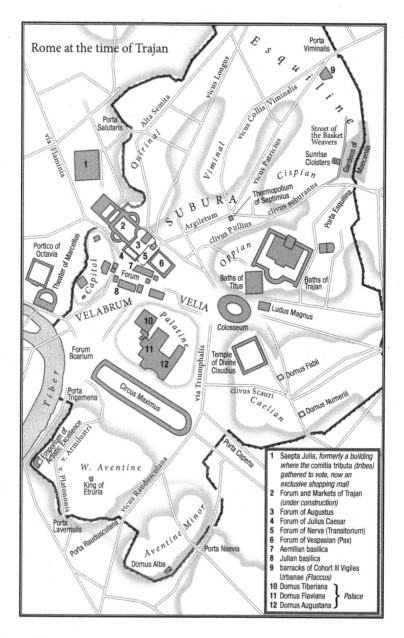

Rome at the time of Trajan

1 Saepta Julia, *formerly a building where the comitia tributa (tribes) gathered to vote, now an exclusive shopping mall*
2 Forum and Markets of Trajan *(under construction)*
3 Forum of Augustus
4 Forum of Julius Caesar
5 Forum of Nerva (Transitorium)
6 Forum of Vespasian (Pax)
7 Aemilian basilica
8 Julian basilica
9 barracks of Cohort III Vigiles Urbanae *(Flaccus)*
10 Domus Tiberiana ⎫
11 Domus Flaviana ⎬ *Palace*
12 Domus Augustana ⎭

"Perhaps we might find a free apartment. There are some quite large ones, as I recall. Room for us as well as Dryantilla and Ashur. Let's go have a look, and…" she hesitated and glanced up coyly from under long dark lashes. "Why not ask Tullius Rufio along?"

Quintus looked crestfallen. "I think we broke up."

Vipsania clasped her hands and regarded him sternly. "One: what do you mean, you *think*? Two: why haven't you said anything to me about it?"

"Because I'm not sure how things stand. He was a bit angry last time we spoke."

"But… I mean you jointly own a gladiator. You can't be broken up."

"He's the problem, I think. Regulus, I mean. Rufio's jealous. Which isn't like him, but…"

"But what?"

Quintus gave a great sigh and stared up at the winter-covered impluvium. "It's complicated."

"That's what men always say when they haven't a clue what they think." She huffed impatiently. "Heights of Olympus, Quintus! He's little more than a slave, worse, a gladiator. They're known to be flirtatious if it will get them something, or somewhere. Forget Regulus and send Ashur off to ask Tullius Rufio to meet us there."

"He may refuse."

"I'd send Dryantilla, but I doubt her feminine wiles will excite in the way I suspect Ashur's will do. I'll speak to him and tell him exactly what to say. Then we'll see."

They set off an hour later. The day was set fair, though cold, with a pale cloudless sky glimpsed between the towering apartments above shops lining Clivus Suburanus. Like the adjacent Viminal, the Cispian was a spur of the much greater Esquiline hill, which spread north and south within and without the Servian Wall. At the top of the incline, where Clivus Suburanus bore right to eventually pass through the Porta Esquilina, the small Street of Basket Weavers branched off left, edging on its eastern side the extensive Gardens of Maecenas. Halfway along, opposite this delightful oasis of foliage, lawns, and elegant public buildings, they came across the insula that Quintus now owned (though his father's name was still on the dowry deeds).

"The watchman's called Janus," Vipsania informed him. "Which is appropriate because he needs eyes in the back of his head as well."

"Or because he's typically a two-faced bastard concierge," Quintus said with a grin.

She returned it with one that hardly became a demure Roman matron. "I've met him when I've visited with my father. Just look right at his nose," she added mysteriously. "Ah, here he is now."

A short, stocky man waddled out from the central entryway, a gap-toothed grin of welcome on his face. When he gurned at them Quintus saw the wisdom of Vipsania's advice. It was hard to tell if the smile reached his eyes because they wandered about quite independently of each other. It was obvious why his loving parents named their son after the two-headed god. The left eye almost gazed ahead, though disconcertingly not quite at whom he was looking, while the other roved all over the place as if watching out for low-flying raptors. His nose was the focus point, then.

"Domina, what an honor." He bowed low and held an arm wide to indicate the insula's main step-up entrance. Vipsania introduced Quintus as the new owner of the apartments and shops below. "Welcome to Sunrise Cloister, dominus."

"I like the name," Quintus said, glancing back. "I suppose here on top of the hill and with the gardens opposite it does get the sunrise."

Down the access alley to the left of the four-story insula Quintus could see a second entrance. To the right and back it abutted other properties. The block was a hollow square around a small courtyard. Judging by the litter, this was where those on the upper floors threw their rubbish. He made a note to stop that. The main entrance sat between two shops: one a baker's, the other a seller of leather goods and an odd range of trinket trash. A humid yeasty aroma wafted out from the bakery. Locals were handing over their corn dole in small sacks at one side while at the other a girl took payment from people in a second line before handing out their baked loaves.

"It's handy having a Janus as watchman, after all he is the god of gates, doorways, and passages," Vipsania murmured as they passed into the dimness of a passage leading to a dark stairwell. Janus led the way up brick-laid steps to the second and third floors where hallways ran off the landings to serve the side and rear apartments. Wooden treads connected the third and fourth floors, but everything seemed sound. Quintus took everything in but his mind was on the impending reunion with Rufio… *That's if he turns up.*

A covered gallery ran right along the front of the block on the top floor, providing a splendid view to the east over the Gardens of Maecenas. After a full inspection of the insula, Vipsania asked Janus if any apartments were unoccupied.

"Oh yes, domina. The corner apartment on the floor above the bakery is very nice." His right eye semaphored wildly. "The owner of the Hog in Heat had it but he was too fond of his tripe and offal pies and one of them carried him off this two months past."

"It's cleared of his possessions?"

"Yes, domina. Ready for a new renter."

She looked at Quintus, who shrugged. "Let's have a look."

"It should do us well enough." Vipsania bustled through the rooms. "Spacious, in fact, though we might get sick of the smell of baking bread. See, two large bedrooms, so—"

"You will be able to have guests to stay!"

Quintus and Vipsania whipped around in surprise. Rufio leaned casually against the doorpost. He was first to break the awkward silence. "Ashur's directions were very accurate." He pushed off and came across the empty concrete and tiled floor, right hand clasped deferentially to his chest. "As Quintus doesn't look like he's going to introduce us, I am—" A look of surprise suffused his face. "I— I know you, lady."

Quintus screwed his eyebrows together in matching astonishment. "You do?"

Vipsania looked both embarrassed and coy. "You remember me! Last year," she explained to Quintus, "Tullius Rufio caught me with his lash at Lupercalia."

"Where?"

She tapped her hip. "About here."

"I mean where were you standing?"

"At the bottom of the Velia," Rufio said. "I do remember it."

"I remember it very well." Vipsania simpered teasingly. "There was a lot of you on show, Tullius Rufio!" Her sly wink at Quintus said, *Ooh, I know what it is you like in him... or* on *him!*

Quintus wasn't playing along. "What I seem to remember is that you were in a random whipping mood that day. Loser!" He added in an acid tone.

"Quintus!" Vipsania glared at him.

Rufio suddenly broke into a broad grin. "Well that makes two of us, Quintus—pleb and patrician, losers both. Look, I don't know what got into me that day at the Ludus Gallicus. I apologize for what I called you. And I've really..."

"Missed you," Vipsania finished for him. "It's time to put any differences behind you and make up. Quintus has something to tell you, Tullius Rufio." She glanced at Quintus. "Tell him why we want two large bedrooms, dear husband, and why one's not for guests. Tell him why granting me great fertility with the mark of his bloodied goat thong at Lupercalia was beside the point. Go on." And with that, she swept out into the communal hallway and left them alone.

"She reminds me of someone," Rufio said, "but I can't think who exactly," Quintus gave a noncommittal shrug. "Definitely an organizer. How did I get to promise the loan of Zeno, Phocas, Alexius, and our big handcart the day after tomorrow to haul a load of furniture from your father's store?"

"Vipsania's a bully, I've come to the conclusion. It won't be much of a load and I bet she'll complain how unfashionable everything is. Which is why it got dumped in the jumble room in the first place."

Rufio chortled gleefully and risked a playful punch at Quintus's upper arm. "My oh my, a Gaia-on-Gaia kind of girl you married, Quintus! Does she write Sapphic poetry, ha ha. I can't get my thoughts around that yet, except it means you'll be free to… *entertain*? Regulus well away from ludus or Domus Alba."

Quintus, rubbing his arm absentmindedly, looked uncomfortable. "I'm not sure."

He didn't elaborate and Rufio felt it wise to comment no further. The truce was too fragile to push. *He can't bring himself to admit how deep in over his head he is with Regulus.* They were making for the Colosseum in response to an urgent message an urchin had delivered. "Bebryx wants to see you by the Meta Sudans," he panted heavily for effect. He'd already run all the way up the Aventine only to be redirected to the Cispian, so his demand for an extra fat reward was not a surprise. The clip over the ear Rufio delivered was though.

"Go, both of you," Vipsania had ordered. "I'll be fine. Janus will find a chair to take me back to Domus Alba and I'll look at this furniture you mentioned we might have, Quintus."

They found the Scythian where Clivus Cuprius and Vicus Insteius merged into the pavement circling the Colosseum. He was pacing around the colossal statue of Sol well apart from the circling crowd of gladiators and their hopeful fans around the Meta Sudans. He was not alone. With a shot to his groin, Rufio recognized the beauteous Briton at the gladiator's side. Bebryx glowered. "I thought you weren't coming."

"Well, we're here now," Quintus said flatly. "What's this about?"

"I want you to hear Britannicus. It concerns what happened in Capua when I defeated Capreolus. Talk, tell them." He pushed the boy forward. Britannicus didn't look much like he wanted to tell anyone anything. He looked everywhere except at Quintus or Rufio.

Bebryx nudged him roughly, and after swallowing nervously he spoke in a timorous voice. As still as a statue, Rufio listened to the sad tale and the unwitting part Britanniucs had played in helping kill his former master. Quintus shuffled uneasily, shaking his head from time to time.

When he finished, Bebryx spoke up. "Thing is, he's heard again the voice of the hooded man who gave him the potion that dulled Capreolus and it belongs to someone we've all met."

"Panthera?" Rufio breathed.

"Gaius Fabricius Luscinus?" Quintus asked.

Bebryx nodded. "He's dangerous." He patted his boy's shoulder. "Thanks to Britannicus, Ursus—who is not as dumb as he looks—has told me many, many things. I know the name of the *collegium* Panthera fronts. They call themselves s·a·d·a, *Societas ad divitias augendas*. Very secretive, but like an octopus with tentacles everywhere."

"A group dedicated to the increase of their wealth. Sounds about right," Rufio said. He smiled surreptitiously at sad Britannicus.

"Yes, and there are rumblings in the ludus that two muneraria have crossed them. I think that's you."

Rufio looked hard at Quintus. "I suppose you haven't done anything since that day he spoke to us? No, I thought not, and I certainly haven't. I can't believe Clivius or any of the other club patrons would cave in to a bunch of snobby senators."

"I would reconsider," Bebryx rumbled. He shook his head "Even I have been approached and given a choice: cooperate or face never knowing when another will be provided the means to defeat me. You are in peril. Your Regulus is infected. He will be your undoing... perhaps even your deaths. Go with extreme caution. I wanted you to hear Britannicus and know that I am not deranged."

"I'm not inclined to trust that man," Quintus muttered as he and Rufio walked back through the Velia toward the Forum. "Regulus swore to me that he's never taken a bribe to throw a fight or anything," He looked as unhappy as had Britannicus.

"Perhaps he *hasn't* taken one… yet. But *you* have remarked before now that something doesn't quite ring true. He's too sure of himself, the airs and graces of a patrician."

"Oh leave him alone! He's got a big fight coming up. I'm sure he wants to win. For us as well as for himself."

"I don't know. You must ask him again, Quintus. If it upsets you I'll do it."

"No, it's my task. I still trust him. You don't." In spite of the words, Quintus adopted a gentle tone. "If he lies I know I'll know it. Oh… and I'm grateful for the offer of help with the furniture."

"You mean Zeno, Phocas, Alexius. I'm not lifting a finger! And you'd better go supervise them if you don't want everything smashed to bits."

"Changing the subject, I'm curious." Quintus managed a smile. "What do you think that sweet Briton—and don't think I'm so far gone as not to notice you undressing him back there—had to do to screw information out of Ursus?"

"I think you said it. Screw."

Quintus shuddered at the image.

As Quintus and Rufio crossed the Forum, Bebryx's warning fresh in their thoughts, only paces away rapacious minds were considering their future.

Voices clamored for attention in the confines of the Aemilian Basilica, contracts were waved and exchanged, seals stamped in hot wax, lawyers argued their cases in the petty court, overseen on this day by Atilius Crescens, who as chief of the Centumviral, or Chancery court, handled matters of civil law. He sounded loud and irritable. The Banker was equally put out—not that anyone would notice from his bland features—but addressing the Summa in a back corner of the basilica he kept his voice low.

"I have just received figures through our usual channels resulting from private games up and down the peninsula. They won't set the Rostrum ablaze but they are adequate. However, that is not why

I asked for us to meet urgently. To cut to the quick, we've had no representation from the muneraria of Regulus and time is running out before Ostia. Everything else is in place and we could let this one go for the time being, postpone securing future cooperation… and punishment."

"With respect, friends," Luscinus broke in, "we should not do that. To let these callow juveniles get away with ignoring us and—worse—letting the Crossroads patrons muscle in on our operations would be a fatal error. Other of our assets might see our failure to act instantly as a sign of weakness and get ideas we'd rather they did not."

"I agree." Papus pursed his lips in a gesture of finality.

The Banker fixed his eyes on Virius. Who was less sure of drastic action. He didn't let the uncertainty show in his carefully guarded bearing. Livius would hold him responsible if anything unfortunate should happen to Quintus. Not that Livius cared a shit about his nephew beyond the long-term hope that he'd one day get his leg over the boy and fuck him brainless. But if the boy got hurt and his involvement ever leaked it could harm the deal to supply the marble drums for Trajan's column.

"Fabius Virius?"

"Ah…I will agree with whatever you decide."

"The behavior of the Crossroads Clubs is disgraceful!" Papus added indignantly. "I am sickened to think that anyone should attempt to fund games from the proceeds of criminal operations."

"Luscinus?"

"We can squash two ants with one stamp." Luscinus looked at the other three in turn. "Caecilius Alba is the Crossroads' figurehead. They hide behind his patrician standing. Eliminate him and F·G·O·T will reject the application."

"What about his associate, the Tullius boy?" the Banker asked.

Luscinus dismissed the objection. "A pleb of little consequence. He can't front for the clubs, and if he gets in the way, well worse luck for him."

Virius sighed inwardly. Not much he could do. Just hang in and hope the murder of Livy's daft nephew wouldn't fuck up the Fabii-Caecilii deal, which was on shaky grounds as it was, considering doddery Lucius Caecilius Alba's dislike of him. And he thought Luscinus foolhardy to underestimate the offspring of that cunning bitch Junilla Rufia.

"I'm grateful that you persuaded Quintus to let Rufio visit your new home." Two days had passed since then, and Junilla and Vipsania were enjoying a cup of watered wine and some pastry fancies. They were seated companionably on padded stools around one of the Emporium's tablinum tables.

"It will be our home soon," Vipsania corrected. "I confess, I shall be happy to be away from Domus Alba, not that everyone hasn't been kind," she hurriedly added.

"But it will be so much nicer to be your own mistress in your own place." Junilla smiled conspiratorially. "Free to live your lives as you wish."

Rufio, free as usual with any news concerning Quintus, had told his mother about the astonishing acommodation between his dearest friend and Vipsania. Junilla, free as usual with discussing anything relating to her son and his best friend, had informed Vipsania that she knew. "You remind me very much of myself at your age, my dear," Junilla had said after admitting this. "With, perhaps, the difference of my preference for male anatomy."

It could have been awkward, but Vipsania just burst into laughter, complemented Junilla on her taste in wine ("It's from my sister Velabria's vineyards"), and everything had been plain sailing since.

"It's kind of you to lend Quintus the labor of your slaves today."

"That lazy lot could do with some exercise. Though I note Rufio has made off on 'important business' with my helper Hephaestion and Adalhard, who Rufio thinks is his to command when actually he was given to me. That way he's avoided having to do a bit of lifting! He says the apartment you have picked out is large. In fact his words were, 'big enough for a first-class Neronian orgy.' I ought to apologize on his behalf."

Vipsania's tinkling laughter lit up the room. She had not expected Rufio's mother to be so frank and open, but then, she didn't know Rufio all that well either, in spite of having followed him and Quintus around for some time. She decided to keep her surveillance from Junilla in case she thought it a bit creepy. She had not thought to form such a warm feeling for the woman so quickly—if at all— and yet here they were conversing like friends of long acquaintance.

"You and your sons enjoy a very free life, Lady Junilla. I do envy you."

"You mean Rufio. Cato is firmly under the thumb," she fibbed. "And please call me Junilla. I'm no lady, even though I was a very demure matron until my dear husband died."

"I'm sorry. Was it a recent bereavement?"

"No, some years ago. He died under Zeus."

Vipsania looked puzzled. "Under Zeus…do you mean a slave?" She tried to sound faintly shocked but saw straight away that Junilla wasn't fooled.

"No, Tullius died when a gigantic statue of Zeus in the process of raping Ganymede fell on him," she said dryly. "It had been badly deposited on a high pedestal and he didn't hear him coming—if you'll pardon the expression."

Vipsania's bemused smile indicated that she was aware of the double meaning but she was unsure of the attitude to strike at this oddly cheerful note. "You make light of it."

"On the contrary, my dear, the statue was extremely heavy." Junilla gave a throaty chuckle. "Don't mistake me, I adored my raffish husband, but it was some years ago and I've had the business—two of them in fact—to manage since, which has kept me fully occupied and with no time for extended mourning. However, I have to say that having his father exit this world under the father of the gods busy fornicating with a handsome boy affected Rufio in some way (Cato was too young). He's always been very drawn to handsome boys thereafter. He tore around like a crazed stallion seeking casual companions until he bumped—or should that be humped?—into Quintus and everything has been as smooth as the Via Appia since... well," she hesitated, "until recently."

"I do hope you don't blame me for that."

Junilla gave Vipsania a frankly appraising look. "I did for a while—indeed, Rufio was concerned at the thought of Quintus marrying you (or any woman, come to that!), but since my reheaded rapscallion spilled the chickpeas I can see Quintus's fling with the gladiator was what nearly split them up. So unlike level headed Quintus. Indeed, your good influence appears to have brought them back together. I do hope they resume their closeness. You see, their very differences complement each other."

"I can see by the way you say his name you like him."

"Quintus? He's almost like my son-in-law, in a funny kind of way." Junilla cocked her head to one side, a slip of a smile crossing her full lips. "Have you read any of his poetry?"

"I did attend a reading the Emperor arranged. It was...fulsome."

"This is different." Junilla crossed the tablinum to a vast chest, opened a drawer, rummaged around inside, and produced a large scroll. She turned and unrolled it on one of the three large tables that almost filled the room. "Quintus writes and Rufio illustrates," she said, clearly proud of her son's artistry. "It's almost finished, he tells me."

Vipsania peered at the neat lines of script and then leaned closer. "Well, well. He never told me about these. A pity he's no interest in Sapphic eroticism." Her eyebrows shot up. "By the Three Graces! How on earth can anyone get into that position?"

"Boys," Junilla said in a droll voice, "will be boys."

2nd to 4th days of January AD 109

With a spring in his step, Flaccus felt like a boy again. And one of Lucretia's would do nicely before reporting for duty—on a night promising rain. The barracks of Cohort III Vigiles Urbanae sat at the top of Vicus Patricius, close to Porta Viminalis. The street branched off Clivus Suburanus opposite the Thermopolium of Septimius. Flaccus felt peckish and thought a bite of supper would be in order before nipping over to Lucretia's Lupanar. A quickie fuck should set him up for a dreary stint training recruits in the use of pumps, buckets, hooks, picks, mattocks, and axes—the vigiles' fire watch tools when they weren't hauling in perpetrators and other assorted riffraff.

"Greetings, Flaccus Caepio." Septimius clasped his arm across the spotless counter. "Haven't seen you for days."

Flaccus dropped his official notes on the marble top with a wooden clatter. He elbowed the tablet aside. "Saturnalia kept me busy." Legs tucked over a stool, he glanced at the chalked up bill of fare. "And Cohort IV up on the Aventine were short of officers, so I got sent there a few days."

"Bunked down at the Emporium?"

Flaccus ignored the sly wink. "It's convenient and Lady Junilla is always kind, so long as she gets to boss me about and help her out." *And after that mucky orgy at the start of Saturnalia, Rufio keeps giving funny looks and avoiding me. Still... it was worth it!*

Cloud, thick as sin, threatened to abbreviate the too-short January day. Pregnant with rain, a blustery breeze matched his jumpy mood. Quintus looked up and hoped the weather would remain clement until Zeno and his fellow slaves got all the furniture into the Sunrise Cloister apartment. He was headed there, but in the middle of the Forum Romanum he swerved aside. He knew he shouldn't tarry, but neither could he put off accosting Regulus, and so detoured along Via Sacra and over the Velia to the Ludus Gallicus.

A jolt of consternation flickered across Dolabella's face when they met in the entryway. The lanista bunched heavy brows together. "Caecilius Alba!" he blurted as if it were a question. He swiftly recovered his composure, offered a tight smile, but Quintus could not put aside the idea that the lanista looked as if he had seen a ghost. He put it down to the lateness of the hour, greeted Dolabella politely, still wary of the lanista's relationship to that Luscinus fellow, and announced his intention of seeing Regulus. He asked whether he was at practice or resting and was directed to the inner gate, where a security guard admitted him to the inner sanctum of the ludus.

The impassive rocklike expression cracked minutely. Daroua's rubber lips twitched upward but Flaccus knew better than to think it a smile. The lupanar's Nubian bouncer didn't do humor. The slightest sway of his mountainous torso admitted Flaccus. With little time to spare, Flaccus accepted Lucretia's inflation-linked entry fee without a haggle, and two secundae later he was naked and busy at it.

He pushed the boy face down onto the hard brothel bed, climbed on after and straddled his legs. He ran hands up the smooth skin

of his thighs, forced fingers between his legs and groped at his stiff crotch. The lad moaned in professional protest. Within a few breaths, Flaccus was lost, in part to the rented body, in part to his dreams of doing Rufio again, glorious Rufio...

I turn him and pin his wrists above his head. So slim. Golden skin, dark nipples perked up, tight belly button. He groans, wet lips glinting. I rear up, and jut my cock against his chin. My wet knob nudges pert lips. My balls caress his chin. I feel his mouth wet against the root of my shaft. He moans. With a quick finger squeeze on his jaws I get his glistening lips to open up to me. His teeth graze my knob as I edge inside and slide my shaft into his hot mouth. Boys look so fucking pretty with their face stuffed full of big cock. I feel his tongue trying to make room, nudge against the clenched muscles guarding his throat. I'm only halfway in, but...

I haven't time for foreplay. I want his ass. Now

It hadn't gone well. Regulus played obstinate, denied everything Bebryx accused him of. "The Scythian is envious of my youth and vigor, my good looks, of the way the crowds cheer me." The strength of the bluster more than the content rang a sour note. Quintus kept hearing Rufio inside his head; Rufio who had ever been a loyal, trusty friend, sounding warnings in a tentative voice cautious of pushing them both into another argument. Trust cracked. He drew a breath and struck Regulus a hard blow. The gladiator staggered back and collapsed onto his bed of rushes under a thin blanket, hand to his jaw.

"You lie and in doing so you make me a liar!" Quintus growled. Regulus examined the smear of blood on his hand and then glared back. "Admit it. You have been bribed..." A sobbing laugh broke from Quintus's lips, a sound of frustrated anguish. "It's not as if you're alone. This whole filthy business is corrupt." He clenched his fist again, but slammed it against the wall.

* * *

Gripping his ankles, I twist his legs, flip him on his tummy. I elbow his thighs apart, thumb his boy butt wide open. I focus on the vulnerable little rosebud, pink and twitching in the baby-white hollow of hairless flesh. The darker ridge, leading to the delicate balls, curves down into shadow. My hard-on jerks painfully as I imagine it plowing into Rufio... no, this boy whore. My balls ache with lust. I press the blood-gorged head

273

against the little twitching hole. He groans. He wants it. Holding him firm by his cock and balls, I push some more and edge inside, feel his sphincter clutch at me. He gasps. Another push, he yelps, eyes aglow with pleasure. He doesn't want me to stop. I keep pushing and my cock disappears from view. Snap! I'm in. His muscle tight around the top of my shaft...

"Oh fuckit!" Coitus interruptus hit Flaccus in mid-thrust. He just realized he left his note tablet at the cookshop. "By Minerva's minty minge, if it gets nicked the tribune will have my balls, if the centurion hasn't already hacked them off."

His deflating erection plopped free. No creamy orgasm for Flaccus, but at least Lucretia's boy got his money.

Regulus remained on the floor, looking up at Quintus with a baleful stare. "Corrupt, you say, dominus, but then so is Bebryx," he muttered sullenly.

"Possibly," Quintus admitted. "But at least he's open about it. How much were you offered, and for doing what?"

Regulus pushed up into a half-sitting position. The floor rushes whispered under his weight. "I haven't taken any bribes."

Quintus wondered. This was a different voice, perhaps telling the truth. And yet the gladiator's demeanor argued against it. Maybe Rufio had the right of it, perhaps he hadn't yet been bribed. A turmoil assaulted Quintus's breast. He no longer knew what to do. In the end he had shaken his head sadly and left his man rubbing a sore chin where the unexpected punch landed, and words that they would meet again in Ostia.

No, it hadn't gone well. Perhaps Rufio would be able to discover the truth. Yet Quintus still pined urgently for the embrace of his gladiator. Rain hammered down as he hurried around the Colosseum's skirts and into a darkened street beside the Baths of Titus. He wasn't thinking much about his direction and paid no attention to two men who turned into the street ahead of him. The Subura was more Rufio's world than his, but some geography had rubbed off over the months. He had a hazy idea of a shortcut to Clivus Pullius through the tangled alleys below the building site of Trajan's new baths. From there he could cut across to Vicus Patricius.

He raised the cloak's hood and waded near blindly through all kinds of filth caught in the river running over steep cobbles. He barely recognized Clivus Pullius or saw that the two men he'd been following earlier had paused to look into a store on the corner and now followed his path. He crossed the wider street and plunged headlong up the narrow alley he hoped would take him to the intersection of Clivus Suburanus and Vicus Patricius.

"Oh forgetful Flaccus," Septimius exclaimed. He was wiping the counter top and almost swept aside a note tablet the vigilis had left behind in his rush to get to Lucretia's. "He'd forget his prick if it wasn't well screwed on." He grabbed the tablet, making sure the two wooden leaves were tightly shut against the downpour, and turned to his apprentice chef busy chopping root vegetables for a heartwarming stew. "Keep an eye on things, Appulus, I won't be long."

Septimius hoped to catch Flaccus on leaving Lucretia's, since he hadn't made any secret of his next destination. Lucretia's squatted on the corner of a cramped street that ran steeply downhill between Clivus Suburanus and Clivus Pullius. After the brothel's doorway it narrowed until it was little more than a passage. Septimius cursed the rain. He turned down the alleyway.

It was an uphill struggle in the dark alley's confines. Quintus slipped on uneven stones and thanked his prudence in wearing full boots. Rain impeded his sight; the deluge hammering the cobbles deafened. He never heard the sudden rush of feet, but he felt the sharp blow to the side of his head. At the instant the assailant struck, his heel skidded off a raised stone and the cudgel fell with less impact than its wielder intended. Nevertheless, Quintus crashed down. Stars filled his vision. A dark figure loomed over him, arms lifted to deliver more abuse. Instinct took over. He rolled away from the worst, only to meet a painful booted kick in the ribs.

As the law demanded, he was unarmed but for his eating knife, and even that was now trapped in his sodden cloak's folds. Not so for his attackers. A distant brazier glinted dully off the brandished blade. Whoever they were, they wanted him dead. "Grab him!" Strong hands under his armpits hauled him up. "Hold tight so I can stick him!" Quintus writhed, but the first blow had blunted his senses. He cried out before a hand clamped over his mouth. The assassin with the blade drew his arm back for a killing stab…

A gasping cry rang out accompanied by a loud oath, followed by an obscenity in a different voice. The knifeman staggered back, pulled by a mighty force, and fell to his side on the cobbles. "By Apollo's ancient ass-crack!" yelled Flaccus as he delivered a swinging boot to the downed man's head. He followed it up with another to the chest. At the same time the hands holding Quintus squeezed harder for a moment and then suddenly let go. His would-be killer yelped in agony as Septimius drove a nasty looking kitchen knife into the meat of the man's shoulder, simultaneously kicking his feet

from under him. He too followed up with a boot to the balls. The cry of pain echoed off the enclosing walls.

Flaccus gave Quintus a hand up and gasped in shock when he saw who he'd saved. "What in Hades' name are you doing in a place like this on such a horrid night?"

Quintus coughed, shook his head to clear some of the birdies still tweeting away in there. "I— I was on my— oh, never mind. I'm most thankful you were here… and, is it Septimius?" he asked in wonder.

The former imperial agent made sure both assailants were unlikely to slink off into the gathering night before coming forward to clasp Quintus by the arm. "I am happy to have been of help. Are you all right?"

"Damp and bruised and a bit dizzy, but fine otherwise."

"Who are they?" Flaccus demanded.

"Never set eyes on them before." *But I'm sure I know who sent them.*

Septimius handed Flaccus his tablet. "Ah, I am very happy to see that, much gratitude. I'll have their worthless asses hauled in for questioning, but you know what it's like. Won't give up much." He eyed the bedraggled state the rain and the fall had left Quintus in and waved the confiscated blade. "Nasty weapon."

"I'd better get back to the shop," Septimius said. "But if you need aid, you know where to come, Quintus." As he turned to go he added over the shoulder, "I'll sound the alert for more vigiles, Flaccus."

Several deep breaths restored Quintus to a semblance of normality. He gazed at his would-be killers, for he had no doubt his elimination was their task. The man Septimius knifed gripped his bloodied shoulder and groaned. Flaccus had a foot firmly planted on him to prevent his running off. His abettor, struck by Flaccus, would be counting stars for some time to come.

"I'd be ball-busting mad if anyone tried robbing me at knife point. Ah, here comes the cavalry."

"I'll be on my way, then. And… thanks, Flaccus. I owe you one."

"Is that a *one* with Rufio?" Flaccus smiled evilly as two of his fellow nightwatchmen strode past Lucretia's Lupanar toward them.

Quintus grinned, gave him the finger, and resumed his trek to Sunrise Cloisters. As he climbed Clivus Suburanus, busy in spite of the rain, his primary concern was for Rufio. If they'd come for him, they might equally have a go at Rufio, and Quintus couldn't bear the thought of that. He liked the feeling: his first thought was of Rufio… But he didn't want Regulus harmed either, at least outside of an honorable gladiatorial fight, and even then preferably not. He almost hoped Regulus had taken whatever bribe it was he denied having taken. Refusal clearly meant putting oneself in harm's way with these ruthless bastards. They thought they ran the games. Well it was time to teach whatever toad squatted behind his hired muscle a lesson. Gaius Fabricius Luscinus—Panthera—would be a start… next time he dared stick his greasy head over the parapet.

* * *

Uproar rocked the King of Etruria. An attack on one of the brethren was an attack on all, and as honorary members of the Western Aventine Crossroads Club that sentiment extended to Quintus and Rufio (who had been appalled when Quintus dashed into the Emporium, a warning on his lips). "And Dannotalus Dolabella is in on it, I'm sure," he insisted to the jam-packed tavern. "That's why he was astonished to see me. He must have thought I was already dead."

Rufio had been far less concerned for his own safety than that of Quintus after such a narrow escape. "I would kill anyone who harmed you," he'd cried, finally unclasping Quintus from his embrace. "We

must go see Clivius now!" But it was late, the weather had closed in again, and Junilla insisted on Quintus staying the night. So it was a whole day later that the boys alerted Ostiensus and his lieutenants.

"We were warned." Quintus was speaking as the hubbub his news had caused quieted. "Told we should not mess with something called *Societas ad divitias augendas*, or s·a·d·a."

"It's true," Rufio added. "And the man claimed this bunch of crooks was everywhere, much bigger than all the Crossroads Clubs put together."

"Which man is this?" Ostiensus demanded.

"A low equestrian called Luscinus." Quintus glanced around. "He also goes by the name of Panthera."

"*Panthera*! I know of him." All eyes turned to an elderly man urging a young man in front of him through the press of Crossroads soldiers. The similarity of their features marked them out as father and son, a fact he he quickly confirmed. "I am recently arrived in Rome from Nova Traiana Bostra in Nabataea—apologies friends, it's now the province of Arabia. My name is Aurelius Aquila and this is my son Nicantinous, a fine fighter of the arena but condemned to humiliation by the command of this…*Panthera*." He spat the word as an obscenity.

"I confirm his people have agents in many places, including distant Bostra," he went on. "They are greedy, corrupt, cruel, and above all ruthless. I have made the best time possible to flee my home before Governor Severus prosecuted me on charges trumped up by the creature of Panthera when I refused to accept a bribe for my son to throw a fight. As a provincial citizen, only Caesar can hear my petition, so I come to Rome."

He turned his gaze on Clivius Ostiensus. "I am deeply indebted to you for your assistance."

"It is the least I could do," the club patron responded, with an affection in his voice that must have surprised his hard-bitten men.

Aquila turned to the gathering. "We are distantly related, you see."

"It turns out that he's one of my father's distant cousins by various marriages," Felix related quietly to Quintus and Rufio. "I suppose you could take on Nicantinous as a second gladiator in your troupe."

"I think one's more than enough," Rufio retorted. "Shush, listen."

"I hope to clear my name." Aquila shook his head sorrowfully. "But I fear you cannot go against the power of those who govern the games from their secret dens of vice."

"We'll see about that," Ostiensus countered hotly. "When next are games of consequence held?"

"At Ostia," Quintus and Rufio said as one, not really answering the question.

Decimus the accountant added his reedy voice. "Ides of January. Big event. Vindex is candidate for praetor. There will even be lions to execute criminals." Decimus gave phlegmy chortle. "That should be fun in the confines of the theater orchestra. It's not that big."

"Then Ostia's where we will marshal our forces. My brother is patron of the Ostia brethren."

"I just hope Regulus is ready," Quintus muttered to Rufio. "For whatever…"

"My nephew was attacked, almost killed," Livius shouted at Virius.

"Ah… I hadn't heard."

"You expected it?"

Virius sighed deeply. "You are as responsible as anyone for your nephew playing with fire. Which he is. According to Luscinus, the men watching Regulus report he's behaving like a Miss Goody Two Sandals. If it's a front to fool officials, well and good, but Luscinus is convinced it's not and that your nephew is influencing him… in the wrong way." He sniffed. "Besides, do you really care?"

"For his welfare? No, but I care that he and his vagabond friend have a relationship with the Emperor. If Quintus has heard too much he might tell Trajan. And then we'll all be for the mines."

Virius sneered coldly. "Then it's a pity his assassins failed. We shall have to hope that the stupid boy sees sense and cooperates… or hope better of the next attempt to eradicate the nuisance."

T·W·E·N·T·Y | XX

14th day and Ides of January AD 109

At the second hour of the day three ponderous ox-drawn wagons rumbled up Ostia's elegant, arcade-lined Decumanus Maximus. The lumbering vehicles turned off into a street sandwiched between the theater and a long row of shops and warehouses. These backed onto the city's main baths—built by Domitian of damned memory—in which bathing facilities were reserved for the use of the visiting gladiators from the Roman ludi, currently gazing out through the barred ends of the covered wagons.

Pieces of painted scenery and props partly filled the warehouses sited opposite the theater, and here among the theatrical paraphernalia the gladiators and their guards were to be penned for three days. Dolabella and his doctore had traveled in some better comfort on their wagon driver's bench. They climbed down to supervise unloading the Ludus Gallicus gladiators, among them Regulus and Bebryx. The boy kept his distance from the Scythian, whose continuous dark looks threatened trouble.

Joined to the rear of the theater's tall *scaenae frons*, its elaborately decorated architectural stage, the Forum of the Corporations stretched toward the river. Merchants from all over gathered here—the center of commerce for the Imperium—to sell anything from shipping services and slaves to elephants and giraffes, but most importantly grain. The open-air market was now temporary home to various species of wild animals contained in an assortment of wheeled cages. The unmistakable roaring of lions could be heard across the street in the warehouses. Lions didn't much bother gladiators who never faced them, but caged in the Forum alongside their hungry executioners were prisoners condemned to die by claw and fang. Listening to the prowling beasts, their last night on earth would be a living nightmare.

At first glance the two-story insula was a handsome building. "But it's supposed to have four floors," Quintus complained. Appearances, however, had misled. The street's narrow width and the surprising height of the two lower floors conspired to mask the third and fourth levels. Above regularly spaced doorways and windows a second row of mezzanine-floor windows sat below arches cut into a very deep cornice, and from the street this huge overhang effectively concealed the upper apartments.

Quintus and Rufio had taken to horses for the journey to Ostia, accompanied by Ashur and Zeno on donkeys. They now stared in wonder at the large block of apartments Vipsania had brought Quintus in her dowry (or would when his father handed it over). It was in fact a mirror of the House of Diana where the company had stayed prior to embarking on the voyage to Alexandria last summer. Situated in Ostia's most fashionable district, one short lane off the Decumanus Maximus, three shops faced the street that ran toward the Tiber. At its junction with a lane parallel to the Decumanus, a large thermopolium-cum-tavern occupied the corner.

Rufio whistled in admiration. "Well, your father-in-law has done you proud. Tucked just behind the curia and across the way from the forum, a short walk from the theater and the main baths. Very nice. Even a fine looking eatery to pop down to for a midnight snack after a good fu—"

"Let's see if I can commandeer some rooms," Quintus cut him off.

As a traveler's inn, the tavern even boasted some stables at the rear, and at the advertised arrival of their new owner two stable lads dashed out to take the horses and donkeys into their care.

Rufio grabbed his light saddle pack and checked his pugio was safely secured. "These last few days I've felt a wee bit naked—and I don't mean in a good way. It's worrying, not being allowed to carry a proper weapon in Rome when you're faced by a death threat."

In answer, Quintus raised his matching dagger. "I'd prefer my spatha, but even though Ostia isn't Rome, it's too respectable to allow sword wielding—"

"Thugs like us being rowdy in the streets, blades drawn. Well, hopefully it won't come to that!"

"Famous last words," Ashur muttered darkly to Zeno.

Following a standard midday meal of barley mash washed down with a vinegar and plant-ash sports drink, each of the training schools was given a familiarize-yourself tour of Ostia's theater. The fights were to take place on the floor of the orchestra, a half-moon shaped area in front of the raised concrete stage. Regulus looked all around with interest. It was quite different from being in a full arena. A grand, centrally placed tunnel cut through underneath the upper rows of steeply rising concentric seating of the cavea. He counted up from the ground eleven rows, cut in two either side of the tunnel by access steps; a further nine divided into five sections by access steps in the upper level. A semi-circular back wall closed off the auditorium. To either side the lateral stage entrances had been barred by tall wooden gates, one side for the entrance of wild animals, the other for the gladiators when their turns came. In the same way, the three ornamented doorways cutting through the scaenae frons for actors' entrances and exits were closed off. The restricted combat area meant there would only be a maximum of two pairs fighting at a time, though presumably no one would be prevented from leaping up onto the stage if tactics demanded.

For once, the magistrates and other civic dignitaries would have to park their bums on hard stone because the two wide steps at the front where slaves placed comfortable chairs for their masters was occupied by a barricade. To his eye the spaced timber uprights and stretched rope netting looked like a flimsy protection for spectators

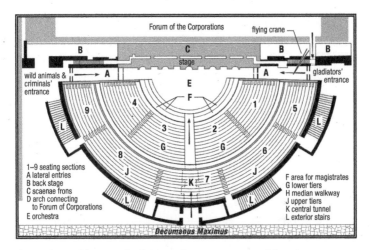

Forum of the Corporations

flying crane

B   C   B   B

stage

wild animals &
criminals'
entrance

A   A

gladiators'
entrance

E

F

9   4   1   5

L   3   2   L

G   G

8   6

J   J

K   7

1–9 seating sections
A lateral entries
B back stage
C scaenae frons
D arch connecting
   to Forum of Corporations
E orchestra

F area for magistrates
G lower tiers
H median walkway
J upper tiers
K central tunnel
L exterior stairs

Decumanus Maximus

from the wild animals during the venatores and bestiarii events. Regulus shrugged. Not his problem.

Scanning the theater's features, he espied Bebryx staring fixedly at the scaenae frons. The stage backdrop was an architectural feature rising three high floors, decorated with columns, pediments, niches for statues, blank windows and real ones with balconies from which an actor might call down to his fellow players on the stage. At the very top toward one end a crane arm stuck out. Its cable curled down and was tied to a balcony balustrade. It was this device which seemed to be of interest to Bebryx and, for a moment's merriment, Regulus tried imagining the brute gladiator playing a god, flown on the wire into a play's action, as he'd seen once before at a pantomime.

Tomorrow there would be plenty of blood spilled, but little of it gladiators'…unless Panthera decided to make an example of someone, maybe him, perhaps Bebryx for being such a nuisance to the aims of those who really controlled the outcome of games from behind the scaenae frons. Whoever they were. He hadn't seen sight of the man, yet knew instinctively that he was not far away.

* * *

Regulus was right. As the gladiators were touring the theater, Panthera was less than a shout away, tucked in the shade of a shopping arcade opposite the baths in the company of two lieutenants. They were keeping watch. At some point in the afternoon everyone passed into and out of the baths. It wouldn't be long.

"There!" he said after a wait he reckoned to be almost an hour.

"What seats have we got for tomorrow?" Rufio called out to Quintus, who just then emerged from the theater's main entrance. He crossed the pavement to where Rufio, Zeno, and Ashur waited.

"As usual, there are some allotted for muneraria," Quintus answered. They began to stroll toward the baths. "Ours are in section four, lower tier, row seven, places one and two. That's against the aisle steps, so it'll be easy for you to get out without disturbing anyone when you need the latrine."

"Says you! You're the one can never hold in a piss."

Ashur giggled and received a cuff from Quintus for his pains. "Shut it! The theater augur says the weather's set fair for tomorrow and the signs bode well for Vindex to gain the votes he needs."

It had been a short walk from the newly renamed *Domus et Taberna Caecilii* and an even shorter one to reach the bathhouse entrance. Rufio yawned. "Do we really have to be there for the early stuff? I'd prefer a lie in. We could miss the wild beast hunts and then get there in time to see lions tearing apart a few crooks. But I suppose you'll want to go see Regulus before the main fights start?'

Quintus shook his head. "He won't need my good wishes. I'll see him when he takes the sand." He led the way up the steps and into the moist warmth. "Still, I suppose we could give the venatores a miss, if you insist."

"Oh goody, a nice lie in," Ashur piped up. And perhaps a chance to get his master's thoughts off wretched Regulus. Ashur had several ideas in mind for that and wondered how he might inveigle delectable Rufio and husky Zeno to join in the action.

"See! Those two." Panthera hissed. "Just come out of the theater. They're muneraria, so I want to know what seats they have reserved. Find out Fronto! They're entering the baths; slaves following. Mark their appearance. Make sure your men know who they are looking for tomorrow. Canus, you take the redhead. You know what to do. Timing will be important. When the shit starts to fly, pin the little prick down. We can deal with him later. He's a pleb. They're all venal in the end and if he doesn't take the bait…well that's his problem. Naso, the dark-haired patrician is yours. Get him to me. I'll be at the farthest end of row seventeen, almost at the top of section five where there's standing room. That's the end overlooking the baths," he emphasized so there could be no mistake.

As the auguries promised, the Ides of January dawned fair. Viewed from his eyrie on a balcony high up in the thickness of the scaenae frons, the scattering of off-duty hired-on soldiers below looked like lazy ants to Bebryx. He laughed gruffly. "There to guard the barricade in case a wild beast decides to jump it and snack on a fat citizen."

Britannicus was nervous of the dizzying height. Weighed down by a secutor's armor, his sense of balance was awry. And then there was the damned sword. Bebryx called it a gladius but it was half the Briton's height! He cocked an ear to the cacophony of growls, rumbles, roars, and howls rising from behind (to his perspective) the theater's right-hand side entrance (left-hand to the gathering spectators). The animal and prisoner cages had been wheeled earlier into the courtyard of buildings on the other end of the access, ready for their cues to enter the arena. In their place, gladiators were free to wait in the Forum of the Corporations, to warm up, practice, consider their advertised opponents' tactics.

"I don't want to be stuck with the all the others waiting our turns," Bebryx had told Britannicus, who trotted after his master toward the arch which accessed the theater's lateral entrances and back-of-stage area. Being the Hero of Capua and many laureled Ludi Plebeii victor had advantages. The guard at the foot of the stairwell rising into the scaenae frons' left wall instantly recognized him, gratefully accepted one of the small horn tablets Bebryx had had carved with his sigil ("Gratitude, Bebryx, for my son, you understand…"), and granted the champion his right to view the fights from "the Gods."

Bebryx leaned big hands on the balustrade, right beside the iron ring to which was loosely fastened the rope dangling from the flying crane. By leaning over the rail and looking up to his left he could see the crane's arm sticking out at the farthest reach of the stage. No actor-god would be flying today. Lower down there was a view over the roofs of the warehouses where they had spent the night into the open spaces of the bathhouse complex. Immediately ahead, the highest tiers of the cavea were a few paces below and across the gap of some fifteen paces that was the lateral passageway to the orchestra the gladiators would use. Excited spectators slowly filled the cavea's graceful curve.

Suddenly, Bebryx stiffened. His gaze hardened. He stepped smartly away from the rail, pulling Britannicus with him. "Get back!"

"What is it?"

"There. Walking up to the end nearest. Panthera! Almost opposite. And if I'm not mistaken he has minions with him." Even as he spoke, one of those at Panthera's side turned to peer across the width of the auditorium. He raised a hand, gave a strange wave. Three-quarters of the way around the cavea, a man in a group of four standing on the median walkway semaphored back. To a casual observer it might have looked like acquaintances exchanging greetings, but Bebryx saw it as a signal, as if they were saying, "We're in place, how about you?" Panthera nodded curtly. Evidently satisfied, he seemed to be scrutinizing people descending from the four entrances at the very top descending to their seats in the upper and lower tiers. Because of the animal barriers the central access tunnel normally reserved for Ostia's elite was not in use.

"What evil is he up to?" Bebryx muttered, still keeping back as far as possible to avoid catching the cheating bastard's attention.

Ushers showed guests of the candidate praetor to the pulvinar, which because of the theater's structure was perched above the mouth of the central tunnel rather than the more usual amphitheater position on the elite lowest level. Rousing cheers soon announced the arrival of Octavius Vindex himself, splendid in his *toga candida*, which had been rubbed with chalk to a dazzling *candida*—the "pure white" of a man campaigning to win an election. The beast hunts were due to start any moment.

Quintus and Rufio strolled along the Decumanus toward the theater unaccompanied by Ashur and Zeno. Since there were no seats for them they had the day off to roam the city. The savage sounds of animals at bay comingled with an approving crowd's roars rose like a physical force from behind the theater's tall walls.

"We're too soon," Rufio complained. "The venatores are still thrilling the crowd with their skill at killing exotic African beasties."

"By the time we've found our places a pack of cheetahs and panthers will be devouring the *damnatio ad bestias*."

"Poor bastards."

"Convicted criminals," Quintus retorted.

"Even so, I bet you wouldn't enjoy being gnawed on by a big cat."

Big cats—a constant distraction to the convicts—held little interest for Regulus. Even the upcoming fight with the rising hoplomachus star Invictus wasn't bothering him much. Invictus the Unbeaten, hah! But something was eating him: an uneasiness in his gut after he'd spotted a familiar figure among the spectators making their way into the theater. The men of Ludus Gallicus were being shepherded by guards from the warehouse to the Forum of the Corporations. He'd glanced up the street at the crowded Decumanus and seen him. The senator who suborned him at Ludus Magnus to seduce

Quintus, the senator who thought he was anonymous but Regulus knew to be Publius Fabius Virius. As much as Panthera, the slimy bastard's presence signaled that skullduggery was afoot.

Bebryx and Britannicus had a fine aerial view of the slaughter. A score of condemned men, women, and children secured by their arms to two staggered lines of stakes made a bloody frieze across the width of the orchestra. The claws and slavering jaws of big hunting dogs held in some check by long leashes had torn chunks of flesh from many of the victims. With the dogs dragged away, snarling panthers soon finished off the poor souls. The lithe cats used the bent knees of their sagging victims as a handy step up to close jaws around tormented faces. The crowd's enthusiastic cheers rang from side to side of the theater, coming back from the rising scaenae frons like a physical assault.

Bebryx shook his head in disapproval at the carnage. He had a wary eye fixed on Panthera, who had just been joined by another, not one of his strongarm boys though—this man was quite expensively dressed, patrician and probably a senator by his haughty posture. The fixer stood on the side aisle steps, up against the low wall that followed the cavea's steeply rising side of the entrance passage and warned the unwary of the precipitous fall into its depths. Ventores came on to round up the satiated panthers, lassoing them with flexible collars affixed to long poles. As the yowling beasts were removed, attendants unshackled the ragged corpses and dragged them off. Out came the stakes, ready for the next bestiarii event.

To sighs of admiration and not a little fear, three female and two male lions were released onto the orchestra floor. They prowled around the confines until the gate behind them opened again to admit a dozen or so men, goaded on by sword point and spears: miserable men convicted of treason, murder, or atheism.

"The fools think keeping in a close group will save their wretched hides," Bebryx spat contemptuously. Britannicus shuddered.

Bellows of laughter greeted the antics of individuals who broke free when a lion approached, sniffing and growling. At first, the beasts seemed more confused than dangerous, until a female lazily tripped one man and slapped a great paw down, pinning him to the sand. Claws tore apart the flesh of his back. His agonized screams aggravated the other beasts, and suddenly the orchestra became a scrum of flying limbs and bounding felines.

Britannicus didn't wish to look, and cast his eyes higher, over the howling mob. Suddenly he nudged Bebryx and carefully pointed at the far reach of the auditorium. "Isn't that the redhead? Tullius Rufio?"

Bebryx narrowed his eyes. "It is, with that patrician friend of his, Caecilius Alba." The two boys, having emerged from one of the central stairwells at the top of the cavea, paused to take in the packed theater, obviously looking for their seats. From the corner of his eye Bebryx saw Panthera straighten like a hound scenting its prey. He tapped a lackey on the shoulder. The man immediately repeated his odd wave and received acknowledgment from across the cavea's wide half-bowl. Over there, the group had remained standing in a clutch on the median walkway, almost indistinguishable from the surrounding spectators, all on their feet, wildly cheering, shouting encouragement, and hurling insults to criminals and lions alike.

The brightness of Tullius Rufio's hair made following his progress a simple matter, even across the width of orchestra and auditorium. Bebryx watched him begin to descend the aisle steps toward the median walkway. On reaching it, he bore away from Bebryx's viewpoint over the top of the access tunnel, evidently aiming for the lower-level aisle on the other side of the cavea.

After that, events unfolded very swiftly…

T·W·E·N·T·Y-O·N·E | XXI

Ides of January AD 109

Rufio nodded briefly at three men who were blocking the walkway. They were on the other side of the aisle so they were not in his way. He started down, looking for the empty space on row seven, which was not easily seen since no one was actually sitting. A few steps down on the left he found the vacancy. He assumed without looking around that by the clatter of his dainty footwear Quintus was hard on his heels. As he slipped into their places, he turned to grin… only it wasn't Quintus. He instantly recognized the man pressing in after him as one of those who had been up on the walkway. Surprise turned instantly to anger and, when the rude fellow shoved him up against the next spectator on the bench, anger. "What the fu—!"

"Shut it!"

A sharp jab in the ribs. The man behind grasped his wrists and bent his arms back painfully before he could reach his own pugio. A trap! He glanced sideways through a sea of weaving heads and arms, frantic at seeing Quintus walking in the other direction along the median pathway between two strange men.

"Act normally. Keep your trap shut and you won't get hurt," the knifeman hissed, not that any would have him above the hullaboloo.

There was no room to maneuver, so closely pressed were they on all sides. Either the man gripping his arms so painfully or his murderous companion could have killed him on the spot and none would have been the wiser until the show was done.

As Rufio had turned to descend the aisle Quintus almost trod on his heels. But then a blocky figure on the walkway ahead pushed in front cutting him off. The man followed Rufio and at the same time two others stepped forward. One accosted Quintus in a polite but firm voice. "Caecilius Alba? This is Helva and I am Naso, a representative of the *Foedus gladiatorum orbis terrarium*. We desire an urgent word with you about your man Gaius Regulus."

"Is there some problem?"

"Not at all, I assure you, but Senator Livius Caecilius Dio requested our support, so my colleagues over there need to talk to you. We won't keep you from your friend very long." He smiled, held out an inviting arm, and then went ahead along the walkway toward the other end of the cavea. Puzzled, Quintus followed, uncomfortably aware of Helva closing in behind. He felt trapped. His neck prickled and the sensation only heightened his concern at what on earth Livy could be up to—again.

Panthera abruptly turned his back on the auditorium. The move almost caught Bebryx out. *He doesn't want someone to recognize him!* In turn, to prevent his own discovery he ducked back against the balcony's side wall, pulling Britannicus with him. It was only part concealment, but Panthera seemed too concerned with his no doubt evil plans to take notice of anything else. Peering out cautiously, Bebryx saw Tullius Rufio reach his row, easily spotted because the late morning sunshine burnished his red-gold head. Suddenly another man obscured him. But it wasn't his friend. And then Bebryx saw Caecilius Alba much nearer to hand, coming along the walkway in his direction. He was sure the thung leading the way was the distant signaller of earlier. *What's going on here?*

Boredom. The bane of a gladiator's life. Exercising, training, sparring every day never prepared a fighter for the wait before a contest. Regulus wondered where his patrons were. Quintus had last said they would see each other at Ostia. Well, this was Ostia. Seeing Virius was a reminder of how he was supposed to have split Quintus from

Rufio. Had he succeeded? He wasn't sure, and what was the point? Were he and Rufio a part of the game fixing conspiracy or not? Too many questions. But his mission was all that needed answers.

Bored with waiting and speculating, Regulus wandered idly through the connecting arch to the backstage area. Screams of agony and terror coming from the other side of the scaenae frons roused his curiosity. Carrying his myrmillo arms and armament in a neatly belted bundle at his side, he wandered toward the barred central stage door and raised his voice above the din at the two soldiers there. Heads together at the generous grill set in the door, they were obviously fascinated by the carnage.

"Can't go out there, mate," said the younger one, twisting around.

"Them beasties'd gobble a mite like you in a flash," the older man added in a hoarse guffaw. He gave Regulus a good once-over that turned into a leer.

"Can I at least have a peek?" Regulus treated his admirer to his best winning smile.

After a bit of cheek chewing, there was amiable agreement and space between them made at the door. "S'pose it can't hurt. Room for three."

The sanded orchestra floor glowed white with sunshine between carmine streaks painted over its surface. Regulus sucked in a breath at the butchery. Lions were singling out the prisoners clinging to the fearful cluster's periphery. Those dragged off were made short work of, their frantic cries for help soon choked off.

Not a death he'd wish on anyone.

Quintus and his escort ran the gauntlet between curved lines of wildly animated spectators. Flushed faces greasy with sweat rose to the theater bowl's rim, backs of heads fell away below in narrowing ranks down to the killing floor. Feet stomped, fists beat the air, mouths agape screamed for more blood and butchered limbs. It sickened Quintus. Looking ahead around the figure of Naso, he saw a group of four men—two in lightweight togas—standing perilously close to the cavea's end wall on the rising side aisle, a few steps up from where the median walkway ended. Oddly, the togate pair were looking out over the adjacent baths complex, apparently uninterested in watching lions maul criminals. Only the two attendants beside them stared at him.

As they reached the end, Naso stood aside, a step down the aisle. Helva slipped around Quintus to join him, pointing up at the four figures silhouetted against the sky. Quintus frowned but stepped up the side aisle and waited with impatience for Naso's superior to open the conversation. One thing for certain—there was no Uncle Livy here, no one fat enough. The nearest man turned and stepped closer. To Quintus's surprise he was staring into the glowering eyes of his family's arch-rival. And then the other, taller man spun on his heels.

Quintus gasped in shock.

For a brief respite the few criminals who still lived or were intact could shiver in fear while four of the five lions busied themselves feeding greedily on the piles of torn corpses; a mess of blood, protruding bones, and coils of intestine lay strewn on the sand. As Rufio watched in dread fascination, a female dragged away a carcase from the diminished huddle of paralyzed men and began tearing chunks of meat from it. As if bored with the entertainment, the other male wandered off toward the side entrance the gladiators would later use. The beast paced up and down in front of the passage.

Rufio's agitation mounted with every human scream: at his imprisonment and his concern for Quintus. Every time he squirmed round to look up and hopefully catch sight of his friend, he was reminded of the knife at his ribs. He wondered why they hadn't searched him for his own blade. Stupid. He risked another twist and from the corner of his eye saw a group on the far quadrant of the cavea, among them... Quintus! And...

"Oh fuck! That's Panthera and that prick Virius."

Bebryx could not miss the tension, the raised level of threat when the two turned on Caecilius Alba. The young man's body language changed from nervous to defensive, but also angry; that of Panthera coldly sneering, aggressive; and that of the well-dressed patrician vacillating between fury and... fear? The thugs closed in. The patrician waved his arms angrily, shouted, the words lost in a gale of audience acclamation, but his gesture spoke loudly enough.

Quintus stepped back defensively when Virius spat out words emphasized by vicious stabs at his chest. "See sense you stupid boy. If you refuse to listen to the tune you will still have to pay the piper!"

"Enough!" Panthera's voice cracked like a whip.

Quintus felt the presence of Panthera's henchmen Naso and Helva at his back—no representatives of the Federation for sure. The other two pressed down past Panthera and Virius in a rush and hemmed him against the low retaining wall. He teetered, slipped, scrabbled desperately for a footing. Next, two things happened simultaneously: a curious leonine growl came from below and a massive shove sent him over the edge of the drop.

Rufio cried out and leaped to his feet.

"Canus, grab him!" Knifeman shouted. They slapped him down viciously, but not before he'd seen Quintus surrounded, struck, and vanish from sight. Terror filled his heart for his friend, his lover, the only person who made him whole. Hands hauled him down on the stone bench from where he could see nothing from the press of spectators all on their feet. Fury like he had never known burned in his breast, fueled by the aroused shattering roar of a male lion— *Panthera leo...*

Bebryx stared in mute horror at the spectacle unfolding only twenty paces distant and a bit below where he stood on the balcony. He felt helpless at seeing young Caecilius Alba clinging by his fingers to the edge of a drop the height of three men into the lateral entrance passage. A swirl of dirty buff mane caught his attention briefly. A lion's roar confirmed his worst fears for—

"He's called Quintus," Britannicus wailed. "Save him!"

What to do? And then it came in a blinding flash of lightning sent by Jupiter. Bebryx snatched the fastened end of the crane rope and with a mighty tug freed it from the ring buried at the end of the balustrade. Britannicus gasped as Bebryx sprang up onto the rail, pulled the rope taut and then launched himself into space with a bellowing Scythian warcry.

He swung out in a graceful descending arc, a human pendulum, twin battering rams of boots stretched out in front. Britannicus barely registered that his master had sailed into battle unarmed before Bebryx slammed into Panthera. As he impacted, he let go the rope and delivered a hefty backhand to the patrician.

* * *

From his precarious hold, Quintus witnessed Bebryx collide with Panthera. The bastard was hurled to the concrete steps and Virius felled into a seething mass of spectators. And then big hands reached for him. Bebryx to the rescue! But as he bent, hands outstreteched, the thug Helva lowered his head and lammed into the gladiator's midriff. Bebryx fell back for a moment, enough time for Naso to stand over Quintus and stamp down on his fingers. He couldn't hold on. With a tearing of fingernails and a cry of dismay, he fell.

Recovered, Bebryx swung around and shoved both assailants back with sufficient force to send them stumbling down the stepped aisle's steep incline. He heard the warning shout of Britannicus in time to whirl round and confront Panthera, back on his feet, snarling in incoherent rage at the insult of being struck by a slave gladiator. Bebryx backed down a step from the sword in Panthera's hand. He reached to his waist for his own. Not there. Of course. The yell from above came again. He glanced up at the balcony, at Britannicus waving his long gladius with evident effort. And then the boy raised his arm and threw the sword as hard as he could.

Panthera came down one step. Two steps. Sword point wavering.

Bebryx reached up with his right hand, calculated the twists and turns of the arcing blade, timed precisely its trajectory so the ivory grip slapped exactly into the palm of his hand. His fist closed. He flexed knees on the turn to lower his center of balance and closed in under Panthera's downswing. He launched uphill, all his massive weight behind the tip of his blade. The gladius tore through toga, tunic, and flesh deep into Panthera's gut. For good measure, Bebryx twisted the sword savagely to tear up the man's innards.

Panthera collapsed onto those spectators nearest, setting off shrieks of terror that spread outward like the ripples from a stone thrown into a pond. The patrician he'd punched staggered away, face contorted with terror, unleashing a new wave of shouts from

the audience, some in fear, others in annoyance at the disturbance. The bruised thugs scattered as best they could, only to run into brethren from the Ostia Crossroads Club, finally aroused to action.

Quintus groaned and staggered to his feet, half-stunned by the drop. His side hurt where his pugio had dug into his hip on the impact. He turned and froze in mute horror. He'd landed on the wrong side of the barred gate! The lion lowered its head and crouched. Its tail flicked left and right irritably. He unsheathed the pugio, aware of what puny defense it offered against such a powerful, fiercesome opponent.

The dun-colored brute blocked the way out into the orchestra—which given the snarls coming from there didn't sound like the best escape route anyway—and behind him the gladiator's gate was tall. He looked at the end of the stage, some fifteen paces away. Was it a possible opportunity? Dark brown eyes fixed him. The lion stooped even lower, poised to charge. Quintus moved. He ran at the monster and took it by surprise, a hesitation sufficient for Quintus to swerve aside at the last moment and jump up onto the stage. And run. He was aware of the horror picture to his left, but no time to dwell on the massacre. The beast whipped around and was coming up behind him. It kept pace along the floor of the orchestra and twice reared up to slap at Quintus with huge splayed claws, and twice Quintus jinked back out of reach. He knew this could not go on long. The damned brute was going to get him. He was desperate to find a way out. That's when the shout rang in his ear, coming from the central stage door.

"Open it! Open it!"

Rufio's relief at seeing Quintus appear from behind the end of the cavea to run along the stage was short-lived. When the great lion loped into sight from the side passage after him, it was time to act. He shot upright, catching out the goon pinning his arms. His right arm came free. He raised the elbow, smashed its point against the nose of the man on the aisle. The gangster barked in pain.

"Jump, Tullius!"

The cavalry at last. He recognized two brethren from the West Aventine Crossroads Club. One pulled him free of his second captor's attempts to grab his arm again while stamping down hard on the knifeman's instep. Another squeal of pain. The knife clattered to the step. As Rufio dashed out, the second Crossroads soldier fell on his former captor with a heavy fist to the face.

At last able to free his pugio, Rufio hurtled down the aisle, gaining speed from the sixth to the second rows. Without calculation, he aimed at an enthralled spectator in the front row, lifted his left foot high enough to plant it on a heaving shoulder. And then with a last burst of power, he pushed up off the startled man to vault clean over the barrier. If it were so easy, he fleetingly wondered, why hadn't any of the lions tried jumping it in the opposite direction?

He didn't know which of the soldiers unbarred it, but suddenly the central stage door burst open with sufficient force to crash into a framing column. Regulus shot through the gap. The lion had just jumped up onto the stage after Quintus, but the sharp sound startled the animal, as did the gladiator's sudden appearance. At its deep snarl, Regulus grabbed his gladius and dropped the rest of his kit.

The commotion alerted Quintus. He halted his dash, spun round. His eyes went wide on seeing Regulus and in the same instant he crouched beside him to confront their nemesis. "Make for the door!" Quintus yelled. But too late. The frightened guards slammed it shut and the snick of bolts said they weren't going to open it any time soon. "This is no good. We need to make for the end of the cavea where there's a chance of getting over the lower end wall before these fur-rags eat us."

Regulus freed the gladius of its scabbard and the hiss of steel on leather seemed to energize the lion. He flung the scabbard aside and followed Quintus in a hasty retreat down to the orchestra floor, unheeding of the wall of sound from the frenzied crowd. The lion paused at the stage's edge as if uncertain how to proceed. Its to and fro hesitation might have been comical under other circumstances, but Quintus saw nothing funny in the way the rest of the pack sprang to their feet with renewed interest.

"To me!" Quintus commanded, and Regulus obeyed. Back to back they crabbed toward the far side of the orchestra, away from the pile of eviscerated human remains. Two females slunk forward in cautious investigation, sniffing and growling, and then fell back at a sudden disturbance. A flying body cannoned into Quintus's side.

"Rufio!"

"Gods, but I thought I'd lost you again."

"You may have yet."

"Nice to see you again, Dominus," Regulus added dryly.

"Couldn't you have at least kept a hold of your shield," Rufio groused.

"It wouldn't be much use against lions."

Shoulder to shoulder, they formed a strange three-sided creature, bristling with blades, but not steel enough. The pack closed in. The two females Rufio's whirlwind arrival had scared off loped around to come behind the three-legged crab, cutting off a retreat to the barrier. The other male trotted up, crouched briefly, tail twitching angrily. And then it attacked. In three great bounds it sprang, claws spread, at Regulus. The gladius came up. There was a tearing sound of ripped flesh and a deep, shuddering roar. The lion thumped down among them. A claw caught Quintus a glancing blow on his arm. He cursed, but the cloak saved him from the worst damage. They split apart and fell back from the wounded animal to swiftly reform and present a solid front to the lions. Two arena attendants appeared from the animal enclosure end, but timidly remained well back.

"Cowardly curs!" Regulus shouted. He brandished his sword in taunt.

Rufio laughed crazily. "I don't think you can shame them in to doing anything."

"To live, we're going to have to get ourselves out of this," Quintus added, with patrician disdain for the obvious.

"Did I yet say: 'this is another fine mess you got us into'?" Rufio gasped, as he jabbed his pugio ineffectually at the third female.

"I'll tell your Ma you blamed me again!"

The injured lion ended any further conversation. With a yowl of outrage, it sprang to all fours as if the sword slash Regulus had delivered mattered not at all. Its bellowing call finally encouraged the male that had attacked Quintus to leap off the stage and join the fray. The persistent female closed in and began snatching the air with raised claws, slavering jaws alive with wicked, bloodstained fangs. Rufio lunged at her with his pugio. She backed off, but clearly this wasn't going to prevent her final victory.

Quintus felt the first pangs of true despair. "We must keep trying to reach the barrier at the end of the cavea." But encircled as they were, it appeared to be an impossible task. Praying to all the gods, the three boys prepared to take as much feline flesh with them as they could. And then the pressure suddenly eased. A disturbance in the crowd at the other end of the cavea from where beleaguered Quintus, Rufio, and Regulus defended their hopeless position attracted the big cats' attention. Leonine heads swung around. A huge figure leapfrogged the lowest part of the cavea wall and, wielding a sword resembling a spatha, flew across the corpse-strewn orchestra—he jumped the slaughtered to engage their executioners.

"Bebryx!" three voices chimed with renewed hope.

"Quick," Regulus bellowed to his brothers in arms. "Give him a chance. Distract the lions."

Rufio yelled at the top of his lungs at the lioness standing between them and the enraptured audience. He threatened again with his dagger. She snarled, backed off, and then attacked. "Oh fuck! That worked well— *ughn…*"

Quintus whipped around to his aid, while Regulus made short dashes against the other of their tormentors. In a fury of stabbing motions, Quintus and Rufio drove off the lion, and she slunk away, but not far.

Bebryx found himself confronted by both males. The Quintus chaser growled deep inside his outthrust chest. The lion Regulus had slashed crouched on his haunches menacingly. Which one posed the greatest threat? The boys could see Bebryx weighing up his chances. He chose the wounded animal. It was an error. The aggression was a diversion. As Bebryx moved in for the kill, his back momentarily turned, the other great cat, tail whipping angrily, readied to spring. The boys' shouted warnings came too late. The lion took two tremendous springs and a single rake of lethal claws opened Bebryx up along his back and side. In a trice the wounded lion was on him. It seized the gladiator by the shoulder, shook him as a cat worries a mouse, and then threw him on the sand.

Regulus cried out. Instinct took over. He rushed out from the mutual protection to reach the fallen man in a few strides. His sudden attack surprised the lion that had attacked Bebryx first. As it reared up, Regulus struck clear at its exposed throat and sliced it open. Without pause, he turned on the lion worrying lifeless Bebryx and dealt it a tremendous blow to a foreleg. The beast lifted its great head, long mane flying. Saliva and blood flicked from its massive jaws when it roared at him. Undeterred, the young gladiator thrust his sword between its raised paw and shoulder, and plunged the blade in behind the lion's neck. The claws lightly grazed him as he dodged the blow, and the lion staggered back from unconscious Bebryx. Its haunches gave way, and it slumped in a lifeless tawny heap.

The attendants now found their courage boosted and began closing in, quickly followed by a handful of soldiers. Banging swords against shields, they managed to cow the four lions and round them up against the stage. There, a surprise appearance of Praetorian Guards armed with spears soon dispatched them to rousing cheers from the thrilled spectators.

Bloodied, lightly wounded, Regulus turned to see Quintus and Rufio in an embrace that spoke loudly of an affection he could never have shared. He walked back to the stage to retrieve his gear, passing medics rushing in to see to fallen Bebryx.

T·W·E·N·T·Y-T·W·O | XXII

Ides of January to the Kalends (1st) of April AD 109

"What the…?" Rufio's brow wrinkled in uncertain surprise. He swept a sweaty lock of hair back as though it might help him understand what he was seeing.

Quintus was amazed too, but less so. He knew that Regulus had been summoned to the palace at least once before. The greater cause for surprise was Trajan's presence in Ostia. With the end of the lions, bruised and battered the boys had made their way through the backstage area to the Forum of the Corporations, where they came across bloodied Regulus in conversation with his Emperor.

Rufio nudged Quintus. "Do you see over there, behind Trajan, under close guard?"

"Yes. Fabius Virius." Quintus glowered. "Serves the cheating bastard right. I hope Trajan has him executed. And I see they got Panthera's scum as well. But what have Regulus and Trajan got to discuss?"

They found out the moment Trajan spotted them and called out. "From what I hear you have done well to still live." He waved them through the cordon of his Batavian bodyguard. "I am relieved to find all your limbs, digits and…" he glanced down from one to the other, "all the other vital bits still in place." He paused at the clatter and and rattle of armor to glance around at the entry to the enclosure of more Praetorians. "It seems I am unable to leave you two anywhere without your causing an earthquake."

"Caesar! That's not fair!"

"Hush, Rufio. I came today to lend support to Octavius Vindex to discover uproar, chaos, murder, mayhem. I think you both owe a debt of gratitude to Gaius Atilius Regulus here."

The name dropped into the sudden silence like a thunderbolt exploding. If Regulus had punched Quintus in the solar plexus he couldn't have been more winded with shock. *Deceit and betrayal!* A curtain of cold embarrassment wrapped around his shoulders when he contemplated how easily Regulus had taken him in.

"You… you are a patrician?" Rufio exclaimed indignantly.

Regulus stared defiantly ahead, not really engaging anyone's gaze. Rufio looked from one to another in bewilderment. Trajan came to his rescue. "Atilius Regulus is a son of Atilius Crescens, chief of our Centumviral Court, and he has rendered a great service not only to his father but also to me."

"But I thought… you… I thought you were fallen on hard times?" Rufio said. Quintus remained shaken and mute.

"That was what we wanted everyone to think. Though you were a bit suspicious Rufio, you never guessed the truth." Trajan squeezed Regulus on the shoulder and explained that in his civil law role the father's attempts to penetrate the worst of the crime syndicates had proved more difficult than anticipated. "These despicable crooks and their match fixing are corrupting the noble tradition of gladiatorial combat." He told them how Atilius Crescens had obliged his youngest son to work under cover, posing as a volunteer gladiator. "We felt a novicus inducted into a training school would gain a better understanding of the machinations at work, and where better to begin than the Ludus Magnus at the start of a major festival like the Ludi Plebeii?"

"And it worked," Quintus said quietly, his eyes boring into Regulus, who finally had the grace to shuffle his feet in discomfort.

"It worked better than I ever imagined, thanks also to his sister Atilia Crescens acting as go-between on those days the gladiators roamed the Meta Sudans." Trajan clapped Regulus on the shoulder again. "And so the wretched Gaius Fabricius Luscinus—Panthera— is dead and his gang rounded up wth the useful intervention of the Crossroads Clubs. Once again, I am obliged to turn a blind eye to some of those rogues' less salubrious activities." He jabbed a thumb at the bedraggled senator in the grip of two hairy Batavians. "Fabius Virius is uncovered and…" he raised his voice, "he will happily reveal to us the names of others who yet remain hidden.

"Now I must go to Vindex for the rest of these games, in which the gladiator Gaius Regulus is no longer on the bill, by the way. Oh, and I meant to say…the intention was for Atilius to get taken up by a munerarius who was hopefully deeply involved in the corruption. And then you two stepped in! Oh my Firehound and my Mars, I never in my wildest imagining thought you would spend my gifts to you on the purchase of a gladiator. What were you thinking of?" And with a burst of laughter, Caesar and his chortling German bodyguard (who understood not a word of Latin) swept off out to the street ready for an imperial entrance to the theater.

"No congratulations for us getting ourselves out of the shit, huh?" Rufio muttered rebelliously. "And what gifts? We haven't had even a bent semis yet!" He turned his sneer on Regulus. "A fucking patrician. Gods save us!" The words were aimed like a spit. He shook his head in disgust. "I'm going to give Virius the toecap of my boot. Nothing like kicking a lying cunny when he's down." He stalked off, leaving Quintus holding the gaze of a shifty and yet unrepentant Regulus.

"Would it help if I offered apologies?"

"For making me feel devalued? Taking me for an idiot? Making me out a fool? For taking my… my affection and shoving it into a cesspit? Oh how you must have laughed behind my back."

"They made me do it. The pathetic prick that Tullius Rufio is kicking ordered me to seduce you, split you away from him. He must have been very frightened of the bond between you two. In my role I could hardly refuse him, and I was being watched. We all were." He fell silent, gazing back at Quintus. "You know the real irony? I'm not much removed from other patricians who—as Tullius Rufio put it— fall on hard times. I am a sixth son. Do you know what kind of life the sixth son of a family boasting seven consuls and two dictators in its ancient, virtuous history can expect? When it comes down to it, my father is very little better than that carcase of shit Fabius Virius."

Quintus sniffed. He did sort of know, being the fifth son, well fourth son with Tertius dead in infancy.

"And the other cruel irony is that though I did not want sex with you…" His mouth tightened into a tiny smile. "I enjoyed it anyway. Go well, Quintus Caecilius Alba. You have your Rufio and I now have the leverage of imperial favor to better my status within my family."

"Did he fuck you?"

Regulus knew who Quintus meant. He huffed sour amusement. "I was 'hauled in' as a cover so I could report to him, but as it happens, yes. And of course I'd have to say I loved it, wouldn't I?"

Ever since the murder of the Divine Julius Caesar on the Ides of March, the date was held to be one of infamy, but it was not unlucky because in a long month the Ides fell on the 15th day. And so it was an auspicious date for the funeral rites of Bebryx the Scythian. The gladiator had clung grimly to life but his wounds proved too much even for his great strength. For his part in striking off the head of the s·a·d·a snake, the *Foedus gladiatorum orbis terrarium* had paid extra sums on his behalf to the Ludus Gallicus burial club, and so when he succumbed to his injuries on the seventh day of March, the quality of his funeral and his burial spot was assured.

After the traditional nine days of mourning, his ashes were interred with great ceremony. Quintus composed the eulogy, which Rufio declaimed (it was felt that a trained upper-class orator like Quintus wouldn't come across well with all the fellow gladiators assembled). Men and women from all walks of life listened tearfully. Britannicus shed tears of his own. It was hardly a surprise that a gladiator should fall, but the man he'd hated he'd come to admire. In an ungainly scrabble, Dolabella and Gracchus of Capua laid claim to him, but with both lanistas under investigation, Bebryx's will was honored—Britannicus was given to Rufio.

"By Vesta's velvety vulva," he exclaimed on hearing of the bequest. "Quintus, I have to be sensible. I have enough boy problems as it is, even though I'm first to admit a healthy lust for the beauteous butt of Britannicus. But really wouldn't it be better if you had him, I mean took him into your house... whether you have him or not, or..."

And so Britannicus was passed to the Caecilii and added to the growing household at Sunrise Cloister. Quintus anticipated an eruption from Ashur, but from that smoking volcano of Syrian jealousy there came no complaint; on the contrary. "Will we have to share a cubicle, Quintus?" Ashur asked in all coy innocence. "It is a little cramped, but I think we can fit in together. Somehow. Top to tail probably, you know. Tight, but I'm sure it will work." Britannicus, it transpired, had no gripe with the arrangement either.

"Nice," Rufio commented. "You'll be the meat in a Syrio-Britannic sandwich."

Life was not as pleasant for Publius Fabius Virius. The threat of being put to the question by a Praetorian *carnifex* loosened his tongue. His spillage unveiled the mysterious Banker, also Cornelius Aemilius Papus and the part Livius Caecilius Dio had played. These and several more senators and upper-class equestrian figures were hauled up before the Emperor. Trajan and Crescens were agreed that there was little to be gained in undermining the Senate's reputation, and so their unlawful activities were hushed up, although Trajan threatened exile for any further breaches of good order. There was, however, punishment suitable to each individual.

"Fabius Virius," Trajan intoned, "you are let off lightly for your crimes. You will supply through the offices of Lucius Caecilius Alba the required number of A-Class marble drums to my architect Apollodorus of Damascus to complete my victory column. And you will do so at your cost. Dismissed. Livius Caecilius Dio, you are a wretched creature. I have decided that having to live with your cowardly self in the shadow of your brother-in-law Lucius will be sufficient punishment... oh, along with your removal from the list of Conscript Fathers."

"He's no longer of senatorial rank," Quintus explained to Rufio.

"That won't stop him hankering after your ass, you know."

Those who avoided the subsequent round-up went to ground. And so the practices of syndicates bribing, bullying, and blackmailing gladiators, referees, lanistas, and muneraria were ended… for the time being. "After all," Clivius Ostiensus told his lieutenants and brother-soldiers of the Crossroads, "those cheating patrician ponces were making fortunes. Shame to let that all go to waste, eh?"

"Are you over Regulus?" Rufio asked tentatively as they walked away from the funeral. It was two miles from the better part of the Esquiline necropolis to Sunrise Cloister.

"I was *never* into him."

"For a self-proclaimed historian you have a very short memory."

Quintus drew breath to reply and then thought better of his response. He sighed. "He tricked me. Us."

"In a good cause."

"A Titan's testicles to that."

They strolled back through the Porta Esquilina in companionable silence until Rufio couldn't resist. "Was he a good fuck?"

The nonchalant shrug, a lifting of one shoulder that managed to push against Rufio, suggested: *satisfactory but could have tried harder.* Quintus grinned with sudden affection for his companion. "Regulus was all right." He glanced sideways at Rufio from under lowered long black eyelashes. "But not as good as you."

Quintus was just returned from a paternal summons to Domus Alba, where he'd had to face the inevitable—yet it was still a shock to the system. Vipsania took the news well, perhaps a bit too well, a miffed Quintus thought; a touch of feminine regret might have been appropriate, at least a smidgeon of Rufio's appalled reaction would have been welcomed. He hadn't gone straight home to Sunrise Cloister but detoured to the Emporium and burst in on Rufio, who was in the throes of the final illustration to complete their first porno-scroll book.

"Britannia!" Rufio cried with a horrified expression.

Quintus nodded, unable to elaborate for a moment.

"B–but that's across the Ocean. You'll be gone for ever," Rufio wailed. "No one comes back from the Romans' Grave."

"Ah, my boy, come in," Lucius had said when Quintus in answer to the summons appeared in his father's tablinum doorway. "I have wonderful news for you. As one of the consuls of this year, my dear friend Pompeius Falco has been awarded the British Isles to govern. I have brought my influence to bear and he has agreed to take you with him for your military service. Isn't that wonderful?"

"Er… yes, father. Quite wonderful." *Stunning, in fact…*

"You will attend the general at his home on the 23rd day of this month to collect your orders. That should leave you sufficient time to set your affairs in order because you're still a boy, so you won't have much to do. I shall ensure your wife is well chaperoned and supported in your absence. This is a splendid opportunity, Quintus, and I know you will do your duty to help bring civilization to the wretched natives of those benighted islands, as well as honoring your patria, your family, and your Emperor. Now go see your mother and say your goodbyes today. I don't want her upset nearer the time. You know how she always cries."

"That's so soon." Rufio dashed a sudden welling of moisture from his eyes. "What will I do without you, Quintus?"

"You'll cope." But instantly he regretted the shortness of the words and added in a tone of fond amusement, "After all, there is Adalhard and Hephaestion and Felix to soften the blow—"

"And you will have the lovely Britannicus… you will take him, won't you? After all, he's a native of those far-off lands, which will be useful. He must speak some of the barbarian lingo, surely?"

"I hadn't thought. Are junior tribunes allowed slaves? I must ask the general when I see him."

"And who is this famous general? Another pansy patrician prick no doubt."

Quintus smiled. "Ah, this you will like. You remember the prefect of Legate Similis in Alexandria, how we laughed at his having too many names? Lucius Junius Quintus Vibius Crispus—"

"Oh yes, and his pompous notary. Lucius Pomponius Bassus Cascus Scribonianus."

"Yes, well my general is…" he took a deep breath, and launched in. "Quintus Roscius Coelius Murena Silius Decianus Vibullius Pius Iulius Eurycles Herculanus Pompeius Falco."

That gave Rufio pause. He stared vacantly for a moment. "He shares your praenomen. And imagine—there's enough of him to form an entire harpustum team and have substitutes over to spare!" And then he fell about with a fit of terminal giggles, swiftly joined by Quintus as the two boys buried sadness under hilarity and a sense of rekindled love.

Vipsania by contrast was sanguine. "My darling husband, I shall shed a tear for you—remind me to ask your mother for her tear cup—and tell my dear, dear father-in-law that his haste to tear us apart has prevented the early conception of his first grandson."

"Oh." Quintus smiled conspiratorially. "There is that. It does postpone a tricky little problem a while." He turned a serious patrician mien on her. "Just please, dearest darling, don't cause a scandal while I'm away bashing barbarian brains."

"Me?" she retorted with a coy smirk.

"I was so upset when you told me we're to be torn asunder that I forgot to tell you something," Rufio began.

Quintus had come to take his leave of Junilla, Cato, and Rufio, who had organized Woof-Woof Felix to be present for the farewells. They and Hephaestion had been sworn to secrecy about the important surprise Rufio had to impart to Quintus. After a light lunch, he had sequestered Quintus in his bedroom, away from the others.

"I happened to bump into Scorpus just after you told me about Britannia and when he heard you were off there he dragged me to the Velabrum to see the Greens' main horse-doctor. He's also their weird man who fends off evil magic from the stables and he's an adherent to that strange cannibal sect, you know, the Christians. So I told him about your imminent departure for the Isles of Mist and he went all funny and excited about some Holy Chalice thing, whatever. Supposed to have been taken to the 'Isles Beyond the Ocean,' which means Britannia, I think."

"What's so fabulous about this Holy Chalice thing, whatever?"

"I'm a bit hazy about atheistic matters, but it seems that their demon-king, after eating body parts, used to drink human blood from the cup, which made it holy. They call it the Grail, for some reason. The horse-doctor says it's worth a fortune. He says the cult's pontifex will pay anything to put his hands on it. There's a legend that the Grail was hidden among the hoard of Caractacus, or Caradoc in the Britons' outlandish tongue. I'm sure you'll be able to get wind of it and bring back all that gold as well as this grail thingy."

With furrowed brow, Quintus said, "And that was the 'big surprise' you wanted to tell me?"

Rufio looked put out. "What? How did you know about a surprise?"

"Have you ever met a certain Cornelius Tullius Cato?"

"He didn't let on?" Rufio said, outraged. "That little fucker. I'll tan his hide for—"

"He said 'surprise.' He didn't say what or that it was about some madcap religious cult symbol."

"Well, it wasn't." Rufio's face flushed to match his hair. The color heightened the sprinkle of freccles across his burning cheeks. He gazed intently at Quintus. "You won't have to search for Caradoc's gold or that Holy Grail thing alone."

Quintus froze. They stared at each other. Something lurched deep inside his chest. "What's that supposed to mean?" he asked, hardly daring to hope.

"I'm going as well."

Quintus continued staring, a question slowly forming in his eyes.

"You know my Aunty Velabria owns several vineyards up in Liguria? Well, her agent in Gaul passed away inconveniently. He didn't even give her any advance notice. She's got talents of wine in warehouses waiting for distribution in Britannia and no one to do it. So Ma suggested I go and look after you, I mean after things for Aunty Velabria for a year."

Like a legionary ordered to be at ease, Quintus came to sudden life with a stifled guffaw. "What do you know about selling wine?"

"I know how to drink it, and if I can help Ma sell fake Myron, Phidias, and Praxiteles bronzes to Roman connoisseurs I'm sure I can flog Aunty Velabria's crappy vintages to provincial hicks in Britannia. Besides, your military comrades will drink anything to prevent drowning in ghastly native beer. What do you say?"

Quintus didn't say anything. He stepped up close and threw his arms around Rufio in heartfelt relief at finally shaking off the gladiatorial dizziness. He pushed until they both tumbled to the bed and there discovered a renewed joy in their love made all the sweeter for their reconciliation.

In less time than it took Cato to lose Eutychus on the Canopus Way, the two boys were rolled up naked in each other's arms. Quintus's recent aberration underwent a magical transmutation, the effects of which were to smother Rufio's skin with licks and kisses, starting with his delectable ears, his neck to either side and the enticing hollow just under the Adam's apple, and then those longer convexities above the clavicle bones. He worked with lavish attention down over Rufio's silky smooth pectorals, first left, then right, in turn and again to find and nibble the erect nipples; breathing in the familiar scent so recently absent due to his own blindness as to who really mattered in his life.

Rufio seemed to understand Quintus's need for him to lie passively and react with the abrupt, but contained body movements

of received pleasure. In his atonement, Quintus made the intensity of his ministrations all the more pleasurable for both partners. And Rufio sighed in response to the increased flickers of tickling fingers, saliva-wet brushing lips, the coarser whisk of dark, crisp hair over his tense skin, the feel of Quintus's lips finding and, with a sigh, relishing Rufio's cock, so hard, so smooth in texture, the slick cock head ready for engulfment. The sucking, tip to base, lipped and tongue-squeezed in a controlled frenzy, went on until Quintus sensed his partner's orgasm mounting.

As the afternoon drew on Quintus repeatedly took Rufio to the pinnacle of release, only to calm the pace before picking it up again. Eventually he drove his partner to a fury of lovingly resentful retaliation, and by dusk they had taken each other turn and turn again, finding in the other their perfect reunion.

"What will happen to our *magnus opus eroticus* if we're both absent from Rome?" Quintus asked as he recovered his breath.

"Worry not, O versifier amorata. Ma has Sosius well under her thumb. She'll be watching him like an Egyptian kite watches mice rustling the riverbank reeds. If he fails to publish *and* pay up on time she'll have his—"

"Balls minced up with herbs for a terrine. You're right. I can't think of anyone better to guard our interests. Poor Flaccus, though. What will he do without at least a weekly sight of your sweet ass? Oh, and that reminds me of something."

Rufio yawned and stretched languorously. "What something?"

"Britannia is said to be a horrible, cold, damp country of bogs and endless forests, full of gray fogs and evil wraiths, but there is a silver lining. I'm not like you who can keep an entire menagerie on the go so I'm thankful that I won't be here in Rome when Sekhemkhet Adonis arrives to claim his prize!"

Rufio snuffled in amusement.

"But in Britannia, I will be with my military duties in one place and you will be selling amphoras of wine somewhere else. How will we ever actually meet?"

The bed covering rustled as Rufio rolled back over to hold Quintus. He closed in until their mouths met and spoke softly into the parted lips. "Don't worry. I promise I will find you." And they kissed.

A cool breeze blew the wall hangings about in the gloomy depths of Domus Tiberiana. The fluttery motion made Pancratius nervous as he nodded to the secretary guarding the chamberlain's offices. He passed through the open doorway.

"Ah, Pancratius. Thank you for coming." Athenos was seated behind a desk neatly piled with scrolls and tablets. "So, what progress have you made with Caesar's gift?"

Pancratius coughed twice to clear his throat. "That silly old goat Callias at the arearium sanctius has lost the paperwork."

Anthenos frowned in puzzlement and scowled. "In the name of charismatic Cybele, how did it end up there?"

Another phlegmy throat clear. "Long story, Athenos. Suffice it to say that it will take years for Callias to locate it before we can arrange to pay Caesar's gift."

For several moments Athenos hummed to himself while Pancratius waited for the execution order. "Hmm, well, perhaps it's for the best."

"The best?"

"Under the circumstances. You see, the two beneficiaries are being sent to the province of Britannia. I'm sure we can't expect to see either for at least a year. Besides, you know what the savages who infest those islands are like… If we're lucky Quintus Caecilius Alba and Junius Tullius Rufio may never return."

But, hey, we're sure they will…
…after the quest for *Caradoc's Gold*

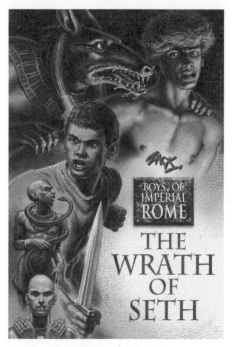

Zack: THE WRATH OF SETH
Boys of Imperial Rome 3

320 pages, soft cover
5¼ x 7½" / 13 x 19 cm
978-3-95985-155-8
US$ 16.99 / £ 10.99 / € 14,99

The Roman Empire, AD 108. When emperor Trajan
sets sail for his province of Egypt, his mind is on
sightseeing and the acquisition of art and antiques
to adorn the city of Rome. Little does he imagine
that he is heading toward his own potential doom…
Deep in the western desert, a sinister cult plans to
return Egypt to its past glory, and Rome and its
empire stand in the way… Traveling with Trajan are
lovers Quintus and Rufi o, along with his mother
Junilla and younger brother Cato. Together, they
encounter fabled wonders of the past, the quirks and
threats of the natives both human and animal--and
repeated attempts to assassinate the emperor…Amid
the dangers, exotic erotic encounters keep Rufio
and Quintus busy even as they strive to avert the
disastrous wrath of the god Seth.